A HAND CLOSED ON HER SHOULDER, SPINNING HER AROUND UNTIL HER BACK PRESSED INTO THE DOORFRAME.

A cold drizzle misted her face as an even colder shape pressed into her throat. She could not see it, but she knew what it was: a blade. A little longer than two hands. Sharp enough that the very edge of it was turning warm from a sliver-thin split in her skin, leaking blood. Too sharp even to hurt. Tomorrow it would itch.

The angle of the blade was such that she could see only her attacker's chest, but sewn into the cloak was the royal guard insignia. The surge of relief that it was not an outlaw made her lightheaded.

"Unhand me," Renna hissed, not wanting to reveal herself to anyone else on the crowded Nottingham street.

"Unhand you?"

She recognized the distinctive voice—low, with gravel in the very back of it.

Her assailant shifted but did not remove the weapon, and her gaze flicked up to the face of the high sheriff of Nottingham. Now the cold slice was in her gut instead: dread.

Renna bared her teeth in an approximation of a smile. "It is considered treason to threaten the life of the future queen. You'll release me, immediately and quietly. You're making a scene," she whispered.

Draic adjusted the blade, forcing her to tilt her chin higher. For a moment she was reminded of the way he used to tap the flat of the dagger against her sternum when he'd won a sparring match. "My knife is subtle, Princess; to everyone else, we're lovers in the rain."

Copyright © 2025 by Brittany Hansen.

All rights reserved.
Cover art by Alice Powers
Map by Andrés Aguirre Jurado
Cover and Interior Design by Abril Sainz (Abrilas Art)
Line and Copy Editing by Alison Cherry
Intimacy and violence coaching by Thorns N' Roses and New York Combat Stage & Screen
Interior art by Avendell and Incendiosketches
Author photo by Brooke Janette

No part of this work may be reproduced, stored in a retrieval system or transmitted in any form by any means, electronic, mechanical, photocopying, recording, or otherwise, without written permission of the publisher.

This is a work of fiction. Names, characters, places, and incidents either are the product of the author's imagination or are used fictitiously. Any resemblance to actual persons, living or dead, events, or locales is entirely coincidental.

NO AI TRAINING: Without in any way limiting the author's [and publisher's] exclusive rights under copyright, any use of this publication to "train" generative artificial intelligence (AI) technologies to generate text is expressly prohibited. For rights and permissions, please contact: brittanyhansenauthor@gmail.com

ISBN 9798991546904 (Hardback)
ISBN 9798991546935 (Paperback)
ISBN 979-8-9915469-1-1 (E-Book)

THE OUTLAW WITCH OF SHERWOOD

ALSO BY BRITTANY HANSEN

The Abandoned Realm

THE OUTLAW WITCH OF SHERWOOD

BOOK ONE OF THE RENNA HOOD DUOLOGY

BRITTANY HANSEN

CONTENT GUIDANCE

This is novel contains depictions of ritualistic cutting in religious context; fantasy style violence; sexual content; mentions of torture; general violence/gore; adult language; religious abuse; panic attacks; oppression of certain magic users; PTSD; emotional and psychological abuse from authority figures.

For those who have lost their voice. And are fighting to get it back.

PRONUNCIATION GUIDE

Alaini	aa-LANE-ee
Aurem	ORE-um
Bogdanik	bog-DAHnik
Draic	DRAY-ick
Druidhen	DRUID-en
Garen	GARE-en
Gisborne	GIZ-born
Kirin	KEER-en
Koravik	CORA- vik
Loxley	LOCKS-lee
Much	muhch
Nastasia	nah-STA-see-uh
Osric	OZ-rik
Renna	REH-na
Rennavera	REH-na-vAIRa
Trissaia	trii-SAY-uh
Ulrik	UUL-rik
Vedra	VED-ra
Velmir	VEL-meer
Wendsvik	WHENdd-svik
Yana	YAA-na

A woman's first blood doesn't come from between her legs but from biting her tongue.
-*Meggie C. Royer*

If the waters move, if the ground does quake,
Be it a storm unseen or forested straits— therein lays a magic most dark,
A false flame corrupting the vedra heart.
Cast out their kind, remove their tongue, let not them bleed the Truth from us.
With Silence we pay, our blood we give, for the Mother to hold us in her grace.
Fire and foresight, aurem most pure—
These are the blessing we must pray for.
Truth shall light the way.
Truth is in the Blood.
We thank the Mother this day for the Trissaia's way.

- Trissaian Nursery Rhyme

Vedra **(VYEH-dra) noun:**

 1. witch

 2. one who draws from the unholy magic source Velmir.

 3. see also: Great Culling

Velmir **(vel-MEER) noun:**

 1. unholy source of magic used by vedra and druidhen that's forbidden by the Mother.

 2. power drawn from the nature.

 3. see also: the False Flame; witchrot; rot

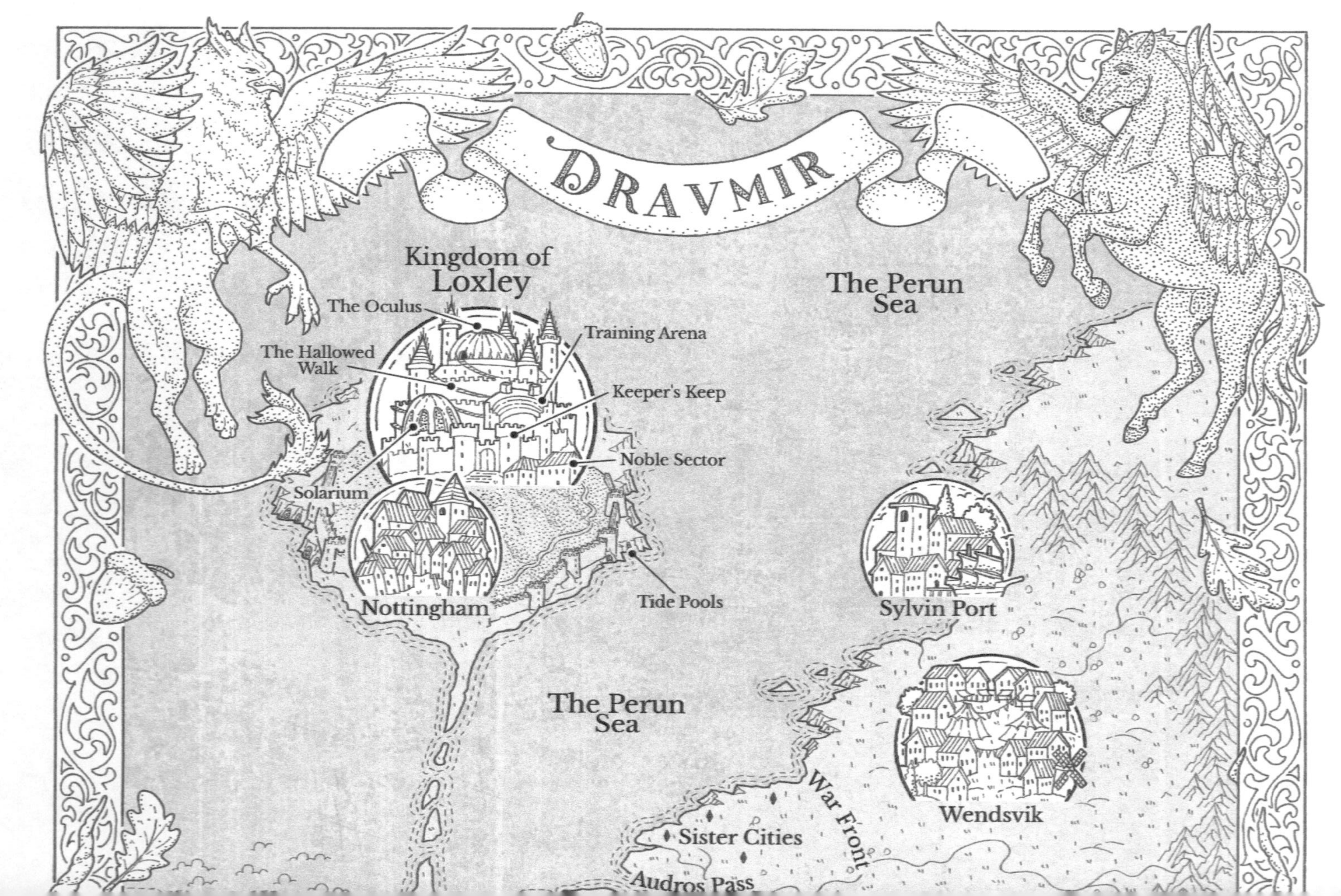
Dravmir
Kingdom of
Loxley
The Oculus
Training Arena
The Hallowed
Walk
Keeper's Keep
Solarium
Noble Sector
Nottingham
Tide Pools
The Perun
Sea
The Perun
Sea
Sylvin Port
Wendsvik
War Front
Sister Cities
Audros Pass

Trade Road
Oakheart
Training area
Falsehood Stronghold
Willow Pond
Sherwood
Forest
Hearthtree
Thorne Crown
Rowan Reach
The Spine of Kaerenthal
Kingdom of
Bravik
Branimer
Misty Meadow
Blood Lake

PART
ONE

CHAPTER 1

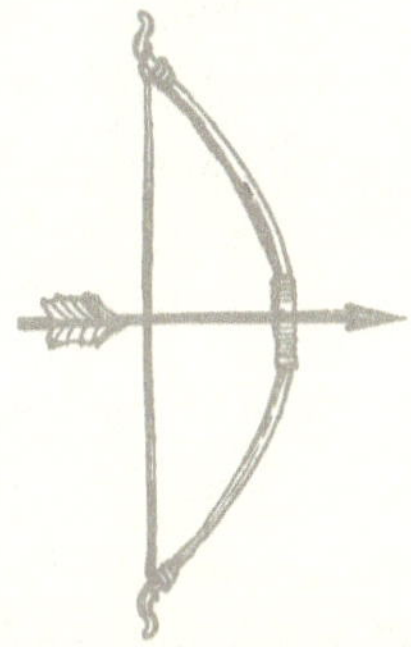

Tʜᴇʀᴇ ᴡᴇʀᴇ ɴᴏ ᴛʀᴇᴇs, ᴏꜰ ᴄᴏᴜʀsᴇ. Renna waited for the priestess to pierce her skin with the enchanted blade as she took in the view from the temple window. Not so much as a sapling interrupted the scene. During the Great Culling, all the trees had been cut down or burned, but on clear days, if she squinted, Renna could make out the far-off smudge on the horizon.

Sherwood Forest.

It felt dangerous to look at it even under regular circumstances, but while inside the temple, preparing to tithe before the Silent Hour? Blasphemous.

The castle of Loxley crowned the mountain it was carved into, and the rest of the kingdom sprawled below. Outside, storm clouds rolled toward the palace spires and the sea rushed in to seal off the tidal island from the rest of the land. Within, the cathedral walls were adorned with the holy aurem mined from the mountain, the dark mineral flecked with deep red, silver, and gold veins. Massive pillars hewn from stone held up the high ceiling. There were reinforced storm windows and private alcoves all along the length of the room, and aurem lanterns holding precious offshoots of the Mother's Flame bathed the entire sanctum in a soft reddish light. A dozen or so of the church's esteemed members were gathered: red-robed Trissaia—Truth Sayers, the Mother's voices; Keepers of the Truth and newer novice Head Trissaia and regent until Renna's coronation; and Lord Gisborne, his consort. A priestess re citing the Tome of Truth stood on the dais next to the stone sculpture depicting the Mother holding Her Flame in Her palms, ready to bestow it upon the people of Loxley. The statue's curved cheeks and strong nose reminded Renna of her mother's face. Looking at it now brought a sense of loss and longing.

A familiar twisting pinch at the base of her skull signaled the mental connection of mettlemancy. Many priestesses and nobles had the ability to a certain degree, but she and her cousin, Nastasia, were more skilled than most. They could easily communicate with their thoughts, though Renna found it somewhat uncomfortable. That pain was supposed to have gone away eight years ago, but…

Her cousin spoke inside her head. *You are supposed to be preparing your mind, Ren.*

Renna pulled her gaze from the window, smiling gently at the priestess approaching with the ritual dagger. The dagger had a bloodstone siphon embedded in the hilt. Tiny grooves and rivulets along the blade allowed the tither's blood to fill the siphon. Her cousin believed in the sanctity of the ritual. Renna believed in the necessity of it, a difference that was subtle but important. She relied heavily on Nastasia to add spiritual weight to it.

And how do you know my mind isn't prepared?

Renna pushed up her sleeve and offered her arm, and the priestess cut into the skin just below her elbow. The bloodstone siphon was warm and buzzed faintly against her as the vial slowly filled. It was difficult to imagine how life would have been had her Foretelling been different. How strange it would've been to tithe only once a year or when the need arose for additional guidance from the Mother, like today. The Blood Tithe was only one month away, and it would be her last before she underwent her crucible and took the throne. Others might not have noticed the building anxiety surrounding her as the days slipped by, but Nastasia did.

It's normal to be nervous, Nastasia continued as Renna focused on breathing steadily through her nose. *You know the influences of the vedra are strongest before the Blood Tithe. The darkness fears the light you bring, Ren.*

A prayer rippled through those gathered. "We thank the Mother for Her Flame. Truth shall light the way. Truth is in the blood. With Silence we pay, and blood we give to the Mother to hold us in Her grace." The litany ended there, but Renna's silent addition was rote. *Do not let the darkness inside you snuff out the light.*

Tithe complete, a second priestess bandaged Renna's arm as the first hurried off to take the full siphon to the lowest level of the castle, where the blood would be tossed into the Mother's Flame. The ever-burning, goddess-blessed finnikfire was a gift of favor bestowed upon the people of Loxley centuries ago for their obedience in burning down Sherwood Forest.

Renna shifted against the hard pew, mindful of her back, still tender from her daily private tithe. The rest of the kingdom was no doubt holding Silence somewhere much more comfortable. She already had plans to sink into a hot bath later, the finnikfire-heated aurem warming the water perfectly. In the years following her Foretelling, Renna's back had become a map of her devotion, constellations of piety cut carefully into her skin to beseech the Mother to let her wield the church-sanctioned magic.

Ulrik crossed to the dais, his robes the pristine white of the Head Trissaia. "As we begin the hour of silence, let us ask the Mother for guidance. We must remain ever vigilant against the wicked who seek to sully the Truth, the vedra who touch the False Flame." He fixed Renna with a paternal smile. "The crucible for our crown princess Rennavera Koravik draws near. We pray for the Mother to bless her so that the Light may go forth. Let us not forget the Almost Queen."

As if it was possible to forget the cautionary tale of the only queen to have failed her crucible. She had touched the False Flame, exposed her witch blood, and been sentenced to the pyre. Renna forced away the thought of the Almost Queen being swallowed up by flames.

If she wasn't found worthy…if she failed her trial…

The familiar walls felt suddenly suffocating as the Head Trissaia finished his sermon. *Can we go to the stables after this, Stasi?* Nozdravian horses were mouthy creatures, always nibbling and biting, and Alita's playful nips kept Renna's dark thoughts away.

We have an audience with Gisborne, and then we're overseeing preparations for the Blood Tithe feast, and then Tomes. I'm not sure there is time.

What is the point of being royalty if I never get to do what I want? Renna knew she was being childish, but it could not be helped.

Duty to your people, Ren.

My people *are in Nottingham.* She'd been eight the last time she'd been allowed out among her people, joining her mother on a parade through Nottingham during the Fire Feast. The celebrations had stretched on like a leisurely yawn. Her mother had stopped to accept handmade stone tokens and knitted scarves, hold chubby babies, and ask what the fishnets had yielded lately. And even though they'd consumed their weight in kolaches, her mother had continued to sample each proffered pastry with enthusiasm.

When Renna's parents had been murdered by False Flame rebels shortly afterward, Ulrik had restricted her movements to the castle.

Nastasia was unmoved. *You know we can't do that, Ren.*

Sparring, then. Surely you can quote the Tomes at me while we spar.

The bells rang out, and as the Silent Hour began, Nastasia released their mettlemancy. Not so long ago, they would have secretly communed throughout the Silence. But that was before Nastasia had donned the purple robes of a priestess. Though they both wore surcoats of finnik leather—flame-resistant and designed to pull away heat from the body to avoid burning up—her cousin's robes beneath were stark reminders of how things were changing, how both their paths were laid out before them. Renna envied Nastasia's sure path toward the church, so much simpler than hers. Because she was tied to the throne only through a long-ago second marriage, Nastasia was not subject to the responsibilities and expectations that Renna had been born into. More than that, Nastasia was already pure; her training only made her more so. Whereas something inside Renna didn't belong in the kingdom; she had to be forged from something impure into a queen. It was not the easiest thing to make one element into another.

The words of her Foretelling replayed over and over in her mind, reverberating through her soul like the echoing ring of the church bells.

Following the Silent Hour, they'd adjourned to the throne room, where low chaises lined the walls. The rumor was that after one too many nobles had fainted after a tithe, their bashed noses wasting blood on the floor, a royal decree had gone out that every room and hallway must contain a fainting couch.

Lord Gisborne had been lecturing her for the better part of an hour in a tone that had Renna daydreaming of the lord toppling in such a way: nose crooked and leaking blood, stoic nature shattered, unable to continue his speech. An ungenerous thought, but whenever she was around him, Renna felt like a scared sixteen-year-old and not a woman of nearly twenty-four who was about to take the throne. Gisborne, along with Nastasia, and Ulrik, was among the few who had been present for Renna's Foretelling. It was he who had discovered the obscure bloodletting ritual, different from the Blood Tithe, that could drain an unwanted element from a person's blood.

Her attention came back as Gisborne offered her an aurem necklace in the same collar-like style as the one he wore. Most of those who served the church wore their aurem as arm cuffs, like the aurem bracer around Nastasia's wrist, and studs pierced below or through the lips, but those were traditional, not utilitarian.

The metal vibrated gently against her palms as she took it. The thick choker was more ornate than the one Gisborne wore, with a near-invisible clasp at the back and an uncut bloodstone set at the front. Flecks of gold and crimson swirled in the gem. The bloodstone seemed to pull in the light around it, pulsing with an inverse glow.

Renna could tell that she was supposed to admire it, but she didn't find it particularly handsome. She preferred the sculptures in the temple: stone so expertly carved that it looked buttery soft and veil-like, or delicately worked copper that reflected light like the setting sun scattered across the water at high tide. Even the meticulously woven tapestries depicting Loxley's history excited her more.

Gisborne's tone carried a hint of self-satisfaction. "Soon we shall have enough forged for all the Trissaia. With your blessing."

Ah. So this was not a lecture, but rather a sales pitch. These ceremonial endorsements were her only true regal responsibilities until she became queen; Ulrik, as regent, handled most of the important matters of the throne. While she needed this time to prepare for the crucible, Renna didn't particularly enjoy feeling more ornamental than useful.

"Tell me what it does," Renna said.

Gisborne's lips pressed into a thin line, most likely an attempt to conceal his irritation. "Your Grace, I just did."

Renna refrained from snorting. His idea of an explanation was an hour-long lesson on finnikfire with idioms like *the only church-sanctioned magic; the Mother's light; our greatest weapon against vedra rot.* "I do not need you to wax poetic on our kingdom's history, Gisborne. Tell me plainly."

With this break of decorum came a pinch at the base of her skull as Nastasia asked, *What are you doing?*

Renna, focused on keeping at bay the gnawing thoughts regarding her crucible, did not answer.

Gisborne dipped his head, the motion making the light catch on the studs of aurem along his ears. "My apologies, Your Grace. What I mean to say is that we have discovered a way for aurem to amplify the natural abilities of firefinniks and Trissaia."

His words were carefully bladed, the collar in her hands suddenly heavy. This aurem would aid Trissaia in channeling finnikfire and speaking Truth, their most sacred ability.

There were mundane instances during which a Trissaia could be consulted for Truth: matchmaking, predictions about crops, or guidance on which vocation to choose, when to take a vow of silence, what to do if one's neighbor was harboring vedra materials. But speaking Truth occurred most often during someone's Foretelling.

Truth was inexplicably tied to one's fate. It was the prophecy indicating the height of one's potential and warning about the potential depths of their failures.

Renna handed the necklace back and delivered the expected response: that all the higher-level Trissaia should have them by the Blood Tithe.

Gisborne bowed, taking his leave.

What was that all about? Nastasia asked.

Perhaps it was the reminder that despite all her tithing, she could still become the next Almost Queen. Or the fact that she didn't share Nastasia and Ulrik's confidence that her Trissaia powers would manifest fully once she went through the crucible. Even these new aurem necklaces may not help bolster her abilities. Whatever the reason, panic rolled over her like the dark clouds that had formed hours ago before the flash storm. Her firefinnik leathers suddenly felt too tight, too *wrong*. Her palms buzzed, fingers clumsy as she tugged at the buttons of her high collar.

Nastasia took her hand, then turned under the guise of fixing the surcoat and looked at Renna—really looked at her, at her throat and the hidden ritual scar there. They'd never spoken aloud about it, only through mettlemancy. Even then, they always skirted the topic, looking at it as if from the corners of their eyes. *Renna, you come from a long line of Koravik queens, all of them firefinniks and Trissaia. You'll be ready.*

The next audience was ushered in. "Your Majesty," began a familiar voice. It was Yana, the head cook. The woman smoothed her hands over her apron before dropping into a curtsy several paces from Renna. She kept her eyes lowered.

Renna frowned at the unusual display of formality. She'd been visiting the kitchens since she was a child, ever since her mother had discovered her love of Yana's cinnamon scones. *Those scones didn't appear out of thin air,* her mother had said before accompanying Renna to the kitchens to meet and thank the cook. Renna had spent many hours in the kitchens that summer, Yana teaching her how to make the scones herself.

Renna descended from the raised dais and took the woman's hand, callused and warm and shaking. "Peace, Yana. What is it?"

"There's a new lass in the kitchens, my lady. Her ma was like a sister to me. I look after her and—she's young, Your Grace. She didn't mean anything by it. I know she didn't mean anything by it. She's naïve, and she's from the country, where ways are different. She broke Silence."

The ways are not so different in the country, Nastasia said stiffly. Having been raised in the annexed villages herself, her cousin knew better than most. Silence was perhaps the simplest of the Mother's requirements. Every child learned it from the moment they could understand *shhh*.

"Lord Gisborne ordered that she be taken to the dungeon, Your Grace." Yana's voice wavered.

Nastasia said, *If the girl broke Silence, then Gisborne made the proper choice.*

"How old is this girl?"

"Twelve, Your Grace," said Yana.

The age Renna had been when she'd received her Foretelling. When she'd begun her duty.

Nastasia's tone was sharp, even through the mettlemancy. *Keeping Silence is a pillar of the Mother's Truth, is it not?*

It was, and by the Tomes of Truth, no one would question Gisborne for punishing the girl. But a memory washed over Renna: her mother sitting on the throne, listening to someone who'd been brought in for a similarly minor transgression. There'd been a furrow between her brows, though her deep ocher skin was otherwise smooth. Marian, Renna's royal governess, had found her spying on the proceedings from an alcove. When Renna had asked why the audiences always took so long, Marian had pulled her into her lap, the familiar warmth of the woman's arms immediately soothing her anxiety. Her governess had stroked Renna's hair before answering.

"The Mother is merciful with us, Rennavera, and so the crown is also merciful to the people. The queen must weigh the severity of the crime and the willingness of the wicked to repent."

The emotions that had churned inside Renna all morning now felt like they were crystalizing into a single powerful thought: this was a moment when she could behave like the queen she would become. This was how she could embody everything her mother and Ulrik and Marian had taught her. This was how she could live with herself at night when her doubt chewed on her legs.

With mettlemancy, Renna said to Nastasia, *The girl wasn't summoning a storm with vedra runes or attempting to channel power from the False Flame, Stasi. It should cost her an extra tithe, not her tongue.* Then she raised her voice, motioning to the nearest guards. "See to it that this woman's ward is released back into her care. Perhaps time in the company of the priestesses would serve her well."

Tears flashed in Yana's eyes before she dropped to her knees, forehead bowed over their still-clasped hands. "Truth is in the blood, Your Grace."

As Yana and the guards dispersed, Nastasia remained silent—not her usual silence, but an oppressive quiet that made it obvious she was withholding her words. Renna tried to quash the feeling of guilt, hating when they disagreed. *Well?*

Is it foolish to hope that the future queen will hold the Truth in as high a regard as I?

The words crackled down the mental tether with a dangerous undercurrent. Renna stilled, balancing on the edge of something precarious between them that she wasn't ready to traverse.

Nastasia must have felt it too, because she dropped swiftly to her knees, her aurem bracelet clinking against the floor as she braced her hands against the flagstones. "Forgive me, my lady. I forget myself."

Her cousin's dramatic drop, an overt reminder of how different their ranks were, felt like walking through an unseen cobweb that clung to her skin. The day she would take the throne was fast approaching, but how she longed to hold on to their youth and sisterhood a little while longer. To not have to worry about her worthiness or the crucible or the crown.

"Peace, Stasi," Renna hissed, pulling Nastasia back to her feet. Her cousin was still pale with her transgression.

"I will make it up to you, my lady."

An idea struck her, and Renna looped her arm through her cousin's, falling into the old familiar way they draped all over each other. Ignoring the pain, she reached out with mettlemancy. *If you want to make it up to me, a trip to Nottingham seems like the appropriate penance.*

Nastasia sighed through her nose, looking skyward, but Renna caught the twitch of her lips. The tension from a moment ago dissolved as her cousin replied, *Was this your plan all along?*

CHAPTER 2

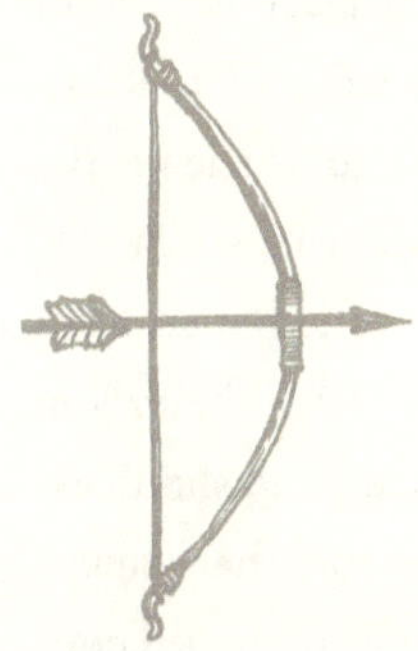

Touch not the powers from the oaks, rivers, sky, or sea. Do not be tempted by
False Flame, as the druidhen and vedra would have you be. Ward yourself
against those who do, for they seek to destroy the Mother's Truth.
—Truth given through Osric, First Trissaia

Fɪʀsт тнеу had то lose the guards. Sɪɴce her parents' murder, Renna had been escorted everywhere by red clerics, the palace's royal soldiers. They trailed her from her rooms to the stables to sparring practice. When she grew too tired or sore from tithes to train or the gaze of courtiers clawed at her neck, she retired to the temple, letting the red clerics believe it was devotion that made the soon-to-be queen sequester herself for hours. It was common knowledge that there was a private royal alcove in the temple for reflection and prayer.

What wasn't common knowledge was the false wall in the adjoining chamber.

Renna sensed the moment the temple's sanctity loosened the tension in her guards' shoulders, when they allowed their attention to wander and they peeled off to wait in the wing. She stepped behind the privacy screen of the royal alcove, where an aurem lantern cast shadows on the table holding an offering bowl and bloodstone dagger. A low velvet couch was tucked into the corner next to vellum prayer scrolls—any vestiges of poisonous trees, including paper, had been put to finnikfire centuries ago. The walls had intricate carvings that caught the light of the red flames. When Renna had been younger, the effect had seemed to twist the images, filling her mind with thoughts of the beasts that had wreaked havoc on Loxley centuries ago, before the Culling: fearsome stags with teeth as long as her forearm; demonic winged horses that ate flesh; foxes cursed by vedra, whose tails could spread unholy wildfires; tree spirits that would lure you into the forest only to strangle you slowly with their roots.

Renna touched her fingertips to her mouth and heart, silent gratitude for the Mother's favor and the knowledge of the threat the trees posed to the Trissaia's powers. She was attempting to extricate the aurem circlet from the braided coronet around her head when Nastasia slipped into the alcove. Her cousin's mouth quirked into a smile as she batted Renna's hands aside and began to pull out the small pins and let the braid hang long down Renna's back—undone, it would halo out around her head and shoulders like a cloud.

Nastasia's features were soft, her olive skin lighter than Renna's golden brown. The sides of her head were shaved completely, the remaining raven tresses bound into a high knot. In her novice robes, her cousin had a solemn, austere look most days. But here, hidden away from the rest of the court, about to sneak out of the castle, Renna could see the more playful version of her cousin seeping through. For a moment, Renna imagined the two of them back before Nastasia had donned her robes, when her cousin would help Renna sneak away for quick trysts with whichever noble she fancied. Back when Nastasia had a wicked talent for coming up with bawdy nicknames for their retinue of red clerics.

Renna ran her hand along the back wall to find the familiar groove, nearly invisible alongside the ornate carvings in the stone. When she was younger, she'd assumed that finnikfire was temperamental for everyone, but training with Nastasia had quickly disabused her of that notion. It was the opposite for her cousin, her fire eager to spring to life, waiting just below the surface. Each time Nastasia cast finnikfire, it was something beautiful, something like art.

Renna called up her finnikfire, internally coaxing the spark to life. The magic stirred in her veins, rousing like a slumbering beast. She sent a pulse of fire down through her palm, and the stone shifted in answer, drawing back to reveal the dark opening to a tunnel. Cold, sulfur-scented air wafted out.

They had discovered the tunnels quite by accident. After a failed attempt to speak a Truth, she'd fled to the private chamber, and Nastasia had followed, wringing her hands, not knowing how to comfort her. Renna had pounded the wall with her fists, tasting salt from her tears. Anger and frustration had swelled inside her, hot through her palms, until her finnikfire had flared and the stone gave up its secrets. Panic had spiked her veins when she'd first entered the labyrinth, but then she'd felt something—or rather, an absence of something. Here in the dark and quiet, away from the cloying eyes of the court nobles and council members, she could be just Renna.

After that, she'd explored forgotten alcoves, listened through the walls as nobles bickered about infidelity, brought treats to an owl who frequented the window of a secluded corridor, and played countless games of hide-and-seek with Nastasia. Ulrik knew—there was no way to keep secrets from such a skilled mettlemancer—but he'd never tried to stop her. They'd never spoken of it, but she assumed it was a kindness. After all, she'd always stayed within the confines of the castle walls, as was the rule.

Well, until today.

It was awkward to lower herself into the crawl space in a dress, but she'd done it plenty of times before. Ducking her head to avoid knocking it on the roof of the passageway, she moved farther in to allow Nastasia to drop down lightly behind her. Above them, the door closed, plunging them into darkness except for the concentrated red flame of a lantern. They picked their way forward in silence, taking the well-known turns to a few crude steps that led up to another false wall. A second pulse of flame from Renna's palm shifted the door, and the two slipped out of the passageway.

The corridor was empty except for a long plinth of bloodstone positioned a few paces in front of a massive tapestry. The intricately woven depiction of the Great Culling covered the entire wall. There were smaller tapestries with similar renditions of the holy war throughout the palace. The unbroken line of Trissaia casting finnikfire at the cowering army of druids, witches, and monsters. The enemy falling before the Mother's Flame as the trees around them caught fire. Druidhen and vedra, two sides of the same coin, drawing from the dangerous and perverse magics that corrupted the Mother's Flame. The druidhen had been more organized in their opposition to the First Head Trissaia's teachings, openly defying the Great Culling.

The druidhen were all dead now. Nearly all of Sherwood had been destroyed, taking the creatures and rot with it. But, as Ulrik frequently said, rot left untended will always spread, and small groups of vedra had fled the forest to Wendsvik, where they'd begun spreading dark teachings of the False Flame. The residents of Loxley had long attempted to spread the Mother's Truth to the neighboring pagans in Wendsvik. As the church proselytized, Loxley's armies fought to keep the kingdom and the Mother's Flame safe from the vedra army of Falsehoods.

"Truth shall light the way," Nastasia murmured.

"Truth is in the blood," Renna replied, and hung the aurem lantern on one of the empty hooks that lined the wall.

The abandoned hall led to a large, bustling corridor. Servants milled about, carrying away chamber pots, dusting the aurem lanterns, fluffing the cushions of the chaise lounges. Renna nicked two cloaks from a pallet of fresh laundry as a maid chatted with a man in livery. She tossed one to Nastasia, who caught it effortlessly. They weren't the deep purple of the Keeper robes but a dark green denoting a commoner. They threw them around their shoulders, Renna pulling her thick braid free, and made their way to the gatehouse.

The Mother's Flame burned below the castle, cradled by the mountain itself. As such, the palace had been constructed around it for protection. They traversed the complex series of bridges, towers, and barriers to the bone portcullis at the top of the fortress. Renna kept her chin tucked as they approached the guards on either side. The officers look bored, though, and were only really paying mind to those coming *in*. No one looked their way as the crown princess and her lady-in-waiting slipped out of the castle in the guise of two commoners who had been visiting the temple.

Immediately Renna felt better.

The fresh air filled her lungs. The smell of salt water flooded her nostrils. The long stone staircase before them was carved into the outermost wall of the battlements. Nearly the width of a dozen men, the steps wound around the fortress like a snake. The pilgrimage was referred to as the Hallowed Walk, but Renna knew from eavesdropping on the palace maids that most called it the *Harrowing* Walk. The only thing keeping people from falling over the edge and plummeting to their death was a half wall fashioned from bloodstone and aurem, a symbol of the city's devotion to the Mother.

The din of the city below grew as they melted into the crowd of citizens making the trek down. Renna found the jostling of elbows and shoulders oddly comforting, and she let herself be pulled along with the current. The sun was a hazy blot in the grey sky, the storm from that morning long over. After the Culling, the violent shift in the ecosystem had resulted in the intense storms and flash flooding Loxley now endured, but such was the price of protecting the Mother's Flame from the vedra forces that sought to eradicate the Light. Now at high tide, the Perun Sea sealed off the kingdom from Wendsvik. As a tidal island, Loxley was surrounded by water at high tide and connected to the mainland at low tide. The constant shift in how to access the kingdom made any siege—by land or by ship—nearly impossible. Loxley was impenetrable. Spires atop stone turrets pierced the sky, the structures adorned with thin slotted windows that would hold even in strong storms.

Down they went, a cramp steadily building in Renna's side, but the vast expanse of open sea tugged at her, and she let the pain fade in the background. It was no more than she was accustomed to daily. Her energy swelled, bright and vibrant. Renna grabbed Nastasia's hand, squeezing as she reached out with mettlemancy. *Last one to the bottom buys drinks.*

Ren, you promised to be discreet—

Renna released her hand and their connection. As she darted through the crowd, holding her hood secure, a laugh burst from her. The noise of the crowd swallowed up Nastasia's protest. Renna bumped into a group of young girls making their way up and called out an apology over her shoulder, taking the stairs two at a time, letting momentum direct her feet. She wove around people, aware of Nastasia at her heels.

She didn't see the group of Keepers stepping out of the throng until she was practically on top of them. Renna threw her arms out, and she and the priestess in front gripped one another as they both tried to maintain their balance. Nastasia darted past, disappearing around the curve of the stairs. The priestess's hair was dark as the night sky save for one streak of silver. The lighter lock framed her face, which was a perfect picture of disapproval. Renna ducked her head, hoping she hadn't been recognized, and altered her voice as she muttered an apology.

Renna was winded and sulky when she reached the bottom of the stairs, well behind Nastasia.

"You can't win them all, Ren." Nastasia threw an arm around her shoulders.

While Sherwood Forest had burned outside the walls, the city inside had been torn apart to cleanse Loxley of wood. Homes and churches had been rebuilt using stone, brick, clay, or aurem. Trees had been ripped from the palace gardens. Occasionally, a wooden relic still turned up, one that had either survived the Culling or been smuggled in from Wendsvik by False Flame zealots. Gisborne was always beside himself with righteous anger when this happened. Just last month a whole row of houses in Nottingham had turned out to be harboring arrows made of wood. Renna had bitten her tongue to keep from asking if she could see them as Gisborne's yells had filled the private council room. "What if these had been allowed to infiltrate the kingdom? We might as well have invited the Night Watchman to dine with us. This new high sheriff is a disgrace."

New was bit of a stretch. The current high sheriff of Nottingham had held the position for five years now. Garen Draic, Renna's old sparring partner, had held the role until he'd been given command of a small battalion and sent to the warfront five years prior. They'd certainly not been friends—more rivals than anything, as Draic was arrogant and had no qualms about leaving Renna bruised and bared after lessons. His reputation was such that when he'd been named high sheriff, the word *nepotism* did not cross anyone's lips. But two years ago, when the news had come of his capture and subsequent death at the hands of the Falsehoods, Renna had felt haunted by a sense of loss.

The aurem-rich architecture of the noble sector slowly petered out as they traveled farther down the mountain, giving way to crowded homes piled high atop one another, crafted from worn bloodstone and rusting metals or bricks made of sand and dirt. Plastered to the stone were thin vellum sheets bearing a sketch of an acorn with a slash, reminding the citizens of Loxley of the dangers posed by trees.

Renna tried to recall if the city had looked this bad when she'd last seen it. Surely not. Worry knotted in her gut. Ahead of them, a crowd blocked the way. Royal guards stood in front of a dilapidated doorway as a man and woman were dragged into the street. Tear tracks carved paths through the dirt on their faces. Renna's stomach tightened as if she was the one being dragged. Metal clanged loudly as a guard nailed a thin sheet of copper to the door: another crossed-out acorn.

There was poisonous wood inside.

"For crimes against the Truth and harboring detritus from trees," a Keeper called.

This is no place for you to be identified, Ren, Nastasia said, and dragged her down a side street.

The commotion faded behind them, but Renna's heart was beating painfully fast. She ducked under the awning of a shop, trying to quell her building anxiety. She scrubbed a hand over her face but still could not shake the image of the couple's tears tracing paths down their cheeks. Renna knew they must be punished; it was the only way to keep order in the kingdom, to protect her people here and on the warfront. Loxley prospered because of the Mother's favor. And obedience was the price of Her blessing.

But seeing her people from this vantage point, the consequences felt much more tangible.

Something orange darted through the doorway of a shop, followed by someone cursing *bark off!* A small creature wove between her legs, then vanished down the alley. The shopkeeper appeared in the doorway with a half-eaten loaf of bread in one hand and a dented collection plate in the other. Renna could only stare in the direction the animal had run.

A *fox.*

One less desirable result of the Culling was the rise of feral woodland creatures roaming Loxley's streets. They were common enough, but any sensible citizen knew to shun the beasts, as they were easily susceptible to vedra influences and could be carriers of their impure magics. Hunting foxes for sport had become quite popular of late. Just last week Renna had sat through a long-winded petition for a citywide sanctioned hunt to handle the infestation with a prize purse for the most kills.

A pinch at the base of her skull brought her back to the present. *It's your blessed day, Ren.* Nastasia stood a little farther down street, pointing to the vellum sheets fluttering in the breeze. Renna drew nearer to inspect them. Poster promising rewards for any information about the Night Watchman; news of the most recent victories over on the continent ("YOUR BLOOD TITHE MADE POSSIBLE THIS VICTORY FOR THE MOTHER'S TRUTH"); proverbs from the Tomes of Truth. Renna quickly spotted the one Nastasia was talking about.

TODAY: AUREM PURSE FOR THE WINNER OF ARCHERY CONTEST!

Maybe you won't need to dip into the royal treasury to pay for my drinks after all, Nastasia said.

Renna's mouth pulled into a grin. Her blessed day indeed.

CHAPTER 3

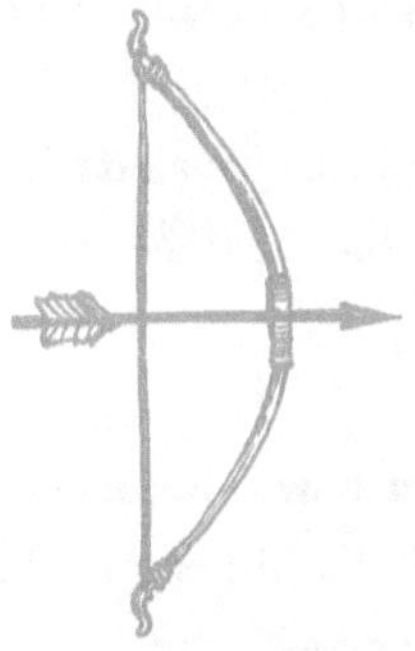

THE ARCHERY CONTEST WAS BEING HELD IN AN OLD CHURCH COURTYARD, THE TARGETS SET UP AGAINST THE FAR SIDE OF THE EMPTY FIELD.

At one time, this had probably been a beautiful, dangerous place; lining the lawn were charred sections of ground where the stumps of massive old trees had been burned. Oaks, probably—the worst of them, the trees that drained Trissaia of their ability to see and speak Truths and poisoned the mind against the Mother. Now tufts of grass grew sparsely in the dirt, and the smell of sour ale clung to the air. Renna wrinkled her nose.

Are your royal sensibilities offended? Nastasia teased.

In truth, they were. The presentation was woeful in comparison to the competitions she regularly participated in back at the palace. But wasn't that why she'd demanded they sneak out in the first place? She'd wanted to be with her people. And judging by the stench, she was about as close to the people as one could get.

Two men were taking entrance fees at the side of the field. Extra bows were piled on the stone wall behind them, scuffed and stained with grime. Before the Great Culling, bows and arrows had been made from wood. Now they were crafted from bone, sinew, and aurem. The men were nothing like the courtiers in the castle. One had a mouthful of rotten teeth. The other was short and twisted with bowlegs.

"Name?" asked the bowlegged man. There wasn't a lick of politeness about him; this was different from the castle too.

Renna had been feeling nostalgic all day, and the false name fell easily from her lips: "Marian." Her governess, Mother rest her soul, would have approved of her subterfuge.

"Two aurems an entry."

"Any charge for a loaner bow?" Renna changed the cadence of her words, attempting to hide the noble lilt in her speech. She jutted her chin toward the weapons, careful to not let her cowl drop.

The second man bared his rotten teeth at them. "Another three. Each."

Nastasia tensed beside her, but Renna merely plucked the additional coins from a pocket in her cloak. She was careful not to let the remaining money jingle as she paid for both of them. This day wouldn't be fun if it ended with a robbery.

With bows and quivers in their possession, they moved aside to let the next people in line pay. Renna gently tested the point of an arrow with her thumb: dulled from use, but serviceable. An official-looking woman announced the rules in a booming voice. Each contestant would have one shot to make their best hit. Showmanship and tricks to impress the judges were encouraged.

For all that was different between Nottingham and the palace, this was the same: with a bow and arrow in her hand, Renna was supremely confident of who she was.

A woman who could land a bull's-eye.

Fellow competitors, many of them boisterous young people, gathered to discuss strategy and jostle one another like puppies. Renna grinned as she took in the crowd; their faces were smudged and lined with exhaustion, but their eyes were alight. Dirty children clung to their mothers' skirts, mugs of ale were shared, and someone whistled a tune. A few villagers joined in, singing the lyrics to a tavern song off key: *witches and outlaws sitting by the trees, R-O-T-T-I-N-G.*

"Taters! Half a coin. Taters!" a young boy yelled over the tray he brandished.

The potatoes were lumpy and half shriveled, but Renna grinned, exchanging a coin for one a little larger than her fist. She tossed it to Nastasia. "What do you reckon, Stasi? Catch and fire?"

A snort from beneath the cowl. "Hardly seems a fair fight."

"But think how pleased Devana would be."

Nastasia cut her a sharp look. "She would light her own blood on fire from her grave, knowing we'd snuck out like this." Grudgingly she inspected the potato before slipping off to find twine.

Their old weapons master *would* have been horrified. It had taken months of pestering Ulrik to secure Devana Draic as her teacher. Archery wasn't typically taught to nobility, but Renna could shoot arrows after tithing and not be struck with a headache or fatigue the way she was when they used swords or daggers. She could train for longer stretches of time or even practice while astride Alita and not wear herself out as quickly. Devana was an archer of high renown, known for her unrivaled ability to split arrows and her signature flair with a bow. But she was retired, staunchly claiming it was the Mother's wish for her to spend her final years with family. Which was why Devana's only grandson, Garen, had become Renna's sparring partner even though such a thing was not traditional.

Nastasia returned to her side. Sweat beaded between Renna's shoulder blades as the sun beat oppressively down on them; the sea breeze never made it into Nottingham. The first contestants began to take their shots. The archers nearest them were whispering and glancing over their shoulders at the other competitors. A young boy took his turn, sending an arrow into the bull's-eye after a complicated acrobatic leap, earning a cheer from the spectators. As the line of people ahead of her dwindled, Renna's spirits lifted. She felt Nastasia's enthusiasm bubbling, too. There was nothing quite like having someone else believe in you, even if it was for something that didn't matter in the long run.

When Marian was called, Renna stepped up to the firing line. Fingers loose at her side, Renna waited for Nastasia to get into position opposite her, just in front of the target. Snickering raced through the onlookers; it was quite a sight, the woman standing there with a potato secured on top of her head with twine tied off under her chin. The first time Renna had seen Garen similarly posed, she'd laughed until tears leaked from her eyes. It had boosted her mood for an entire week, even when Devana had scolded her for acting childish and when Garen had bested her at splitting arrows. Renna did not begrudge the spectators their laughter, especially because it shifted to sharp intakes of breath as their understanding dawned.

Renna turned her back to Nastasia. Feet planted apart, bow held loosely at her side, she waited as her cousin nocked an arrow, readying her aim. The hair on Renna's neck prickled, the excitement in her veins dulling the sharp pain at the back of her skull.

Catch and fire was a risky play, even with mettlemancy at their disposal. Timing was everything. In the heartbeat of time between Nastasia releasing the arrow and its metal point burying itself in Renna's back, she would need to spin around, snatch it from the air, and return fire. She'd have a split second for a shot that required absolute precision.

The burdens of the world slipped off Renna like a loose cloak. No weighted glances, no bows of deference. No whispers of duty. No demands that she display her firefinnik abilities. The anonymity and recklessness warmed her body like too much wine. This must be what it felt like for everyone else after the Blood Tithe.

I say this with all due respect, Ren: You do *realize you're a tree-brained fool, yes?*

Renna grinned. *Won't be the last time I'm called that.*

Nastasia's tone was withering. *Three…*

Renna shook out her right hand.

Two…

Renna exhaled.

One.

Even without the mettlemancy, Renna's body was tuned to the subtle *twang* in the air, the shiver of premonition.

Someone screamed, but everything was blurred except for the arrow shooting straight toward her as she spun on her heel. Renna whipped out her arm. Her palm stung in protest as she snatched the arrow, but the pain was nothing to her. In a fluid motion, her bow was up, arrow nocked. The fletching briefly touched the side of her mouth, and she let it fly.

The potato exploded in a wet mess, leaving one large chunk skewered by the arrow now buried in the dead center of the target.

The crowd roared in disbelief and pleasure. Renna's arms trembled as she held her hood in place while hands clapped her on the back in congratulations. The judges' deliberation was brief before they declared a winner: Marian. The heavy purse of aurem was pressed into her palms. A surge of belonging went through her as Nastasia appeared at her side, eyes crinkled in a grin. But the atmosphere shifted. The crowd, drunken and riled, swayed together like clothes tumbling in the large laundry vats back at the castle. Someone jostled her hard, an elbow digging into the soft spot between her ribs. There were mutterings about the clean state of her cloak and what would a highborn be doing down here and do you recall Devana Draic? Someone booed. Faces twisted into sneers, and panic laced tightly through Renna's chest.

"—obviously some noble bitches come down here to steal what's rightfully ours—"

The words were dripping with hatred and struck Renna like a blow. The speaker was one of the competitors: the acrobatic boy. An older woman snatched his arm, begging him to keep his voice down. The boy snarled, ignoring the insistent tugging from his companion, features screwed up in righteous rage. "Don't you take enough?"

Nastasia pressed close. "We should leave. Now."

Red cloaks and armor flashed, and Renna's heart leapt into her throat as guards began pushing through the crowd. She stood frozen in place at the sight of the angry tears streaking through the grime on the boy's face. The image seemed to be inescapable today. There had been no such tears when her mother had walked these streets. Was this to be Renna's legacy? Up close, the older woman's cheeks were sunken inward, and her skin looked like it could peel right off the bone. The boy's arms were peppered with badly healed tithe marks, and the jut of his collarbone was clear through the threadbare tunic.

Ren, we must go. Now.

Renna found her voice. "Wait." Her body acted of its own accord, holding out the purse. "I meant no harm. Just…please, take it."

The guards were nearly to them, bogged down by onlookers, and dread swooped through Renna's gut. Warring emotions flickered across the woman's features, torn between the promise of the aurem that clinked in the bag and fleeing before the guards could question who dared to speak out against a noble. Bleeding Mother, what was the punishment for that? Never mind that Renna wasn't just a noble but the heir to the throne. She thought of mutilated tongues, chains in a dank dungeon. *Shit.* She should have never left the castle. Any chance to do something *good*, to do something her mother would have done, would vanish the moment the guards realized the crown princess was in the middle of an unsettled and drunken crowd.

Renna pushed the purse into the woman's hands. "Take it."

The woman's slender fingers closed tightly around the purse. "May the Mother bless you with Truth," she said. And then she and the boy disappeared into the crowd.

Nastasia's fingers twitched subtly. Finnikfire burst a few paces away, startling the guards, and she hauled Renna away.

They were several streets over before they stopped to catch their breath. Renna's head was beginning to ache, and she had no fewer than three blisters on her feet, but she no longer felt ornamental, like something made of glass that needed to be protected behind the castle walls.

She should have known the feeling would be fleeting.

CHAPTER 4

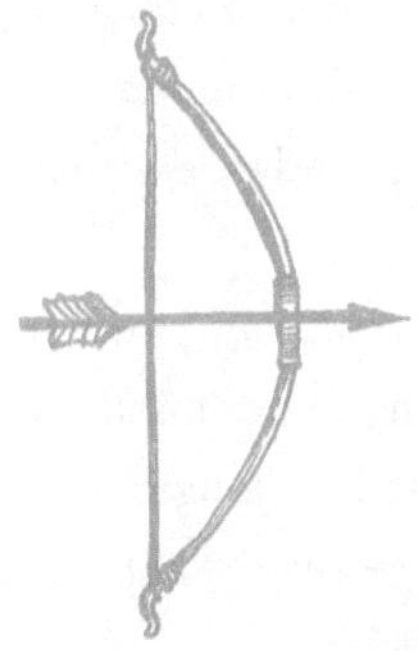

RENNA STOOD IN THE THRONE ROOM ANTECHAMBER IN WHAT SHE HOPED WAS A STANCE OF CONTRITION. Her nails bit into her palm. They had been caught. She had emerged into the royal chamber in the temple just in time to come face-to-face with Ulrik. Any hope of clemency disappeared when she saw the disapproval on his face. Nastasia had been made to wait outside with her guards. This conversation was meant for her alone. He hadn't said anything to her yet, though her head pulsed with the mettlemantic connection.

Ulrik loomed over the large bloodstone table, knuckles pressed into the map of Dravmir etched into the dark rock. He looked like a wrathful god looking down on the world below, carved pieces of aurem representing the citizens of Loxley arranged across its surface like a giant game of chess: their troops on Wendsvik across the Perun Sea; missions of Keepers spreading the Mother's Truth; cities that recognized the Mother—and therefore Loxley—as their sovereign and contributed to the Blood Tithe. A deep groove in the stone showed the trade route to Wendsvik that skirted the edge of the forest. The road was the only way to access the narrow causeway leading to Loxley during low tide, but it was dangerous, frequented by outlaws and vedra who sought to thwart and oppress the Truth.

Renna's gaze traveled across the small strip of water between Wendsvik's edge and Sherwood Forest—or rather, what remained of Sherwood Forest. In vivid aurem, the art on the table showed the large swathes of forest that had been burned in the Great Culling, leaving miles of land that alternated between marshy plains and unbroken sea, depending on the level of the tide.

Ulrik looked up at Renna from under furrowed brows. "Every time I think you're getting closer to being ready—*every time*, Rennavera—you do something that undermines our mission."

Renna swallowed her reply. Shame twisted in her gut, Ulrik's mettlemancy dictating the memories playing in her mind: overturning Gisborne's punishment for the kitchen maid; running headlong into the group of Keepers; the archery contest in Nottingham; giving away the aurem purse; and finally, the angry crowd she'd run from.

"There are reports that the crown princess was gallivanting in the slums, taunting her people."

"That's not—" Renna blinked against the heat in her eyes, digging her nails deeper into her palm.

The tokens representing their army blurred as Ulrik sighed, boots scuffing along the floor. Large hands rested on her shoulders. "The Falsehoods have advanced and gained territory at Wendsvik's edge. Loxley is at risk. Do you understand the danger you put yourself in? You might've been killed if you'd been recognized. You could've been ransomed. You would've been Loxley's weak point."

Renna couldn't bring herself to look at him. Ulrik grasped the high collar of her jacket, tugging it open to reveal the scar along the left side of the column of her throat. His finger brushed the raised skin and sent a memory into her mind— his memory. Renna had her own version of this one, but it was Ulrik's she saw now, clear as the day it had happened.

She looked so small on the bloodstone altar, only sixteen. Ulrik's anxiety threaded the memory as Gisborne stood at his shoulder, speaking in hushed tones. She was just a child. He had to protect her, would never forgive himself if he didn't. They'd spent the last four years searching for a solution, ever since that damned Foretelling.

"Will it work?" Ulrik cut off Gisborne's string of words. "Will it cure her blood of…the darkness?" He couldn't bring himself to say it aloud.

"Yes, my lord."

A sense of knowing, of Truth, washed through him, the same sensation he felt when he peered into the Mother's Flame and was gifted with a vision of the future. Ulrik would do whatever was needed to honor the late king and queen, to fulfill his oath that he would protect their daughter. Renna would lead Loxley in the way of the Mother's Flame, spreading Truth to the pagan vedra across the sea. Rennavera Koravik was to be the next firefinnik queen.

Ulrik gave a curt nod, and Gisborne placed a bloodstone dagger into his hand. The hilt was cold.

As the palace physician and another Trissaia held Renna down on the stone, Ulrik placed a thick strip of leather in her mouth. "Bite down on this, Rennavera. It will be over quickly."

Renna obeyed. She was an obedient girl. Her parents had raised her to be trusting, and she trusted him now. He would not let her down. He smoothed a hand over her hair, just once. Renna didn't flinch, but her pulse fluttered in her neck. Ulrik steeled himself. *Truth is in the blood.* They could not afford to be weak.

The edge of the dagger cut easily through her skin, blood welling up and spilling. Ulrik held his hand steady, careful to not go too deep or to hit the main artery. Gisborne and Ulrik murmured the ritual words together as blood pooled beneath Renna.

The present snapped back into place as Ulrik released her from the mettlemancy hold.

Renna swayed, nausea roiling her stomach. She reached for something to say to repair her mistakes. "Forgive me, my lord. I wasn't thinking. I…I want to be better. I *will* be better." She was dismally aware of having heard Yana say something similar earlier that day about the kitchen maid who had broken Silence. She wasn't exactly sure how to say that she deserved mercy when Ulrik didn't feel the kitchen maid was owed the same.

Behind Ulrik was a smaller table strewn with vellum, bloodstones, and a collection plate. In silence, he rifled through a small chest atop it before finding what he wanted: an aurem stone, uncut, fist-size. Each facet caught the light differently, crimson, gold, silver, and onyx. It was heavy in Renna's palm when he handed it over, and she tested a sharp edge with her thumb, careful not to slice her skin. Anticipation hummed in her veins.

"You know what this is." It wasn't a question.

How could she not? Each Koravik queen before her had proven her worth through the crucible: a trial of aurem. The intense heat that resulted from channeling finnikfire directly into the aurem would reveal the wielder's true nature. If a queen was chosen by the Mother, the aurem would remain whole, unbroken under the pressure, and be alchemized into a bloodstone gem that would be embedded in the royal crown. It sat now on a plinth behind Ulrik, resplendent and dripping in the bloodstones of Renna's ancestors. Not for the first time, she wondered just how heavy it felt.

Ulrik gestured to the aurem gripped in her fist. *Your mother's flame burned bright as the sun the day of her crucible.*

For a moment, Renna had the uncanny feeling of gazing into a warped mirror as another image bloomed in her mind. But no—her mother's face, though younger, was unmistakable. Nastasia always told her how much she looked like her mother, and while the resemblance was strong, Renna felt nothing like the poised, determined woman in the memory. Her mother had been incandescent in her youth, a paragon of faith: skin of deep ocher, hair regally braided away from her face, freckles dusting the bridge of a strong nose, eyes bright with conviction.

Leida Koravik. The Mother chose the people of Loxley as Her stewards over the aurem. It is through our devotion to the Truth that we continue to receive Her blessings and guidance. Today, She will speak through the aurem. Let the crucible begin.

Renna strained to see exactly what her mother was doing to the aurem in her hands, but it merely looked like Leida was deep in prayer, head bowed over the sacred stone. Sorrow rose in Renna's throat, sharp as the day she'd lost her parents, the years unable to dull the pain of their deaths. Oh, how Renna wished she could speak to her again just once, to question her. *Did you ever have doubts? Did you ever wonder if you were enough?*

Finally the aurem began to change, morphing and shrinking into a sparkling gem, golden and red and beating with an internal light. The glow reflected off the smile on her mother's face, and the crowd cheered as she held aloft the gleaming bloodstone.

Abruptly, the memory ended. Renna felt so small, the vision cutting as surely as the dagger had cut her arm this morning for her tithe. She swallowed against the grief lodged in her throat.

"The Mother chose the people of Loxley, Rennavera. The mountain of aurem beneath our feet is a testament to that. You must trust the truth running through your blood."

Renna kept silent as, in her mind, Ulrik reminded her of the only one ever to fail the crucible. At least he spared her the shame of saying it aloud for anyone outside the doors to overhear. The Almost Queen had not ridden herself of darkness, and her vedra blood had been exposed when she'd failed the trial.

The Almost Queen had been burned on the aurem pyres. Renna wondered what the dead woman would make of her life being used as the cautionary tale for future queens and children alike.

Her skull ached as Ulrik continued to speak inside her mind. *I am trying to tell you that I will not be able to protect you should you fail.*

Her stilted nod of acknowledgment felt like it came from someone else; Renna watched the conversation as if from somewhere far away.

Finally Ulrik spoke aloud again, gesturing to the aurem in her hands. "The time for your crucible is fast approaching. Use this to prepare. I have done everything I can to help you. The rest is between you and the Mother. There is unrest in Nottingham. I've tried my best to shield you from this burden until after you take the throne, but these vedra outlaws are growing bold. We've had particular trouble of late with the Night Watchman."

A fist tightened in her stomach at the moniker.

The Night Watchman had terrorized the church and the crown for decades. They had lost count of how many red clerics the man had killed or how much he had stolen from the royal coffers. But the way Renna saw it, the Night Watchman was responsible for so much more than those crimes. His lies and deeds acted like weeds in the vulnerable hearts of her people, taking root and slowly strangling the light out of them.

She thought of Marian's face that early morning, twisted with shame and fear, as Renna had pleaded, *You must not say such things.* The memory of her governess sent a pang through her, like pressing on a fresh bruise. No, the Night Watchman had far more blood on his hands than anyone knew.

Ulrik saw the thought flit across her mind. "Ah. I forgot about your late governess. I am sorry, child. I know how fond of her you were. Rot will always spread if unattended." He paused, giving her shoulder an awkward squeeze. "There are reports that he is in the city again, trying to free vedra from the dungeons."

Renna looked up sharply. "Then we should double the guard." Ulrik inclined his head.

She shoved the aurem into her pocket and strode toward the door. Marian's face in her mind morphed into the faces of the citizens with tear tracks down their dirty cheeks.

One more thing, Rennavera.

Renna stopped, glancing over her shoulder. The years had etched themselves on Ulrik's face. Exhaustion pulled at his shoulders, and worry cut lines across his forehead; Renna suspected that even more bracketed his mouth under his fading red beard. His years as regent had taken a toll. She recalled the terror he'd felt while performing the ritual—the fear that he would fail to protect her as he had failed her parents. Her heart squeezed painfully.

Now is the time to turn away from any…lingering darkness. Only then can the Mother choose you as queen.

Outside, her guards lined the wall, eyes straight ahead, and she was grateful for their studied blank gazes. But as she looked around to find Nastasia, the guard nearest her cleared his throat. "She is receiving her own punishment from the Trissaia, Your Grace."

She remembered Nastasia's grin at the archery field. The trip into the city didn't seem worth it now. She didn't feel like saying anything at all, but she whispered, "Thank you."

It was what a queen would do.

CHAPTER 5

For the righteous there is only this: the Mother, her Flame, and her Truth.
Those seduced by the False Flame will claim there are many gods, and many
powers, and many paths. Do not let yourself succumb to rot.
—excerpt from the Tomes of Truth

THE NIGHT WATCHMAN SURVEYED THE CLUSTER OF GUARDS FROM WHERE HE PERCHED HIGH ABOVE ON A ROOFTOP, KEEPING TO THE SHADOWS, AVOIDING THE MOONLIGHT THAT SPLASHED ACROSS THE CITY OF NOTTINGHAM.

He was preternaturally still, swathed in an ink-black cloak and cowl, features obscured by an obsidian half mask. No stranger to waiting, like all good hunters. He'd been tracking them through the streets for the better part of an hour. The prey in question this evening—the guards dragging the bound prisoners along— had stopped to take a piss.

The vitriol they'd been spewing had only increased as the night went on. Every threat and insult punctuated with the word *vedra*. As if the abilities of a witch were dirty and not the same as the prowess that firefinniks displayed. As if there were something inherently wicked about pulling power from the well of magic buried in the land of Dravmir, pulsing through the trunks of trees like a living heartbeat or hanging in the air, so rich you could taste it. No, the twisted bastards up in the temple decreed that anything other than the vein of finnikfire was blasphemous.

His grip on his bow tightened. It was made of rowan wood, and merely possessing it was treasonous enough to have him burned alive. He pulled an arrow from the quiver on his back, notching it into place with the same ease as one might turn a page of a book. Not that anyone in this godsforsaken kingdom would know that feeling. There was a phantom itch in his fingers as he wished for one of his novels that was a world away now, another possession that would have him executed here.

A vicious smack rang out as a guard struck one of the prisoners, and he shoved all thoughts of books and home behind the mountains crafted in his mind, meant to keep others out and his secrets protected. The Watchman decided the handsy guard would be the first to die and placed two more arrows against the bow, deftly holding all three between his fingers. The struck prisoner spat on the boots of the guard. His words were too soft for the Watchman to hear, but the sentiment was clear. Respect and reproach tugged at the Watchman in equal measure as he shot the first arrow.

Handsy was dead before he hit the ground, and the other two quickly followed suit. The Watchman swung down using a drainpipe, crouching as he dropped to the street, cloak billowing behind him like a winged shadow. He cut the prisoners' ties quickly, noticing that their wrists were an angry red. The image seared into the trench where his heart had been carved out. He noted the young child peering out of an alley, eyes wide, taking in the scene. The Watchman raised a finger to his lips and watched the transformation take hold—the child's chin quivered but lifted. A firm nod, and they disappeared.

Blood trickled from the split skin of the prisoner who'd tried to stand up to the guards. He looked like the color had been leached out of him, his skin a pallid grey, stretched waxy across his bones. No one fully understood the effect of this hellscape, the weakening of stamina, like something vital was being drained from you constantly. Gods, he hated this place. The other prisoners weren't much better off. They all trembled, and one of their legs was twisted unnaturally, the bone broken. The Night Watchman quickly relieved one of the dead guards of his scabbard; if he lashed it to the man's leg, it could serve as a splint until they were safely out of Loxley. It would have to do for now. The pain would end, but not for hours yet, and nothing he could say would take it away sooner.

Merely freeing the prisoners who were to be burned or Silenced was simple. It was smuggling them out of the city that was the difficult feat, making sure no one called the guards as they ran through the streets—the Watchman had learned long ago that greed and desperation made innocent people into harsh weapons against their fellow man. And then there was the matter of timing the tides correctly so they *could* flee. All this he explained in an urgent tone as he set to work finishing the crude pageantry he would leave behind.

The brave one objected. "We can't—we can barely walk, let alone make that journey."

The Watchman tried another tactic. "What's your name?"

"Muchovik. I'm called Much, sir."

"Much, I saw how you stood up to the guard. I need you to find some of that fire for a little while longer. Can you do that for me?"

"Are you the Night Watchman?"

"Listen carefully. If we get separated, you must get to the eastern edge of the city, past the tide pools. There's a small cove in the rock about forty paces from there. A friend of mine will be waiting. You are to ask, 'Where is the fun in a lie?' The safe reply is, 'When it's the truth that's outlawed.' Do you understand? Repeat that back to me."

"What if they don't answer with that?"

The Watchman resisted shouting at the lad. None of this was his fault. But the truth was that if the rebel fighter had been compromised, they were as good as dead. "Say it with me, all right? Where's the fun in a lie? When it's the truth that's outlawed."

CHAPTER 6

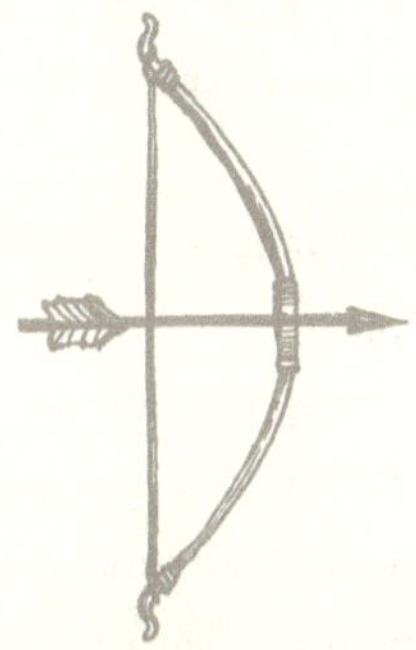

WITH THE SUN BLAZING OVERHEAD AND NOT A CLOUD IN SIGHT, THE COURT WAS TAKING ADVANTAGE OF THE RARE WEATHER AND HAD FLOCKED TO THE LUSH PALACE GROUNDS. The field stretched wide, comprising the stables, the training arena, and the raised stands, typically used for viewing royal punishments. Today they were strewn with nobles soaking in the sun. The kitchen staff had set up finger food and kvass as refreshments for the gentlefolk. Renna had spotted Yana and her ward fussing over the presentation of the kolaches—savory should be separate from sweet so as not to confuse anyone.

But that had been a few hours ago, and Renna's mood was souring as she stared at the piece of aurem in her hands. Over the fortnight since Ulrik had given it to her, she'd spent every day working to channel finnikfire into the stone. A few times it had seemed as if the aurem were shifting, morphing into a bloodstone, but the full transformation had never taken hold. Perhaps it wasn't meant to, being a practice one and all, Nastasia had said more than once.

Still, it dug at Renna like a burr in her shoe that she couldn't get rid of.

The Night Watchman had left the message NO TITHES TO TYRANTS written in the blood of red clerics all through Nottingham. Vedra influences were strong before the Tithe, Renna reminded herself. It was only a fortnight away, her crucible and coronation another fortnight after that. Stability was just around the corner. She just needed to be patient.

They were stretched out on the grass, Nastasia twirling a small spark between her fingers, which meant she was bored. Renna sighed, setting the stone aside, her gaze flicking across the yard to where Ulrik sat in the shade. She wanted to go to the stables—it had been a week since she'd visited Alita.

Horns blared.

Dozens of guards spilled into the open yard, followed by cowled Keepers and a retinue of Trissaia. Ulrik appeared at her side as Renna clambered to her feet. Three men cloaked in black, weapons glinting, strode out of the tunnel. Behind them, shackled at the wrists and ankles, was a line of prisoners. The first figure, taller than all the others and with broad shoulders, tugged down his hood. Renna's blood shifted in recognition, and she was suddenly light-headed, as if she'd stood up too fast.

His icy-blond hair was swept back, ending with a faint curl at the nape of his neck. Grey eyes pierced her, bruise-like shadows underneath them on his pale white skin. His face was all harsh angles: a tight jaw, mouth pulled into a severe line. His left hand rested on the pommel of a sword, swathed in bandages that were tinged dark red, his right arm in a sling strapped tightly to his ribs. Peeking out from under his collar and snaking up his neck were barely healed abrasions. A courier announced his name and those of his men, but he might as well have been speaking underwater, for all Renna comprehended as Garen Draic approached.

Commander Draic stopped several paces from Renna and dropped to his knee. He moved with surprising grace, not only for a man who was supposedly dead but for one who'd clearly been beaten within an inch of his life. Renna blinked rapidly to clear her thoughts as the returning commander brought two fingers to his mouth, then his heart.

"We heard you were dead, Commander," Ulrik said. Into Renna's mind, he said, *The Mother has blessed you with this opportunity.*

Draic's voice was heavy with exhaustion. "We escaped captivity two months back but had to remain hidden until we met up with our forces in a small village in Wendsvik." Draic gestured behind him. There were six men and three women, all of whom had also been beaten recently, judging by their split lips and bruises. Bloody gags were shoved in their mouths. "Please accept these captured vedra as a show of loyalty to the crown."

"The Blood Tithe is near, and the vedra are keen on trickery, Commander." Ulrik's tone was casual, but each word carried an unmistakable weight.

Draic dipped his chin. "Of course, Your Grace. We will willingly submit to the Head Trissaia so our tale can be verified with mettlemancy."

"The crown and I will verify your story, Commander." Ulrik waved a hand as if brushing away a fly.

Draic had hardly looked at Renna for the entire exchange, but when his eyes flicked over to hers, they were flat and cold. "As it pleases you, Your Majesty."

Still a prick, then. He'd always needled her with titles said like they were insults when they sparred. She rolled her shoulders back. "*Your Highness* is sufficient until next month when I take the throne. I am glad to see the war has not changed you too much, Draic."

"On the contrary, Your Highness, the Mother's grace has changed me. I am able to see Truth more clearly now."

Renna had spent her whole life attuned to the nearly invisible shift around mettlemancers: the way their pupils shrank, the smell of salt in the air, and the occasional blank expressions that followed. She wondered briefly if Draic marked any of those on Ulrik or herself as they sank into his mind. A headache permeated her skull as the scene before her faded, replaced by Draic's memories. Renna forced herself not to flinch as they rushed over her as clearly as if she had been there.

There were five people huddled in a ditch, rain churning all the dirt to mud. Draic's collarbone was broken, and he had to lean forward, or else he'd pass out again from the blinding pain of the still-weeping lacerations on his back. She felt his panic at the sound of footfalls, not knowing if their captors had finally found them. Hunger gnawed at his stomach, and dehydration made his brain sluggish; his lips were in an unending cycle of cracking and healing over, only to crack again. The copper tang of blood in his mouth felt almost normal. Kirin was delirious with a fever that had lasted too many days.

Relief flooded through Draic, as visceral as a balm on a burn, when the banner of Loxley became visible in the distance.

His consciousness faded in and out; a stiff cot in a dark tent, bones being reset, the cuts on his back being cleaned out as he swore at a nurse.

Then he was on the highway road, the sunshine above at odds with the chaotic scene before him. An overturned caravan, screaming, metal ringing against metal. Three Keepers lay dead on the ground, their robes stained a deep crimson. The faces of the outlaws attacking the remaining Keepers matched those of the prisoners, Renna realized, each twisted with hatred and anger.

Draic and his men called for surrender, but then the man closest, his eyes burning, began chanting in a language Draic didn't recognize. The man's hands stretched forward, fingers weaving an intricate pattern. The sky darkened. The air chilled and thunder rumbled.

"*Storm vedra!*" Ilya bellowed, rushing toward the man, sword raised to stop him, but then a thrown dagger caught him on his shoulder. It knocked him off balance just as rain began pelting down. Each drop cut like a small blade, splitting the skin all over their bodies. The ground shook beneath their feet, and Draic struggled to stay upright. Every muscle groaned in protest, weak from all the months of torture, his endurance nearly nonexistent.

An outlaw slit Warrick's throat. A harrowing scream tore from Draic as he called up his finnikfire and sent a large ball of flame at the outlaw. The battle continued, and another companion fell, then another. They'd survived years of being tortured in captivity only to be slain by these vedra bastards. Finally they brought the vedra to heel, binding them all. Draic methodically Silenced them: one vicious cut each, severing their tongues. Blood sprayed his face again and again and again.

Renna broke the connection.

Draic's eyes were locked on hers. Renna repressed a shudder at the agony—*his* agony—that she'd felt only moments ago. Anger now radiated from him, and he flexed his hand as if barely containing the finnikfire that simmered there. "My men and I know firsthand the lengths to which vedra will go to cause suffering to those loyal to the Mother, Your Highness."

She took in the three of them for a moment, marveling that they'd survived: Garen, Kirin, and Ilya. Renna knew who they were now from the memory, had tasted their fear as they'd battled the enemy together. Kirin's hair was shorn close to his head, his skin a deep brown except for a white birthmark that started above one brow and traveled to the opposite cheek. Ilya, the shorter of Garen's companions, had the same muscular build, high cheekbones, and deep-set eyes behind sultry lashes. His sleek pin-straight hair was pulled into a queue at the nape of his neck.

Draic gripped the hair of the prisoner who'd killed their friend Warrick and roughly shoved him to the ground. There was a sickening crunch as the prisoner fell on his face, bound hands preventing him from catching himself. Gasps came from the crowd. The man rolled onto his side, spitting dirt and blood, his nose twisted at an unnatural angle. Renna could not summon any sympathy for the prisoner, Draic's scream at watching Warrick die still ringing in her ears.

Ulrik watched Renna, waiting. *An opportunity*, he had said. Understanding dawned on her. This spectacle was for her benefit. She sought Nastasia's face, needing to see something familiar. She could practically feel the nobles salivating from where they hungrily watched. War heroes returning safely with enemies in tow allowed her the opportunity to demonstrate the throne's commitment to the Mother's Truth. No sign of weakness in their soon-to-be queen. That they were already gathered in the stands by the aurem pyres suddenly felt clandestine instead of happenstance. How long had it been since an execution this size had taken place? She couldn't recall.

There is a darkness in you.

She knew what was expected of her and pitched her voice louder. "I have seen the Truth of what you say, Commander. The magic these outlaws possess is an abomination to the Mother's chosen finniks and Her Holy Flame. The Tomes of Truth forbid magic of the sky, trees, and water. These things alone are enough for them to be Silenced. But for the murder of our Keepers and soldiers…by my blood, I sentence these vedra to burn for their crimes."

Let the commander be the one to carry out your orders, Ulrik said.

Her mind tugged back to Draic witnessing Warrick's last breath. Retribution for that moment, then. "As thanks for your loyalty, Commander, we grant you the opportunity to light the fires."

With his back straight and his face impassive, he managed to look regal even in a sling and covered in bruises. For a heartbeat, his eyes went to Ulrik, as if seeking confirmation, before returning to hers. The slight nettled her, and she said sharply, "Do you require me to say it again?"

Draic surveyed her, then bent at the waist. "No, Princess. I do not. Thank you for your generosity."

This is justice, this is justice, this is justice. Renna clung to the words like they could absolve her. Her ears rang with the cheers and shouts from the gathered nobles as the prisoners were dragged to the aurem pyres and secured to the stakes. Draic's uninjured arm stretched before him. A ball of fire danced in his palm, causing the prisoners to pull at their restraints. Heat rushed toward her face as Draic lit the aurem piled beneath their feet, the holy stones greedy for the finnikfire. The faces of the prisoners contorted in pain as their wails pitched higher, more frantic. Deep crimson flames grew, reaching waist height.

The smell of burnt flesh stung her nose.

This is justice. Renna couldn't take a full breath. *If I fail, this is my fate.* Spots appeared at the edge of her vision as the wind picked up. She trembled, shoulders tight. *Please,* she pleaded to the Mother as the vedra burned. *I am a Koravik. Their blood runs in my veins. Truth is in the blood. Truth is in* my *blood.*

The twisted prayer stung the backs of her eyes. Her hand twitched as if she wanted to reach toward the dying.

The words of her Foretelling burst free from the corner of her mind where she kept them locked away.

There is a darkness inside you, Rennavera Koravik, that will destroy this kingdom and its people if you let it. Vedra blood runs in your veins. Only the Mother's Truth can cure you of this darkness. Obey the Light, and if you are found worthy, your finnikfire will be a beacon to your people. Do not let the darkness inside you snuff out the light.

The air turned sharp and metallic. Something roiled under her skin as storm clouds blocked the sun and darkness swept over the area. Lightning flashed, and the sound of swords being drawn rang out. The crowd's cheers morphed into screams as a storm hit, the rain battling with the flames. "Vedra! Mother save us! Witch! Storm witch!"

Horror held Renna in its net, a question roaring in her mind: Was this her doing?

"Seize her!"

Renna flinched as red clerics surged forward—but not toward her. Toward the crowd.

Toward Yana. Yana, who'd fallen to her knees, palms outstretched to the sky. Her fingers bent in jerky movements, calling down a storm.

Renna took one step toward the cook.

Don't move. Ulrik's mental command was like a whip.

Ulrik, please, I know that woman—

Silence, child. Do you wish to undermine everything you just accomplished? You must honor your word.

The storm subsided so quickly that she could almost pretend she'd imagined it. But then Yana was gagged and bound, and it was all too horrifyingly real. She struggled against the guards, thrashing her legs, tears streaming down her face as they dragged her before Renna.

Better to be Silenced than burned at the stake, Ulrik reminded her, as if it was simple. *The Mother knows the weight of the crown, child, and will bless you for following the*

Light. Darkness seeks to snuff out the light at every turn, and we must stay vigilant for the good of all the people.

Nastasia's question from weeks ago rang in her mind: *Is it foolish to hope that the future queen will hold the Truth in as high a regard as I?* If she backed down from her decree immediately, what would that make her in the eyes of her people? Weak. Untrustworthy.

Her blood turned to wet sand in her veins. The pyres still burned brightly, casting cruel light on the woman at her feet. Renna knew the consequences. She looked just above Yana's head, eyes unfocused so as not to see the tracks the tears made down her cheeks. Her lips formed the necessary words again: "The Tomes of Truth forbid magic of the sky, trees, and water."

Don't look away, she thought. But she could not bring herself to watch as Draic stepped forward, dagger glinting. The sound of the blade severing Yana's tongue would haunt her dreams.

CHAPTER 7

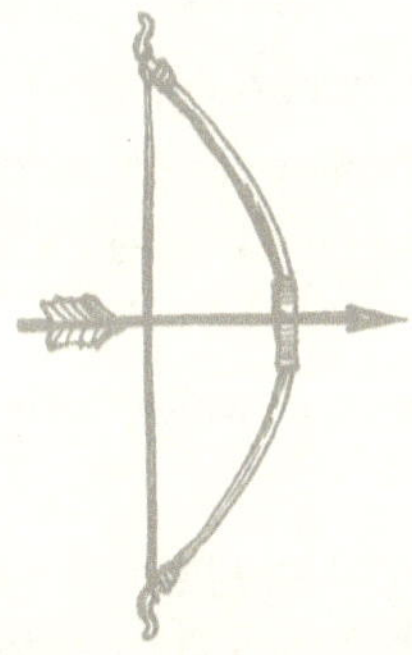

*Truth is in the blood. As such, to use blood for anything other than an offering
to the Mother is an abomination.*

—excerpt from the Tomes of Truth

RENNA SHOOK OUT THE CRAMP IN HER RIGHT HAND. "I don't understand what I'm doing wrong." She and Nastasia were in a lower wing of the castle in what had once been the solarium. The arched wall of windows had broken long ago in the high winds of storms, leaving only the stone ruins interlacing overhead to form an open cathedral. The cobblestones were cracked, and bits of grass and moss covered the ground. Nastasia had wrinkled her nose when Renna had suggested coming here, saying she'd never understood what she liked about it, and honestly, why hadn't it been torn down decades ago? But with the Blood Tithe only a few days away and the Night Watchman leaving a trail of bodies in the streets, the entire population of the castle was on edge. Renna needed to let off some steam and was unwilling to visit the training yard after the executions. So they'd retired here, her red clerics waiting outside the ruins.

They'd set up two targets on the opposite end from where they stood, Nastasia's burnt black and smoldering while Renna's remained unsinged. Her attempts to call and command flames had not improved; she had managed only to hold a ball of red fire in her palm for several uninterrupted minutes, nothing more.

"Let's take a break," Nastasia said, straightening up from where she was leaning against one of the stone pillars. She traced complex patterns up and down her arm with her finnikfire—the flame moving as if it was alive—with such a bored expression that it made Renna want to kick something.

"I'm doing everything I can." Nastasia furrowed her brow as Renna continued, emotion clogging her words. "I'm doing the extra tithes, and I observe Silence daily." Renna unwound the flame-resistant bandages from her wrist, tossing them to the ground with a huff. "And for Mother's sake, it's meant to be my birthright. I am to be a Koravik queen."

There was flint in her cousin's voice. "Not everything is meant to be easy, Princess."

The title sounded close to an insult, and her ears burned with embarrassment. Nastasia worked on her magic. When she wasn't with Renna, she studied with the priestesses in the hope of climbing the ranks and becoming a Keeper of the Truth. It would take years of training and service to the Mother to become a Trissaia, which was her ultimate goal.

"I didn't—"

Nastasia waved away her words. "You're thinking too hard." She snagged two practice daggers from her sack and tossed one at Renna, who caught it, shoulders slumping.

"I'm tired, Stasi."

Nastasia smirked, adopting an opening stance, the tip of her dagger moving in small circles as she beckoned Renna with her free hand. "Then you better disarm me quickly."

And that was all the warning she gave before she lunged.

Renna blocked her blow, falling into a defensive stance. Nastasia swiped again, and she absorbed the blow with her forearm to protect her shoulder.

"You're focusing on the mechanics too much. Stop reciting the Tomes of Truth and let the fire act as an extension of you." Nastasia punctuated the sentence with a quick jab and cut from above, her free hand sending a few harmless sparks toward Renna's center. Renna barely spun out of the way in time, the heat warming her hip, and attempted to parry the next cut, knocking Nastasia's weapon arm wide to give her an opening. The flat of Renna's dagger grazed Nastasia's hip, and her cousin laughed softly. Nastasia adjusted the golden aurem bracelet on her wrist as they stepped apart to reset, both breathing audibly.

"Now, let's see that Koravik fire." Nastasia shifted ever so slightly, signaling the lunge that was coming.

Renna called the fire to the fingertips of her free hand and let go of the recitation she usually kept in her head as she parried and struck an inside cut. Red sparks shot from her hand in a sudden burst, leaping toward Nastasia's clothes. A laugh of triumph tore from her chest. Nastasia tried to spin away but couldn't without opening herself to another attack. Renna dropped her guard arm as she pressed her advance, dealing another blow, sending another shower of finnik sparks at Nastasia.

A wave of red flame arced toward Renna and filled her vision, heat caressing her face.

Renna faltered, and in that split second, her cousin's dagger hilt collided with her jaw. In a heartbeat, Renna was on the ground, the forearm pressed into her throat cutting off her breath. Stars danced in her eyes, and her head throbbed.

"You let your guard down." Nastasia leaned close, still panting.

"You cheated. That was more than finnik sparks."

Nastasia sat back on her heels, and Renna struggled to her elbows. "Don't assume that your enemy won't use every advantage they have against you."

Renna rubbed the tender spot on her jaw. "Yes, well, we're *not* enemies, so I assumed I wouldn't need to worry about that."

"Did you cast your fire farther?"

Renna scowled but conceded, "Yes."

"I don't see what you're complaining about, then." Nastasia gestured to the still-untouched target. "Try again."

Renna was still frowning, but she faced the target, trying to let go of the steps she usually followed. She exhaled slowly, swinging her palm up and out. A shiver went down her spine as the red flame built in her hand, and then, without any hesitation, a ball of fire flew at the target, eviscerating it in one hit.

Nastasia clapped her on the back and smugly whispered, "You're welcome."

Channeling finnikfire took more out of Renna than most people; Nastasia was always too kind to point out that it was most likely because of her vedra blood. The healer ward was just down the hall, so when Nastasia left to study with the Keepers, Renna made her way there to get some balm for her back and see if they had any of the tonic she liked for recovery. Her clerics following like silent shadows.

The healer ward walls were lined with metal braziers holding aurem stones, the light of finnikfire bathing the corridor. Stone benches topped with leather cushions, small copper sculptures of the veiled Mother holding Her Flame aloft, and clay urns full of extra supplies dotted the hall. The doors were not solid but made of thin wrought-iron lattices with curtain inlays to allow for airflow. Tendrils of smoke seeped out of hanging thuribles, and a smell like slightly bitter sage suffused the corridor. Mugwort, she thought.

The hall opened into a small cavern where five healers shuffled around, checking charts on thin sheets of vellum or bundling herbs. With a start, Renna recognized the priestess who was waiting patiently for one such bundle: the woman she'd barreled into on the stairs the day she'd snuck out. Her midnight hair cascaded past her shoulders save for the one white lock. Renna dipped her chin as the woman curtsied, the look on her face confirming to Renna that she had indeed been recognized that day. A snippet of conversation between two of the healers, heads ducked together and brows furrowed, floated over to her as she waited for her items.

"…nails completely ripped off, yes…just the one hand, correct."

Renna shuddered at the mental image. She didn't need to ask who they were speaking about. In the days since Draic's return, Renna had only caught glimpses of him. Ulrik was so pleased with Draic's *outstanding display of loyalty* that the commander was to return to his position of high sheriff, effective as soon as he was healed. Draic had been given a room near the healing ward so he could be treated by palace physicians. Though she had heard a few servants whispering that the returning soldiers wanted to forgo healing time, anxious to be put to work again.

Men—honestly. Perhaps she could convince him to rest. Loxley had run perfectly well in his absence, no matter what Gisborne said.

Renna quickly drank the recovery tonic and took a few tins of balm, thanking the healers. She was halfway down the hall when a curse uttered from behind a closed door brought her to a halt. A sound of frustration, or perhaps disgust, came next. Her tunic stuck to her back uncomfortably, and she wondered if one of her unhealed tithes had reopened. Grateful she'd chosen to wear one made of dark fabric, Renna knocked once, then strode into the chamber.

The room was narrow and sparse, containing only a front-facing bed with an iron frame, an aurem lantern, shelves carved directly into the wall that held bandages, herbs, several glass jars, and a bloodsiphon dagger. A hanging thurible steadily leaking a dizzying combination of lavender, mugwort, and something she couldn't place. Renna's eyes watered, and when she blinked away the tears, she was greeted by the sight of Garen Draic facing the wall as he sat on the edge of the bed.

More to the point—Garen Draic *nearly naked* with no more than a strip of cloth between his legs, attempting to pull on a pair of loose trousers with his one working arm. His chest was covered in pink-tinged bandages. Yellow-and-purple bruises bloomed across his moon-pale skin. There were scars and healing lacerations all over his arms and broad shoulders, which were tattooed with a design she couldn't make out. White-blond hair stuck to his forehead with sweat. Renna registered all this in half a breath before finding his eyes locked on hers, burning with vexation.

Renna was not a prude, nor had she ever been. True, no one had seen *her* fully disrobed (the risk of her scarred back raising questions was too great) but Renna had experienced many passionate exchanges with men and women both. She was familiar with the human body. But on those occasions, both parties had been expecting the nudity.

Surprise, then, was the only explanation for the embarrassing sound that came from her and the heat rushing to her cheeks. An absolutely filthy word came from Draic as he threw the bedcovers over his lap. Renna looked away so quickly her neck ached.

"What are—"

"Sorry! I just—I didn't—" Renna turned her entire body away, wishing she could walk into the sea, trying to ignore the rustling of clothes.

"May I help you, Your Highness?" His words came out through gritted teeth.

"Please, my apologies, I did not think—I came to see how your healing was progressing." Silence, except for a pained grunt. "Do you…should I call someone? To assist you, I mean. It seems like you're not well enough to—"

"I am perfectly capable of dressing myself," he snapped.

Renna longed to walk back out the door in the awkward quiet that followed, and nearly did, but he spoke again, gruffly. "I am decent, Your Highness."

Renna took her time turning back around, inspecting the room as if it endlessly fascinated her before letting her gaze fall back on him. A pillow was propped between his back and the headboard, legs stretched long with one ankle crossed over the other. He would've looked the very picture of a dutiful convalescent if not for the muscle that kept popping in his jaw, as if he was biting back what he really wanted to say, and the sheen of sweat on his forehead from the exertion of dressing. *Decent* apparently meant only pants because he'd not bothered with a tunic. The sling probably made pulling on a shirt rather cumbersome, but knowing how his abdomen tapered into a v before dipping below the waistband of his trousers felt anything *but* decent.

"My apologies, Princess. Being away from court for so long has affected my manners. I offer you my services."

Renna reigned in an undignified snort. "Your *services?* You are to rest until you are well."

"Our enemies do not rest, so neither shall I, Your Highness."

"I think Loxley can spare you for a few days more while you—"

"The blood of the red clerics painting the streets of Nottingham would suggest otherwise. The only thing that gave me the strength to endure torture was my devotion to the Mother and the Truth. So you'll forgive me if I don't accept your invitation to rest, Highness." He practically bit the title out. "I intend to root out all the rot in Loxley."

There was an audible click of teeth as Renna shut her mouth. Draic was watching her closely. The hair on the nape of her neck prickled. Despite herself, Renna found her eyes drawn to the hand of the arm supported by his sling. The nails looked wrong, too short, and the flesh underneath them was redder than the rest of his hand. She swallowed down the rising bile, averting her gaze from his brutalized fingernails. Finally, hoping to end the conversation and take her leave, she said, "Your devotion commends you. Truth shall light the way. I pray that you will capture the Night Watchman."

Draic hummed, eyes assessing her. "I remember hearing of your governess. Vedra sympathizer, yes?"

Renna crossed to the shelves and picked up the ritual dagger, studying it to buy herself some time. Her heart constricted painfully as the memory of that night played in her mind.

"Marian, please, you mustn't say such things," Renna whimpered. She was crying just as much as her beloved governess, who knelt on the floor, a crumpled piece of paper in her hands. Renna had cried out when she'd seen it—paper was forbidden. What had Marian been thinking?

"Throw it in the fire, Marian, please! I can't send you away, I can't lose you too." Renna wiped her nose, her snot and tears mingling.

"Oh, Rennavera—" Marian had reached out as if to stroke her hair, like she so often did, but Renna did not want the comfort. She backed away. How could her governess do this? How dare she let the lies of the Night Watchman poison her faith?

"Why, why did you have to bring it in here?" Renna stamped her foot, knowing she looked every bit like the thirteen-year-old she was.

The door swung inward, and Nastasia stopped dead, taking in the scene: Renna, face wet and screwed up with frustration and fear; Marian, kneeling, head bowed over the damning piece of parchment clutched in her hands. Renna hadn't even gotten a good look at what was on it. What could possibly have been worth her life?

Without a word, Nastasia's fingers made a delicate twirling motion, and the page burst into flame. Marian screamed—was it from pain or the loss of the relic?—and with one last tearful look at her, fled the room.

Later, Renna had found out that someone had informed the Head Trissaia of Marian's treason. Nastasia had made sure Renna was not implicated. None of Renna's tears or pleas to Ulrik had mattered. Her governess had been taken down to the dungeons soon after.

The healers were surely giving him balm, but Renna placed one on the shelf with a click anyways before facing Draic again. "Rot unattended spreads."

"Thank the Mother, then, for your diligence, Princess. And thank you for the opportunity to light the pyres."

The sound of screams, the smell of burnt flesh…

There was an ugliness to his words that sent a shiver down her spine. The hard set of his mouth and the way his grey eyes glinted in the afternoon light gave him a haunted expression. When they were younger, Garen had always been arrogant and competitive, and while she'd never admit to such a thing, it had made him the perfect sparring partner. She'd valued the fact that he did not treat her like something that would break. That when she bested him, she could relish the victory because she knew it was earned, not given. Even having glimpsed only a small portion of what he had endured in captivity, Renna knew one thing for certain: the cold and calculating man before her wanted nothing more than retribution against those who had harmed him.

Those with vedra blood.

Feeling like she was walking atop the battlements in a storm and any misstep could send her plummeting to her doom, Renna neatly accepted his gratitude. She was nearly through the door when he called after her.

"My men have told me all about that fearsome display you arranged in Nottingham after your little excursion. I look forward to seeing it myself."

Nearly two decades of royal etiquette lessons were the only thing that kept Renna from coming apart at the seams and demanding what he meant. Instead she clasped her hands to keep them from trembling as dread and confusion flooded her veins. With a gracious nod, she fled.

CHAPTER 8

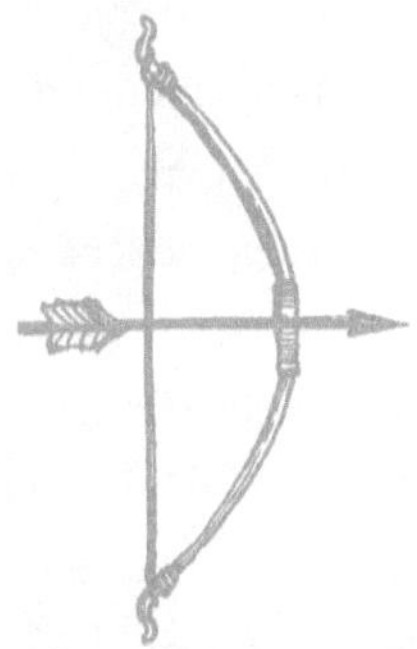

"If there are any among you who doubt that the Trissaia are the Mother's voice, remember that when those who had touched the False Flame sought to drown the kingdom with an endless tide, it was the Trissaia who knew to gather the people on the mount."
—*excerpt from the Tomes of Truth*

DOUBT WAS A RELENTLESS BEAST, SLINKING ALONG THE CORRIDORS OF RENNA'S MIND. It smelled of burning bodies and looked like tear-stained cheeks. It prowled, searching her mind for weak and rotting points so it could slip in and rob her of her faith. Draic's parting words the previous fortnight had struck her like an arrow. She truly had no idea what *fearsome display* he could mean. Ulrik was consumed with preparations for the Blood Tithe in three days, and when she asked, he said only, "We discovered that a group of con men ran the archery tournament, and we saw that it was dismantled, thanks to you."

When she asked Nastasia, her cousin left her feeling foolish. "With only a little more than two weeks to finish preparing for the crucible, *this* is what you want to spend your time on? Nottingham is as it ever was, Ren."

But it could not be helped. Draic's words had chilled her, nudging something in the back of her mind, prodding at the fear that there were, and always would be, things that were kept from her. There was a pull in her gut as if she were an unsuspecting fisherman lured by a rusalka's otherworldly song. She had to follow. She had to see for herself what was happening in Nottingham.

Making the decision released the pressure that had been building inside her, and Renna felt light as she crept from her bed around midnight. Her guards were several paces down the hall, engrossed in playing a game of stones. Their distraction allowed her to slip by undetected—they were more worried about people trying to get into her rooms than out—and Renna took it as a sign of the Mother's favor. Through the tunnels and out of the castle walls she crept.

By the time she reached the streets of Nottingham, a thin sheet of rain cloaked the city. Despite the weather, citizens spilled through the streets, dancing and cavorting, the proximity of the Tithe shaking something loose inside everyone.

The city looked different at night—harsher and more dangerous despite the celebration. There were no fainting couches, nowhere soft to rest if you'd given too much blood, just packed dirt roads and dark alleyways. Such a stark difference to what she and others in the castle would have after the Blood Tithe in a few days' time. If she failed to prove herself worthy, if the wickedness in her blood snuffed out the holy fire, the Foretelling was clear: she'd doom the entire kingdom. Already, Loxley hung in such a precarious balance. Across the sea, the front lines grew increasingly lethal as the vedra forces multiplied, while here in Loxley, the Night Watchman continued to leave behind morbid tableaus: red cleric guards pierced through with wooden arrows, their mouths stuffed with gnarled roots, words scrawled on the street with their blood: NO TITHE TO TYRANTS.

Renna would find out what Draic had meant, and then she could get some sleep. The Blood Tithe would bolster the whole kingdom, strengthen everyone's faith, and wash away the fear that was always thickest beforehand.

A drunken passerby weaved suddenly, and Renna sidestepped to avoid a collision. Her heel caught on a step, and she flung out her arms to brace herself against a doorway. A rebuke she was about to utter died on her tongue as something grabbed her attention. Tucked under a small archway, the door hung halfway off its hinges, streaks of red paint cutting across it in vicious strokes. Nailed to the surface was a sheet of metal etched with an acorn.

Renna jerked her hand away as if burned. She looked around, realizing she'd been here before. This was where she and Nastasia had watched those people being dragged from their home. No one was paying her any mind. Renna turned back to inspect the door, eyeing the acorn warily. Did traces of tree poison linger? If so, why had they not just burned the place down? She took a step closer, craning her neck to see through the gaps and into the home.

A hand closed on her shoulder, spinning her around until her back pressed into the doorframe. A cold drizzle misted her face as an even colder shape pressed into her throat. She could not see it, but she knew what it was: a blade. A little longer than two hands. Sharp enough that the very edge of it was turning warm from a sliver-thin split in her skin, leaking blood. Too sharp even to hurt. Tomorrow it would itch.

The angle of the blade was such that she could see only her attacker's chest, but sewn into the cloak was the royal guard insignia. The surge of relief that it was not an outlaw made her lightheaded.

"Unhand me," Renna hissed, not wanting to reveal herself to anyone else on the crowded Nottingham street.

"Unhand you?"

She recognized the distinctive voice—low, with gravel in the very back of it. Her assailant shifted but did not remove the weapon, and her gaze flicked up to the face of the high sheriff of Nottingham. Now the cold slice was in her gut instead: dread.

Renna bared her teeth in an approximation of a smile. "It is considered treason to threaten the life of the future queen. You'll release me, immediately and quietly. You're making a scene," she whispered.

Draic adjusted the blade, forcing her to tilt her chin higher. For a moment she was reminded of the way he used to tap the flat of the dagger against her sternum when he'd won a sparring match. "My knife is subtle, Princess; to everyone else, we're lovers in the rain. But I wonder why the crown princess is sneaking through the slums in disguise, and poking around a traitor's condemned home, no less? The Night Watchman is said to have been seen in this area, and then I find you skulking around. I'd say that's more than a coincidence."

Renna let out a shaky laugh. There was an unexpected release of the tension in her body. He thought she was a vigilante trying to stir up trouble, which felt far less dangerous than him knowing the truth: that vedra blood perhaps still coursed through her veins. "*That's* what you think? Everything I do is for this kingdom, Sheriff. So if you want to keep your position and your life, I suggest you unhand me. Right. Now."

A heartbeat passed, his breath warm on her face.

Draic stepped back swiftly, the pressure at her throat easing.

Renna rolled her shoulders back. She would not give him the satisfaction of knowing that his parting taunt earlier was what had spurred her into action tonight. "Not that I owe you an explanation, sheriff—"

"High sheriff," he corrected, sounding bored, and irritation heated her chest.

"I'm here because I want to understand the conditions of the poorest in my kingdom. I don't believe I should wait until after I am crowned to know the details about those I'll rule. I challenge you to disagree."

"I don't disagree. Tell me, then, what you have learned about poverty during your excursion."

The heat in her chest went to her cheeks. She'd expected him to patronize her, and his agreement threw her off balance. "A high sheriff interrupted me just as I was starting my journey."

Those grey eyes of his narrowed, regarding her, considering. He was aggravatingly tall. She had to crane her neck to meet his gaze. Draic scanned the street, filled with revelers, and said, "As the high sheriff, I cannot allow you to wander the streets without protection. I propose that I help you find sufficient poverty for one miserable night's education, and then you accept an escort back to the castle."

Renna carefully controlled her voice. "Surely you have better things to do."

"Most assuredly. Shall we begin?"

Annoyance chafed at her, but it was clear that if she refused his offer, he'd ensure that she was taken home immediately. His sling was gone, and silvery scars crisscrossed the moon-pale skin on the back of his hand, disappearing up under his sleeve. Ungraciously, Renna hoped she had given him at least one of them all those years ago during their sparring sessions.

They navigated around a cluster of Trissaia giving personal Foretellings. Renna tried to lengthen her steps to match Draic's. Memories of their mettlemancy rose: the pain wracking his body as he fled from his vedra captors. The horror of watching his men be slaughtered, unable to stop it. The barely healed gashes on his back reopening under the sharp lash of the whip. Renna wanted to ask about Warrick, his slain comrade, but it felt too personal. She got the distinct impression he would not welcome the question.

A large stone statue sat in the middle of the next square, carved into the likeness of Osric, the first Trissaia. A plaque at the bottom reminded every passerby of the Foretelling he had received from the Mother, warning against an imminent flood—the Endless Tide. A stone marked how high the tide had risen. Renna knew the story, of course, but she'd not seen the marker herself. She shivered, looking at the sprawling city below that had once been a watery grave for those who'd not heeded the warning to climb to higher ground. Renna pulled her cloak tighter against the chill, peering out through the steady drips coming off her hood.

They crossed to a more somber street, and the noises of celebration faded into the night. When citizens caught sight of the high sheriff, they changed direction.

"It would appear there is love lost between you and the people of Nottingham."

"One does not need to be loved to be effective. In cases of power, it is almost always the opposite."

"And that's what you want, is it? Power?"

"I do not expect the heir to the throne to comprehend someone wanting to improve their station. But to answer your question, no. What I want most is retribution against those who have wronged me."

Here, deeper into Nottingham, the houses were stacked high atop each other, each holding as many people as possible. Guilt fluttered through her as they went, elbows held tight to her sides. The muddy streets were churned up with boot marks, each hole promising a twisted ankle. The hem of her cloak was filthy, soaking up the puddles of rainwater like a thirsty kitten. If the storm got any worse, the streets might flood, she realized with a spark of panic. They passed another home marked by an acorn painted in red. Barbed wire crisscrossed the door. Outside it sat two beggars, soaked through with rain and mud. Their faces were lined with deep creases, their eyes downcast. There was dried blood around their mouths and on the front of their clothes.

Renna averted her eyes. "And what of mercy?"

Draic was unmoved. "I am but a humble weapon for the crown to wield. I leave mercy to the Mother."

Down an alley, a man loomed over a motionless body, a jar half filled with something dark clutched to his chest. The stench was putrid. "Is that—"

"A leecher," Draic confirmed, his hand encircled her upper arm as he steered her away from the alley. She'd heard tales of those who hung around the injured or dying, circling like vultures. They used leeches to drain the victims of their blood. A few red clerics were down this street, and Draic must have spoken to them with mettlemancy, because they strode purposefully in the direction of the alley.

Renna made a sign to the Mother. "That's an abomination. Who would do such a thing?"

"Surely the crown princess is well informed about the black market in Loxley. No? There are those who are unable to pay the tithe to the nobles who oversee their sector, or whose blood had been deemed unfit because of a disease or an infection of the skin. So they turn to more unsavory methods of procuring blood."

Renna flinched as if struck. Shame unfurled within her, hot and sharp across her chest. She had not known. Were things so dire in Nottingham that this was inevitable? Draic had not let go of her arm, which was good, because when they turned down the next street, she felt woozy for a moment.

Here was the fearsome display he had mentioned.

In the square, no fewer than a dozen citizens stood hunched with their heads and arms in metal stocks. The dirt below each prisoner was already stained with blood and piss. A crowd had gathered, jeering, and tossing bits of rotten food. Something foul-looking struck one prisoner and left a dark smear. A missive next to the stocks proclaimed: FOUND IN POSSESSION OF OUTLAWED MATERIALS. BY ORDER OF THE KORAVIK BLOOD, THEY SHALL BE SUBJECT TO SILENCING AND KEPT IN THE STOCKS FOR SEVEN DAYS.

Draic's eyes were on her, piercing and searching. Hunting for weakness. She thought of how calm he'd been lighting the pyre, the smell of the bodies burning. She recognized the men who'd taken her entry fee at the contest, their faces swollen with bruises, blood dripping in congealed ropes from their lips.

Renna unstuck her tongue from the roof of her mouth. "Tell me what the con men's ruse was."

"They'd place acorns inside the money purse, then follow the winner home. They had a few guards that were in on the scheme, who they would send in to raid the homes. Then they would divide the winnings between them, never having to pay out to the contestants. They had built up quite a treasury running their charade."

The person in front of her shifted, providing a view of the final prisoners.

It was the boy and the older woman.

The ones she had given the prize purse, which had apparently contained acorns. They were shackled next to the con men. Renna wanted to run, to scream, to say she had not ordered this, that she had not known—

"And you still punish those who are victims of this ruse?"

His eyes flashed. Gone was the boy Garen Draic had been. Only the high sheriff stood before her, cruel and ruthless. His face was a mask of cool judgment as he said, low enough that only she could hear, "They were found in possession of treasonous materials. As you say, rot left unattended will spread. Being Silenced is a mercy, is it not?"

Renna wanted to defend herself, to wipe the condescending, self-righteous look off his face. This was not the same. What had happened the day of Draic's return had been justice, had been a mercy. Better to lose your tongue than be burned at the stake. She swallowed the hatred coating her throat, fought to keep her face unaffected like his. Ulrik's words cut through the rage churning inside her—he would not be able to intercede on her behalf if she was found out. Renna did not doubt Draic would be just as calm lighting a pyre meant for her if he discovered the truth.

"Shall we continue the tour, Your Grace? Or have you seen enough?"

Renna steeled her spine, a pillar of royal strength and conviction, even as thunder raged beneath her skin. "I've seen enough."

CHAPTER 9

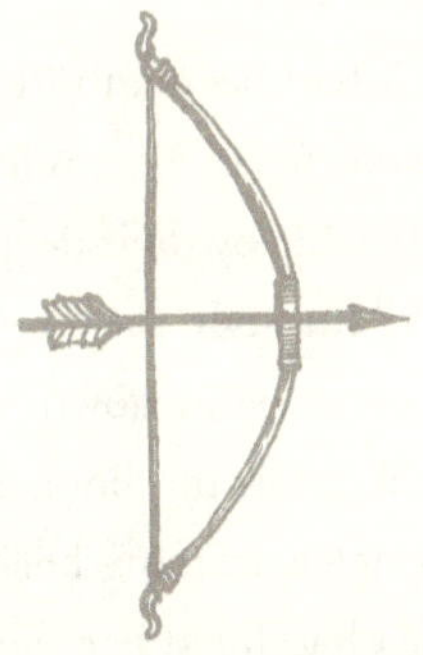

And so it was that the Mother found the people of Loxley to be faithful to
Her words, and She blessed the mountain with precious aurem and a spark
of Her essence. The stones forged from the holy fire would raise Her people
in esteem for as long as they were faithful to Her ways. Let the flames be
kept at the heart of the kingdom, resting on a hearth carved directly into
the mountain, that nothing shall be below, and in this the Mother is our
foundation.

—excerpt from the Tomes of Truth

AUREM WAS THE LIFEBLOOD OF LOXLEY. AFTER THE GREAT CULLING, THE MOTHER HAD BLESSED THE PEOPLE WITH KNOWLEDGE OF THE PRECIOUS STONE THAT WOULD SOLVE THEIR IMMEDIATE PROBLEM NOW THAT THE TREES HAD ALL BEEN BURNED: WARMTH. Not only could the aurem be used to forge weapons stronger than steel and be crafted into jewelry finer than gold and diamonds, but the people also no longer needed flint or kindling. Aurem kept the finnikfire burning, warmed the water in the castle, and provided both metaphorical and literal light to the kingdom.

The kingdom prospered as demand for aurem rose throughout all of Dravmir, securing Loxley's place as an important trade center. But mining aurem was slow and dangerous, so the Mother spoke again to Her Head Trissaia, telling him She would reward their offerings of blood with more aurem. In their blood She would see their Truth, and in this way, She would know if they were worthy. The crown and the church crafted the first bloodstone siphon. Once filled with an offering, a bloodstone siphon would not reopen until it was tossed into the goddess-blessed fire, where the blood would alchemize to bond and infuse the raw aurem, creating more bloodstones.

Thus the first Blood Tithe began.

Renna liked to imagine it had been a more intimate ritual back then, unlike the roiling mass of people who filled the castle to bursting now. The corridors were packed. Trissaia, recognizable by their deep red robes and the aurem collars around their throats, moved through the crowd, taking last-minute offerings before the Tithe. Renna's ceremonial gown was cream brocade, the sleeves dagged at the wrists and trailing on the floor. Her hair was twisted away from her face and plaited, a few ringlets framing her temples. An aurem circlet rested on her forehead, and Nastasia had lined her eyes with kohl before they'd left her chambers to head to the throne room. Several pale noblemen lay sprawled on chaises while their blood filled the vials in the hilts of ritual daggers. They could afford to lie around, lightheaded and dizzy from the loss of blood that left a tang in the air.

None of them would be forced to lie in the mud.

Guards dotted the hallway, looking for signs of trouble. Several noblewomen strode by wearing masks of delicate chains and beads woven together: an elaborate display of Silence. A courtier with a plunging neckline bumped into Renna. Hands ran down her arms as hot breath hit her face, carrying a tittering laugh with the smell of wine.

"They say it's a blood match," she slurred her words, evidently unaware of who Renna was. "Father will have to accept his proposal now." She staggered as a guard appeared from the throng, gripping her by the elbow as she continued to blather. "Did you hear what the Triss said? He and I are a match!"

"Where is the royal retinue?" Nastasia hissed at the guard, scanning the crowd.

"It's all right, Stasi."

Nastasia scoffed as the guard led the woman away. "Personal tellings aren't meant to be performed until *after* the Tithe."

"Yes, but did you hear? They're a match," Renna teased. "You can't begrudge them their fun."

Nastasia mumbled something about propriety, but it was lost in the din. They maneuvered around a cluster of youths who seemed to be waiting for a Keeper. Priestesses in purple, their faces shrouded in half masks, scurried around with collection bowls filled with bloodstone siphons. An overlarge stone table ran the length of the room, right down the middle. Large clay jars were stacked in every corner, filled with sparkling aurem-infused kvass; pillars of solid aurem had been carried in by groups of burly men for decoration; the air carried the mingling scents of scones and stew wafting from the kitchens.

Tonight there would be dancing, feasting, and drinking; the chaises would be draped with light-headed and giddy citizens reveling in post-tithe belonging and euphoria. Renna's personal experience of the Fire Feast had always seemed good enough until she'd witnessed Nastasia's metamorphosis the previous year. That was the first time she'd worried that everything she was doing might still be for naught, that no matter how obedient she was, how many supplications she sent to the Mother, she would still be missing something vital. The feast had been the happiest she'd seen Nastasia in years; her cousin had transformed into a wilder, more vibrant version of herself, like the person she'd been before she'd donned the robes of a priestess, when she'd frequently left Renna gasping for breath with a stitch in her side from laughing so hard. Nastasia had danced all night, received personal Foretellings, and shed tears of joy, the peals of her laughter echoing like music through the castle.

Renna wondered if she would feel that euphoric after the crucible.

A Trissaia stood elevated on a low platform, a Tome of Truth before her, reciting over the heads of citizens already deep into mugs of mead and wine. "A worthy Trissaia will have Sight. A worthy Trissaia is incapable of causing harm while performing the Blood Tithe."

As the crowd bottlenecked at the doors to the throne room, someone fainted. Renna was jostled to the side as several noblemen tried to catch the man who'd given too much blood and hadn't made it to a chaise. Nastasia's arm was ripped from hers. Renna wished fervently that she'd waited for her guards to escort her, for now the crowd, too closely packed and too drunk already, was becoming a seething, wild thing. She fought to remain steady on her feet, casting her gaze around for a uniform or armor.

A large hand clasped her upper arm, and Renna blinked away the sense of having lived this moment already as she looked up into Garen Draic's scowling face. Her skin was hot under his touch. A crease appeared between his brows, his mouth a tight line. She'd not seen him since he'd escorted her back to the palace three nights ago. His words had kept her awake: *What I want most is retribution against those who have wronged me.* What would happen should the high sheriff discover that she herself was a witch carrying the same vedra blood as those who had wronged him?

She sent another prayer to the Mother that she'd done her duty.

"You aren't in the Ember Seat." His voice was so low it was almost a growl.

Renna pulled away from his grasp, a flush climbing up her neck, taking a moment to gather herself by straightening her skirts. Ulrik was no doubt making his way to the Ember Seat, the private anointed room near the Mother's Flame, to hear Her voice. "Excellently spotted. I can see why you're such an asset on the battlefield."

Draic opened his mouth, but Nastasia reappeared, cutting him off. "Finally. Her Highness shouldn't be without an escort, and I'm meant to be meeting with the Trissaia." Nastasia made a show of waving at Draic's looming height. "Make yourself useful."

As they pressed through the throng, Renna felt the ghost of Draic's hand on her lower back, never touching her but creating a barrier against the unruly courtiers. He kept his head down as they made their way to the dais at the front of the throne room. "I was under the impression that the crown princess would be involved in the Foretelling."

Renna's temper crackled like lightning at the reminder that she still had yet to prove herself. "Until I perform my crucible, I will remain out here. Only the Head Trissaia and crowned monarch enter the Ember Seat to receive the Foretelling."

Draic didn't respond, offering his hand as she climbed the three steps to the throne. His fingers brushed the scar on her palm.

There is a darkness in you that would destroy this whole kingdom.

"Truth shall light the way," she said to Draic as a dismissal.

"Truth is in the blood." But instead of retreating into the crowd, Draic stood off to the side of the dais, hands clasped behind his back, his eyes roving the crowd and flicking to the oculus above as she took her seat on the throne.

A Keeper approached, bowing low, offering a tray of ritual daggers arranged just so. At Renna's gesture, the Keeper first took the high sheriff's tithe. With practiced movements, Draic undid the laces at his wrists, rolling his sleeve up three times to reveal the corded muscles of his forearm. He stood as if he were made of stone as the blade pierced his skin just below his elbow. The bloodsiphon filled quickly, and then it was Renna's turn. She pulled up her sleeve, letting the Keeper take from the vein at her elbow. Blood flecked her white gown. A fitting symbol, she thought. She sensed Draic's focus on her and resisted the urge to clear her throat. Tithes complete, the Keeper took their offerings and hurried away.

Nastasia stood at the front of the crowd, half mask now drawn over her mouth and nose, her eyes shrouded by her purple hood. A Trissaia stood at the podium of solid aurem, reading to the congregation from the Tome, familiar passages that Renna knew by heart. *The first Foretelling showed us the poison that would destroy the Trissaia; the Great Culling removed trees from the kingdom; as Her show of favor for our loyalty, the Mother provided Her Flame and aurem to keep us warm; Truth shall light the way; Truth is in the blood.*

A chalice blocked her view. Renna blinked at the proffered cup.

"Your Highness looks rather pale." Draic pressed the drink into her hands.

The knots in her stomach loosened as soon as the mineral-enhanced liquid hit her tongue. She wiped away the kvass dripping down her chin with the back of her hand before clutching the chalice to quell her shaking. The sun was nearing its zenith. Soon the Silent Sacrament would begin and last until the sun went down, while the Head Trissaia would be sequestered in the Ember Seat. There he would hear the Mother's words for the upcoming year on behalf of the entire kingdom.

When she was young, Renna would get hungry and antsy during the Tithe. She'd been chastened by priestesses on many occasions, as if the fact that she was the crown princess should take away a child's need to fidget. The hour of silence each day was meant to help prepare the citizens for the Silent Sacrament.

The large aurem bells rang out. The vibration went through Renna's bones, and the chatter in the throne room ceased. The hair on her arms stood up, as if aware of the silence falling all through the castle and spreading through the streets of Loxley like a cloak. The crackling of the Mother's Flame in its hearth at the lowest level of the castle could be heard.

Keepers began the procession to cast the tithes. Their palanquins were piled high with the collected bloodstone siphons. Everyone over twelve—the age at which one could receive their Foretelling—was expected to give an annual offering that would be cast into the Mother's Flame. An unsettling thought whispered in the back of Renna's mind: How many of those tithes had been procured by a leecher?

She wished the ceremony were over already. After the Tithe, the Mother would bless the entire kingdom by taking away the anxieties, fears, and doubts that had crept up over the last year—rot seeking to ensnare their souls. Renna had come to rely on the post-Tithe bliss over the years. While others like Nastasia had an easier time tending to their faith like a burning, growing thing, Renna needed the Blood Tithe just to keep her spark alive. She wiped her palms against the fabric of her dress. Her crucible was a fortnight away and when she was found worthy, her faith would be bolstered. She would ascend the throne as a beacon of the light to her people, as her personal Foretelling had said.

The rapid clinks of bloodstone siphons being poured into the heart of the Mother's Flame created a symphony of crystal raining into the fire. This was normally Renna's favorite part, but today it felt like tiny pebbles striking her skin. As the offerings were cast, the Mother's Flame grew higher and higher, reaching up from the depths of the castle. The growing pillar of goddess-blessed fire breached the opening in the floor. The massive flame column grew until it extended up through the center of the castle and out the oculus in the roof.

The throne was cold against Renna's back as the air shimmered with the heat of the roaring Mother's Flame. She imagined the crowds gathered in the streets, their attention rapt on the castle, on the flames billowing from the dome like a giant torch. How strange it must feel, Renna thought, mind muddled from the heat, to be so far away from the warmth of the Flame, yet still stand in reverence and silence.

Hours slipped past. The red flames crackled, swirled, and soothed. Images flitted through Renna's mind. Was this a small taste of the Foretelling that Ulrik was seeing in the Ember Seat? Once, after kneeling before the Mother's Flame for hours, head pounding and knees aching, Renna had asked Ulrik what it felt like to see a Truth. *A calm sense of knowing will wash over you. To tell someone their Truth is an honor we must safeguard.*

Renna let the wonder of the Mother's Flame speak to her mind. The fire seemed to call to her, an old friend reaching out for connection. Her palms hummed as finnikfire simmered in her blood. Her eyes were unfocused, tension seeping out of her. The nobles were strewn across lounges, leaning against the stone pillars as the Mother relieved Loxley's people of the burdens they'd carried all year. Renna relaxed on the throne.

The sky overhead was a bruised color when Ulrik returned to the throne room, signaling that the first part of the ritual was complete. He had heard the Mother's words and would now address the kingdom.

Inside the pillar of flame, images unfurled for all to see as the Foretelling began. Ulrik narrated alongside the images—crowds of people, tears of joy in their eyes; Loxley's flag flying proudly over a steadily marching army. His words, a soothing prophecy, washed over Renna. The Mother's Flame would continue to expand into Wendsvik through the diligent proselyting of the Keepers. Those who touched the False Flame would either bow to Her Truth or experience Her rage. The Flame presented an image of an aurem crossbow, but it had more gears than those the army currently used. A stirring of excitement rippled through the congregation as Ulrik spoke of the advancements in aurem weaponry, the reward for their faith. A new era was on the horizon for the Mother's chosen.

The vision shifted again, and Renna saw herself looming larger than life in the fire. Her corset felt too tight as she watched the vision of herself channeling finnikfire into aurem, transforming it into a bloodstone to be added to the crown.

"This shall be the year a Koravik queen ascends to the throne, strengthening the crown and the Mother's will. Her fire will be a blazing beacon to the world."

The same words he'd used to admonish her after her outing to Nottingham seemed portentous now, full of bright promise. She found Nastasia's face in the crowd, an anchor point. Nastasia's eyes were glossy with unshed tears, crinkled at the sides as she grinned. Warmth spread through Renna, tingling in her limbs in the telltale fashion of post-Tithe bliss. She bit back a sob of relief. *This* must be what it felt like to look into the Mother's Flame and see Truth. It swirled in her throat, the words blossoming and seeking an outlet. Her chest swelled, and she straightened against the throne, barely registering what Ulrik said, so distracted was she by this blessed relief and sense of *knowing* and truth and—

"It is the Mother's will that the crown princess, Rennavera Koravik, not wait to perform her crucible. She will do so tonight so that she may usher in this new era for us all."

80　BRITTANY HANSEN

CHAPTER 10

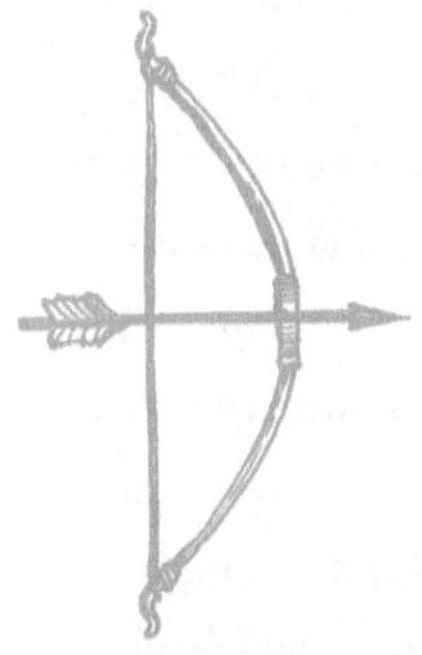

Even as Ulrik spoke the words aloud, he spoke directly into Renna's mind: *Do not fear, Rennavera. You are ready. Let us use this moment to instill faith in the people's hearts.*

The atmosphere was brimming with anticipation and euphoria and drink as Keepers moved quickly to procure the aurem for the task. Ulrik's voice filled the large throne room, floating up through the oculus, reminding the people of the rites of the crucible. The ceremony hadn't been performed since Renna's mother's ascension to the throne, after all. Most history had been passed down orally through the Trissaia after all the parchment was burned; only essential documents had been rewritten on vellum or thin copper sheets. To Renna, Ulrik sounded as if he were speaking underwater—*must channel finnikfire into the stone and let the aurem and Mother reveal the wielder's true nature.* She fought to keep her breathing even.

Once when she was young, a horse in the stable had broken its leg. It was shortly after her parents had died, and she'd yelled at the Keeper who was with her, demanding that they use their magic to heal the mare. The Keeper had gotten so close to her face that she could see the veins pulsing in his forehead as he told her that such vedra magic was wicked. Renna's mouth had tasted of ash as she'd stared into the mare's eyes. The magnificent beast had not struggled or cried out, just lain there, big eyes boring into Renna's soul, accepting its fate. The Keeper had used a ritual bloodsiphon dagger to cut the horse's throat. *We cannot allow such royal blood to go to waste*, he'd said before hurrying off, leaving her alone with the dead horse.

Standing frozen in the throne room, every eye trained on her, Renna thought of the horse, silent and unmoving, waiting for its fate.

Remember what I have shown you, child, Ulrik said inside her head, projecting the image of her mother's triumphant crucible into Renna's mind.

A Keeper positioned an uncut aurem stone at the front of the dais on a narrow altar, displayed on a black satin cushion. It was larger even than the one Ulrik had given her for practice. Next to it sat the crown, dripping with the bloodstones of queens past. Awaiting her addition.

"Rennavera Koravik, the Mother has chosen the people of Loxley as Her stewards over the aurem. It is through our devotion to the Truth that we continue to receive Her blessings and guidance. Today She will speak through the aurem. Let the crucible begin."

Come, child, he said gently, just to her. He swept a hand toward the stone.

This was the moment Renna had imagined a thousand times, the image that kept her up at night until she gave in to uneasy sleep, what she prepared for as she bled each morning. On the surface, it was a straightforward and simple task: channel her finnikfire into the aurem like a blacksmith pouring hot ore into a mold to craft a desired shape. The aurem would become a polished bloodstone, proving her mettle, her worthiness. It would be over quickly.

Renna's hands were cold as she reached for the aurem.

The weight of it pulled on her limbs like a sudden current. The power emanating from it swept her up in its path. Outwardly, nothing had changed: she stood before the citizens, gazing into a large aurem stone. The rest of the room fell away as her jaw clenched, her muscles strained.

The world went black, then exploded into fire around her.

Here in this in-between place, her form was ablaze. The Koravik blood coursed strong through her veins, her birthright pulsing hot like a second heartbeat. *Channel it into the stone*, said a calm, quiet voice in her mind. Was it hers? Her mother's? Ulrik's, perhaps. It didn't really matter. She'd done her duty. This was her moment to reveal her worth, to shine as bright as a beacon for her people.

Renna drew the fire up, swirling it into a vortex that scalded her throat, singed her skin, and blazed through her mind. The finnikfire raged hot and wild, demanding an outlet. She focused her attention on her palms and the weight between them that tethered her to the physical world. She poured the finnikfire down her arms, letting it burn away her impurities, letting it forge her into something new, something stronger and brighter.

The aurem fought her.

The heat building in her palms became blistering, but the aurem did not yield to her. Like the moon eclipsing the sun, she was plunged into darkness for a heartbeat. *Please, Mother,* she begged, unsure if she meant the goddess or her own. But there was no answer, only howling wind in her ears. Pressure swelled inward and out simultaneously. Her fire sparked again. A clash of storm and flame swirled around her, ripping at her soul, each demanding something she couldn't understand. Pain rang through her knees as they struck the floor.

There is a darkness in you, Rennavera Koravik.

Not worthy, not worthy, not worthy.

Her finnikfire abruptly snuffed out.

Someone was screaming. *She* was screaming.

Renna tore her eyes open, wrenching herself out of that in-between space. The atmosphere was no longer one of reverence but of fear. Blood marred her empty palms. Her fingers trembled as she bit the back of her hand, choking on a sob.

The aurem stone lay broken before her, cracked viciously in two as if struck by lightning.

Pain carved through her body, which bowed as the realization hit. Hisses of *witch* raced through the congregation. The guards at the foot of the dais stood poised to move. The crowd had pulled away.

In her mind, Ulrik said, *What have you done?*

I don't know, I didn't—

Her bones were vibrating.

"High Sheriff, seize her," Lord Gisborne ordered from somewhere behind her.

Rough hands gripped her upper arms hard enough to bruise. She was hauled to her feet, her weight sagging. The High Sheriff's hold was the only thing keeping her upright.

"Please," Renna begged, voice raw. Tears dripped off her cheeks, her chin. *Forgive me my weakness, Mother.*

The destroyed aurem sat at her feet, proving the words of her Foretelling: *Vedra blood runs through your veins.*

You force my hand, child. Ulrik's voice cut sharp as a knife.

Renna could hardly breathe around the ache in her throat. She would be burned alive like the Almost Queen. What would they call her, she wondered distantly.

Help me. She threw her mettlemancy out, searching for Nastasia, but she couldn't find her.

Please, she said to Ulrik. *Just tell me what I must do.*

It felt like an eternity before Ulrik said, *There might be another way.*

CHAPTER 11

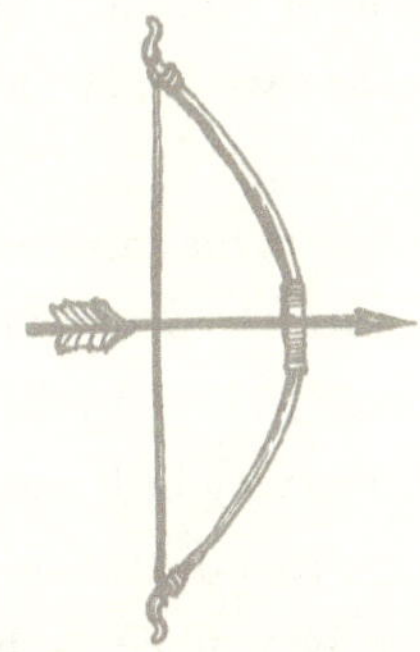

E XILE.

It was a simple thing to relinquish her kingdom. They did not require her blood. Not now that everyone knew what coursed through her veins. It was done merely with words that she said aloud to the crowd as Ulrik spoke them into her mind.

"I, Rennavera Koravik, renounce my claim to the throne of Loxley. As I have failed my crucible and been deemed unworthy to rule, I abdicate the duties of the crown to Head Trissaia Ulrik Varin. It is by his mercy that I accept banishment and keep my life. Long may he reign. Truth shall light the way. Truth is in the blood."

A line of guards and Trissaia now stood between her and her people, as if witch blood was catching. She was to be taken to her rooms to gather her belongings. Her exile would begin immediately. After all, when had the wicked ever been given more time?

Having failed the crucible, Renna's finnikfire and mettlemancy would be taken by the Mother. She'd never asked how it worked. She should have.

At least she didn't have to pretend anymore.

Draic gripped her arm, ushering her from the throne room, a few of his guards trailing them. Aurem lanterns flickered around them. Renna tripped over her feet, staying upright only because of his tight hold on her upper arm as he led her down another hall. A blade in Draic's hand caught the light. The hair on her neck rose, and Renna twisted, trying to find a familiar marker.

This was not the way to her chambers.

"Where are you taking me?"

"To be Silenced."

A manic laugh threatened to burst from her, but she swallowed it. Oh, the cruel irony. She thought of Yana, of Marian. How many people had she sentenced to this exact punishment over the years? Now she would suffer the same fate. It no longer seemed a mercy.

But when they came to a split in the corridors, they veered away from the one that led to the Silencing chamber. Deeper and deeper into the castle they went, taking too many turns for Renna to keep track. She tried to pull free of Draic's grip, but her body was weak. Warning bells were blaring in her mind. Why had she let herself be dragged away from the throne room, from Nastasia and Ulrik? Anyone would have been more sympathetic to her fall from grace than the high sheriff, whose personal vendetta against witches fueled his ruthless measures to sniff them out, to inflict such suffering as only one who had suffered could exact.

Renna forced herself to breathe through her nose, to keep her composure, as Draic shoved her through a door. He spoke in low tones to the other guards, his back to her. The room was small, with only a grate over a drain in the corner. No window. Nothing to use as a weapon. Just an empty room that held a lethal promise.

The guards took their leave, and Draic took a step toward her. She retreated as she threw a hand out, desperately calling her magic. But the finnikfire was dormant in her veins. It seemed the Mother's judgment was quick.

Draic advanced another step. Her back brushed the far wall. "Didn't you say everything you do is for the kingdom? Why fight what is best for this kingdom, then?"

"King Ulrik decides what's best for the kingdom, not you." Renna pressed flat against the cold stones as he towered over her.

"You seem to be under the misguided belief that I'm acting in opposition to the king's wishes."

He was trying to get under her skin, to make her think that he was simply following orders. But even as she rejected the thought, a sneaking doubt reared its head. Ulrik *could* have used mettlemancy to give Draic commands. Panic cinched tighter around her ribs, and her mind raced. "I require a moment with Nastasia."

Draic ignored her.

"Did you not hear me, Sheriff? I demand—"

With unsettling speed, Draic was right in front of her, gripping her jaw, angling her head back. A musky, slightly sweet smell filled her nostrils. He dragged a thumb roughly across her bottom lip, pulling it down as if checking to see if she'd sprouted fangs. His gaze roved from her face to her throat, where the edge of his dagger was pressed directly over her scar.

"You're not in a position to be making demands. They've publicly proclaimed you a witch, though it seems they knew that all along. What pretty lies they told to uphold the Truth."

"And yet the truth eluded you." She wouldn't give him the satisfaction of watching her break, even though the blood was rushing away from her head, the room was beginning to spin, and spots danced at the edges of her vision.

"Perhaps. But I intend to remedy that."

Long fingers wrapped around her throat, pushing her head up. The blade bit into her skin, and slick blood wet her neck. Renna tried to thrash, a strangled cry tearing from her. But her limbs were suddenly heavy, dread making her dizzy. Draic kept her pinned to the wall as he carved another cut, deeper this time. Was he going to torture her to death? Wait until all her vedra blood was on the floor of the cell, creeping toward the drain? There was a wrenching sensation, and pain was all she knew.

Then the torment stopped. Her body went cold, and she slumped to the floor. Perhaps the Mother still saw her worthy of a small mercy, because shouts came from far away, and horns trumpeted. A rasping, keening sound escaped her as she fought to stay conscious. Draic retreated to the door, issuing a command to the waiting guards, blood dripping from his hands. Her blood.

A too-sweet smell had burrowed straight into her brain, mixing with the copper tang. She touched her throat, fingers coming away deep crimson. The door swung closed, plunging the room into darkness. Renna's eyes slid shut of their own accord. If she fell asleep, she would die. But wouldn't that be so much easier for everyone?

Wake up, said a voice, cutting through the haze.

She's coming, Renna.

She was going to bleed out here in an unknown room, alone.

Cool fingers touched her palm, then pressed against her wound. White-hot pain radiated from her throat. The world spun, nausea rolling through her. The room tilted again, and a heavy warmth rested around her shoulders. Purple robes. A priestess was lifting her off the floor, which was foolish. She was meant to die. A deep scraping noise—the grate had been pulled aside, revealing a steep set of stairs.

Renna had spent so much time avoiding her duty in these passageways before forsaking them in the name of Truth. And now that she'd failed, someone was bringing her back to them. She wanted to laugh. It came out as a pained whimper. She knew she was straddling life and death. It was nearly too much effort to put one foot in front of the other, clinging to the priestess pulling her along. The tunnel spun as her companion murmured to her. Renna blinked slowly, trying to grasp what she was saying. The walls shrank and expanded as if they were breathing. Then Renna was sitting against the cold stone in the dark, alone once more.

An endless darkness stretched before her, pulling her into its gravity, like that wretched night so many years ago. *Something has happened...I am so sorry, child... wounds too extensive to heal...the assassin has been dealt with.* She saw the leecher, the boy from the contest, Yana's stricken face. She longed for Marian's soft embrace, for her governess to smooth her hair once more.

Renna could sink into the bleak nothingness now. All the pain would cease. Perhaps then her people would be shown more mercy. Perhaps their suffering had been because of her all along.

The priestess was back, retying the bandage around her neck. There was a sharp prick in her arm. Renna tasted the salt of her tears. A rush of warmth flowed through her veins, and her head cleared slightly. Then they were moving again, their labored breaths the only thing passing between them. In the distance, muted footfalls. Had Nastasia discovered she was missing yet?

Renna's eyes fluttered open. How long ago had she closed them? They were out of the tunnels. Crisp air kissed her face, filling her lungs. The moon cast weak light across the ragged mountainside around them. The ground below was muddy. A horse nickered, and the recognition made her knees weak: Alita. The midnight mare allowed Renna to be hoisted up and into the saddle. The priestess was speaking urgently. Alita's hair was rough against her cheek as she forced herself to concentrate. The woman shifted her weight, and the shadows across her face lifted. Dark hair save for a streak of white at her temple. It was the priestess she'd knocked into as she'd raced Nastasia down the steps of the castle. The woman was speaking rushed words that she couldn't make sense of: *The tide is out* and *Alita knows the way* and *Hold on, Your Majesty.* Renna wasn't that anymore—she'd signed away the kingdom—but she couldn't gather the energy to tell her. All she wanted to do now was to sink into the nothingness that tugged at her.

The priestess clicked her tongue, and the world wrenched abruptly, jolts of pain wracking her entire body. Renna clung to the saddle. A fox ran alongside them, nipping at Alita's hooves as if urging them to go faster, and an owl trailed them overhead, or perhaps they were merely hallucinations. Oblivion took her then, but not before the priestess's last words echoed in her mind.

Take her to Sherwood.

PART
TWO

CHAPTER 12

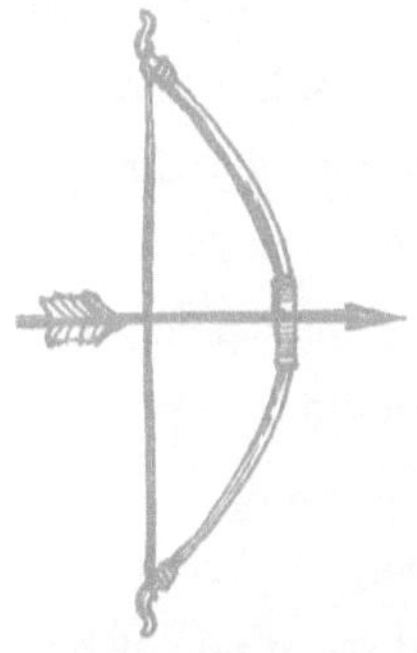

A single oak will blind the believer, silence the seer. If any righteous tarry too long near trees, their strength will be drained, their minds ensnared, and their souls lost. Therefore, it is the Mother's will that the abominations be burned, scorching the temptation from Dravmir.
—*the first Foretelling, given to Osric,*
Obeyed by the first Koravik queen

SOMEONE HAD FORGOTTEN TO LIGHT THE FIRE IN HER ROOM, AND THE CHILL DRAGGED HER FROM A FITFUL SLEEP. Her head pounded like she'd drunk her weight in mead, the normally soft velvet prickling her face as she shifted on the chaise. Pain like a hot knife dragged across her throat, and she jerked fully awake.

Renna was still on Alita, her hair stuck to her face, skin slick with fever, and her fingers nearly numb from being shoved under the rope around the pommel. Her mare had stopped a few paces from the massive expanse of trees stretching before her in both directions.

Sherwood Forest.

Renna pulled the reins to turn Alita away from the cursed woods, trembling, her thoughts tumbling wildly. She tried to command Alita with words, but attempting to speak brought another bright burst of pain that raked across her vocal cords. She pressed her heels into the mare's sides, desperately urging Alita away from the trees, but her horse ignored her. Despair and panic welled up in her. *Get away, get away.*

The sky was a bleak, lifeless grey, heavy with rain clouds, and she could taste the storm rapidly blowing in. Loxley Castle was but a speck in the distance. Renna was on the top of the plateau where Sherwood loomed, above the Perun Sea. She scoured the expanse of water, unsure if she was looking for someone to finish the job or to rescue her, but there was no one. She was meant to be exiled to one of Loxley's annexed villages, but that was before the high sheriff had tried to kill her. She pictured the map of the continent spread out on the war table. There was the road that followed the edge of Sherwood to the Audros Pass, where one could cross over the river that spilled into the Perun Sea and continue into Wendsvik. But surely there would be patrols there sent by the high sheriff, not to mention the bandits who lay in wait.

You seem to be under the misguided belief that I'm acting in opposition to the king's wishes. Draic's words seemed more potent now that she was so far from home. Was it possible Draic would have done something so drastic without the king's knowledge? Would there not be a dire punishment for such an act? Or perhaps he thought to curry favor with the king, disposing of a problem so the crown need not sully its hands.

Renna had nowhere to go. She was an outlawed witch. Grief clawed up her spine as wind whipped the cloak she had on—the purple robes from the priestess. Her eyes burned. Perhaps she could ask for refuge with the vedra on the continent, though there was the risk that they'd recognize the fallen queen. She didn't trust the Falsehood army not to use her as leverage against the crown.

A flash of orange darted past the tree line, and a fox crept from the forest's edge. The animal had an intense gaze, so solemn it was almost reproachful. Was this the fox she thought she had imagined during her hurried escape? Green moss and ferns covered the floor. Renna eyed the trees warily. Why hadn't the nearness of them killed her? At the very least, she'd anticipated some draining effects. *Because you have vedra blood,* a snide voice said in her head.

The rain began to fall, hard and sharp. Below, the Perun Sea was a choppy riot, waves tossing and crashing. An ominous roll of thunder cracked the air. The fox disappeared back into the trees. The reins dug into Renna's palms as Alita shook her head. The temperature dropped rapidly as the storm rolled across the land. The Blood Tithe took place at the shift in the seasons, the Fire Feast landing on one of the final mild nights before the winter chill took over. If she stayed out in the storm, she'd be soaked through in minutes and would quite possibly freeze to death. Alita was restless, each step sending hot pokers of agony through Renna's neck. Lightning flashed not too far off.

I did not die in those tunnels, nor under Draic's blade. I'll be damned if I let a storm kill me.

Renna's rescuer had sent her to Sherwood. Why go to all that effort if only to send her to another death?

Perhaps the forest recognized the darkness in her.

Perhaps this once, her witch blood would not bring her ruination.

Renna urged Alita into the trees. Rain still speared through the tangled mass of branches and leaves, though it lost some of its force. The vicious wind dropped to a low moan. It was pitch dark inside the forest. She shivered against the chill, all her senses straining. There was a flurry of wings, and Alita veered away, a raven's screaming caw sending Renna's heart racing. The trees here were close together, like skeleton fingers twisting in a macabre prayer. The branches overhead looked like spiderwebs of tar or the spine of some monstrous creature that had swallowed her. The smell of petrichor hung heavy in the air, conjuring images of the training yard in Loxley when there was a sudden downpour: metal and ozone, loam and crushed nettle. Alita kicked up wet detritus in her wake. The trees creaked and swayed, living, breathing things stretching toward her, whipping her face, snagging at her cloak. A chittering sound swirled around, the source invisible.

There was something lurking at the edge of her vision. There, a movement in the corner of her eye, but it was gone when she tried to look straight at it. Something—or perhaps many somethings—was watching them. Following them. Renna's heart was in her throat, her breath a rasping wheeze. She wound Alita's mane between her fingers, her legs suddenly numb. With every snap of branch under hoof, her nerves ratcheted tighter. To her left, moonlight glinted off predatory eyes, and Renna swore she saw a flash of teeth as long as her arm. The determination from only moments ago was ripped from her, just as her powers had been. She was going to die.

Up ahead, a spark of fire. Not red like the Mother's Flame, but a deep green. It wove through the trunks, coming closer. The green flame twitched in a way that felt familiar, and then the fire *leapt*, a streak of unholy flame shooting straight toward her and Alita. Renna had just enough time to think *How fitting that I'll die by vedra fire* when the rest of the creature became visible under the halo of green light.

The fox spun around in a tight circle, easily staying clear of Alita's hooves, looked Renna dead in the eyes, and then took off in the opposite direction, its green flame leaving a fading viridian trail in its wake. It was leading her away from the thing with teeth.

Renna did not think, did not stop to question, just pressed her heels into Alita and followed. The thing with teeth gave chase with an uneven cadence.

Renna pictured massive paws, claws dripping with blood, a mangled head, and grizzled maw. Water and mud splashed as they dashed through rivulets that were beginning to swell with rainwater. The green flame bobbed in and out of sight. Branches hung low, forcing Renna to lie flat against Alita's neck, weeping with pain and fear as they trampled through the wild, overgrown forest. She could smell the creature's rank breath behind her. The harrowing sound of its pursuit flayed every nerve raw.

I should never have come here, Renna thought as they brushed roughly against a thicket of thorns. Her leg and arm stung. A snarl, low and unlike anything she'd ever heard, came from behind, branches and leaves snapping as if being torn from the trees.

The forest floor sloped down suddenly, the rush of water drowning out the beast behind them. The fox dashed to the riverbank, flitting across an overhanging branch before jumping from stone to stone to reach the other side. Alita, bless her, charged into the river, heedless of the water. Renna bit the meat of her palm to distract herself from the searing pain the jostling movements caused in her neck. She kept her eyes on the fox, who waited on the far side, still radiating green fire.

They reached the other side as a bellow ripped through the air. A hulking mass rippled out of the dark line of trees, unfolding itself to stand on its hind legs. Its front legs were so long that even at full height they brushed the ground. In the dark, Renna could not make out its face, only the enormous tusks jutting over its bottom lip. The monstrous creature stopped short of the water, emitting a low screech of frustration, and Renna sagged with relief as understanding dawned: it would not, or could not, cross.

The fox led, and they followed. Minutes or hours passed, and the adrenaline wore off, leaving Renna numb and drained, like she was tucked away in a deep corner of her mind, hidden within her body.

A fugue state: she'd heard one of the palace healers whisper of such a thing. Her mind had retreated to protect itself. They mostly saw it with soldiers returning from Wendsvik. In the weeks following the ritual to drain her witch blood, Renna had been numb save for the constant pain in her neck, watching everything around her as if through a rain-streaked window. Days had passed without her permission. On one occasion Nastasia had found her watching Draic's weapons training. Nastasia had attempted to coax Renna out of her haze by asking which of the drills he'd been practicing, but Renna had found she didn't even know how long she'd been leaning against the battlement wall, let alone what Draic had been doing.

Alita stopped walking. Vacantly, Renna slid off her horse, limbs moving without thought. Sometime later, she became dimly aware that she'd crawled into an enclosed space. It was warmer than outside, though only just. Alita had positioned herself in front of the opening. Renna's eyes passed over the full saddlebags, the bow and arrow; there was a shape that could be a blanket, but fetching it seemed impossible. She was sinking into her surroundings, becoming a part of them, unmovable. She felt a flicker of fear, recalling tales of roots that would pull you into the ground, bury you alive, but it vanished when a soft green light bathed the walls around her—no, the *tree* around her.

She was nestled inside a hollowed-out trunk. Turning sluggishly, Renna blinked down at the fox curled at her feet. Its tail burned gently, a whisper of the bright flame she'd seen as they'd run through the woods. Warmth seeped into the soles of her shoes, spread to her legs and arms, thawed the chill in her torso. If only her people could see her now.

The great Koravik queen, unable to start a fire.

When unconsciousness came, it felt like nothing.

Birdsong roused her. She was slumped against rough bark, the ground covering leaving indentations in her palms. Moving carefully, every muscle protesting, Renna crawled out of the trunk, squinting against the sunlight. The forest floor was carpeted in soft green moss, bursting with ferns, draped in vines: life exploding and growing.

And the trees.

Above her, branches and leaves twisted into an intricate canopy. She had assumed there would be mostly green hues in the forest, but there were more colors than she'd imagined: maroons, verdant yellows, pale and vibrant crimsons, olive so deep it looked like pooled shadows. No two trees were the same. There were ones with bone-white bark, rich browns with knots and swirls, ones with tiny clustered buds, others with limbs that reminded her of a mother reaching down to hold her children. There were heart-shaped leaves larger than her face, others like a bird's fluttering wings, still more that looked like needles. The smell of flowers and loam and something she'd never experienced before forced her lungs wide open, and she took in a fuller breath than she'd drawn…maybe ever.

Her sinuses burned. Renna dashed the back of her hand across her eyes, her heart and insides feeling like butterflies bursting forth. She felt a sense of being watched, but it was different from the stare of the monstrous beast from last night. This was the feeling of woodland animals she couldn't make out peering at her, wondering who she was. Rustling, buzzing, chirping, and croaking mingled with the now-distant sound of the river in some strange orchestra. The hollowed-out tree she'd slept in was massive and had a gravity to it that made it seem very old. It was carved out enough that she could fully stand up inside it.

This, said a small voice in her head, *this* was how the temple was meant to feel.

There was no sign of the fox, but Alita looked up from where she was grazing and ambled over immediately. Renna pressed her forehead to the horse's side, waiting for the world to stop spinning. Alita chuffed but stayed still. Moving slowly, Renna looked through the saddlebags, biting down a sob when she pulled out a familiar tin of healing salve. There were extra bandages, dried meat, cheese, a bundle of scones, and three full waterskins: two with water and one filled with some type of broth. Renna's mouth watered at the aroma, recognizing flavors from the Fire Feast. Her chapped lips smarted as she brought it to her mouth and drank. The motion of swallowing sent pins and needles through her throat. She choked and coughed, sending more fire through her veins. Carefully she touched the bandage around her neck. No blood came away on her hand, which was something, at least.

Pouring a little water on her fingers, she cleaned the dirt off her neck. A stuttering breath escaped her at the wretched sensation of unwrapping the bandage. Dark dried blood stained the cloth. When she gently touched the wound, she could tell there were stitches, hastily done by the jagged feel of them, holding the split skin together. The cuts ran diagonally down the column of her throat, shallow enough that she hadn't bled out when Draic had left her for dead.

Renna was well acquainted with the effects of a blade on skin. These wounds would scar badly: two scars for all to see, to serve as visual reminders of her failings. To look at her would be to know she was unworthy. She gingerly applied some of the salve to the wounds, hissing through her teeth. The task kept her mind from spiraling. She wrapped fresh gauze around her neck, adding an extra strip right over the deepest wound. The salve and bandages would have to be sufficient, as it was all she had. How long would it take for her to heal? She tried to recall the months after the ritual, but those memories were clouded and grey. There was enough food to last her a week if she rationed carefully. And then what? Renna eyed the bow and arrow still strapped to Alita.

So much thought and care had gone into packing all these supplies. Nastasia must have hastily gathered these things for her when her exile had been announced. Her cousin would have realized something was wrong when Draic did not return her to her rooms. Nastasia must have found the priestess and told her of the tunnels before sending her to find Renna.

She held on to this thought like a Truth. Her cousin's face surfaced in her mind along with a fresh wave of grief, and Renna scrunched her eyes closed, refusing to let the tears come. If she allowed herself to cry, she would never stop. The emotions would overtake her, pull her under, never let her back up.

As she repacked the saddlebag, her knuckles scraped against something. There was a hidden pocket, and tucked inside was a small bundle. Frowning, Renna unwrapped the parcel with unsteady fingers. The worn velvet fell away to reveal two items. She dropped them as if they'd bitten her. Alita shook out her mane, and Renna pressed her palm to her chest to calm her racing heart.

A torn page folded hastily, thicker than the vellum sheets they used in the castle: parchment. And a leather cord necklace with a token carved from wood. Renna stared at it, frozen in place, unable to bring herself to touch it but crouching to get a better look. The token was an owl, delicate lines cut into the wood for the feathers. Ink was seeping through the parchment; something was written on the inside. She shook out her fingers and slowly reached for the page. Nothing happened when she touched it; no holy fire from the sky struck her down, and the pads of her fingers remained unharmed.

It's because you are a witch, she told herself.

The parchment crackled as she unfolded it to read the four scrawled words, the ink blotched and messy:

Find the druidhen, Ren.

But the druidhen were all gone, wiped out during the Culling. She balked, wanting to dismiss the message. She needed to focus on staying alive, not chasing down a myth. With jerky movements, Renna wrapped the note and the token back up in the cloth, careful to not touch the wood with her bare skin, and shoved them to the bottom of the pack.

CHAPTER 13

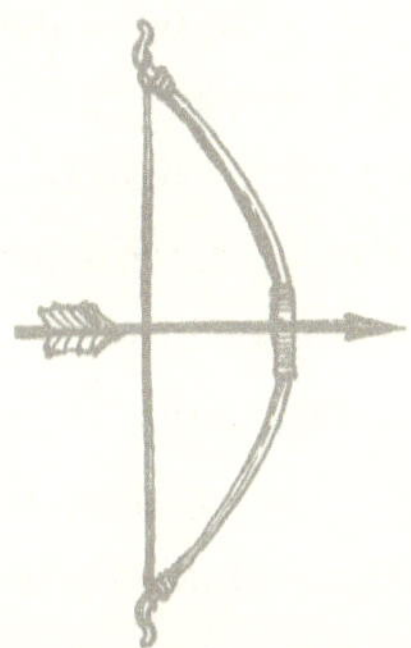

PUSHING THE DRUIDHEN TO THE BACK OF HER MIND PROVED SIMPLE, FOR A TIME. Renna would stay curled up tightly upon waking, not moving as she swallowed down the tears that always lived just under the surface and until the chill in her bones demanded that she get up. Unwilling to return to the river that had kept the beast away, Renna had followed Alita in search of fresh water on her first day in the woods; the fox had not returned. The midnight-colored mare had found a nearby stream quickly, and Renna had greedily filled the waterskins, relishing not needing to ration her sips. One less weight on her mind.

She'd expected the forest to turn fearsome again at night. Instead, the fireflies danced each evening as a blanket of calm settled over the woods. Without the Mother's Flame or the aurem lanterns to compete with, the stars seemed to explode from the sky, more numerous than the grains of sand surrounding Loxley. Renna whispered constellations to Alita, pointing out ones she knew and discovering ones she'd never seen.

The chill once the sun set was a concern, though. If not for the fact that she had woken up with lingering warmth that first morning, Renna would have thought she'd hallucinated the fox and his green fire. Each night, Alita blocked the entrance to the hollow tree, providing a barrier against the night air, and Renna buried herself in two cloaks, mentally cursing the library in the castle for not having any records on how people used to make fires. It was supposed to be possible with wood, but so far, her experimentation had been as unsuccessful as her attempts to call finnikfire. The moon was only a sliver now, and their breath hovered between them as Alita nudged her shoulder. Gratitude for her horse pierced her heart as she drifted off to sleep. *I'm not alone.*

Renna was aware that she was dreaming, but it was unlike any dream she'd had before. It felt not entirely dissimilar to being shown someone else's memory through mettlemancy, but without the pain that accompanied that method. The background was blurred and dark—a large field she didn't recognize, twisting trees not too far off. A caravan pulled off a dirt road. She stood by the horses—by Alita, she realized, giving the mare soothing pets on the shoulder as she looked around. A group of people huddled together, their words unintelligible, their accents guttural and sharp, but the laughter and obvious ease between the speakers let her know it was all good-natured. Alita drew nearer to the people as they crouched around a pile of broken sticks, her eyes trained on their hands like she wanted Renna to do the same. Someone held a small flat stone in one hand. Striking it downward against a piece of wood created sparks, which finally leapt to a larger pile of leaves and debris that lit up quickly. The bright golden fire crackled loudly, the smoke drifting lazily up into the sky. Renna watched the smoke, and then she was the smoke, fading and becoming the night.

The next morning, Renna studied Alita while chewing on a strip of dried meat. Back in Loxley, there'd always been whispers of the strange connections witches had with animals, particularly foxes, certain birds, and cats, who were more susceptible to vedra influences. She'd never heard anything about dream sharing, if that was even what she'd experienced last night. Still, Renna debated all morning before finally steeling herself for what she had to do.

There was some time before the food ran out—she was still unable to bring herself to eat the plants and berries that Alita ate—and now that she had a clean water source, she needed to focus on warmth. Even if winter weren't on the horizon, she would need a way to cook whatever meat she hunted once her food was depleted. On a hunch, Renna checked the deep pocket of the saddlebags again; her fingers brushed against the owl pendant, then found something sharp. The same flat rock the dream people had used to start their fire. Renna hesitated, then retrieved the pendant too. If she was going to die from touching wood, she was already doomed, so she carefully unwrapped the necklace, studying the intricate detail. It was a work of art, really, tugging at something behind her ribs.

This was perhaps her only connection to her cousin now. How had Nastasia—pious, righteous, rule-following Nastasia—come to have this? The thought that her cousin had kept secrets chafed at something deep inside her, but there was no other explanation Renna could come up with.

Find the druidhen, Ren.

She pulled the necklace on, the owl resting against her sternum, then turned her attention back to her task. Apart from the one she slept in, Renna was hesitant to touch the trees. She was already exiled, so the act couldn't very well be treasonous. Still, she had to work to keep her breathing even as she knelt, hands outstretched and hovering above the fallen branches, trying to reason with herself. If they were no longer connected to the trees, they were probably less harmful.

Her hands remained unscathed as she piled a stack of sticks high in her arms. Starting the fire took nearly all day. Ironically, Renna's mind played over the first time she'd successfully cast finnikfire—the months, even years, leading up to that moment. It had been shortly after she'd healed from the ritual, and it had been just her and Nastasia in the solarium. She could picture it so clearly: Nastasia, face rounder with youth, in her finnik leathers, her hair pulled into a sleek tail. She spoke in calm tones, but the way she fidgeted with the aurem bangles around her wrist betrayed the nerves she hid on Renna's behalf.

Come on Ren, you can do this. Find the spark inside you and unleash it.

How strange it was to coax a spark to life outside her body rather than within it.

It was nearly nightfall when she produced a flame and her fire leapt to life. The popping and cracking noise made her burst into relieved laughter. Renna danced around the flames, whooping loudly, tears burning behind her eyes.

She threw her arms around Alita's neck, breathing in her comforting scent. Then Renna collapsed next to the fire—*she'd done it*—and stared at the golden, orange, and yellow flames, so different from the crimson red of the Mother's Flame. It sent a spire of smoke drifting up between the treetops. The smell clung to her hair, coated the back of her throat, leaving her enchanted by the dance of the flames.

It almost felt holy.

A few nights had passed since that first successful fire when a stranger barreled into her camp.

The shock of seeing another human quickly escalated to panic. Renna jumped to her feet, brandishing the small dagger she kept in her boot, mind racing. Perhaps this was someone coming to finish what the high sheriff had started, or maybe it was an outlaw ready to take everything she had.

The young man halted at the sight of her, throat working as he swallowed. "I mean no harm. I was just following Kit, is all."

Renna's scoff sounded more like a growl, her vocal cords stiff with disuse. He looked about her age, with brown hair that fell in messy waves around his heart-shaped face. There was something skittish about him; it seemed like he was more afraid of her than she was of him. She took a step toward him, and he flinched, which made no sense for an attacker.

Then the fox sauntered out from behind him. Her mouth clicked shut, and for a moment she could only look between the man and the fox: the former dirty and nervous, the latter smug and unbothered. The same fox who'd led her to the hollow tree now came over to wind through Renna's legs. "Kit?" she croaked, unable to think of anything else to say.

"My fox."

"*Your* fox?" Something strangely like jealously bubbled up inside her, which was preposterous, because she did not own this animal.

"Yes, *my* fox. He's my fa—my friend."

He'd clearly meant to say something else and thought better of it. Kit, apparently satisfied that the two humans were not going to kill one another, trotted over to Alita (who'd been calmly lying down through the whole exchange, the traitor), and curled up with the Nozdravian. For a moment, Renna wanted to laugh at the absurdity of this tense standoff, two people testing if they could trust each other, with only the attitude of a fox to go off of.

Renna kept scowling but dropped her weapon arm to her side; her upbringing demanded civility. "Well, your *friend* saved my life, so… so it appears I owe you a debt."

A smile split the stranger's face, and it relieved some of the tension in the air. "Kit has a way of doing that. He… he wanted to come back and find you. Kind of a stubborn asshole like that. I'm Much, by the way."

"Renna." The truth slipped out before she could think better of it. But there was no stiffening of surprise, no gasp of recognition. Much merely dipped his head, unslinging something from his shoulder. Her mouth watered at the sight of the dead pheasant, her stomach choosing that exact moment to let out a grumble.

"Hungry?"

Much sat down at the fire and began plucking the feathers. When he was finished, he pulled out a sorry excuse for a dagger and casually began to remove the guts. Renna gagged. Watching the process, she became aware of just how woefully unprepared for the task she would have been, the delicate moves required to not nick the intestines and ruin the meat. She busied herself with fashioning a spit to roast the pheasant on. The fire crackled as fat and juices dripped from the bird as they rotated it to cook evenly, mixing with the sound of crickets and owls.

Neither asked after the other's past, as if their presence in Sherwood was enough to indicate what kind of life they'd each lived. They spoke of Alita and Kit, the changing weather, and stories that meant nothing. Much's face had a boyish quality to it, and when he spoke, his hands moved as quickly as his lips. It was simple to be lulled by the easy excitement he exuded, and Renna found herself nodding along as he prattled about his time in Wendsvik. He described whole buildings made from wooden boards, food that you could pluck right off the trees, magic and non-magic folk alike walking the streets. He'd once seen a small band of outlaws steal from two royal guards *right under their noses*, like they had their own kind of magic. Renna tried to keep her face impassive at the casual way he condoned thievery, and she nearly managed it.

Much switched topics. "And then, of course, there's the Night Watchman. I've met him, can you believe it?"

Renna's spine stiffened, remembering the dead guards with roots in their mouths, NO TITHE TO TYRANTS written in their blood. Marian's face flashed through her mind. "The man who's killing people in Loxley?"

Much snorted and poked at the embers with a long stick, his expression darkening. "I'd hardly call red clerics *people*."

Renna wished she'd said nothing as they fell into silence again. Finally Much raised his gaze. "He saved my life. I was headed for the dungeons, or the pyre, maybe. He rescued me and some others and smuggled us out of the city."

Renna turned his words over in her mind as Much set about carving up the cooked bird. Yes, she'd heard that the Night Watchman had been helping vedra escape from Loxley, but she realized now that she'd never stopped to picture the individual people. If she had, they certainly wouldn't have looked like the man across from her, who was cheerfully plating their portions (a piteous amount, really, for all his work) while speaking in soft tones to Kit and Alita.

Who did you picture, then?

Shame curdled in her gut at the incredibly naïve depiction of witches and blasphemers she'd conjured in her head. In truth, the only vedra she'd known personally were Marian, Yana, and herself…and now, it seemed, Much.

Headed for the dungeons, or the pyre.

"Is Kit your familiar, then?" She wanted to ask what kind of magic he possessed, but it felt like too personal a question. Instead, she guessed at what he'd almost said about Kit before, hoping her lack of knowledge wasn't too apparent.

Much's cheeks flushed a shade darker, and he gave her a shy grin as he rubbed the back of his neck. "It wasn't my intention to keep that from you. I've not been out of Loxley long, and some habits are hard to break. But yeah, he is my familiar. He's saved my life plenty of times, so when he said there was someone who needed us, I followed."

The phrase *when he said* elicited a thousand more questions, but she held them back temporarily as they began to eat. Renna had never tasted anything as delicious as that plain pheasant; no royal dinner, no roast pig from the Fire Feast compared to the meal they shared that night.

Much leaned over to stoke the fire, his shirtsleeve pulling higher on his arm. Renna sucked in a breath at the scars covering his forearm. Much paused, a bit of color darkening his cheeks again as he rotated his arm so she could see better. "We didn't have a lot of money growing up, and my da struggled to keep up with the levied taxes."

Renna peered closer at the scars, so like the ones that covered her back, but his words didn't make sense. "What does that have to do with tithes?"

Much looked at her like she'd made a joke, his expression shifting to shock when he realized it was a real question. "Did your family never have to do extra tithes to offset what they owed the barons? Must have been well off, then."

"So…so you're saying you didn't just tithe at the Blood Tithe or when you needed guidance from the Mother?"

Much's brows shot up to his hairline, and he laughed, incredulous. "Osric almighty, who can afford that? Most folks on my street in Nottingham went every other day. I'll tell you, the Night Watchman is right—no tithe to tyrants."

She'd been such a fool. Her people were bleeding themselves dry to pay the taxes levied by the crown. And she had thought that everyone was just managing their money poorly. She'd no idea that so many people were forced to tithe or starve. Of course there were leechers in the city. They could turn those bloodsiphons for a huge profit. Renna's appetite soured, and she gave Much her last few bites of pheasant, which he acceptedly happily.

Much indulged her questions about Kit, though it seemed his knowledge was limited to his own experience, which was still new. Their familiar bond had developed as he'd fled Loxley. While one of the Night Watchman's contacts was leading them across the marshy expanse in the dark, Much had fallen ill.

"It was like my skull was on fire," he recalled in a haunted tone. "I could only concentrate on the green fire picking out the path, making sure no one fell into the bog or a spot of quicksand." As if aware that they were speaking about him, Kit came up and pushed his head into Renna's palm. She petted him, hanging on to every detail as Much went on. Upon reaching Wendsvik, he'd collapsed, near death, and was unable to recall the first few days except that Kit had been with him the whole time. He'd been able to hear the creature's thoughts, distant though they were, and when he'd pulled through the crushing headaches and body tremors, Much had found he could send his own thoughts back.

"Leaving Loxley felt like…like stripping tar from my veins." The firelight danced in Much's hazel eyes as he turned to her. Renna felt a tug behind her ribs, the desire to be seen by him. Much tapped his heart. "Kit was the tether that pulled me through. I thought it would feel awful to leave my home, to be cast out, but…the truth is, I feel like I can finally breathe."

His words, spoken like a confession, brushed against her psyche like a slinking cat. During her time in the forest, Renna *had* felt that internal scraping and shedding of grime, of extricating rusted talons from her mind. Perhaps her increase in energy was not only because she was no longer giving blood daily, but also because some part of her belonged in the forest.

"Fingers just like that. Yes. Good. No, don't draw until you're ready, you'll waste all your stamina holding it."

"I don't have any stamina to begin with," Much grumbled, adjusting his stance, holding Renna's bow awkwardly. They stood in a small glen. The leaves were changing color, deep greens giving way to burnt oranges and yellows and rusty reds until the forest looked like a flickering fire. They fell from the branches, twirling and gliding through the air until the ground was covered in a thick carpet that crunched under their feet. Alita was nuzzling some withered-looking fruit on the ground a few paces off while Kit sat like a solemn sentry.

A fortnight had passed since they'd formed their strange alliance, falling into an easy rhythm with one another. Their combined stores of food had finally diminished. Much was good at foraging for edible mushrooms and plants, but even those were getting harder to find as the season progressed. Her attempts to string her bow still caused immense pain in her neck. They needed to be able to hunt—they could hardly rely on Kit to provide them a pheasant for every meal.

Renna imagined the curve of the bow, warm against her palm, the arrow fletching whispering against her cheek, the release of the arrow mirroring a release in her soul.

Much looked like he was holding a snake that would bite him.

"Try again," Renna said.

By the time they traipsed back to camp, Much had made a few accurate shots. They were about the same height, and Renna threw her arm over his shoulders. Her cheeks hurt from the smile plastered on her face. The spark of hope that had been simmering in her chest was catching—slowly, but she was warmed by it all the same. She felt a surprising amount of pride and fulfillment after her day of teaching. Perhaps this feeling was partly why Devana Draic had agreed to tutor her.

Thoughts of training with Devana shifted to thoughts of sparring with Nastasia, which inevitably turned to thoughts of the parchment she kept hidden in the saddle bag. *Find the druidhen, Ren.* Potentially the last words Nastasia would ever say to her, and she'd been adamantly ignoring them.

That night, after retreating to their own shelters (Renna, the hollow tree; Much, the overhanging rock he'd draped with woven moss and leaves), she played with the carved owl around her neck. *I'll try, Stasi.* She sent the thought out like a prayer, even though the task was impossible.

There was no way for her to know that before the next full moon, the druidhen would find her.

CHAPTER 14

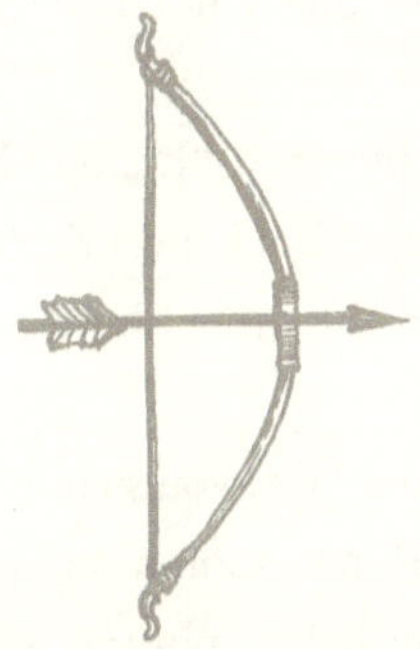

RENNA WASN'T ENTIRELY SURE WHAT ROTTEN WOOD LOOKED LIKE, BUT SHE IMAGINED THE BRIDGE YAWNING BEFORE THEM OVER THE RUSHING RIVER WAS A GOOD EXAMPLE. Holes pocked the weathered slats of wood, the rope strung between them fraying in places. The river, swollen from rain, let out a roar that beat against Renna's ears. It was so much bigger than the stream near where she and Much camped. On the other side was an open meadow with large flat boulders directly under the beaming sun.

Renna glanced at Much, who stood next to her with his arms crossed. For a moment Renna felt like she was catching a glimpse of herself in a mirror. It wasn't just their builds and complexions that were similar; their clothes hung loose on their frames in the same way, their faces both lacked vitality, and both had a thin layer of grime in their hair that seemed impossible to wash off. Currently Much had the bow and arrow slung across his back, and Renna carried a few daggers and leaned against a staff Much had fashioned. It helped her keep her footing on the uneven ground, and with their food supply dwindling, it helped conserve her energy.

"You're sure about this?" she asked.

Much had been scouting the day before and had found a sheltered meadow where a herd of deer were living. He wet his lower lip, which tended to split when dry. "Do you fancy dying of starvation?"

"You're telling me you crossed that thing?" Renna jabbed a finger at the precarious bridge. It creaked in the wind, sounding like a wounded animal.

The tips of his ears flushed darker, which Renna had learned meant he was hiding something, though not out of malice. Embarrassment, maybe? Worry?

Whenever Much got close to discussing the magic he possessed, he would fidget and fumble over his words.

Renna didn't press him. She'd not noticed any vedra magic surfacing in herself.

Much chose his words carefully. "I…found my own way to cross, but we'll need to use the bridge this time. But I saw others use it. It's safe."

"Well, wait until I'm on the other shore to start. I don't fancy going for a swim."

Much quirked an eyebrow. "*Can* you swim?"

The bridge swayed as Renna took a tentative step. She tapped each piece of wood lightly with her foot before putting her weight on it, then peered over the edge and immediately regretted it. The distance to the water brought on a swooping sensation in her stomach. She was all too aware that one wrong move could make the whole bridge collapse into the freezing water below. Her meager experience with swimming in her youth wasn't much more than wading in the water at high tide, and even then, she was accompanied by guards, Nastasia, and Keepers. But that was not going to stop her from reaching the other side. They *needed* those deer to last through the winter.

She'd made it halfway across when the entire bridge swayed, sending her stumbling, as someone at the far end stepped onto it. Peals of laughter and conversation drifted to her as she squinted, wondering who had the arrogance to not wait until she was across. Even at a distance, she could tell the stranger stood a good deal taller than her. Broad shoulders, slender hips, and dark hair chopped short. In their hands was a large quarterstaff.

"Go back and wait until I've crossed," Renna called out to the figure ahead, trying to keep the steadily rising panic from her voice.

"I've as much right to this bridge as you. *You* go back and let *me* cross first."

Renna narrowed her eyes at the stranger, taking another step. The stranger matched her with one of their own.

She'd clearly been here first. Perhaps they just needed a little incentive to behave decently. The bridge swayed beneath their feet as she plucked the dagger from her hip.

They twirled the quarterstaff expertly, lofted it at her like a warning finger, and said in a singsong voice, "If you do that, I'll beat you till you're black and blue."

Her anxiety transformed into fury in an instant. "You're talking like an ass. I'd stick this between your eyes before you could take a swing."

"I'd rather be an ass than a coward. You'd strike with a dagger when your opponent has only a staff?"

Water sprayed up around them. The bridge groaned in protest as if sensing their impending foolishness. She sheathed the dagger, hefting her walking staff—paltry in comparison to theirs, but no matter. "You want a fair fight? Fine."

They threw their head back and laughed. It was loud and unapologetic, commanding notice like a bear moving through the woods. But the gentleness in it buzzed beneath Renna's skin: not a threat, but an invitation to join in. They came closer, each step sending a shudder through the boards. A sleeveless tunic, baffling in the winter chill, revealed muscled arms like small tree trunks. Several piercings in their ears glinted in the weak sunlight. They had a strong jaw and cheekbones, tight dark curls shorn close on the sides with a little more length on the top. The gleam in their eyes matched the mischievous look Marian used to get on her face when trying to cheer Renna up. And that hint of a grin hovering around their mouth was exactly the same as Nastasia's when her competitive side took over. The memories flared hot behind Renna's sternum but faded quickly, leaving a warmth of nostalgia in their wake.

The stranger said, "I'm going to enjoy sending you for a swim."

Adrenaline pulsed through Renna's veins, and she let herself smile. They both set their feet as wide as the narrow planks would allow. From the opposite shore came a whoop, and the two other figures waiting to cross began calling out.

"Come on, Little Jon!"

"Looks like a fine day for a swim!"

"They could snap her as easily as that bloody branch she's got."

The first attack was quick and blunt, swinging from low to high. Renna leaned away, but they were too fast. The end of the staff caught her chin. She stumbled back, jaw smarting, and brought her walking stick up, batting the incoming staff away before adjusting her grip to strike. The stick cracked on her opponent's shoulder, and Renna felt the reverberation all the way in her chest. They grunted and returned the attack, Renna meeting the staff with renewed fervor.

Blow after blow sounded, adding to the river's din and the bridge's creaking. No more verbal sparring, just heavy breathing and quick calculations. The width of the bridge gave little to no room for footwork errors. Renna had only rudimentary training with a quarterstaff. Her opponent was highly skilled, using both sides of the staff to rain down incessant blows, sliding their grip to manipulate the staff with finesse.

Little Jon—really, what kind of name was that?—clearly knew how to navigate the bridge, stepping over gaps without looking down, keeping their weight distributed in a way that Renna could not fathom replicating. It was too narrow to wield the staff as she'd been trained to do, to move around her opponent. On the swaying bridge she was forced to duck and crouch, blocking a downward strike meant for her shoulder. Much called out a warning, and Renna barely maintained her footing as she stumbled over a loose board that Little Jon had been pressing her toward. She executed a strong parry, sweeping the staff away. Renna was momentarily distracted by the sight of the symbols carved into their staff and the pale crystal strapped to the fore end—before the butt end of Jon's staff snapped forward to crack her upside the head.

Stars burst behind her eyes, and she nearly fell into the river. Renna staggered back, eliciting whistles and cheers from the far shore. She touched her brow, and her fingers came away slick with blood.

Blood dripping from her palm.

Blood rushing from her throat, coating her neck and shirt.

Staining the dagger pressed to her throat.

"Now, where did you get that?" Little Jon's words cut through her stupor. Their eyes, dark amber, were fixed on her owl pendant, which had shifted during their fight and now lay on the outside of her tunic. Faster than she could comprehend, Little Jon had stepped into her space and plucked the small carving up between two fingers. Their eyes widened.

Renna jerked away, protectively clutching the necklace. "None of your concern."

Little Jon's expression shuttered. "Interesting."

Form forgotten, Renna thrust the quarterstaff like she would a longsword. A strike to Little Jon's gut doubled them over, followed quickly by an upward swing from the other end of Renna's staff. The crunch of bone when the staff met their nose sent a shiver down Renna's spine. Little Jon spat, their nose crooked and leaking red, and drew themself up to full height.

The grace and fluidity with which they moved momentarily transfixed Renna, the whip-like movements giving the impression of a dance. She could not tell where Little Jon's next blow would land; the staff wound and unwound too quickly. The rhythm of their attack changed. The crystal warped the air around it, blurring the staff in a way that defied reason.

Then she felt two strikes in quick succession: one to the gut, one under the jaw. Renna's head snapped back, her feet skittering. A crack of wood split the air as her stomach dropped like a rock.

And then she was falling into the river.

Cold swept in, filling her mouth and ears, piercing her brain, robbing the air from her lungs, stabbing her with a bone-deep chill. The current was so much stronger than she'd anticipated—though she hadn't *really* anticipated entering the water at all. How sure and arrogant she'd been. The sting of defeat mixed with the cold and began to swell into panic. This was how she was going to die—alone, choking on water like a fool in a too-swift current.

Her feet smacked against a large rock, her ankle barking in protest, and she propelled herself in the direction she thought was up. When she broke the surface, she dragged in air, pain searing her lungs, her head spinning. She violently coughed up water, sputtering and fighting to stay afloat.

"Oi!" A shout from above, joined by others.

Water covered her head once again, muffling the world. Such a strange and eerie silence. Not unlike the Silent Hour, she thought, the edges of her mind feeling fuzzy.

A hand grabbed hers, and another yanked at her collar, but not before she slammed against something solid. Her rescuer was pulling her against the rushing current that tore at her hair and limbs.

She broke the surface with a ragged breath in. Much was beside her, yelling in her ear—"*You can't swim?!*"—holding tight to her tunic, the other arm wrapped around a fallen tree that stuck out of the river at a strange angle. Renna grabbed on, relishing the rough bark against her skin as she tried to catch her breath. Her lungs were on fire. She let out a half sob, half hiccup, her stomach too full of swallowed air and water. She clung to a tree like she was moss. Much was still cursing her out, and her heart squeezed with affection.

"Thank you," she panted, "and sorry."

Much scowled at her, but he stopped shouting, and Renna realized how shaken he looked.

"Do you have a death wish?" he asked.

Renna pressed her cheek to the bark, ignoring the spray hitting her face. Her eyelids were heavy as she mumbled, "You could have let me drown. Maybe *you* have a death wish." She cracked one eye to look at him. "You do get that look sometimes, you know."

Much sputtered rather indignantly for someone drenched and clinging to a log.

Her eyes closed again, and she was smiling now. "It's an 'I'm about to do something entirely foolish and brave' face. Like waltzing into a stranger's camp, unannounced and unarmed, with dinner."

"I was hardly alone. Kit can hold his own." A pause. "Don't do that again."

"I promise I won't get into a sparring match on a bridge over water ever again."

Shouts and motion reached them from the opposite shore. She'd acted like an ass and broken their nose, and still, Little Jon was charging into the current after her. The other two hovered on dry land. If not for the fact that her pride was completely broken, Renna might have felt embarrassed at the ease with which Little Jon swam to them, head held high, broad strokes working with the current until they grabbed onto the trunk beside her. She must have looked miserable, she thought, soaked and shaking, bloodied and bruised. Her teeth chattered despite her best efforts.

"You're either incredibly foolish or very lucky," Little Jon said by way of a greeting.

"F-foolish. Foolish and f-freezing."

Little Jon laughed, and again, it was not at her expense, but in that way that seemed to invite her to join in. They confirmed that Much could swim, which Renna found strange, because he had just swum out to rescue her, hadn't he? Much gave her a withering look before confirming that yes, *he* could swim. Little Jon instructed Renna to hold on to their shoulders, and the three of them made their way to the opposite shore. Two women waited for them, offering hands to steady them all. Much had left the bow and arrows on the other bank.

The duel had been foolish. Renna had lost her walking stick in the current, and she had only a few items of clothing to her name. If things got too wet, they never fully dried in the cold air. Already she was calculating how much time she had before the sun set. Renna began to wring out her sopping tunic.

Little Jon touched their nose, wincing. "It would seem you're not an easy person to beat or to drown."

Renna barked out a laugh, her throat aching. "It would seem you're not an ass at all, and one hell of a fighter." (Much muttered something that sounded like *pair of asses.*)

"I must say, that's the most fun I've had in a while. You're a right better fighter than these two." (The two women muttered something that sounded like *instructor failing*, and *other talents*.)

"Hang on." Much's head swiveled to take in the group. "I know you lot. I saw you in Wendsvik, I mean. Stole some coin from royal guards. You overpaid the shop owner for your food and said to see that it got to those who needed it most."

His words tickled a memory from what seemed a lifetime ago: a drunken crowd, a winnings purse, a whisper to give it to those in need, a young boy and an old woman, the same boy bleeding in the stocks. Renna slammed an iron door shut on the memories.

The first woman, with dark hair chopped just below her chin, had the build of the acrobatic performer that the palace sometimes employed, only the blade at her hip looked more utilitarian than ornamental. She cocked her head at Much. "Of course. You're the wind-walker."

The what?

Much glanced at Renna before nodding. She wished they were alone so she could ask for an explanation. This did not seem like the appropriate time.

The second woman groaned playfully, tipping her face—which was striking—toward the sun, red hair slipping down her back in a thick sheet. She draped an arm around the other woman. The gesture tugged at Renna's heart. The three interacted in a way that spoke to shared trust and fondness.

"Dammit, Scarlet, how much do I owe you, then?" the pretty one asked.

"More than you can afford," Scarlet replied. Her eyes, like two emerald chips, scrutinized them.

With a start, Renna realized that the bandage on her neck had been ripped away in the water, her scars on full display. Too late now. She wanted to ask what the wager had been about and what in the name of the Mother a wind-walker was, but she could feel Little Jon studying her—or rather, her owl pendant. Their expression was the same as when they'd held it for a moment on the bridge: recognition tinged with sadness or longing. It felt like looking at the back of a tapestry, pulling tight a stitch to complete a pattern without knowing what the final design would reveal as Renna held the carved token up. "How is it that you recognize this?"

There was a flicker of pain on their face, and then Little Jon said, "I made it."

Every eye fixed on Renna, who was trembling now from more than just the cold. *Find the druidhen, Ren.* "This was given to me by someone who was looking out for me." Someone who wanted her to find the druidhen. Someone she desperately wanted to be Nastasia. She would've given anything to know that her cousin was still watching over her, that Nastasia had saved her life and given her this necklace.

"May I?" The way Little Jon picked up the owl from Renna's open palm was reverent. They closed their eyes, their fingers curling gently around the token, the picture of prayer.

She held the air in her lungs, waiting for whatever came next. Renna had so little experience trusting herself. She was still so uncertain, wary of a trap, the sharp edge of a smile. But this was what Nastasia had wanted. She could trust this.

Little Jon exhaled long and slow, opening their eyes again. They ran the backs of their fingers along their jaw, looking between the carved owl and their companions. They moved their hands in a series of subtle gestures, a silent conversation.

Suddenly Renna was sixteen years old and unable to speak after the ritual. Compulsory silence was an opportunity to get closer to the Mother. Those born deaf or mute were seen as exalted souls, unable to speak or hear falsehoods, and they were typically taken in by the temple. But after ten days without speaking, Renna could stand it no longer. She'd started to come up with hand gestures to talk to Nastasia, but then a Trissaia caught her practicing. He'd struck her on the back of the knuckles hard. Focusing on the sting kept her tears from falling. "Silence is sacred. You would tarnish the Mother's gift of this opportunity to draw nearer to Her with false sigils?"

Little Jon spoke up again with a simple authority, shattering the memory. "Winter in Sherwood Forest will show you no mercy. Judging by your state, I imagine you've begun to realize that already." They gestured between Much and Renna, ragged and half-starved.

The pretty woman with the long hair reached into a deep pocket in her coat and pulled out a fruit the size of her fist. The skin was a deep green that shone when she polished it on her tunic. She tossed it to Renna, who barely managed to catch it, and another to Much.

Renna stared at the fruit like it might sprout a head.

Much chuckled and took a bite, then held it up for Renna to see. The crunching sound made her mouth water. "See? It's not poisoned. It's an apple."

Renna brought the apple to her lips. *Sweet bleeding Mother.* The flavor—crisp and sweet and juicy—exploded over her tongue. The sound she emitted made the woman cackle. "You'll always remember your first."

Renna's cheeks warmed. "Where did you get this?" Nothing had been growing.

The woman's eyes sparkled, her easy smile coaxing one from Renna. "Rowan Reach isn't like other parts of the forest. I'm Alaini, by the way. That's Scarlet, and you met Little Jon, of course."

With manners that would have sent her etiquette tutors to an early grave, Renna and Much each gave their name in return around a mouthful of apple.

Little Jon said, "We're a small group, but most could stand to learn how to fight. If you'll join us and teach the others how to spar, we can offer you food and shelter for the winter. Our camp is protected by more than just trees. Rowan Reach is warded with druidhen magic."

Much whipped his head around so fast that Renna swore she heard it crack. "But the Druidhen are all gone."

"Loxley would have you believe that." Little Jon's voice carried an edge.

Find the druidhen. A knot of emotion was tangled through her ribs and spine. "Are you all…"

Little Jon shook their head. "Just me."

Scarlet made a show of inspecting her nails. "The rest of us are just boring witches and outlaws."

Renna hugged her cloak tighter, still chilled from her dip in the river. She'd changed into one of her other two outfits when they'd gone back to retrieve their belongings, Alita, and Kit. She had felt an unexpected sadness when she'd said a silent farewell to the little camp she'd made, even if the others had looked horrified by the inadequate shelter.

Little Jon seemed to take the lead on most matters, the other two seemingly happy to defer to their judgment. They walked in a loose line as they traipsed deeper into the woods. Scarlet's lips pulled in a soft smile as Much and Alaini talked over one another, swapping their favorite stories about the Night Watchman. They were so alike with their easy words and laughter. Even back in Loxley, Renna had never experienced this kind of free and easy talking between so many people; it had only ever been her and her cousin. Little Jon whistled a tune that Alaini eventually added words to.

They traveled for most of the day. Then Little Jon halted, turning to face Renna and Much. "You cannot find Rowan Reach unless you've been proven worthy and shown the way."

Worthy.

The word stung like the slice of a blade. Renna struggled to keep her breathing even, her body running hot and cold as Little Jon held up a simple cloth. They reassured her that it was just a blindfold; it was the same for everyone; it would be over before she knew it, she had their word.

Renna wet her lips. The forest around the clearing seemed to stretch higher, branches bending to loom over her. The wind through the woods suddenly sounded like the crowd at the crucible. She could refuse, go back to the hollow tree for the winter and take her chances.

Much squeezed her hand. It grounded her back in her body. Softly enough that only she could hear, he said, "No one should suffer alone in the forest."

"And what if I deserve to suffer?"

A sad smile crossed Much's face. "I doubt that very much, Renna."

She wanted desperately to believe him, but she always left destruction in her wake. She hated the way her chin quivered. Much held her gaze, unblinking. "What is it those bastards in Loxley are always preaching? Truth recognizes truth. Well, suffering recognizes suffering."

Little Jon asked in a voice that was almost too understanding, "Why would we drag you all the way out here just to be rid of you?"

Because I deserve it. Because you're going to sacrifice me in some vedra ritual. Because you've figured out who I am.

Alaini asked, "Do you trust Alita?"

The question centered her in the internal storm. Renna lifted her chin. "With my life."

"You ride Alita, and we'll lead her. If something untoward is happening, she'll let you know, yeah?" Scarlet said.

"And if she doesn't, this one will," Much added, tossing a piece of dried meat toward Kit. The fox caught it easily. The bizarrely normal exchange made the circumstances feel even more confusing. But Renna knew that with their familiar bond, Kit would be able to warn Much of any danger without the others knowing.

Sitting astride her mare was preferable, but the idea of her eyes being covered made her skin crawl. Shame curdled in her stomach as she reached for a rational explanation and came up empty. "I can't be blindfolded," she said.

Again, the others shared a look, and Renna hated the flash of pity underneath. Scarlet broke the silence. "Little Jon, do you have a sleeping draught?"

"I refuse to be blindfolded, yet you expect me to allow myself to be drugged?" Renna's voice pitched higher.

Scarlet studied her, head cocked, then said, "I'll do it with you. I'll drink it first to show you it's safe. We won't have to blindfold you if you're asleep. We can both fit on Alita, and the others will lead us in."

The petite woman accepted a small stoppered vial from Little Jon, drank half the contents in one gulp, then held out the rest to her.

Renna's mouth moved wordlessly. Why did they care? Why go to such lengths for someone they'd just met? In the castle, there was always a hidden agenda, a policy to push through, favor to curry. The owl pendant was the only thing recommending her and Much to these people, and she focused on its comforting weight on her sternum. Much gave her a thumbs-up as his blindfold was secured.

Suffering recognizes suffering.

She'd found the druids. She's survived the forest thus far. Rennavera of Loxley was dead—had been left to bleed out in a dank, unmarked dungeon. Renna was an outlaw now. Just like them.

Her fingers, always cold, felt tacky against the glass.

She downed the contents of the vial.

CHAPTER 15

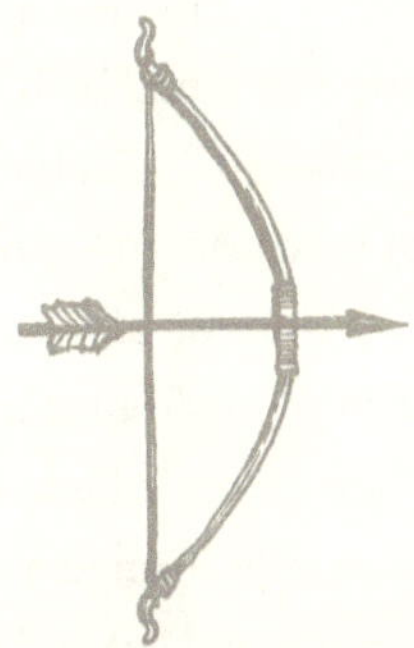

Wake up, Renna.

Warmth cradled her as she sank back into her body. A hand gently rocked her shoulder, her limbs tingling. She kept still as the moments leading up to the deep slumber came rushing back. She'd drunk the potion, her body turning sluggish and fuzzy like they'd said. Little Jon and Alaini had held her weight…

"Good morning, sunshine. Feeling all right?" That sounded like Alaini, speaking just above a whisper.

She heard a yawn. "Best sleep I've had in weeks." Scarlet, then.

Something was pressed up against her leg—Kit. Alita whickered nearby. Renna's heart squeezed. She cracked an eye against the brightness of the sky. She was lying on a bed. No, that wasn't right…Her fingers flexed against soft carpeting, and she blinked rapidly, bringing the world into focus.

Gone were the dead leaves and muddy earth, the swiftly falling shroud of winter. The forest floor was a lush mossy carpet, tiny wildflowers peeking out. Overhead, the canopy of trees, green and vibrant, latticed across the sun-soaked sky. Renna's lungs filled effortlessly with the fresh air. Tiny creatures darted through the brush and hopped between trees. Leaves shivered in the soft breeze. Birds called to one another, a melodious cacophony she'd never experienced before. Plants with leaves nearly the length of her arm fanned out. There were so many hues and shades of green, yellow, burnt orange, and red. Flowers bloomed, and clusters of berries weighed down branches. In this forest, it was a perfect spring.

"Welcome to Rowan Reach," Little Jon said.

"How…?"

Her question trailed off as she saw the tree houses. Planks of smooth wood had been secured to some of the thicker trunks so one could climb to raised platforms built into the trees themselves. Ropes twisted into nets were slung between trees and filled with blankets, serving as floating beds. More ropes crisscrossed through the tops of the trees, forming walkways high above the ground. Runes were carved into the trunks, cut deep with precision and care. Garlands of gemstones, strung on thin threads, splashed tiny rainbows all over the encampment. There was a roaring fire in the round hearth made from stones, and a large pot was hanging over it between slanting tree limbs whittled into poles, a delightful aroma wafting from it. Smaller boulders and stumps formed a seating area, moss or animal pelt softening the surfaces. Wind chimes tinkled in the breeze—some wooden, some a tarnished metal—plucking at the cords of Renna's heart.

She could feel the magic in the air. It was so different from the magic she was used to, but undeniable all the same, like the atmosphere just before a storm, or the taste of salt, or the feel of moonlight on your skin. Renna managed to unstick her tongue from the roof of her mouth.

Figures were approaching, materializing out of the trees. Eleven people including Little Jon, Scarlet, and Alaini. Much and Renna made thirteen. One more than the holy number—the thought came as a reflex. *Twelve Trissaia to uphold the Truth; twelve years of age to receive a Foretelling, and then twice holy to prove your worth.* At first glance, the people living in Rowan Reach were much like those in Loxley: complexions of copper, white, black, and brown, every variation of gender and age. But everyone here was so much more vibrant. It was like Renna had spent her whole life looking at muted colors, and here was the full rainbow.

She half expected cries of outrage at their presence. Little Jon introduced them, making signs with their hands as they spoke. Everyone began talking excitedly, jostling each other, several of them signing as well. The chatter poured over her like a waterfall, staggering and loud and wonderful.

"Got to get your asses in shape before the next tourney."

"I brought in my share all right, I'll have you remember."

"Can you teach me how to wind-walk?"

"Aye, but then you moped around, complaining about how sore you were."

"Can I have a go with your bow?"

"Do not give this one a weapon."

"That was *one time*—"

"Gods, give them a moment to breathe."

"She can share my tree!"

"No one wants to share with your stinky feet."

"I thought you were searching for owls, Little Jon, not more mouths to feed."

The afternoon bled into night, the crew slipping effortlessly into roles and routines as they prepared supper, and Renna tried to absorb it all, tucking away all her questions for later. Alaini explained that the main gathering area with the fire, the cauldron, and the circular seating was called the hearthtree, and that was where they had their meals. The towering tree for which the space was named was covered with moss, the branches stretching up out of reach of the smoke and flames before bowing back down to create a cozy feel around the stone and log seats. Behind the hearthtree was a second smaller fire and a large table covered in pots, pans, cooking instruments, and spices. Bundles of herbs, animal pelts, and a large salting barrel were stored under an overhang. It was more cheerful than the kitchens back in Loxley, albeit it humbler.

This preparation space was bustling with energy. A woman named Edwine reminded Renna of a mother hen as she fretted over the state of Renna's clothes and shooed the outlaws away from the cooking area, brandishing a wooden ladle like it was a sword. Her fawn-colored skin was heavily lined around the eyes and mouth, a lifetime of laughter and tears etched into her kind face. She moved around gracefully with a beautifully carved cane, one leg stopping just below the knee.

"Infection when I was younger," she told Renna as she shoved up the sleeves on the knit sweater she wore. Then she handed Renna a dull knife and steered her to a pile of vegetables before moving to give Much a task.

A young girl with bone-white hair and alabaster skin came over to the table, watching Renna work. Renna tried to recall the child's name but couldn't. When she asked, the girl smiled, fingers tracing quick movements in the air.

"She can't hear, dear. She speaks with signing," Edwine said, hands moving in tandem with her words.

The girl replied with signing, and Edwine translated. "My name is Sif. What are you making?"

"Oh, er…" Renna looked down at the chopped vegetables, then at both Sif and Edwine. "I think it's for the broth?"

Sif smirked, retreating, hands moving.

Edwine laughed, the sound reminding Renna of bells. "She says, 'don't let Little Jon know you called it that.'" The older woman handed Renna a large sweater, much like the one she wore, and whispered conspiratorially, "Little Jon gets rather sentimental when it comes to their stew."

The sun had sunk lower, cooling the air, and Renna gratefully pulled the sweater on. It was lumpy, the sleeves long enough that she had to keep shoving them up her arms, and it hung down to her thighs. Renna had never loved a piece of clothing more.

Task finished, she wandered. It was strange and wonderful, the way all the people in the camp interacted seamlessly and comfortably with one another: Alaini and Scarlet's quips, the good-natured bickering, the youngsters getting scolded for being underfoot, and Little Jon singing a tune all the while. Alita was grazing a little way off, and Kit scampered through the trees. It all swirled together in a messy mosaic, sparking in Renna a fierce desire to belong. Not the kind of belonging she'd experienced after the Blood Tithe. Surrounded by the cathedral of trees, even the memory of that post-Tithe rush felt…unnatural.

Renna moved through the camp as if pulled by an invisible thread. An alcove was carved directly into a small hill. Inside were slats of wood, expertly shaped and secured to the earthen walls with support brackets, creating shelves that ran along the interior walls. Her hands shook as she reached out and trailed a finger along the spines of the books that covered every inch of the shelves.

The library was crammed with bound books, loose-leaf pages, and scrolls. The dirt was soft on Renna's knees as she knelt, pulling one volume free and opening it carefully. With so little written down in Loxley, her mind tripped over the letters briefly. The book was about three fingers thick, the text about a creature called a peryton. There was a picture made with careful brushstrokes: the body and huge antlers of a stag, but the face and wings of an owl.

The shadows stretched long as she knelt there, pulling down more texts to read. There was a particularly worn leather-bound book that caught her eye, the front carved with a massive tree. The crown of branches overhead matched the roots below, the massive trunk decorated with vines and grooves. The parchment crackled when she turned the pages to read the meticulously written text.

The Velmir is the well from which druidhen and witches draw their power. In some spaces of potent magic, where the boundary between worlds is thin, even one who does not possess the ability of a veldra may dip into the river of power.

Renna frowned at the word *veldra*. Perhaps it was another term for vedra. Velmir, in this instance, sounded like witchrot or False Flame. Renna traced the words with a finger. *Even one who does not possess the ability of a veldra may dip into the river of power.*

"I see you found the library."

Renna jumped at the sound of Little Jon's voice, hand flying to her heart. "I've never seen so many books before." To admit she'd never seen a single book felt too much like admitting something more.

Little Jon leaned against the knoll, eyes roving across the shelves. "Rescued a lot of these off a caravan of Keepers last spring. They were returning from Wendsvik, and they surely would've burned them when they met up with their Trissaia." Little Jon's brow furrowed before they shook off the memory, gesturing to the book in her hands. Then their tone shifted to one Renna was used to hearing when someone spoke of the Mother or gave a Foretelling. "Smell the pages."

Renna brought the book in her hands close, inhaling. Her eyes fluttered closed as the aroma filled her nose, seeping into her brain and taking root. It was old, earthy, and it felt familiar in a visceral way. That made no sense; she'd never been around parchment. But still…holding the book felt like reuniting with a long-lost piece of herself.

Little Jon chuckled. "They'll be here after dinner. Come."

Everyone was gathered around the fire, chatting and eating. Scarlet handed her a bowl of stew. Basil and pepper flavored the bits of meat and the large chunks of carrot and potato she'd cut. Broth dribbled down her chin, and she tried to catch it with her tongue. Alaini smirked, passing her a torn loaf of bread. "Such manners," she teased.

Renna ducked her head, feeling sheepish, but she continued to eat ravenously anyway. Scarlet moved to sit on the ground between Alaini's legs. The other woman immediately shifted to accommodate her, fingers playing with the ends of Scarlet's hair. Scarlet drank deeply from a flagon, smacking her lips before passing it to Alaini. With an easy rhythm, like they'd done this a thousand times, the adults passed the drink around.

When the flagon came to Renna, she took it, sniffing delicately. It burned her eyes, but she brought it to her lips and took a hearty pull. The liquid was crisp, just this side of sweet with a smokey aftertaste. It warmed her body all the way through.

The man who'd handed it to her—Bazyli, she thought—grinned knowingly. "Apple mead."

Renna's cheeks soon flushed from the drink, feeling pleasant and fuzzy under her fingertips. Sif appeared at her side, handing her a deck of cards.

Renna turned the cards over in her hands. Each one had a word with a corresponding hand gesture drawn on it. Sif pointed to Renna, then plucked something unseen from her palm and brought it to her temple, and pointed at the deck. Renna realized the cards were for learning how to sign and speak to her.

Renna pointed to her chest. "For me?"

Sif made a motion like knocking a door, smiling.

The warmth spreading through her ribs had nothing to do with the apple mead, and Renna spent the next several minutes poring over the symbols until Much plopped down next to her, peering over her shoulder. Kit curled at his feet.

She turned to face him squarely, emboldened by the mead. "Much, what's a wind-walker?"

Much looked at her with that lopsided grin of his. Then his form flickered, and he vanished. Renna yelped as Much reappeared three seats over, on the other side of Little Jon. This was met with whoops and cheers from the others. Renna gaped at him.

Much gave an exaggerated bow, and the flagon exchanged hands again. Alaini pulled out a lute, plucking a quick beat, and several people joined in singing a bawdy song. Renna sat rooted to her spot. She'd never imagined anything like wind-walking. What else did she not know? Perhaps the passage she'd read earlier went into more detail of the kinds of powers veldra, or vedra, possessed.

Distracted with thoughts of magic, witches, and books, Renna missed the beginning of what sounded like a well-loved and often-told story.

"It's your own bleeding fault for trying to blend in with those bastards so you could sneak into Loxley in the first place," Scarlet was saying.

Little Jon grinned. "I've never tried to blend in a day in my life."

Renna frowned, looking toward Little Jon. (Well, more *leaning* toward than looking toward. Her head and chest were oddly warm. She rather liked the apple mead.) What was Little Jon's connection with Loxley? Who had they made the pendant for, and how had Renna ended up with it? Did they know Nastasia? She couldn't help but ask, "You were trying to sneak *into* Loxley? Why?"

Little Jon stared into the fire, brow pinched. "Nothing important."

Alaini sighed, stretching dramatically. "That's because nothing too important could have happened before I joined you all."

Scarlet clicked her tongue. "Hard to believe that our lives contained nothing of note up until the Fire Feast."

Renna whipped her head around, everything haloed in a fuzzy blur. That was the same time she'd arrived in the forest. But Alaini seemed so…essential to the crew. Like they'd all existed together since the beginning. Renna felt a twinge of jealousy, wishing it were that easy for her to make friends. "You've only been here since the Fire Feast?"

"I make quite an impression." Alaini winked.

"Or you just never shut up."

One by one, the others said their good nights until only the five of them remained: Renna, Much, Alaini, Scarlet, and Little Jon. Crickets chirped quietly. An owl called out. The leaves on the trees shivered like a bird ruffling its feathers. It struck Renna as beautiful. Nailed to the trunk of the hearthtree—hung like trophies, almost—were a dozen or so posters fluttering in the breeze. A poster for an archery contest to be held in Wendsvik. A missive promising bounty for information on a crew of outlaws tied to several robberies. Tacked next to it, a sketch of a figure in black, masked and hooded. WANTED: NIGHT WATCHMAN, ONE THOUSAND AUREM AND THE FAVOR OF THE KORAVIK THRONE.

Renna averted her gaze to the twigs and fallen leaves creating random shapes on the ground. Dirt clung to her shoe where some mead had spilled.

Scarlet said, "How long have you known you're a wind-walker?"

Much exhaled in a puff. "Not until recently, to be honest. The first time I did it was by accident. I'd been caught nicking some bread, and the shopkeeper called the guards. They were just about to put some shackles on me when *poof*, I was across the street. Ran for my bloody life after that. Was sick for days. I still had no idea how I'd done it."

Much had not told Renna all these details when they'd met, but something about Rowan Reach seemed to loosen his tongue, relax his guard.

"I always knew I had magic," Scarlet said. "My mother was a witch—knew how to use plants for enchantments, glamours, and potions. She wanted us to leave, go to Wendsvik. I think a neighbor was desperate for coin and turned her in. She refused to be Silenced."

An unnerving knowledge settled over Renna as Scarlet paused, eyes unfocused as she stared into the flames. If someone refused to be Silenced, the only other option was to burn.

"I wasn't home when the guards came round to collect her. I came back to see the last of the fire being doused. Didn't even have a chance to stop them."

Alaini's arms wrapped around Scarlet's shoulders, giving a gentle squeeze as she leaned forward. Her whispered words came to Renna in snatches: *would have suffered….same fate…mustn't, love*. Scarlet murmured something back, like this was a practiced dance.

Renna looked away, suddenly feeling like she was intruding on a private moment.

Scarlet cleared her throat, breaking the spell. "Didn't want to stick around for the sheriff's men to find me, so I ran. Sherwood seemed like the only place they wouldn't come looking for me."

The firelight threw shadows across Alaini's high cheekbones and muscled lithe limbs. She held out her palm, face up, curling her fingers in a gentle beckoning gesture. There was no breeze just then, but the branches overhead moved, stretching toward the woman. A few flowers turned as if seeking the sun. The tufts of grass beneath her feet shivered with excitement and grew two hands taller for the space of a breath before returning to their previous length.

Alaini's eyes danced in the afterglow of the magic. "I decided I'd leave before they could call me a witch outright."

Perhaps if Renna had accepted the Truth of her Foretelling years ago, she'd have saved everyone a lot of time and heartbreak.

"And you?" Alaini held out the mead to Renna, and the woman's gaze trailed down her neck, no doubt picturing the wound hidden by the sweater. "Can't imagine they give those out to the Mother's Blessed."

If only you knew.

Renna shook her head, memories clinging like cobwebs. Perhaps she could be just like the others here: another outlaw of little consequence. Not a disgraced princess or a failed finnik. Not someone whose unworthiness could destroy a whole kingdom. Someone the trees could not harm, because whatever darkness they carried, so did she. She'd made her choice, signed away her kingdom, accepted the punishment of exile. Granted, she hadn't thought she was agreeing to a dagger to the throat.

The silence had stretched on too long.

Renna held the apple mead up in a salute, forced a smile she didn't quite feel. "If I teach you to fight, maybe you can teach me to know when to quit."

CHAPTER 16

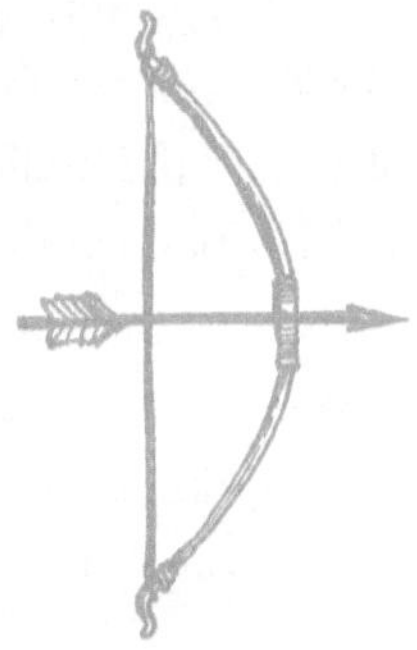

Over the weeks that she'd been in Rowan Reach, Renna had devoured the outlaws' extensive collection of books: novels with romance and passion; studies on the medicinal uses of plants; histories of cities and places she'd never heard of; even a pamphlet on weather patterns.

Her fingers were often smudged with ink when she joined the others for breakfast. Nastasia had always rolled her eyes when Renna had suggested asking the maids for the tales they'd heard at the taverns. *Don't you think there are better ways to spend your time?*

Once she'd wielded Renna's love of stories like a playful barb in front of the Trissaia. It had made her feel small and foolish. So Renna bristled when Alaini caught her reading a certain book for the third time—a tale about a woman who catches the eye of a cruel prince. Lured by an invitation to a ball, she spends the first half of the book in captivity in his dungeons, until she escapes with the help of her step sisters and the handsome stableman. The prince begins hunting for the woman with the shackle scars around her ankle. The ensuing revenge, romance, and reclaiming of freedom was exquisite. "I know it's silly to read it again when I already know how it ends," she said.

Alaini shrugged. "Why should that matter? It makes you happy and does no harm." The next day, Alaini gave her another book without a word before they began to spar.

One morning, like so many mornings, Renna woke to Little Jon whistling a soft tune, joining in with the songbirds. Faint morning sunlight crept in through the curtains woven from ivy, catching the dust motes swirling in the air. Her pack and weapons were hung neatly in the corner of the small tree house she'd selected. It was a short walk from the hearthtree, nestled in a small grove covered in moss and wildflowers that Alita had immediately taken to. The structure was built directly on the thick trunk, and a platform jutted out from beyond the three walls—the tree itself acted as the fourth—providing a private balcony. Handholds and footholds carved from fallen trees made climbing up the trunk easy. Scarlet had shown her a thick mat of vines braided together that could be placed over the branches to create a roof, but seeing the stars through the gaps in the treetops was a novelty she didn't think would wear off, and as such, Renna declined. An ivy curtain covered the entrance and the small window. The bed took up most of the room, which suited her just fine, and the rest of the space was mostly filled with books.

The smell of mushroom kaffi—nutty and earthy—lured her from her tree. Slipping on boots and pulling a sweater over her head, Renna hopped down the ladder with an ease she'd only recently cultivated—she still cringed remembering how awkward those first attempts at climbing the trees had been, all the scraped shins and blistered hands—and headed toward the hearthtree.

Alaini was stretched out on a log, one boot dangling, tuning a lute. Bazyli and Little Jon fussed with mugs and porridge while Tora and Much stoked the fire. Baz passed a steaming mug to Renna, his salt-and-pepper hair styled in tiny braids and tied off at the nape of his neck. His manners and attention to others reminded Renna of Marian.

"Renna!" Tora bounded over, throwing her arms around Renna's middle. She was startled, but warmth spread through her heart all the same as she squeezed the young girl back. Tora was usually with Sif, though the non-hearing girl was likely still in bed. Tora's words rushed as swiftly as the river after rain. Renna sipped her drink, the rich flavor pleasant on her tongue, and tried to keep up, humming when it seemed a response was appropriate. Apparently, a beehive had been kicked over.

"Tora, love," Alaini called in a singsong voice, "Renna doesn't know why the honey is special."

Tora's mouth popped into an O, eyes lighting up. "It means that when we go into Wendsvik we can get ingredients for honey cakes." She didn't notice the way Renna stilled at the mention of the region, going on to explain how the honey cakes melted in your mouth and stuck to your fingers. When Baz cut her off, saying they might not have enough coin, Tora pointed an accusatory finger at the man. "You said last time that the honey is the most expensive part. Well, now we have some for free, don't we?"

"I don't dictate the price of food, Tora. By all means, take it up with the king."

Tora put her hands on her hips. "He doesn't rule over Wendsvik."

"No, but that bastard King Ulrik is dead set on everyone bending the knee or burning at the stake. Wendsvik needs their bloody aurem, so half the lords and nobles pay taxes to Loxley. Which means they gouge their people over the price of grain."

At the mention of Ulrik, Renna swallowed wrong. Coughing hard, Baz eyed her as she waved a hand to indicate that she was fine.

Alaini plucked a minor chord, groaning loudly. "Oh, cheer up, Bazyli. We'll acquire more coins to replenish our stock."

"That's one way to put it."

"It's only stealing in the most technical sense. 'Relocation of goods' has a much better ring to it, don't you think? Besides"—a sly grin spread across her face—"we only take from the rich."

"I have always admired an outlaw opposed to thieving," Little Jon mused, beginning to scoop porridge into bowls. Renna helped to pass them around.

The idea of thievery still did not sit right with Renna. But was that only because she'd never truly gone without anything? Her eyes drifted to the food stores. They were by no means empty, but they'd been steadily dwindling. While they could still forage inside the wards, there was not an infinite supply of food. Scarlet had mentioned that they would need to stock up on grain, dried meats, and other basics in Wendsvik soon. Outside of Rowan Reach, winter would have the land fully in its grasp.

The Great Hunt must be any day now, Renna realized with a start. She'd always hated the days leading up to it, which meant more secret tithes, more prayers, more fear, more worry, more cuts. Last year she'd been so tender from the extra tithes that she'd not even left her chambers, terrified the wounds would seep through their bandages, staining her clothes. The chaos that would have stirred up—the crown princess bleeding on a night when the vedra were at full strength, when the windows were shuttered and no one went outside and every howl of the wind sounded like a witch come to take your soul.

"Don't fret, the winter solstice fair always has the biggest purse," Little Jon continued. "I can't imagine we won't bring home some coin with all Renna's taught you lot."

Renna frowned. "Winter solstice?"

"Bleeding Mother, were you raised in a cell?" Asher joined them, hair mussed from sleep. "How can you not know what winter solstice is?" While most of the others had welcomed her in quickly, Asher was prickly. Unfortunately, it made Renna all the keener to win his approval. Her face heated.

Alaini jumped in. "Winter solstice isn't recognized by the Trissaia or the throne. It's hardly her fault if she's not familiar with it. Loxley has the Great Hunt instead."

"Bloody gods, I always hated the Great Hunt," Much groaned.

Alaini's fingers flew across the strings of her lute in a haunting melody. "According to the Trissaia, on a certain night in the dead of winter, the ghosts of vedra are released from their graves in the forest. They ride the skeletons of wicked horses." The music quickened. "Then they scour the streets for naughty children to steal away in the night."

"Winter solstice," Little Jon cut in, "is a midwinter festival celebrated by the vedra and the druidhen. It's about honoring the dark that will give way to light."

Without faltering, Alaini shifted the song to something playful and joyous. "Scarlet says everyone has huge bonfires and drinks ale and dances the night away. And"—she paused with a dramatic flair, letting the last note ring in the air—"everyone gets gifts."

"How do *you* expect to buy gifts, Alaini? You planning on winning that purse in Wendsvik?" Asher crooned.

Alaini threw a pine cone at him. The conversation devolved rapidly from there.

Renna picked half-heartedly at her breakfast. It shouldn't have surprised her that there was a holiday she knew nothing of—there was still so much she was learning. But she hated how it stung; she was mortified by the gaps in her knowledge and feared the others would find out why those gaps existed. Though even that dread had begun to melt into the background here in Sherwood. How was it that she'd grown up with the Great Hunt while others had winter solstice? While she'd been shut away, terrified of her failures being revealed, others had been celebrating something wonderful. That sensation alone made her feel like more of an outsider in the woods than her hidden past did.

Renna leaned close to Alaini. "What sorts of contests do they have in Wendsvik?"

"All sorts. Long sword, fist fights, falconry, drinking. Archery has the biggest purse, though."

Renna's mind turned, a plan slowly crystalizing as those training today headed out.

The sparring field was about a ten-minute walk through the forest. One side of the meadow had an array of targets ranging in size and difficulty. The other was covered in obstacles: a thick rope pulled taut between two poles a few feet off the ground; a path of pillars shaped from trunks, cut to various heights; a rope wall; boulders to move from one end to another. Beyond the course was a swimming hole lined with trees and long grasses sprouting at the edge of the blue water. Several rope swings hung from high branches. Nearly every training session ended with taking a dip to cool off.

Renna mentally sorted everyone into groups as they stretched. Though they'd all been working on sword fighting, archery, and quarterstaff, they each needed to play to their strengths if they were going to win big in Wendsvik. And Renna wanted to win big. It was the buzz of competition, of having a target to hit, something to focus on, that had the rest of the world fall away.

Scarlet was easily one of the better close combat fighters. She moved with an acrobatic grace that distracted her opponent from the wicked sword she carried. It had a gently curved blade and a green stone embedded in the hilt and had caught Renna's attention early on. The stone was only a shard, striated lines of deepest emerald and light mossy hues. Apart from Scarlet's sword, which only she was allowed to wield, the state of the weapons in the camp appalled Renna. "None of these are even properly balanced," she'd complained as she'd tested them, yet another sword tipping sideways on her fingers. To which Alaini had grumbled, "You're not properly balanced," and they'd wrestled until Renna had pinned her. They'd made do with what they had so far, though now that the prospect of going to Wendsvik loomed, Renna wondered if perhaps they could take the weapons to a blacksmith. She made a mental note for later.

They started by the swimming hole to practice climbing the ropes, first with their arms and legs and then, for those who could manage, using only their arms. Everyone took at least one fall into the water below, so to dry off, they did sprints across the field in the sun. Next, they practiced throwing large stones and walking on their hands. They followed all of this by dragging the targets out of the meadow and into the forest, where they tried to make difficult shots from up in the trees.

Renna had them all hold deep lunges, tapping their back knees on the ground and then straightening their legs again.

Renna's own legs shook, but she relished it all, even as the others complained. "Stop whining," she commanded. "Don't you want to be able to outrun…the other competitors?"

Her pulse spiked as her near slip registered. *Don't you want to be able to outrun assassins? Your parents could've used these drills.* The first time Devana Draic had said it, Renna had held her tears back until practice had ended. Then she'd fled to the stables, the back of her throat burning, and sobbed silently, messily. Snot and tears had stained her pants as she buried her face in her knees, curled up in the dark.

The memory hit her hard now, and Renna wobbled, remembering what she'd forgotten: how Garen had found her.

When he'd barreled into the stables, she'd thought he had come to mock her. But he just stood there, looking entirely uncomfortable and out of sorts. A horse whickered. The skin on his knuckles was bone white, pulled taut, and a bruise had formed on his cheek that she didn't remember him getting during sparring practice. She'd noticed that he flinched when his grandmother's voice carried a specific kind of steel. Garen stared down at Renna, then spun on his heel and fled back the way he'd come, obviously desperate to get as far away from her as possible. But a few minutes later, she heard him snarl *bark off* at a stable hand. He didn't look at her as she reappeared, face dry but surely swollen. When he spoke, his tone was clipped and matter-of-fact, like he was reciting proper fighting technique. "She shouldn't have said that. About your parents."

Alaini yelled over her shoulder, pushing thoughts of the high sheriff out of Renna's mind. "I don't give a shit about that! Is this going to make my ass look good or not?"

Renna put them out of their misery shortly after they began to shout, "How did you even come up with this?" and "Yeah, who hurt you?" Alaini collapsed onto the forest floor next to Little Jon, who was inspecting the blisters on their hands. Baz looked one soft breeze away from falling over, and Asher was…well, in about as good of a mood as he ever was.

Renna brushed the sweat off her forehead. "Tomorrow we'll take turns shooting at the target while riding Alita."

Her words were met with groans.

"Or we could just run sprints again."

She dodged several thrown pine cones.

In Loxley, the seasons bled into one another with no flora or fauna to mark the shift between them; the sweltering heat and humidity would give way to biting cold with hardly any warning. Summer storms became windy squalls, then snowstorms that blanketed the ground with layers of powder and ice. Dried fish, caught in the warmer months, then salted and preserved to last through the winter, was served at nearly every meal, as the price of imported foods from the continent put a larger dent in the royal coffers.

Over the next fortnight, Rowan Reach transfigured, the forest releasing a long-held breath. Leaves shifted from verdant emeralds to crisp yellows, reds, and golds; the sea of moss covering the ground darkened to richer hues; spring surrendered to fall with the gentleness of two lovers reuniting. Renna watched the trees with fascination, the slow changes stirring something inside her. She enjoyed the nip in the air when she woke, relished pulling a thicker sweater over her head, watching the steam rise from her mug of kaffi as the woods shimmered with the new palette, only the pines holding on to their deep color.

"I think I could die happy in fall," Renna said, admiring the foliage as they walked back to the hearthtree from the sparring field.

Little Jon tipped their face up to the sun streaming through the golden leaves. "Spring always spoke to me of hope. Fall is about surrendering to what is, the beauty in change, and letting go." The leaves crunched underfoot. As they did most days, Little Jon asked, "Would you care to join me at the river?"

Renna had yet to accept Little Jon's invitation to join them at the river for their daily ritual, but she had to admit, the druid always seemed much more settled afterward. Even though Little Jon surely had things that haunted them, they moved through the forest with an enviable peace. That fact, mixed with how sore her muscles were from training, made Renna follow Little Jon this time. They came around a bend that dipped closer to the riverbed, where the current calmed and water collected in an alcove to create a small pool. The sunlight dappled the leaves and forest floor, shining like diamonds off the water. Little Jon removed their tunic and trousers, keeping on their undershorts and the tight band they wore around their chest. They gave Renna a pointed look, and she eyed the water warily.

"Must I?"

"Why did you follow me if not to join?"

"Curiosity," Renna said.

"Lies."

"Boredom?"

"Try again."

"Must you make me say it?" Renna whined.

Little Jon just stared at her.

Renna groaned and began shucking off her trousers. Still conscious of the scars on her back, she left the short linen chemise on as well as her knickers. Little Jon walked directly into the river until they were submerged to their neck. Renna stalled, whispering encouragement to herself on the bank. She stepped into the water and yelped, hopping immediately back onto the shore. "Bloody mother, that's freezing!" Her voice was pitched embarrassingly high.

"Don't *stop*, you have to just get in. Otherwise your brain will talk you out of it."

"Yes, well, I happen to agree with my brain in this instance," Renna huffed. "It's completely ridiculous that you're as calm as you are right now."

Little Jon shrugged, breathing deeply through their nose. "I've done this a few hundred more times than you."

Renna scowled at the water. "And why is that, again?"

"When you learn to control your breathing under physical stress, you are training your mind and body to handle stress in your life. You can quiet your mind, help release what is stuck and what holds you back. Count to three, and then get all the way in." Little Jon closed their eyes. "Unless you wish to return to the others and eat crow. There's a wager that you won't get in."

Renna blew out a harsh breath and jumped, curling into a ball so that her splash would hit Little Jon in the face. The cold enveloped her, robbing the air from her lungs. It seeped into her bones, into her brain, stinging her feet and hands like tiny knives. She broke the surface sputtering. Little Jon was laughing, but all she could concentrate on was trying to fill her lungs, cursing herself for fully submerging. She moved slowly, so very slowly, over the smooth rocks that littered the river floor to get closer to Little Jon.

"W-why?" She didn't know what she was asking, exactly; she just couldn't comprehend that she was willingly suffering this torturous temperature. Her teeth began to chatter.

"You're almost through the hard part. The first minute is the worst, and then you get used to it."

"You m-mean because you g-go completely numb?" She was shivering so violently that her words didn't sound as snarky as she intended.

"For blood's sake, *breathe*, Renna."

With effort, Renna sipped in a shallow breath and forcefully pushed it back out, then repeated the action several times. On her fifth breath, her muscles relaxed, the vise around her ribs loosening with agonizing slowness. Little Jon was the picture of serenity as they relaxed in the water, their breathing deep and even.

"Wh-who taught you this?"

"My mothers. The druidhen regularly practice cold exposure."

Renna went through three cycles of inhaling and exhaling before they continued.

"I was raised in Branimer, the place the druidhen found sanctuary, deeper in Sherwood. Druidhen source their magic from the trees, but there are also smaller magics that anyone can cultivate if they practice enough."

Smaller magics available to anyone. "The Velmir?"

Little Jon hummed in agreement.

Renna shifted and immediately regretted the action, as it exposed new spots of skin not yet acclimated to the cold.

"Drawing from the Velmir can be taught, but a clear mind is vital. The cold sharpens your mind and teaches you how to let go of the scars that mark your soul. I would wager that is something you and my people have in common."

Scars on the soul.

This was why she'd accepted the invitation today. The moment stretched between them, their shared pain palpable.

"In a world filled with magic that you do not have," Little Jon said, "you must create your own."

The cold anchored Renna to the present moment. Her heart had slowed to a steady beat. "Will you teach me?"

They both emerged from the water and sat on the grassy bank, letting the sun's warmth slowly seep into them. Renna's hair stuck to her neck and back.

"Close your eyes," Little Jon said. "Picture the forest. The trees are quiet sentinels, the breeze the caress of a loved one. The leaves shimmer in the sunlight. The trunks are old. They have stood for a millennium already and will still stand when we have turned to dust. They have withstood more than we will ever experience. Feel the rough bark beneath your palm. Feel the warmth, and follow it down to the base of the trunk. Now sink beneath the moss, down into the dirt and the roots. The roots stretch far and wide, tangled with one another."

The smell of rich loam filled the air. Little Jon's words painted a soft picture on the backs of Renna's eyelids, dark roots webbing out in an intricate lattice, reaching deeper and deeper. Birds chirped somewhere above, and the babbling of the river was soothing. She could feel her heartbeat in her fingertips, in the arches of her feet. Renna's body was heavy, grounded. The lines between herself and the grass blurred as she sank deeper.

"See the golden glow around the roots?"

She did. Faintly at first, then building, traveling the path the roots carved. Like a river of golden light beneath the ground, pulsing.

"Picture sinking into the river of gold. Let the strands of light envelop you, cocoon you, pull you in and wash over you. The current is strong and steady, but so are you. Feel the gold threads weave between your fingers. Pull them up, pull them in, submerge yourself."

As above, so below. As within, so without.

The words floated through her mind. The flaxen, blooming river poured into her, swirling in her chest like a small tide pool. The light stretched, spearing down into the ground and out the crown of her head, a gilded vortex. Magic breathed through her as if she was an extension of the forest.

It was so…simple. So natural. Could it really be so easy? This power, this essence, this magic was always there, below and all around her, waiting for her to reach out her hand. No trials, no tests. A drop of water hit her hand, then another. She was crying.

Renna sucked in a shaky breath, her eyes fluttering open. The forest around her was vibrant, sharper, more alive, her veins awash in gold.

Little Jon's smile was knowing and sad. "Shall we make our own magic, then?"

CHAPTER 17

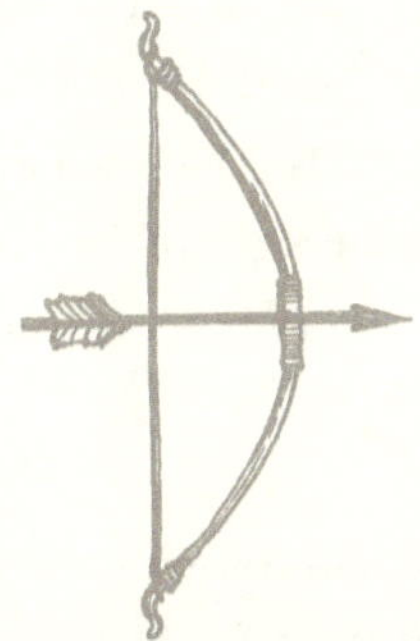

THE MOON HAD WAXED AND WANED AGAIN WHEN THE TIME FOR THE TOURNAMENT CAME. The group traveled through the woods to reach the loch separating Sherwood and Wendsvik, avoiding the trade route that followed the edge of the forest toward Loxley. Multiple ferry points allowed for an easy crossing, and some people braved the shallowest water if they didn't feel like waiting.

Renna's group set out in the early morning, and the journey took the better part of the day, so it was early evening when they arrived in Wendsvik. Though almost everyone from Rowan Reach had come along, only a handful of them would be competing. The archers would be Renna, Much, Baz, Little Jon, and Alaini, while the melee fighters would be Kaja, Scarlet, and Asher.

All Renna's life, Wendsvik had been painted as a country filled with vedra, thieves, and those unworthy of the Mother's Truth or unwilling to hear it. Why else would they gather an army and try to drive the Trissaia out of their lands? Flocks of priestesses and Keepers were sent to spread the Mother's Flame, only to be persecuted. Wendsvik, full of tainted magic users, nonbelievers, and those who defied the Mother's words, conjured up images of chaos and rebellion. Only by the grace of the Head Trissaia did Loxley keep extending its hand, trading aurem and hoping that one day the citizens of Wendsvik would let the Mother's Flame into their hearts, claiming Loxley as their sovereign and contributing to the Blood Tithe.

Renna adjusted her cloak, pulling her hood up to keep her face obscured as she followed her friends through the large marketplace. Buildings made from wood and stone or mud and brick lined both sides of the wide road. Fires burned cheerfully, several older men and women standing near them for warmth.

Children shouted to each other as they climbed a tree, hats pulled down over their ears, and vendors called out to advertise their wares: carved figurines for winter solstice; protection charms to ward off dark magic; herb bundles; apples in every color; firewood; freshly baked bread. Street performers stood on boxes, playing music, and juggling bright objects. One such entertainer had a barrel of water, and Renna stopped short at the sight of her, weaving her hands above it until the water rose in response. Thin ribbons of water danced, echoing the woman's movements.

It was beautiful.

"A water wielder," Alaini said conspiratorially.

Since that first day in the river, Renna had often joined Little Jon in the cold water while visualizing dipping into the magic in the roots below. In Loxley, she'd listened to hours of lectures and then practiced casting finnikfire, but in Sherwood, magic lessons took a different form. Little Jon seemed to think that the best way for Renna to learn the magic of the woods was to meditate quietly, allowing herself to surrender to the Velmir. "You must spend time getting to know it, listening and feeling for it," they said.

They were next to a shop filled with books, crystals, and bundles of dried herbs. Little Jon ran a finger along a few of the stones before plucking up a cloudy crystal that fit easily into their palm as they held it out for inspection. "Scarlet, what would you use this for?"

The woman pursed her lips, holding the stone up to see the fading twilight stream through. It looked like tiny wisps of golden smoke were caught inside, like how Renna pictured the Velmir. "It's some kind of sister to citrine, so I could make a decent glamour of prosperity out of it. But I'd probably make a wand for increased personal power."

"A what?" Renna asked.

Scarlet's eyes glittered with mischief as she reached to grasp something just below her shoulder. Renna stared as a hidden holster materialized rapidly, a slender carved piece of wood tucked inside. Scarlet could usually be found whittling sticks, but Renna had always dismissed it as just a way to pass the time.

"I imbue the wand with a specific purpose based on the properties of the wood. The crystal helps focus the intention of the enchantment." Scarlet motioned to the black stone fixed to her wand, unbothered that someone could overhear them speaking about magic so blatantly. "You can use it to channel magic directly at something, but I prefer for it to cast an aura."

"An aura." Renna's mind was racing.

"So that magic is emitted constantly when I have it on me."

Little Jon said, "Depending on one's affinity, channeling the Velmir will manifest differently. The basic magics of the druidhen are connected to the trees and earth—nature-based abilities. Scarlet has had years of training and practice and is able to bend and harness the magic. She can channel the Velmir into an object, imbuing it with magic."

Channel the finnikfire into the aurem, and your worth will be revealed.

The smell of the herbs turned cloying, the press of the crowd suddenly making Renna's neck itch. No one noticed how still she'd gone. Scarlet chose a few more stones and counted out the coins for payment; Little Jon was speaking to Much; a troubadour belted out a song as they plucked their lute, a small crowd trailing behind them as they paraded from one pub to another.

Numbly, Renna followed her friends as they moved through the market. She focused on the soles of her feet against the hard ground, pictured roots unfurling and digging into the dirt.

I am not there, I am here.

"Anything I can help you find today, miss? Perhaps something a little more dangerous?"

Renna startled out of her daze. The speaker was an older woman in a ratty shawl, a large wooden box clutched in her gnarled fingers. The shop had an impressive array of herbs, dried plants, and leaf clippings. They were all kept in small open crates with neat stamped labels. A heady floral scent, almost too sweet, filled Renna's nose, tickling something at the back of her mind. She leaned closer to inspect the contents of the crates, recognizing some of the plants from her time in the forest: thistle, mint, and lavender; sloe berries, which Edwine had mentioned they would use to make a special drink for winter solstice; perunika, a vibrant purple flower that covered one meadow in Rowan Reach; crushed lotus powder, and poppy.

The older woman shuffled closer to Renna and cracked open a chest filled with samples of flowers divided into sections, names written in shaky handwriting on each individual box: foxglove, belladonna, mandrake leaves, vervain, monkshood. The woman pointed to clumps of yellow flowers labeled rue. "This will protect you from a basilisk's gaze. Perhaps you long for a deep slumber, or you've cast your eye on one whose heart you wish to snare? Or there is moonshade—it plays a little nicer than its sister, nightshade."

"We're all set on poisons today, thanks ever so." Scarlet gripped Renna's upper arm, pulling her away.

Little Jon said something about the Perun Sea, and Renna let herself be led through the city. The smell of the sea bloomed in her nostrils as they passed through a narrow alley that opened onto a long, wide strip of land that met the Perun Sea. The water was an enticing blue, at odds with the nip in the air as the wind grabbed at their cloaks and hair, chilly fingers searching for exposed skin. Far off to their right was a bay filled with white masts of ships anchored by the docks. The crowded homes and shops behind Renna felt incongruous with this expanse of land that could easily accommodate the city's growth.

"Why does the city stop before the land runs out?"

Little Jon pointed to a low wall that ran parallel to the waterline, algae and barnacles crusting the stones. Looking closer, Renna made out ruins that dotted the land: a crumbling stone plinth, a rotting plank of wood that stuck out at an odd angle. "This whole area was underwater when the last Endless Tide came. Scholars say we're due for another soon."

The hair on Renna's neck prickled at the term. But it was Alaini who said, "The Endless Tide? Like the one the church always harps on about?"

Much adopted a stern voice, imitating a proselyting Keeper. "Remember when those who had touched the False Flame sought to drown the kingdom with an Endless Tide!"

Little Jon snorted. "It was hardly a result of magic. The phenomenon happens every century or so due to the position of the moon and sun. Loxley frames it the way it does because it gives the church control over the people. The scholars in Wendsvik and the druidhen all know we are overdue for the next Endless Tide."

The ground felt unsteady under Renna's feet. The story was a keystone of the church. The Mother had told Osric, the first Head Trissaia, about the massive tide coming, an unholy wall of water spurred on by vedra. It wasn't something that could have been predicted by scholars; it was a prophecy given by the goddess.

"How many died?" she asked, dread rising in her throat.

Little Jon spoke evenly, as if they knew this simple truth was shattering something foundational inside her. "The scholars gave everyone enough warning that the villagers were able to retreat to higher ground. There were no casualties."

Renna had been taught that those who did not adhere to the Mother's word had been wiped away when the tide came, that hundreds of people had perished because of their lack of faith. Now she felt sick, the lies and truths muddled in her head.

The sun was dipping below the Perun Sea as they returned to the city proper. Wanted posters and bounty decrees were plastered on building walls and littered the streets, mud tracks marring the crude drawings of hooded thieves. Several were the same ones they had back on the hearthtree in Rowan Reach. Renna now knew these hooded thieves to be her friends.

Little Jon followed her gaze. "Hopefully what we win tomorrow will cover what the forest doesn't provide."

Renna's cheeks warmed with embarrassment. Had her judgment been that obvious?

"Can we not use magic?"

"It doesn't work like that. You cannot make something from nothing, Ren. And just because you haven't lifted the coin *yourself* doesn't mean you haven't benefited from it all these months."

Alaini slung her arm around Renna. "We'll make a proper outlaw of you yet."

Rather than pay for rooms at one of the inns, they pitched tents in a common campground that had been set up to accommodate the crowd for the tournament. At the first sign of light, Renna and Alaini went in search of tea or kaffi before the others woke. They found a stall selling cups of tea at the end of a street. Renna pulled a face at the weak flavor, and Alaini laughed as they continued walking. More people began milling about, the sun rays stretching through low-hanging clouds and mist. The village began to hum with the promise of the day.

When they headed back toward their camp, Renna saw them—a flash of purple, then red robes. Keepers of the Truth and red clerics.

She flinched, dread and wild panic snaking around her, the primal urge to run spearing through her. They'd found her. Alaini tripped over her feet as Renna yanked her friend down a side street, ignoring the shouts of protest from a merchant when they knocked against his table. Renna could see her name poised on the other woman's lips, could see the moment stretch out in horrid slowness: they'd hear the name of the fallen princess and no doubt come find her, finish her off as the high sheriff had failed to do. And what would become of her friends? Surely they would not be spared.

"Bleed me, Re—"

"Don't!" Renna's blood roared in her ears as she clamped a hand over Alaini's mouth. She flushed hot and cold. She'd not thought this through at all. "Just… Marian. Call me Marian here. Please."

Alaini grumbled unintelligibly against her palm, leveling her with a glare. Renna slowly removed her hand.

"Very well, *Marian*. Any other demands?" Her tone was teasing. Renna did not deserve the easy trust.

Alaini grabbed her hand. "Are you all right?"

The concern in her friend's voice made her sinuses burn. Renna wet her lips, searching for an explanation. She wanted to tell Alaini the truth, to confess everything like the sin it was, but the words were stuck in her throat. Alaini gave her fingers a soft squeeze, glancing over her shoulder quickly. Renna was sure Alaini could see right through her, her eyes were too keen, peeling back every secret and deception.

"The first time I came here, I nearly pissed my pants when some Loxley guards came through. We all have shadows that haunt us, Re—Marian. But we look out for each other." Alaini gave her a closed-lipped smile, looping an arm through Renna's, and settled back against the wall.

"We'll take a moment," Alaini whispered, staring straight ahead. "And then we'll go win that purse."

The archery field for the contest was on the outskirts of the village, away from the main market and shops. The air smelled of cinnamon and yeast. Colorful banners flapped in the breeze, designating the boundaries for the contestants. The course looked like the one they had in Sherwood, which was encouraging. There were far-off targets to test accuracy as well as targets contained within various obstacles: crudely cut logs swinging on a pendulum; thin wooden slats over a large muddy pit; a vertical net to climb up and over; dangling chains that shifted unnaturally— perhaps with a bit of magic? Renna craned her neck, trying to find the source of the chains' movement, but could not locate it.

The goal was straightforward: complete each obstacle. Each arrow in its mark counted as a point, and whoever had the most points by the end, won. In the event of a tie, the arrow nearest to the bull's-eye would win that point. Contestants would begin in staggered waves. Little Jon was checking to make sure all the archers had found their way to the sign-ups (Much, Alaini, Baz, and herself). Next to the archery field was a roped-off square where the melee tournaments would take place. Scarlet caught Renna's eye as she warmed up and gave her a goofy salute. The line shuffled forward. A man slumped in a chair, fingers stained with ink as he took down the name of each contestant, motioned to her.

Renna stepped forward. "Marian."

The man looked up from his parchment expectantly. "You think you're the only Marian here, eh? I need your *surname*."

Alaini tugged playfully on Renna's cowl when she hesitated. "Hood," she said.

"Yes, very believable." His expression was one of annoyance, but he waved Renna through, muttering about not being paid enough.

She took her place by the others, fingers twisting on the new bow Little Jon had carved for her out of a yew tree. (For protection and connection to the woods, they'd said. She much preferred it to the old bone and aurem bow she'd used.) She was to be in the second-to-last group, and she was careful to watch the competition. Most everyone struggled with the tasks that required the archer to maintain balance while shooting. Excitement tickled up her spine. In her life before, such a feat would have proved difficult for her too. But now she spent her days traversing branches and rope ladders between trees.

The trumpet sounded, signaling her to begin. Thin rails spanned the length of a swampy pit, none of them much wider than her feet. Renna held her arms out for balance, looking a few steps ahead of her the whole time. To her left, a woman stumbled, arms windmilling to steady herself, but it was no use. The crowd grew loud with jeers, gasps, and laughter as she fell.

A bead of sweat rolled down Renna's back as she reached the first target. It was nestled at the bottom of a ravine on the other side of the net wall, and each archer was to shoot from the top of the ropes. A young man was hanging precariously, arm wrapped tightly around the top rope as he struggled to hold his bow. A middle-aged man beside him managed to balance long enough to take a shot, but the arrow flew wide, missing the mark entirely.

Renna climbed easily, her muscles and lungs used to the effort, and quickly reached the top. She braced herself, the rope cutting into her hips as she hooked her feet securely, one hiked higher than the other for balance. Several arrows stuck out of the target already, but most were far from the center. Renna drew her bow, inhaling through her nose as she focused on the red mark at the center of the target. She held her breath for a beat, then exhaled slowly. The arrow sang as it soared through the air.

Bull's-eye.

Her pride was short lived, though, as a dark arrow split hers down the center. The crowd's applause shifted to cries of shock as Renna swore, whipping her head around to see who was responsible.

The archer's hulking frame was incongruous with the ease with which he perched on the far side of the ropes. His face was hidden behind an obsidian mask, the shadow of his hood obscuring his eyes. He was clad in all black—trousers and a tunic under a leather jerkin and cloak. The daggers strapped to his thighs glinted, and a baldric was slung across his chest. The crowd was chanting, "Night Watchman! Night Watchman!"

So this was the outlaw giving Loxley so much trouble. The judges deliberated a moment, then adjusted the tally, giving them each a point. The Night Watchman gave a mock bow in her direction before launching down the other side of the net.

Smug bastard.

Renna tried to swallow the bitterness that flooded her mouth. Here was the man who had poisoned her governess against the light, led her to harbor treasonous material. *Says the woman who sleeps in trees*, she thought darkly. Dissonance shuddered through her body. Renna pushed away the thoughts of Marian. Slinging the bow across her back, she scrambled down the other side of the obstacle, the rope thick under her hands. When her boots hit the ground, there was a hot knot of anger in her chest.

The Night Watchman moved with precision through the pendulums, diving and rolling to avoid the second log, biding his time to pass the third. Once he was clear, he made his way to the target swinging on a chain. He moved with a fluid, predatory type of grace, but Renna couldn't put her finger on which animal he reminded her of.

It was time to focus. She rolled the tension from her shoulders; counted the seconds it took for the log to complete a full arc. When the pattern started over again, she sprinted forward, clearing the first one easily and mimicking the Night Watchman's dive to clear the second, rolling quickly. The log whooshed past her nose, too close for comfort. She wormed away, heels digging into the dirt until it was safe to crouch. Her breath was ragged as she locked her eyes on the third log. Her mind screamed at her to run, but her body remained still, waiting for the correct moment—

There.

Renna leapt up, legs pumping furiously as she wove through the final obstacles, ducking and weaving. The final target swung on its chain. Only one dark arrow pierced the bull's-eye, the rest on the outer edges. The Night Watchman now stood on the other side of the finish line. She knew his gaze was on her, simmering with challenge. They were tied for points.

Well, an excellent marksman he may be, but so am I.

Her focus tunneled inward, shutting out the noise of the spectators, the tang of blood, the irritating Night Watchman. She sank into the space deep within herself that she'd only discovered while living in Sherwood. Like the eye of the storm, there was a splinter of peace she could reach for. The bow moved as an extension of her, arm swinging in a fluid motion, the air alive like the prelude to a lightning bolt. Renna exhaled and released her arrow. The roar from the crowd was the thunder following a lightning strike as she split the Night Watchman's arrow down the middle, the splintered ends fanning out in every direction.

Almost, but not quite, she thought as she reached back, deftly nocking another arrow. The second shot speared through both embedded arrows, exploding their fragments, leaving her with the only remaining mark. A whoop came from Little Jon somewhere behind her, and her limbs buzzed with adrenaline as she jogged to where her friends and competitors waited behind the finish line. Through the tangle of people, her eyes locked with the Night Watchman's. She gave him a deep, mocking bow.

Renna was jostled by the mass of people, her legs unsteady, as she cheered on Little Jon and Alaini. The rest of the crew was at the archery field now—Scarlet with official winnings, the pickpocketing youngsters looking smug.

Alaini, having finished her turn, was speaking rapidly. "When the Night Watchman showed up, I thought for sure we were done for. And then you used his move against him, not once but *twice*—"

Soon the judges were standing on a crude platform calling for quiet, saying it had been a close race between two specific competitors (someone yelled, "Night Watchman!") but that after the final tally of arrows on the targets, there was one clear winner.

"Marian Hood."

Renna's breath trembled nearly as much as her legs as she untangled herself from her friends. She stepped up onto the scuffed boards of the platform, eyes scanning for the tall cloaked figure of the Night Watchman, but he was gone. The heavy leather purse clinked loudly as a judge handed it to her. A bubble of emotion welled in her chest, spreading across her collarbones, and causing heat behind her eyes as her crew took up the chant of, "Hood, Hood, Hood!"

Asher, eyes glossy from too much ale, was cheering louder than the rest and pulled Renna in for a crushing hug. And then Scarlet and Alaini were hoisting her into the air, calling for celebratory drinks, and Renna had never felt so much like she *belonged* somewhere.

CHAPTER 18

THE NIGHT WATCHMAN STOOD AT THE OUTSKIRTS OF THE VILLAGE, WATCHING THE GROUP OF OUTLAWS MELT INTO THE WOODS. Beneath the obsidian half mask, a smile pulled at his lips. The woman they called Marian—obviously a false name—had won. Truth be told, his pride had been struck when she'd split his arrow, but winning would have merely been a bonus. He'd accomplished his desired outcome the moment they had entered the competition. He had only needed to find them and catch their attention to set up his next steps.

It was too dangerous to approach them in Wendsvik; there were spies for the crown everywhere. The druid had been easy to pick out, their staff catching the Watchman's eye immediately. He'd never seen one like it before, but he had read about the fabled druidhen staffs in an old book, how they could be wielded as weapons or used as focal points to channel their magic. It was rumored that they could even be used for flight.

He had more pressing matters than riddling out what magic the druid possessed. The Falsehoods wanted the fallen princess.

The Watchman focused on the weight of the fox eye stone around his neck. Connecting to his familiar was like wading into a river. Magic lapped around him, a gold-flecked current. Sindri appeared on the far side, his brilliant fur a riot of white, orange, and red. The presence of the Watchman's familiar felt how lotus blossoms smelled at dawn. The fox held all three of his tails high as he entered the river.

Remind me why we must stoop to this level of subterfuge? Sindri sighed in his mind.

You know I'd much prefer to have a candid conversation with the witch in Loxley, but we can't risk the wrong person overhearing. Even the walls in that castle seem to have ears.

And you think this is the best way to gain her trust? In another alley perhaps fifty paces from him, Sindri slipped from the shadows.

You let me worry about that. You worry about finding where the wards begin.

The Night Watchman's fingers strayed to the hem of his cloak, searching the lining until he felt the telltale crinkle of parchment. He watched as the three-tailed fox darted to the tree line and, like a snuffed flame, disappeared into Sherwood Forest.

CHAPTER 19

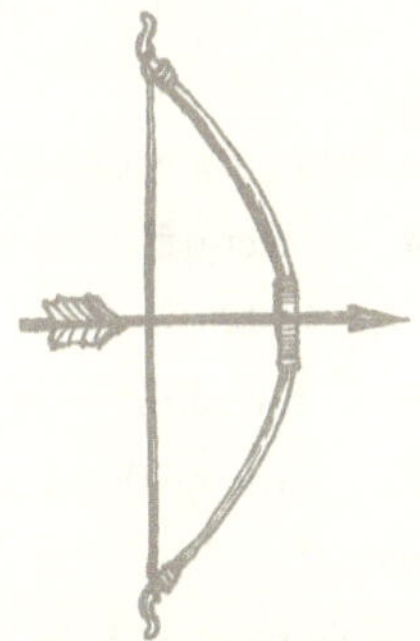

As they reentered the forest, Renna's body seemed to sigh, tension unspooling from somewhere behind her ribs. A gentle whisper wove through the trees as if they were trading secrets. It was a foolish notion, of course, just the breeze playing tricks, and she pushed it from her mind.

The canopy of the forest was a knotted lattice of bare branches. Hardly any animals crossed their path, save for a bright fox in the corner of her vision. But when Renna turned to get a better look, sure that her eyes were mistaken—it looked as if it had more than one tail—the fox took off, streaking through the forest like wildfire. Her breath puffed out in small clouds. She tucked her chin into the neck of her cloak, anxious to return to Kit and Alita and to leave the cold behind.

They had to be close to the wards. There was a subtle shift of pressure in the air, encouraging her to turn another way, and Renna found her mind wandering even as she tried to pay close attention to the forest. Was it possible that the wards weren't fixed in place? Did they move around? And if so, did that mean that Rowan Reach changed locations?

She hadn't given the journey back much thought, but now her palms went clammy as she waited for Little Jon to bring out the blindfold. But they never did.

"You've earned the right to see the way in," Little Jon said.

It was so simple. She'd never earned anything so easily back in Loxley. Emotion caught in her throat. Alaini slipped her arm through Renna's, squeezing her.

The path they took wound deeper into the woods. Alaini jutted her chin, motioning to a trunk that would take three of them to reach all the way around.

At first glance, there was nothing special about the tree, but the others approached one by one, placing their palms over a worn knot. As the crew watched expectantly, Renna repeated the motion. The tree felt warm under her hand, at odds with the chill of the air.

Little Jon whispered something, the words swept up in the breeze that rustled through the trees. The hair on Renna's arms stood up, a tingling, fluttering sensation spreading from the top of her skull to her feet. The spot above her hand blurred and then solidified again, revealing what was carved into the gnarled bark: the rune that was carved into so many of the trees in Rowan Reach, a vertical line with three branches extending out.

The forest rippled to unveil trees rich in color and life: brown-grey bark, knotted and fissured, with paw-shaped leaves untouched by the winter chill. They formed an impenetrable wall, their slender branches covered in thorns the size of Renna's hand.

Little Jon caught the expression on her face. "We call this the Thorne Crown. All these hawthorns are warded with druidhen magic." Crouching down, they dragged a finger through the dirt, writing. Renna's heart beat a sharp rhythm as they drew runes.

A breeze stirred the air, and the limbs of the trees bowed gently, pulling away from each other until an opening appeared in front of Little Jon, only a few paces wide. As the group passed through, the hawthorns closed behind them. The hum of magic skittered across Renna's skin, and warmth like stepping into a pool of sunshine suffused her muscles. Time moved so strangely that they could have been walking through the hawthorns for minutes or hours before the branches in front of them opened to the sunny spring of Rowan Reach.

Little Jon touched her shoulder. "Tonight at moonrise, there's something I want to show you," they said quietly. "Welcome home."

Home.

The forest at night was its own kind of magic. Pale pools of moonlight splashed the roots and shimmered off the leaves. More stars were making their appearance in the sky, winking into existence. The leaves whispered in the breeze, a soft *shhh— shhh—shhh* that soothed Renna as she waited for Little Jon at the base of her tree house. The sound of Alaini's lute carried from where the others sat around the fire, laughter and off-key voices joining in to sing. A whistled tune grew louder as twigs snapped, and then Little Jon appeared from between the trunks, a gentle smile on their face as they held out a fur blanket. The kindness of the simple act brought a dull ache to Renna's throat as she draped it around her shoulders. Their heels scuffed against the rocks and dirt as they began walking.

"What's this mystery you wish to show me?"

"You'll see soon enough." They cast Renna a quick glance, laughing at her expression and pulling her into a side hug. "What, you don't like surprises?"

"They and I have never particularly gotten along, no," Renna grumbled. She could feel Little Jon's gaze on her throat.

Their voice turned somber. "You never speak of it."

Renna kept her eyes trained on the ground. "What's the use of talking about it? It's done. I'd rather leave it behind me." She slipped out from under Little Jon's arm under the pretense of navigating over a fallen tree.

"I'm not sure you can leave something behind if you've chained yourself to it."

"And you're so free, are you?" she snapped. The retort tasted bitter on her tongue. She thought of the storm cloud that passed over Little Jon's face whenever Renna tried to broach the topic of the carved owl necklace. It wasn't fair, but gods, it was so much easier to point out others' contradictions than face her own.

That's because you're weak.

Little Jon didn't take the bait, merely shrugged. "Perhaps not."

Annoyance diffused Renna's guilt. "I'm…it's too shameful to speak of."

Little Jon turned to her, eyes piercing even in the low light. "You have nothing to be ashamed of, Renna."

Her laugh was derisive. They only knew the parts of her that she'd allowed them to see, not the *real* her. They didn't know how cowardly and selfish she was, the pain she'd brought to the kingdom without ever taking the throne. If they really knew… No, it was better that they didn't. Nastasia and Ulrik had truly known her and seen her Truth, and, well… Her stomach went sour as she shoved the memory aside.

Perhaps the conditions in Nottingham were better now that someone worthy ruled. Renna allowed a small twist of her lips, hoping that Little Jon couldn't see the internal turmoil playing out on her face. "That's generous of you, but incorrect."

They didn't push the subject, and their silence was oddly comforting as they led her deeper into the forest. Outside of the Silent Hour, the castle had always had a constant hum of activity, lessons, expectations, and reprimands. Even when it'd been just her and Nastasia in her room, their near-constant mettlemancy meant she was never really left alone in her mind.

A nearby stream, owls calling back and forth, and the rustling of the leaves were the only sounds until Little Jon spoke again. "The king intends to increase the tithe."

"What?"

"It will be soon, if it hasn't happened already."

Renna tried to recall if Little Jon or the others had mentioned hearing news of Loxley while they'd been in Wendsvik. "How could you possibly know that?"

"The trees told me."

"The trees told you." Renna repeated the phrase, watching them closely to determine if they were lying or joking. But Little Jon's face remained serene in the moonlight.

By the time they stopped at the edge of a glen, the moon had shifted in the sky, and a sheen of sweat prickled between Renna's shoulder blades. Little Jon stepped aside to give her a clear view of the grove.

Her breath caught in her chest. Soft moss carpeted the ground; fireflies cast an ethereal glow; an oak tree stretched tall and wide at the center, branches and limbs creating the most majestic lattice against the starry sky; several feet of roots stood above the ground, the base of the trunk digging into the dirt like the fingers of a giant, before reaching down to claim the land.

How—*how*—could anyone have ever been in the presence of this living, breathing wonder, and think it was anything but a gift? Anger and grief twined together in Renna's chest, begging for release, as she felt the indescribable *loss* that had filled so much of her life up until that moment.

As if tree roots had sprouted in her heart and tugged, she stumbled forward.

Renna's earliest memory was that of seeing the Mother's Flame. She'd been barely five years old, taken down into the depths of the castle by a large procession of Keepers, the Head Trissaia, and her parents just after the Blood Tithe. *This is what the crown protects, Rennavera. This is your sacred duty from the Mother.* She'd looked into the flames, willing herself to feel something other than confusion about why so many of the Keepers were weeping with smiles plastered on their faces, and frustration at not being allowed to speak. Her feelings had morphed over the years, though during each Blood Tithe, she still tried desperately to feel the same awe and conviction that seemed second nature to everyone else. She grew to crave the euphoria that came after the Tithe, when the sense of belonging finally flooded her senses, and she worked all year to hold on to that feeling.

Renna wasn't sure when she'd fallen to her knees or when silent tears had begun to make tracks down her cheeks, but she didn't care. Here in the presence of the oak, she knew the truth, more clearly than she had ever known in the temple, in lessons with the Keepers of the Truth, or during a Tithe. Even now, stripped powerless as she was, Renna felt the irrefutable truth.

This tree was *sacred.*

The Velmir overflowed here, coating the ground and the roots in shimmering gold, magic palpable in the air.

Little Jon asked quietly, "Do you recall where the word *Trissaia* comes from?"

Every child knew it meant "Truth Sayer," but Renna said nothing.

"It first meant 'tree sayer' or 'tree seer.' The druidhen were oak seers."

Renna's teeth ached as she clenched them together, trying to keep her feelings in. She curled her fingers into the ground, dirt caking beneath her nails. The truth and the lies scraped against her skull.

Little Jon sat next to her, one knee tucked up to their chest as they gazed at the tree.

"I was raised with the druidhen. They don't typically keep written records; the magic and beliefs are passed down through practice. And when the druidhen were massacred years ago, much was lost. Nearly a whole generation of druidhen. The cost..." Emotion choked their words, and they paused for the span of a few breaths. Renna hardly dared to move, desperate to hear more.

"The way of the druidhen is to let nature run its course. To not get involved with the policies and schemes of men. So they retreated deeper into the woods."

Where were they now? How many were left? Renna kept the words tucked away, knowing this was not the moment to ask. She plucked a fallen leaf from the ground, the veins lined with flecks of gold in the moonlight.

"This is the Oakheart. The druidhen used to meet under it a few times a year." Little Jon pulled a leather pouch from their pocket, spilling acorns across the moss. On each acorn, a different symbol was carved. They seemed to pulse with soft energy as Renna tested their weight in her palm, running her thumb over the grooves of the symbols. Something akin to veneration stirred in her, blooming and expanding as she tried to identify the different runes.

"Acorns from the Oakheart are used for divination. So when I said the trees told me, I meant it. The king is increasing the Blood Tithe, Renna. I don't know the reason, but I know it spells danger for the forest and for us. Feel for yourself."

Little Jon shifted to kneeling, spreading their hands wide before placing them on the tree's roots, their chin tucked to their chest, eyes fluttering closed. Renna stared at them, mind stumbling over their words. Surely they didn't think she was worthy enough to receive such knowledge. But Little Jon just waited, giving her time to wrestle with herself. Her hands hovered over the roots, palms down. The old crescent scar on her left hand prickled, the one from her Foretelling. What if she failed at this too?

Renna touched the tree.

The rough bark scaped pleasantly against her skin. The only noise was the rustle of leaves and chirping crickets, and the clouds shifted so that moonlight bathed the glen. Some of the tension between her shoulders loosened, and Renna closed her eyes, focusing. A faint current moved through the roots, sending a tingling bolt through her system, and she inhaled sharply through her nose. Pulse ringing like a plucked string on Alaini's lute, Renna allowed herself to listen and feel. In her mind's eyes, she could picture the roots tunneling down into the earth, webbing out in a vast expanse, the branches stretching out toward the moon and the stars. Strength—old and tested and true—coursed through the trunk, seeking to pour itself into everything around it, into Renna. The forest's heartbeat caressed her like a mother, humming a constant refrain of *home, home, home*. Tears pricked the corners of her eyes. Relief was a heavy downpour washing away her doubt and fear. She rocked forward, pressing her hands more firmly, starved for more.

A deep sense of knowing flooded her: she merely needed to ask.

Is it true about the Tithe increasing?

A gentle hum floated on the breeze as if the Oakheart was pleased to be asked a question. Images of Loxley brushed against her mind, places she knew and was fond of—the archery field in Nottingham; the tower that had the best view from the castle; the track she'd been allowed to ride horses on.

Then the images warped, their color bleeding into stains of crimson: citizens lined up in droves to give Tithes; slashes of ritual daggers; bloodstone siphons overflowing; homes torched throughout Nottingham; the crack of a whip echoing through a square; men stumbling down alleys, weak from bloodletting, their bodies riddled with leech marks; children crying for their mothers, unanswered; horrified whimpers of *they gave too much, they gave too much* repeated like a prayer over limp bodies lining the streets.

No, not limp bodies. *Corpses.* Renna's nails bit into the bark of the roots; she choked on bile. Corpses of the citizens of Loxley—the poorest—who were taxed for more blood than they could give.

Renna jerked away from the tree, breaking the connection violently; it upset her balance, and she fell back onto the earth. It felt like a boulder was crushing her chest as she blinked, tears slipping from the corners of her eyes to wet her hair, her ears, and her neck. Her extremities tingled, and pinpricks needled the base of her skull. Fear held her tight, locking her muscles, until Little Jon gripped her hand, squeezing gently. Neither spoke, the atmosphere in the grove holding space for the heavy shroud of dread over them both. The oak tree towered over them, creating a haven. They stayed like that until their breathing returned to normal and the presence of the tree grounded them once more.

"Why are you telling me this now?" The ragged quality of Renna's voice surprised her.

"The most powerful truths are sometimes the hardest to say and to hear. If I'd tried to tell you when we'd first met that most everything you grew up believing was a lie…"

"I wouldn't have heard you." How could she have? From birth she'd been taught that the trees would work their poison on the mind, turning one against the Light.

A sound at the edge of the clearing attracted their attention. Much's expression and the way his chest heaved from sprinting brought Renna's thoughts to a halt, her muscles tensed for danger.

"Keepers." Much's voice cracked the air like a branch breaking. "There are Keepers of the Truth in Sherwood."

CHAPTER 20

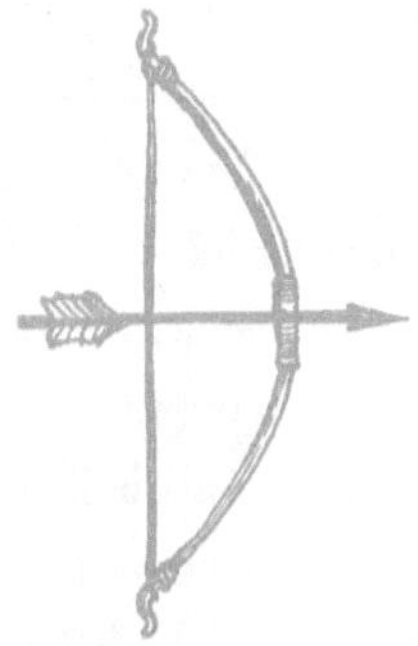

RENNA'S CLOAK WAS DAMP FROM THE LINGERING RAIN, HER TUNIC STICKING TO HER BACK, BY THE TIME SHE FINISHED SETTING THE TRAP. Her thoughts were as murky as the storm clouds above the barren trees. She was outside the wards, kneeling in mud, back aching from digging, and ready to give Much a tongue-lashing for this idea.

A fortnight had passed since Much had spotted the retinue of Keepers clothed head to toe in dark purple, prowling deep into the wilds of Sherwood as if every pillar of the Truth did not strictly forbid it. They'd carried with them a chest of full bloodsiphons and had been singing passages from the Tomes of Truth.

A fortnight since Renna had seen the vision from the Oakheart.

The images she'd seen had sunk into her subconscious, infiltrating her dreams and consuming her waking thoughts in a never-ending spiral. Like a liturgy, they bounced from one to the next in a predictable pattern:

There's nothing I can do for them.

I'd only make things worse.

What I saw might not even be true, just some vedra trickery. (This one brought an intense burn of shame that she didn't want to examine.)

Worse yet was the one that said, *Maybe this is my fault.* What if the people of Loxley were being punished for her failings? She hadn't left soon enough and had brought the Mother's disfavor on all of them for bowing to someone unworthy like herself: a vedra whose darkness would spell destruction and ruin for the kingdom.

Don't think about it, don't think about it. The wave of emotion built, and she pushed it aside.

Renna secured the net over the hole in the ground, then stood back to observe the effect. It wasn't half bad. They'd sewn leaves, twigs, and underbrush into the nets. A moonlit ritual that had consisted of burning incense and weaving runes in the air had made the illusion complete. Throughout Sherwood right now, the others were digging similar holes and covering them with sections of false ground. They hoped to catch any wandering Keepers and ply them for information.

A bird squawked in the distance, as put out by the weather as Renna. She gathered her things, trying in vain to breathe warmth into her fingers, and headed to find Little Jon. As she came across a small clearing, the hair on her neck rose. Renna stilled. The sky roiling with darkness above and the rain obscuring the view of the other side of the glen. Tugging the cowl up over her nose and mouth and adjusting her hood lower, she scanned the area.

There was a flash of dark cloak, and Renna swept up her bow, arrow trained on the emerging figure.

Swathed in all black, face hidden except for a sliver of skin around his eyes, a man stepped into the clearing, his own arrow trained on her. He was just as tall as she remembered him from the tournament, with broad shoulders and a chilling air of certainty around him. The violent urge to punch him in the face surprised Renna. She scowled, her body taut with anticipation.

"Lovely weather we're having," he called.

"And you are?"

"The Night Watchman."

The bastard had the arrogance to say it like that should mean something to her, and even though it did, the presumption irked her. She took a measured step to her right, and the Watchman mirrored her movement.

"Surely you've heard tales of me?" He adjusted his aim, lowering his weapon to point at her feet.

She returned the gesture, but only to aim just below his belt. "State your purpose."

His face was obscured, but by the tilt of his head, she could practically feel him arching a brow. "I should be demanding the same of you. After all, I've given you my name while you have yet to reveal yours. And you are the one setting traps if I'm not mistaken. Perhaps you're trying to get the attention of the Keepers? Hoping to win their favor by catching some outlaws?"

A growl slipped from her throat. "Do not insult me by suggesting I belong to the Keepers."

"When I insult you, believe me, you'll know it." They took another step in tandem, some twisted variation of a dance. Irritation spiked hot through her center. When they'd walked a quarter turn around the clearing, he continued, "Since your words alone would be considered treason nowadays, I assume you are not aligned with the Trissaia or the throne. And you remind me of an outlaw who beat me out of a sizeable purse."

Renna sneered, lifting her chin. "Are you here for an apology? You won't get one."

He chuckled low. "I wouldn't dream of asking for one. But since we understand each other now, perhaps we could lower our weapons?"

"State your purpose, *Watchman*, or I'll get my answers another way. You may have half of Wendsvik fooled—"

"I'm rather popular in Loxley as well."

"—but you're nothing but a vagrant. Have you no care for the people you hurt?"

He cocked his head. "An outlaw who cares for the red clerics?"

Renna scoffed. She was sick of everyone praising this man. There was no one else around to hear her, no one to pretend for. The realization was freeing. Here was a place to direct all her pent-up anger and shame. "Your words and deeds trick decent, kind people into throwing their lives away."

"And who are these decent, kind people?"

"You think you can just do whatever you want and not consider the consequences for anyone else."

He stilled. "On the contrary, I spend a great deal of time considering consequences."

Renna could practically feel Marian's gentle hands running over her hair, the warm arms encircling her after the news of her parents' death. She'd never even gotten to say goodbye before her governess had been sent to the dungeons. Emotion clogged her throat. "Her name was Marian."

"I seem to recall that was the name you gave in Wendsvik."

Her very bones were vibrating. "You have your moniker. I have mine."

"And who was this Marian to you?"

"She was my mother." A lie that felt like truth.

"Then you have my condolences for your loss." Silence fell between them, pulled taut like a bowstring. The he said, "I'm looking for a band of outlaws who are rumored to live hidden in these woods. Ones who have ties to the druidhen. And I believe you can help me find them."

It didn't matter if he was the largest burr in the crown's hide; this was information he should not have. Stalling, Renna said, "And you thought you could just waltz in and submit a calling card?"

He shrugged one shoulder. "I seem to have run out of other options." Slowly and with deliberate movements, he returned his arrow to his quiver and slung the bow across his shoulders. His intense gaze was locked on her the whole time. A raven swooped through the clearing, finding another perch.

Renna swallowed thickly. "What do you want with this band of outlaws?"

"I have well-guarded knowledge they'll want. Specifically the druid." He took a step toward her, and she pulled back on her bowstring. "That, and a proposition that could make you all a large sum of money. But it's clear you don't trust me."

His baiting riled her. "Comes with the territory."

"Well, since you're *obviously* not the one in charge, why don't you point me in the direction of the rest of your merry crew."

The dripping condescension in his tone snapped her control. He flinched as her arrow struck the tree behind him, already aiming another at his feet. He jumped, narrowly avoiding the hit. She tossed her bow aside, and the sound of metal rang in the air as she pulled her sword free, advancing on him.

"See, I told you you'd know when I was insulting you," he said.

The audacity of this man. He'd caught her on a shit day, and she had no other outlet for her bitterness. "Your services and information are not welcome. We do not need small men who've given themselves ridiculous titles to compensate for something. Begone, sir," she sneered, flicking the point of the sword in small circular motions.

His gaze pierced her through his obsidian mask. Then he reached up and unsheathed a large blade from his back. "I see we're not going to do this the civilized way."

"Where's the fun in being civilized?"

Annoyance and anticipation warred inside Renna as she widened her stance. Her muscles screamed for a release. She ignored the voice of Little Jon telling her she was being rash. If this man was arrogant enough to come at her, then his fate was on him. Adrenaline roared in Renna's veins, demanding to move, to cut, to slice, to shut out all other noise. She lunged. The clash of steel reverberated up her arms, biting into her bones. The Night Watchman met her attack with a skilled parry. Renna blocked his return strike and spun away. As he followed her, he stumbled on the roots.

Renna smirked. The forest was hers, and she belonged to the forest.

He thrust again, forcing her to twist away. Using his momentum, he slammed his shoulder into her chest, knocking her off her feet. Her head smacked the forest floor, momentarily stunning her, but on instinct, Renna rolled. His blade sliced through the now empty air and caught on a trunk. Taking advantage of the opening, she kicked him in the hip. He grunted, staggering back as he yanked his sword free. Renna scrambled upright and attacked again, but he met her blow for blow. At one point he batted aside her blade, free hand shooting out. Cool air trickled down the back of her head. The prick had tugged off her hood. She spun away before he could pull the cowl down too. He rolled his shoulders and cracked his neck.

"You're right, this is much more fun."

Renna snarled, outraged, and he laughed.

They whirled, parried, attacked, and lunged, a dance of steel, mud, and rain. Their breathing was heavy, hanging in clouds in the cool air. He pressed his advance, towering over Renna, putting his weight behind each blow, forcing her to give him ground. He drove her to the edge of the glen. Each hit jarred her arms more than the last. Sweat mixed with the rain on her face and trickled between her shoulder blades. She tasted blood in her mouth, though she couldn't remember biting her tongue. If she wasn't wearing her cowl, she'd spit.

He was so much bigger than she was. The ground behind her sloped down into a cluster of trees. *Use what you have*, Renna thought. Silver flashed, his blade swung in a high arc, and she saw her chance. Slightly crouched, she used both hands to parry his blow, sending the tip of his sword toward the ground. As his momentum carried him closer to her, she stepped into him, pinning his wrist against his hip as she gripped his forearm with her free hand. Surprise flashed in his eyes—his weapon hand was trapped between them. The cocky bastard was stunned useless as Renna snapped her elbow up hard, hitting the underside of his chin. The resulting crunch of bone on bone was loud. Pain exploded up and down her arm. His head whipped back, and Renna roughly grabbed the leather baldric behind his shoulder and pulled, twisting her hips to send him down the small hill.

It wasn't an honorable move, but where was the honor between thieves, really? Renna had no remorse as he pitched down into the trees, losing his sword in the tumble. She pulled a dagger from her thigh holster, pursuing him with two weapons. When he rolled onto his back, Renna pounced, her knees holding his forearms to the ground, and her blades crossed at his throat.

They were both panting heavily, the glen behind them torn to a muddy mess. He was trapped beneath her, his chest rising and falling rapidly. A thrill raced through her, but his eyes shone with triumph, as if he were the winner, not she.

"Something amusing, Watchman?"

"Your form is much improved, Princess."

A ringing noise filled her ears, and she flushed hot and cold. She pressed the blades harder. The seconds slipped by like blood from a cut. Memories, old and fresh, blended and reshaped into something horrific and inevitable. The eyes boring into hers over the half mask were steely grey, like storm-tossed waves.

Renna tore off the Watchman's mask, leaving her staring down at Garen Draic.

"*You?*" The word flew from her mouth, a question and an accusation.

"If you'll allow me to explain—" Draic's fingers encircled both her wrists like vises, keeping the blades locked in place where they hovered between them.

"Explain how you attempted to slit my throat in the castle before you were interrupted?" All Renna could see was red as she relived the memory of the knife slicing her neck.

Draic narrowed his eyes. "Why don't you at least *try* to use that brain of yours, Princess. Do you honestly believe that if I'd wanted you dead, you'd be alive? Or that a priestess could overpower me? I had orders to kill you that day, but I never intended to carry them out. I swear to you—"

"You *swear?*" It came out as a snarl. This was a cruel trick—it had to be. She leaned closer. "I should gut you here and now and let you bleed out." Make him bleed as she had bled.

Renna jolted at the unexpected mettlemantic connection.

Did you not recognize the taste of moonshade? I brushed a small amount on your lips to slow your pulse, give the illusion that you were fading quickly, so when others looked in my mind, they were convinced.

The memory came back to her of his thumb swiping her mouth as he'd gripped her jaw, the sickly sweet taste and smell overpowering her senses. She couldn't think straight, her every muscle trembling. "Is that your idea of an apology, *Sheriff?*"

His eyes flicked between hers, a riot of emotions simmering in them. "I apologize"—the word sounded like it physically pained him to say—"for the way in which I had to save your life. But it had to look believable. The moment you abdicated, Ulrik ordered your assassination."

Her stomach threatened to empty itself. Ulrik had ordered it. The man who'd practically raised her, whom she'd trusted explicitly, had ordered her death. "Why?"

"He was threatened by whatever magic you possess."

You will bring destruction on this kingdom and its people. Did he not think exile would be sufficient? Perhaps her death was the only way he thought he could keep Loxley safe since she'd failed the crucible. Maybe the Mother had spoken to him. But this did not explain why Draic had done what he had. Her fingers were numb, and she realized she'd lowered her blades, resting them against his collarbones.

"Why stand against the crown, then?"

Draic's throat bobbed as he swallowed. "I began fighting the crown long ago."

Turncoat. Traitor. Spy. Apostate. Vedra rebel. Night Watchman. But the timeline didn't add up. "The Night Watchman's been around for decades."

"The title is passed down. A name and a mask that represent a common goal."

"And that is?"

"Liberating the people of Loxley."

Renna barked out a laugh. "Says the man who burned nine witches with his own hands."

Draic leaned forward, upper lip curling. "Yes, at whose command?"

The crunch of bone on bone resounded through the clearing as Renna punched him. The skin of her knuckles split, and blood sprayed from a cut on his lip.

"What did they tell you, Renna, about the ritual when you were sixteen? That it was to get rid of your vedra blood, right? But it was never about extracting something. It was an excuse to hide a piece of aurem underneath your scar."

He shouldn't know that—her Foretelling had been sealed, locked away, kept from prying eyes. Every person who knew what had been predicted that day had sworn on promise of death not to reveal what they'd heard. "You lie." Her words were hollow. A cold quiet was settling over her. The calm before the storm.

"The aurem under your skin was warded and enchanted with runes to bind and suppress the magic you possess that Ulrik saw as a threat."

The air was too thin; the trees seemed to crowd in on her. What he was implying was impossible. The head Trissaia knowingly using vedra magic was heresy. She couldn't let Draic leave, not without hearing what else he had to say, like a scab that had to be picked. Taking him to Rowan Reach was out of the question—she would not betray her friends—but perhaps she could bring the others to him.

Of course, that meant revealing her identity.

The thought made dread sweep through her middle. Draic had mentioned a job, something that could earn them coin, and she couldn't turn that down without at least presenting it to her friends—the purse from the contest would last only so long. There was always a risk of illness or infection that would require more medical supplies, and no doubt Little Jon would eventually bring in another stray soul, just as they had her and Much. Everyone shared so willingly in the group, working together as a unit. *As a family*, she thought, and the words speared something sensitive behind her ribs. If she kept this from them purely to protect herself, she wasn't worthy of being part of Rowan Reach.

"What do you want?"

"I told you. I have information for your druid friend. You may tell them Briar sent me."

"And what if I don't believe you?"

Draic's eyes narrowed. "Have you learned nothing useful in your time here? Tell the druid to use their clairvel touch."

Renna bristled, hating how his words made her feel like a scolded child who'd answered a question incorrectly. "If you truly wish to speak to my friends, you are going to do it on my terms. Up." Keeping her dagger at his throat, she searched him, tossing aside hidden daggers so they were out of reach (two in his thigh holsters, one strapped across his chest, another in his boot).

"Don't forget the bracers," was the only thing he said. A little chagrinned, Renna tugged them loose to see five throwing stars sewn into the lining of each. She raised a brow, adding both bracers to the pile. Once she was sure there were no more weapons on his person, she grabbed him roughly by the collar and led him back up the small hill to her pack to grab a length of rope. Something dangerous emanated from him, but only for a moment. Draic held her stare as he slowly lowered to one knee, then both, hands held out before him.

Her blood simmered. She snatched his wrists, winding the rope around them quickly. Her cheeks burned, flushed with adrenaline, and she refused to meet his eyes. Thin silvery scars crisscrossed the backs of his hands and his corded forearms. He grunted as she pulled the bindings tighter than necessary. Renna stepped back swiftly, needing space between them. Her nerves were like the hive of bees Baz had accidentally knocked over last month. She secured the other end of the rope around a thick trunk.

A low growl came from the edge of the clearing as Kit barreled into view, ears pinned back. Draic mouth twisted to the side. "Hello, lishka." He held out his bound hands to Kit, who hesitated for only a moment before dropping his protective stance to accept a scratch under the chin. Renna glared at the fox.

"Perhaps your time in the woods hasn't been totally useless if you've befriended a lishka," Draic said. With a glance at her face, he continued, "Lishka is a northern term for a fox. Clever creatures. They adapt to whatever environment they're thrown into. They survive." His gaze flitted up to hers, then away. "Much like yourself."

The words made her feel too exposed. She pulled a rag from her pack and ripped off a long strip. Draic's nostrils flared as she covered his eyes, clenching and unclenching his teeth. But still he remained quiet, accepting her terms. Her fingers trembled as she tied a knot, accidentally pulling out a few stray hairs as she secured it firmly before gathering up all his weapons and strapping them to her own body. She was still reeling from everything he'd said, and she needed clarity. Renna just prayed she would not regret whatever came next.

Draic's voice rumbled like thunder. "I've complied with your terms. Now you're to take me to Rowan Reach."

She'd never said the name aloud, which could be taken as confirmation that he was telling the truth. Could this Briar be Little Jon's contact in Loxley? Renna bent, her mouth next to his ear, relishing the chance to repeat his words back to him. "I don't think you're in a position to be making demands, Watchman."

At the edge of the clearing, she paused behind a tree. Her hand went to her throat, the ridges of her scars warm under her palm. Several minutes slipped by, and still Draic knelt motionless. Just as she was about to leave to find Little Jon, something shifted.

Draic's chest began to rise and fall more rapidly. He dropped his chin, breathing shakily. His lips moved wordlessly. Guilt churned in her gut as the high sheriff's composure fractured before her eyes, followed immediately by anger. How dare he make her feel sorry for him?

Shaken, she picked her way across the forest floor, keeping silent until she'd put some distance between them. Then a shuddering breath ripped out of her. She pressed the heels of her palms into her eyes until she saw spots. Finally, the tears that threatened to overtake her receded. Renna wiped her nose and straightened. Her churning thoughts were scathing and sharp as she stomped through the woods in search of Little Jon.

"Are you going to tell me why you've tied up the Night Watchman?" Little Jon's voice was barely more than a whisper.

They stood at the edge of the glen, Draic across the way, bound and kneeling, just as she'd left him. His cold and unaffected demeanor was back. Kit lay next to him, not a care in the world. Loathe as Renna was to admit it, the fox's response to Draic had quelled some of her panic. When she'd found Little Jon, they had accepted her word that the situation would be simpler for her to show than explain.

She rubbed her palms on her pants. "I'm worried about what you'll think of me."

"You can't control what others think, Hood."

The nickname plucked a tender chord in her chest. "There are things about my past…if you truly knew…"

They placed a hand on her shoulder, turning her away from the clearing, ducking to meet her eyes. "We all have a past. It makes us who we are. And anyway, it's our choices *now* that matter. Who you are is all right by me, Renna. The dark and the light."

Tears spilled down her cheeks as she squeezed her eyes shut. "You might not think that when you learn the truth."

Little Jon sighed heavily. Their expression—eyes crinkled with a knowing, sad smile—was so open that Renna felt lightheaded. Strong fingers tapped her sternum, right above the carved owl resting atop her tunic. "I know enough, friend, whether or not you've said it aloud. Besides," they continued in a gentle tone, "how I respond is my choice."

Choice.

The word seemed to linger in the air. Shame was hot on her face. Her friends deserved the chance to choose her, and how could they without knowing the full truth? Renna gnawed on the inside of her cheek, looking across the glen.

She couldn't choose her past, but she could choose who she was now: not Rennavera Koravik, the crown princess of Loxley, but simply an outlaw witch of Sherwood. "He said Briar sent him."

Little Jon's posture stiffened, their jaw tightening.

Renna pressed on. "He said you could confirm that with…clairvel touch."

Little Jon sighed, hearing her unsaid questions. "Clairvel touch is a druidic power. I can sense the truth and past around a person with an object of importance. Sometimes it's a strong memory connected to it, but mostly I see glimpses or impressions. It's how I know who you really are, Ren."

Roots seemed to reach up from the dirt, lashing her in place. The memory of that day on the bridge slammed into her: Little Jon plucking up the owl pendant, the strange expression she could not catalogue now clicking into place. This whole time, Little Jon had known who she really was. Did the others? Why had they not said anything to her? Renna's whole body was vibrating, her breath shaky.

Little Jon frowned slightly. "Why will I need clairvel touch for this man?"

"Because he's also the high sheriff of Nottingham."

CHAPTER 21

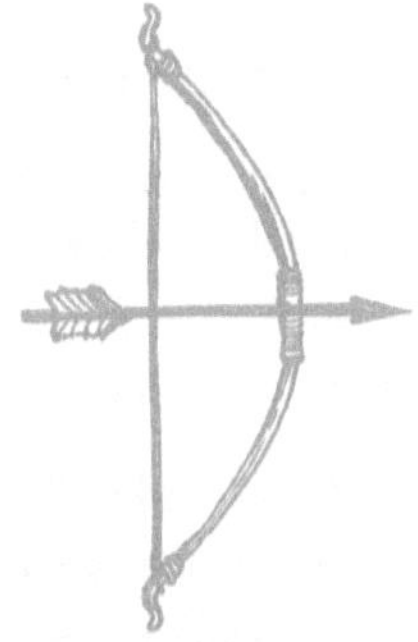

RENNA STAYED QUIET AS LITTLE JON CIRCLED DRAIC, SCRUTINIZING HIM. THE TENDONS IN HIS NECK FLEXED AS HE STRAINED AGAINST THE ROPES AND BLINDFOLD.

"I wasn't sure if you'd decided to leave me here to rot." When they gave no reply, Draic bristled. "Could you at least do me the courtesy of letting me see who I am talking to?"

Little Jon pulled the blindfold off, roughly shoving his head for good measure.

Draic worked his jaw, blinking in the light, then addressed Renna. "Are you going to introduce me to your friend? Or perhaps this is how you prefer men, lishka. Tied up and on their knees before you."

"Fuck you," Renna snarled.

Little Jon cut in, "I wonder what type of death wish the high sheriff of Nottingham has that he let himself be caught and bound in Sherwood Forest."

"Perhaps it's a death wish for those pulling the strings in Loxley." His eyes slid to Renna before returning to Little Jon. "We have a mutual friend in the castle."

"I make it a point to not have any friends in the castle, Sheriff."

"Briar said you might need a peace offering. There's a note in the lining of my cloak addressed to Bjori."

Little Jon stood very still, but Renna could feel the crackling energy beneath their cool demeanor. They jutted out their chin, and Renna knelt, fingers searching along the hem until a dry rustling told her she'd located the note. She tried to ignore his musk of rain and smoke and citrus, grateful to put distance between them again once she'd freed the small parchment. Little Jon unrolled the missive. The handwriting was identical to the note Renna had found with the carved owl.

Bjori,

I won't ask your forgiveness, but I ask that you remember the beginning.

THE TIME IS RIGHT.

Little Jon tucked the note away in their pocket. "What do you have that holds importance to you?"

Draic answered readily. "A pendant. The cord is around my neck."

Little Jon reached for his collar. Attached to a cord with some wire hung a small stone. A fox-eye stone, Renna thought, noting the amber, red, and honey-colored stripes. Draic looked almost pained as Little Jon pulled it over his head. She tried to decipher exactly what sort of magic her friend was doing as Little Jon closed their eyes, leaning against their quarterstaff while holding the stone in a loose fist. Gentle wind wove through the trees, sighing. The atmosphere around the grove turned colder, the trees seemed to grow taller, and the breeze began to sound like an ominous whisper.

If Draic was to be believed... Spots appeared on the edges of her vision. Renna bit down on her tongue, using the pain as a focal point. Ulrik had ordered her killed. The ritual she'd thought had proven her commitment to her duty had in fact been a lie. What exactly was Draic trying to do in Loxley? He had some proposition for the outlaws, but why should he have need of them? She still didn't understand who Briar was or their connection to Little Jon. How many of her friends knew the truth about her? Did Draic have contact with Nastasia? Shame joined the dizzying concoction of emotions as she realized she couldn't recall the last time she'd really thought about Nastasia. She'd been so preoccupied with her life in Sherwood, learning about the Velmir, and exploring Wendsvik.

She kept all these questions tucked behind her teeth as Little Jon returned the pendant around Draic's neck. They looked to Renna, and the sadness in their expression made her knees weak. Her chest constricted painfully, and her friend nodded, confirming the truth of Draic's words.

When Draic spoke, it sounded far away. "The king has increased the Blood Tithes."

"We know," answered Little Jon curtly.

Renna stared unseeing into the middle distance. Her blood roared in her ears, and she couldn't seem to relax her fists. Draic's words reached her in clipped phrases: *masquerade ball* and *perfect distraction* and *royal treasury*.

"What about those memories I saw of you in the war?" she asked. "You said those captives were vedra." The ones she'd ordered burned at the stake.

"Those men and women I burned were not vedra. They were Keepers we found who'd attacked a caravan of mostly starving women and children. They were bleeding them to meet their quota of bloodsiphons."

Horror licked up Renna's spine, followed by hot anger and a twisted desire to watch them burn all over again.

"The church controls the information Loxley has about magic, so they can easily keep up the narrative that there is no way to guard against mettlemancy. But there are methods."

The ground seemed to tilt under Renna, and dizziness swept through her. *Get a grip, Ren,* she ordered herself, but her own thoughts felt far away. Even her lungs were trembling. *Don't think about it now, don't think about it now*—but the words she'd clung to for stability for so long were unraveling.

"There was a kernel of truth in most of those memories you saw, but I was showing you what you and Ulrik both expected to see. I knew a show of loyalty would be necessary, so we removed their tongues and brought them with us under the false pretense that they'd been robbing a caravan of Keepers."

"How could you be sure we wouldn't look into their minds?"

"Kirin and Ilya are quite skilled at mettlecasting—planting false memories in someone else's mind for a short time. That, combined with the concoction of herbs we gave them to muddle their senses, would have been enough for a standard examination. Luckily, Ulrik seemed keen on testing your loyalty. He didn't care to look deeper into the story, so long as it served his purposes." Garen shrugged, the casual movement at odds with his heart-wrenching words. "I imagine he wanted you to display your finnikfire and remind you what would happen if you failed your crucible."

Renna didn't want Draic and Little Jon to see her crumbling, to see her come apart, and she was striding across the glen before consciously deciding to do so. Stray branches whipped her face, snagged on her hair. A panicked laugh ripped from her chest. There was a low rumble from above—a storm gathering. Her breath rattled in her ears, though she was only half aware of the tears streaming down her face. She stooped to grab a fallen branch, then swung it at the nearest trunk.

Crack.

The wood smarted against her palms.

Do not be weak.

Crack.

Air sawed in and out of her lungs.

Don't let them see all your failings.

Crack—crack.

Act like a royal.

The pain is nothing, stop crying.

Keep silent.

Pray harder.

Bleed again, bleed more.

Unworthy, unworthy, unworthy.

Each hit rang through her teeth, her muscles straining in protest, but she kept striking. Rain began to fall. Lightning flashed and thunder clapped, mirroring the storm within her. Her chest heaved with strangled sobs. She swung again, bark exploding everywhere.

Then Little Jon was by her side. They didn't flinch as she dealt the blow that snapped the staff in half, didn't balk as she fell to her knees, digging her nails into the mud, didn't shrink back at the animalistic cry tearing through her. Her fingers had turned to gnarled roots; she couldn't unclasp them. She folded over herself, choking on her sobs, pain shooting through her chest. Everything she'd locked away so tightly was spiraling out of her, and soon it would consume her, crush her beneath its weight.

"Breathe, Ren." Little Jon gripped her arms.

I'm fucking trying, she wanted to say, but she couldn't speak, could barely control her ragged gasps. Panic overtook her, a massive tide that would swallow her whole. Her conscious self was shoved back into a small space in her mind, the internal storm raging at the forefront, and she was not able to speak. The awful churning thoughts were dark tendrils coating her insides.

"This is a wave, Ren. You're in the storm now, but it will pass. The wave will pass. Picture the tree. Find its roots. The tree has been here for an age and will remain here for an age after we are gone."

She fought to slow her breathing, taking exaggerated inhales and exhales. Only the hours of practice in freezing water allowed her the clarity to call up the mental image of the Oakheart.

"Give it all to the roots, Ren. Everything coursing through you, everything you can't hold— channel it into the roots."

Renna imagined thick tar pouring out of her, pictured pushing it into the tree, letting the roots take it from her. It flayed her nerves raw, a weeping wound that seemed to have no end. This was what she'd feared: the inability to stop the storm from rampaging through her if she let it begin.

But…

The tightness around her chest loosened its hold.

The tumultuous waves of sobs died down to a river…

Then a stream…

Then just a trickle of rain.

Left in the storm's wake was a bittersweet quiet, a small respite from the warring thoughts and emotions. Mud caked her hands, drying and sticky. Raindrops clung to her lashes, and her lungs burned from exertion.

Renna pressed the heel of her palm against her sternum, her whole body entirely wrung out. She steeled herself for the lecture that was sure to follow such a garish display of dramatics. *What have you to complain about, Princess?* Nastasia used to tease. *Not all of us have a kingdom bowing at our feet and the Mother paving our way.*

But Little Jon just let the silence fill the space between them, wrapped around them like a blanket. They scooted closer, heedless of the muck, until the two of them sat shoulder to shoulder. Renna's head throbbed sluggishly. It felt like the inside of her skull was bruised. Nothing had been solved—far from it—but she did not feel so alone, sitting there with her friend. She felt…seen, unworthy parts and all.

There was a pained look on Little Jon's face when they pulled out the note Draic had brought, running a thumb over the inked words. "My family name is Bjonir. She used to call me Bjori—little bear." A soft chuckle at a sweet memory turned sour and stale with longing. "I told you before that I was raised in Branimer, deeper in Sherwood, nestled against the Spine of Kaerenthal. Rowan Reach was once the home of all the druidhen, but after the Great Culling, they retreated deeper into the forest. They put protective wards and enchantments in place to keep the Oakheart hidden from anyone but the druids, but…I do not agree with renouncing the rest of the world, as is the way of most of the druidhen. I understand it, of course. But that is not the path I wanted for myself.

"When I chose to come and watch over the Oakheart, I met Briar. This was only a short time after she had left Loxley. I met her when I was still working on the wards around the camp. Briar possesses a certain type of magic that is very rare among witches, and eventually she was able to help me finish the enchantments. We met Edwine and Sif not long after that and invited them to stay with us—we wanted this place to be a haven for other outcasts.

"For a time, we felt untouched by the things happening outside the wards. Living in perpetual spring and fall can make one forget the existence of winter and darkness. Briar would go into Wendsvik and hear talk of Loxley, of children dying of infections from tithing in poor conditions. She was always left unsettled when she saw Trissaia or Keepers in town. She'd get so upset, I worried that..."

Little Jon shook their head, dispelling whatever thoughts were creeping in. They were silent for so long, Renna thought that was the end of their story. But then they continued, "One morning I woke up and she was gone. She'd left a note that said: *If I can help, I must. Please understand. I'll return when the time is right.*" They cracked their knuckles, mouth twisted to the side. Conflict was etched on their face, like they knew they didn't have a right to fault Briar for doing what she saw fit, same as they had. But reason and logic did not always play well with matters of the heart.

Renna ached for her friend. And for Briar, the priestess with the white-streaked midnight hair who had helped Renna escape.

Little Jon cleared their throat. "I'd not seen or heard from her until you showed up with that necklace. I guess I shouldn't be surprised that she's woven herself into the fabric of the rebellion inside the castle walls." Pride and yearning flashed across their face, gone so quickly that Renna wondered if she'd imagined it.

They let silence fall over them again, Renna turning over all the information she'd just learned. It was like trying to understand the war table back in the castle. Everyone's lives were just one large game of chess, everything connected: the increase in the Tithe, Briar sending her to find Little Jon, the bloody Night Watchman sheriff. It seemed that right now, only the Falsehoods knew all the pieces on the board.

"I should have told you where I came from. I'm sorry." Renna's voice was ragged.

Little Jon sighed heavily. "I don't hold it against you. I understand all too well wanting to let the past stay buried."

Renna frowned, pieces of conversation falling together in her mind. "That very first time you brought Much and me through the wards, someone said you'd been out looking for owls."

A smile tugged at Little Jon's mouth. "The trees told me I was meant to find an owl that day. You just weren't the one I was expecting. I suppose we should go collect the Watchman. I threatened him with a slow death by root strangulation if he left that spot."

Renna let out a choked noise. "He isn't tied up anymore?"

The druid shrugged far too casually for the severity of the conversation and situation.

As they returned to the clearing, Draic climbed to his feet, watching Renna like one would eye a skittish animal. When she'd thought him just the Night Watchman, she'd spoken to him candidly and without reserve. A part of her was embarrassed by that now, but another part felt relieved that there was one fewer pretense to keep up.

His eyes roved her face, dipped again to her throat, tension bracketing his mouth. Then he said gruffly, "I am sorry for the role I've played in all this. Up until the crucible, I thought you were a part of the treachery rampant in Loxley. I'm sorry, Ren."

"And that's supposed to make me like you, is it?"

His laugh was devoid of joy. "I don't give two pricks of blood if you like me. I am not here to make friends. I am barely here to make allies."

The matter-of-fact dismissal cut deeper than it should have. "Then why *are* you here? And if everyone thought you dead, why return to Loxley at all?"

"I told you that day in Nottingham: retribution against those who have wronged me."

That horrible tour through the poorest parts of her kingdom. It seemed like it had happened in another life. At the time, Renna had thought he meant that he wanted revenge on the vedra, but now she heard the words with fresh understanding. Garen Draic was not looking to punish witches. He wanted to punish the throne, the church, everyone in power who was responsible for the lies the people of the kingdom were fed.

Draic looked between her and Little Jon before continuing, "Frankly, you have been little more than a thorn in my side, and I would prefer that you were not part of the equation at all. But the Falsehoods seem to agree that the chances of getting Ulrik off the throne are significantly higher if they have the support of the rightful queen. And they're particularly interested in whatever magic you possess that would deem such a threat to the usurper king."

Renna had been saved only so the Falsehoods could use her to gain the throne, like another pawn in a chess game. Was that her only value to people outside this forest? But Draic was wrong about one thing: she did not have any magic, new or old. And when they discovered that, what use would she be to them? She had no crown, no power, no kingdom.

There is a darkness inside you.

"I don't want the crown," she said.

"What you want is of little consequence to me." Draic's words twisted something low in her gut, wringing her out. "But you used to say that everything you did was for your people. Or have you forsaken them as well as yourself?"

Flames of anger rippled across her collarbones. "Forsaken them? I left to protect them. I bled *at your hand* for them."

"Yes. And now I'm asking you to fight for them."

Renna leaned close, her voice low and deadly. "You don't get to ask that of me, Garen Draic."

Little Jon finally broke the tense standoff by holding the blindfold out to Draic once more. "I wager that the full tale will be easier to digest over food and a fire. Shall we?"

Renna steered Draic through the thick wall of hawthorns, avoiding the arm-length thorns that reached for them greedily as the way opened before them. Some of the thorns looked ancient, stained with dried blood. Finally the Thorne Crown parted and Rowan Reach opened before them.

Scarlet, Alaini, and Much sat on the stumps around the fire and jumped up at the sight of them. Scarlet's shrewd gaze took in the blindfold, Draic's clothes, and the additional weapons Renna and Little Jon now wore. Much crossed to them in a few strides, hand on the hilt of his short sword, Kit winding around his legs. Alaini, holding back her usual quips, took in Renna's face, no doubt puffy from tears. Renna's heart squeezed, a sigh of relief rippling through her body. Her friends were like the thorns surrounding the camp: fierce and lethal, ready to protect what they loved, forged from magic, and bound together with blood.

Her thorns. Despite its sentimentality, the term warmed her through.

Draic's breathing stuttered as she removed the blindfold.

"Wait a second, isn't that—"

"—the Night Watchman?"

"—the bloody *high sheriff*?"

In the stunned silence that followed, Draic looked them each in the eye, one by one. "I'd wager you lot would like to hit Loxley where it hurts. I'd like to be the one to facilitate that."

CHAPTER 22

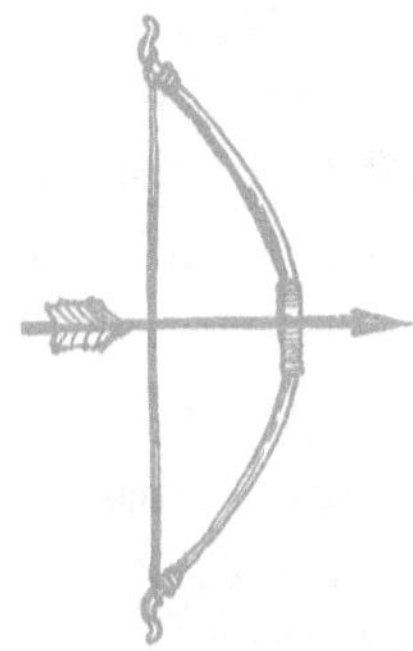

DRAIC WISELY REMAINED QUIET AFTER THIS PRONOUNCEMENT WHILE LITTLE JON EXPLAINED THE SITUATION AS SUCCINCTLY AS THEY COULD.

The high sheriff was indeed the Night Watchman, and he was working with the Falsehoods, the organized group of witches in Wendsvik that was currently fighting Loxley's army. He had contact with the priestess Briar Jain, the acquaintance of Little Jon's inside the palace walls who'd given Renna the carved owl with the instruction to find the druidhen. And he wanted them to break into the royal treasury during the upcoming ball and "steal right from under their crooked, noble noses."

Not for the first time, Renna was in awe at how Little Jon's vote of confidence was good enough for those in Rowan Reach to temporarily withhold their judgment. There was a strange dance of normalcy as supper was prepared. Much and Little Jon fussed over the stew, adding various herbs and spices. The youngsters passed out bowls, stealing sidelong glances at Draic. Edwine poured hearty amounts of apple mead into the collection of mismatched mugs (ones carved from wood or antlers, others made from clay, chipped porcelain, or dented tin). Baz was the closest in size to Draic, but even his forest-green tunic was tight across the Watchman's broad shoulders and arms. Draic had shucked off his rain-soaked tunic right there next to the fire, the hard muscles of his stomach disappearing into the waistband of his trousers. His skin was moon pale against the dark ink across his chest and shoulders. Without his sheriff uniform or Night Watchman cloak, with his white-blond hair falling across his forehead, he almost looked harmless. A blade with blunted edges.

It was disconcerting.

Night fell quickly, and Renna was selfishly grateful when most people went to bed after dinner, tired from a day of setting traps and preparing for the solstice. Now only Scarlet, Much, Alaini, Little Jon, Bazyli, Asher, and herself sat around the hearthtree with the Watchman. An expectant hush fell over the grove, anticipation weaving around them. The fire popped in the silence. Draic's brows drew together, a deep V forming, then he spoke.

"When I was first sent to the battlefront, I learned a great many things rather quickly. As I'm sure you're aware, throughout the rest of Dravmir there aren't the same prejudices against the magics not sanctioned by the church. No one with witch blood is hunted or punished. For the first time in my life, the truth felt… harder to grasp."

The firelight danced across Draic's face, his features alternating between harsh and soft as he told them how adamant the church was that only the Mother's chosen be sent to battle. He had been told that the vedra influence was greater so far from the Mother's Flame. So feeling ill at ease and having doubts was to be expected—a test of your righteousness. To voice those thoughts aloud would have been heretical. When his troop was taken captive by the Falsehoods, he assumed that he and all his men would be put to death. Instead, they were kept as prisoners for half a year. In that time, they saw with their own eyes that the vedra did not always pose a threat. Witches, druidhen, and non-magical people were able to live side by side peacefully.

"Sometimes they kept us tied up outside, forced us to watch the way the world operated in Wendsvik. There was this large wall they would chain us to on the outskirts of one of the villages—they dressed us up like Falsehood soldiers receiving punishment so that no one loyal to Loxley would try to aid us. A skirmish happened one day, and the entire neighboring town was set ablaze by troops from Loxley. I heard women and children screaming for what felt like hours.

"Loxley's army had been so sure of their claim, they didn't even bother to occupy the city. Just set it on fire, hoisted the church's flag, and left. It was the middle of the night, and when the fire died down to embers, I saw shadowed figures coming out of the rubble. Maybe a dozen people limped away from the ashes. I discovered later that they were mostly children. I don't know when Loxley's troops set a trap—perhaps even days before the siege—but nearly twenty armed red clerics emerged from a covered trench and started attacking them, slaughtering three instantly."

Draic's haunting words held them all in thrall. Loxley soldiers lying in wait to kill defenseless children? Renna was horrified, just like when she'd seen the boy in the stocks in Nottingham. *I did not order this.* She should have tried harder to understand what was happening in her kingdom, what was being done under her name. Bitter anger and self-loathing filled her.

"Then, one by one, the clerics start falling, black-tipped arrows sprouting from their throats, their eyes, their hearts. The Night Watchman rode in, leading a few other Falsehood rebels, and killed the rest of the soldiers. He gathered up the injured, buried the dead with final rites, and burned the church's flag when he was done.

"Up until that moment, I had thought that everything I had done was justified, that I was fighting the good fight. But seeing the Night Watchman do the things I told myself I was doing…I realized I was the monster, not him. Not them."

Horror and sorrow and anger simmered in those silver eyes, mirroring Renna's own.

"Soon after that, we were given a choice: defect and fight with the vedra, or die for the lies of the throne. It was the easiest decision of my life. What followed was more than a year of rigorous training in espionage and unlearning the web of lies Loxley had spun. I worked my way up in the ranks until I could request to train with the Night Watchman—he was the fourth man to wear the mask and hold the title, and he was looking to retire to a less dangerous role. My background in combat, my proficiency with mettlemancy, and my old position as high sheriff meant I could be a valuable spy for the Falsehoods.

"When my training was complete, my objective was to reestablish myself in Loxley. I contacted other Falsehoods spies within the castle walls and kept tabs on what was happening; if I sowed seeds of doubt, when the time was right, Loxley would be ripe to fall. For some time, the Falsehoods have suspected that there is something sinister at play in Loxley. Most witches who make it out find their powers easier to access after a detox period."

Renna exchanged a glance with Much, wondering if he too was recalling their conversation about how his powers had felt weaker inside the castle walls, how he was only able to learn to control his wind-walking once he had been in Wendsvik.

Draic's eyes locked on to Renna's again. "Briar was adamant that you didn't know what was really going on. That you were just as much a victim of Loxley as anyone else. So I watched you."

She felt everyone's attention on her like a scorching brand. *Stop*, she wanted to say. But the truth had to come out, like the tide rushing in to cover everything, changing the landscape into something new entirely. Every interaction with Draic in the castle surged in her mind. When she'd thought he was attempting to expose her vedra blood, he'd been trying to determine if he could trust her, to determine whose side she was on.

"The Falsehoods learned that the Head Trissaia and his consort had learned to stifle the magics they saw as undesirable. It's a tricky bit of old magic known only to a few, utilizing runes carved into aurem. There was something odd about the way your finnikfire manifested. You were able to burn only when Nastasia was with you."

No. No, surely he was mistaken. But even as she thought it, doubt crept in.

Draic reached into his boot. A sliver of gold, barely the size of Renna's thumb, flickered between his fingers in the firelight. An inexplicable recognition twisted low in her gut. Renna shook her head as if to stop his words. Stop what was coming. She'd known her identity would have to come out, but not like this. Not wrapped up in this horrific revelation. Draic shifted closer to the fire, all pretense of speaking to the others abandoned, as if he and Renna were the only two souls in the woods.

"The aurem they placed under your skin during the ritual simultaneously dampened your true powers and hid the fact that you were unable to wield finnikfire. This," he held the aurem up, "allowed Nastasia to channel her finnikfire to you."

"I don't believe you," Renna said.

"You do not have to like the truth for it to be so."

He might as well have slapped her. *The most powerful truths are the ones hardest to say and to hear.* The world tilted as she stood, her head tingling. She stumbled backward.

Draic rose as well and spoke louder. "Did you know Nastasia has been made a Keeper? She climbed through the ranks at alarming speed after you abdicated."

Abdicated.

The word rang out, reverberating like a strung gong. Her friends' faces were a strange tableau of concern, anger, and confusion. Renna flinched. She felt like she was underwater, all their words distorted and far away. She was a liar and a coward. Why had she thought she could belong here? The least she could do was to be honest with them before they cast her out.

Sounds of the night swirled around them: crickets and the whisper of leaves. A squirrel chittered, climbing a trunk, then disappeared into the leaves. She envied the animal. Steeling herself against the ax that was about to fall, she spoke.

"I am…I *was* the heir to the throne. I thought I could just forget that life, but I realize now just how unfair that is to all of you. I know the suffering that has happened at my command and in my name, but…" Her throat closed and hot tears burned behind her eyes. "I am sorry. I understand if you want me to leave."

Like all children of noble or royal birth, Renna had received her Foretelling when she was twelve—a holy number. It was the only time one gave a tithe from anywhere other than the inside of the forearm—unless you were the crown princess who harbored vedra blood, she thought darkly, picturing the scars on her back. The scars on her palm reminded Renna of two crescent moons. She liked the idea of having the moon on her body and had said as much to Ulrik before her ceremony. He'd looked at her sharply, eyes narrowed as if trying to see if she spoke in jest.

"It is not the moon, child. The broken circle reminds us that without the Mother, we can never truly be whole."

Ulrik had carved the broken circle into her palm before pressing her bleeding hand to the large oval disc of aurem, the sacred scrying plate used only for official Foretellings. The wait between her hand being cut and Ulrik's eyes glazing over and the words of her Foretelling passing through his lips had been the longest, most excruciating moments of her life.

Until now. Renna pressed her thumb into her scarred palm, hating how her chin trembled. Everything was blurred by the tears brimming in her eyes.

Scarlet finally spoke. "We suspected your lineage, Ren. We didn't know the details, obviously, but we knew you had to be noble."

Alaini blew out a breath, scrubbing a hand over her face. "Bleeding gods, Renna, your cleaning skills are shite in a way that only comes from having money."

A chuckle rumbled through the group, and something like fondness pierced Renna's shield. But she didn't dare breathe until Scarlet added, "The scars you bear commend you, though."

"And your heart," Little Jon said softly.

"Was that done by the king?" Alaini asked, and Renna's hand went to her throat.

The king—it still felt so strange to think of him that way. The truth had been sinking in since finding Draic outside the wards. Ulrik had always known that she was a danger to the kingdom and had gone so far as to tell her that he wouldn't be able to protect her if the people found out about her vedra blood. She'd not thought it possible that he'd ordered her killed, but perhaps he'd seen it as the only way to ensure the safety of the throne.

"If the Watchman is to be believed, it was commanded by the king."

"Do you? Believe him?" Alaini asked.

Draic looked as exhausted as she felt, the dark smudges under his eyes almost like bruises. It was so clear to her now that it had been him competing alongside her at the archery tournament. How had she missed it? He could split an arrow just so, with the technique they'd both learned from Devana. Renna had mistakenly thought that the way he moved reminded her of an animal she couldn't place, but it had reminded her of the insolent sparring partner she'd had all those years ago. That, more than anything else, made her believe him, more than his knowledge of the owl pendant or her Foretelling. She knew it in her bones. Even if she did not understand the complicated threads of everything else that was going on—and there were enough to strangle someone—she knew Draic was speaking the truth.

"I believe him."

Despite Draic's position as high sheriff, he did not know why the Keepers had entered the woods with bloodstone siphons—this was apparently something that fell under the purview of the church. But he did know why the tithe had been increased. A dark look passed over his face as he spoke about the wicked-looking crossbows Renna had seen in the Mother's Flame on the night of the Blood Tithe. It was a weapon forged with a new enhanced aurem that made it possible to load up to ten steel arrows at once and took less than half a breath to reload from a string of arrows being fed into the contraption.

"Bloody gods," Alaini murmured.

"Indeed." Draic's face was grim as he leaned forward on his elbows. "The more uncertainty there is within the walls of Loxley, the less stability the crown has. There has been more unrest in Nottingham, and the dungeons are nearly full. The punishment for vedra sympathizers is now equal to that of being condemned a witch. The people need hope, a display of strength from the rebels. Breaking into the treasury will give them that, as well as depleting the crown's aurem coffers to delay the production of weapons."

The vision from the Oakheart flashed in Renna's mind: people giving too much blood, mangled bodies in the streets. And suddenly they were not just faceless corpses but Alaini, Little Jon, Scarlet. She'd left Loxley to spare her people, had she not? She could not let her new friends put themselves in this kind of danger. But she could see the determination in their eyes, their need to fight.

Draic paused, choosing his words carefully. "There is one more thing. We want you to steal the Tithe."

The thought appalled her for a split second, her strict upbringing rearing its obedient head. Renna quashed it, mortified that even now, after learning about the lies of the church, her body betrayed her mind. As the existential dread spun through her, Little Jon asked why.

"Another crack in the armor of the crown and church."

Again, the blasphemous words scraped against her skin, her emotions warring with one another.

Renna thought of kneeling in the temple, her head throbbing from a prolonged mettlemantic connection. Putting themselves in the king's path would put them all at risk. She had to stop this, and she grasped at the first argument she could think of. "Ulrik is the strongest mettlemancer in Loxley, if not all of Dravmir. There's no way you'll be able to keep him from seeing through your deception, and you'll burn for it. And if we're tied to you, so will we."

Draic's irritation was palpable, turning his words sharp. "If the king is allowed to obtain enough tithe to supply the armory with these new weapons, the entire continent will be in danger. If you think staying in your precious forest will spare you, you're fools." He rubbed the rough stubble shadowing his jaw, seeming to reign in his frustration. Finally, he said, "There are ways to protect your mind: mettlemantic shields, charms, and a ritual that inks protection into your skin."

So the tattoo snaking around his back to his chest and shoulders was a shield against mettlemancy. He began explaining a method that used a spellbound bone sharpened to a point. Understanding dawned on her, dread raising her hackles. "You think I'll ever let you near me with a weapon again?"

Draic studied her, thinking for a moment. "Some amulets can offer lesser protection for a concentrated amount of time. Ulrik will be consumed with the festivities, his mind elsewhere. I suppose those would suffice on this occasion if you'd rather not—"

"Who is to say that the Falsehoods will be any better for Loxley? They can't have purely altruistic motives. Surely they want to seize power for themselves. We might very well be trading one monster for another."

Draic's look said he knew exactly what she was doing. "I'll remind you that the Falsehoods wish to see *you* reinstated—"

"Mutiny in exchange for power may come easily to you, but I wonder how you sleep at night with all that blood on your hands, Sheriff."

For a moment, it was like they were back in the castle's sparring ring and Renna had just landed a blow, only to realize she'd struck too deep. She wished very much that she could take back the words. The glare Draic leveled her with cooled the air, and she braced for a cruel, exacting response. But instead he remained deathly quiet. Shame burned her face.

"The charms, then," Little Jon interceded.

Draic looked at the druid. "I can have them ready within a sennight."

"Assuming we accept your offer." Renna knew she had lost, but she couldn't help herself. He was offering them not only coin but a chance to enact revenge against those who had wronged them for so long. They'd do it, she had no doubt.

"I need an answer by winter solstice to make the appropriate adjustments without arousing suspicion. You can leave a signal for me outside the wards. I'll see it. Each person knowing only what they must and nothing more is how the Falsehoods' movements remain safe and guarded." Then he was rising to his feet. He had to get back to Loxley, to his role as the high sheriff so he gave them instructions on how to signal their choice. As he turned to take his leave, he paused, the line between his shoulders taut like a bow string. He spun back on his heel and crossed to Renna, pressing something into her palm. By the time she realized she was holding the slim piece of aurem that had once been hidden beneath her skin, he was gone.

As promised, the charmed bracelets appeared within a sennight. The Thorns, as Renna had begun calling Much, Little Jon, Alaini, and Scarlet, had left the protection of the wards to check their traps when they spotted the small leather pouch tucked inside a hollow trunk of a hawthorn. Nestled among the braided strands of each delicate metal bracelet sat a black gem. With it was a curt note:

Lishka,

The stone *must* be against the skin.

Eyes will be keeping vigil for solstice.

—Watchman

"Yes, because that's not ominous," Alaini whispered, eyeing the message.

The forest felt more apprehensive as they walked. It was as if it could sense the brewing trouble Draic had mentioned.

They smelled their quarry before they saw them—the reek of blood and sweat and piss made them cover their noses. The trap had been sprung, leaving a large open pit. Two figures in rags lay face down in the dirt a few paces from the gaping hole. They wore clothes too thin for the winter chill, and one of their ankles was twisted at an unnatural angle. Chains secured their legs together. A sharp rock was discarded within reach, and a rope underneath them had been severed.

Weapons drawn, the Thorns approached. At the bottom of the pit were four Keepers, their once-pristine purple robes covered in filth and detritus. They'd cast aside their weapons next to the other half of rope. One appeared to have snapped his neck in the fall, but the others were alive.

Little Jon and Much circled round to check if the prisoners were breathing, but Renna didn't hold hope, given their stillness. They hadn't fallen into the hole but had still been unable to get away. Why? Were their injuries too extensive to run once the rope was cut? Much gently rolled one of the bodies over and swore.

"You knew him?" Little Jon asked gruffly.

Much looked like he'd bitten into something sour. "Aye. A blacksmith in Nottingham. Hadn't a drop of witch blood in his body, but he always looked out for those of us who did. Bastards."

Anger stirred low in her gut as she drew her bow.

"Don't you know these woods are dangerous for righteous followers of the Mother's Flame?" Scarlet called down.

"The Mother protects Her faithful," one of them sneered.

"You definitely look protected," Alaini said, crouching at the edge of the pit. Her fingers danced lightly against her thigh, and some of the roots in the hole lengthened like tiny fingers, reaching toward the Keepers. Renna searched their faces, looking for signs that the trees were affecting them, but aside from what one would expect from people who'd fallen into a hole, they seemed perfectly normal. They didn't even look scared. The difference between these people and the pious believers who'd surrounded her in Loxley left her shaken. How many others did not fear the woods? And why was Ulrik sending them here?

"Why don't you tell us what you're doing in our forest, and we might see about hoisting you out of there," Little Jon drawled, leaning on their quarterstaff.

One of the Keepers whispered something to their companions, eyes locked on the crystal atop the druid's staff. Then, louder, said, "We would rather Silence ourselves than help a couple of filthy vedra."

"We can arrange that," Much growled.

Easy, we need them alive, Alaini signed, and Renna was glad for all the time she'd spent practicing talking with Sif. She found she much preferred this way of privately communicating to mettlemancy.

Much followed her lead and signed back, *They're a bunch of murderers.*

But you're not, Renna argued. Her throat was uncomfortably tight as she remembered Yana's tongue being removed. The thought of Much staining his own hands was abhorrent. *Little Jon, could you use clairvel touch on them?*

The druid nodded before calling down, "We have other ways of getting the information we need."

The Keepers looked at one another, eyes blazing, no doubt speaking through mettlemancy, and Renna realized their misstep with a jolt. *Shit.* She cried out, as if she could stop what was about to happen. In unison, three ritual blades were unsheathed, and crimson blood gushed as they all drew the edges across their throats.

CHAPTER 23

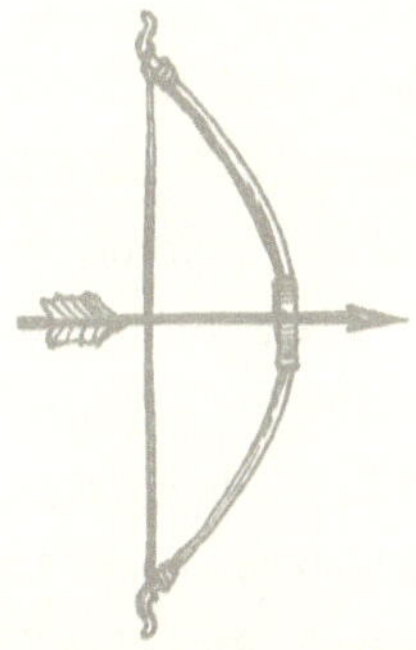

THE INCIDENT WITH THE KEEPERS HAD LEFT THEM WITH NO NEW INFORMATION, AS IT TURNED OUT THE CLAIRVEL TOUCH COULD ONLY BE USED ON AN OBJECT TIED TO SOMEONE LIVING. What they did know was that the circumstances in Loxley were becoming more dire.

Much had insisted they bring back the bodies of the two prisoners. They buried them in a small meadow, one with a weeping willow that dipped into a pond dotted with lily pads and lotus flowers. Little Jon's words echoed in her mind. *Living in perpetual spring and fall can make one forget the existence of winter and darkness.*

On the morning of the winter solstice, Renna buzzed with nervous anticipation for the day ahead. The celebration would be that evening, including a bonfire and a ceremony under the Oakheart, but more importantly, they would each choose if they would accept Draic's offer or not. Renna and Little Jon had emerged from the cold water of the river and sat in meditative silence for several minutes. Renna let the Velmir and the lingering effects from the bracing cold ground her as she pulled out the piece of aurem Draic had left her with. She'd not spoken of it since that day, only pulling it out in the privacy of her room to study it. But she had to know. Without a word, she passed it to Little Jon.

"Are you sure?"

Renna nodded.

Little Jon closed their eyes, breathing deeply, fingers curling around the aurem. The muscles on their neck tightened and they flinched as they used their magic. All Renna could hear was her own heartbeat. Then, as if it had turned scalding, Little Jon dropped the aurem onto the grass.

It felt like tiny thorns were digging into her skin. Sorrow and fury burned bright in Little Jon's eyes.

"It's…that has been heavily cloaked with dark magic, Ren. I couldn't…it was hard to see clearly, but it was enough to know that it was as Draic said: it was repressing your magic and was connected to other aurem."

Her questions were stuck in her throat, but must have been plain on her face, because they rushed on to say, "I cannot say for sure if it was connected to Nastasia, or someone else. Or if the other person was even aware, but…" Little Jon shook their head, then pulled Renna into a tight hug. "I'm so sorry, Ren."

She had never truly wielded finnikfire. Or mettlemancy. Her bitter laugh came out more like a soft sob. It was only after the ritual when she was sixteen that her magic had developed. While she'd bled on that altar, thinking she'd be cured of her vedra blood, Ulrik and Gisborne had been ensuring that she'd have the appearance of a finnik.

There was something odd about the way your finnikfire manifested. You were able to burn only when Nastasia was with you.

Her mind replayed the memory of the dungeon: the wrenching sensation she'd thought was Draic trying to torture her, to draw out her suffering, had been him removing the aurem that now lay on the grass.

Little Jon gave her one final squeeze before they broke apart. She breathed in the smell of pine and wildflowers and dirt, watching the river. Little Jon's words from the night they showed her the Oakheart came to her. *Hard to be free of something you've chained yourself to.* Gods, she wanted to feel free of it all. Renna sniffed, plucking the aurem up, letting it catch the light. Softly, she asked, "What if I don't have the magic they think I possess?"

Little Jon leaned back on their palms, tipping their face to the sun. "You are allowed to take time to discover it for yourself."

Not really an answer, but it soothed some of her anxiety, nonetheless. "I don't want to be chained to it anymore." And with that, Renna tossed the aurem into the river, letting the water wash it away.

When they returned, Baz sprinkled cinnamon into her kaffi, marking the day with a festive feel. Even Asher's stilted nod of acknowledgement felt like a good omen. (He'd been the most upset by the revelation of her identity, but time was helping to heal the wound.) Much and Alaini's usual good-natured bickering was in fine form throughout all of breakfast.

"You're so full of shit, Much."

"You've never played a real game with actual stakes!"

"Oh, don't bring up Carrion Kings again, I beg you—"

Scarlet tossed down a thin stack of rectangles made of bark. "The only way we're getting to the bottom of this is to put your words to the test, Much."

"Scarlet, you clever minx. Have you made us a deck of cards?" Alaini's face split into a grin.

Each strip of bark had a design painted on it. Scarlet's fingertips were the same dark blue and red that stained the bark, and Renna recalled the paints the woman had purchased in Wendsvik. "Happy solstice. Now shut up and put your coin where your mouth is."

After Much soundly kicked Alaini's ass at Carrion Kings, Renna enlisted his help baking fancy scones with cream frosting for everyone. It was the only thing from her past that she knew how to cook and her heart squeezed at the memory of Yana. She hoped she was doing well. Gifts were exchanged at an unhurried pace: Renna received a tiny whittled fox from Little Jon; Edwine had knitted something for each of them; Baz set up a new tightrope course; Sif wove flower crowns; Alaini had gotten Scarlet a secondhand fiddle, which she tried her hand at while Alaini plucked the lute. Tora strung together gilding for Alita and Kit—the former preened while grazing nearby; the latter refused any such decor.

When twilight came, they went to the Oakheart's meadow. Again, Renna was overwhelmed with the sense of being near something sacred. She went to the tree, knelt reverently, placed a hand on the roots, and whispered hello. Little Jon used a golden sickle to cut down mistletoe from the tree, passing small clusters to everyone. They drank hot cinnamon cider and crafted wreaths, which they strung in the surrounding trees.

Floating lights descended in the meadow. Renna's breath caught as she realized they were tiny flying creatures with long, thin bodies just bigger than an index finger, spikes along their spines, and forked tails with sharp points on the ends. The creatures' wings were thin membranes shaped like leaves that glowed like fireflies. One landed on Renna's shoulder. Its body was covered in miniscule deep blue scales, and its eyes were intelligent. Three flew around Kit's head, and he frolicked after them.

"Dragonfae," Little Jon explained, wonder playing across their face as well. "Ancestor of the dragonfly, but extinct outside of the wards."

On a low table they spread honey cakes, apples dipped in honey and brown sugar, loaves of cinnamon-drizzled sweet bread, scones dripping with cream, mead, and berry wine. The twins, Kaja and Vanya, handed out sparkling torches to everyone, the tiny bursts of fire making shadows and glowing trails as they all danced around. They lit the bonfire, the flames dancing to twice Renna's height against the dark sky. Much played hide-and-seek with Sif and Tora, and though his wind-walking was technically cheating, the girls didn't seem to mind; they enjoyed the added challenge. He flickered into existence near Renna, bent over and breathing hard.

"We are going to need to work on your endurance, Much," Renna teased, placing a crown of holly on his head.

This sparked the familiar discussion of what to call the training rig, for every great training course should have a name, shouldn't it? Alaini and Baz were set on the Albatross, while the youngsters liked the Gauntlet. Little Jon insisted it should be called the Trial of Trees, which everyone else agreed was much too corny. Little Jon placed their hands on their hips, looking spectacularly ridiculous with their three crowns of holly, the scarf Edwine had knitted, and their mouth stained dark with berries and mead. Alaini stopped playing the lute to emphasize that it sounded like something out of a bard's song, which meant it was out of the question.

"Aren't you a bard?" Much asked.

"I prefer minstrel."

"Why?"

"It makes the ladies think of the other types of *ministrations* I'm skilled at." She gave a wicked grin and wiggled her fingers. The group laughed and groaned in unison, and Alaini began to play once more, this time a reeling tune. Soon everyone was dancing, spilling wine as they changed partners and tripped over their feet. The moon drifted high in the sky, their veins warm with drink and hearts full of contentment.

The night wore on, and the twins took over the instruments, playing a ballad Renna had never heard. Alaini pulled her down to sit by the fire, the heat on their faces and the cool air at their backs. She pressed a wrapped book into Renna's hands. "This one has a particularly swoon-worthy love interest. Broody, tall, morally grey."

Eventually the conversation and singing died down, crickets and dragonfae offering the only noises. There was an undercurrent of apprehension in the group's silence as Little Jon pulled out the pouch that contained the charmed bracelets. The time had come. They'd all agreed that everyone would have a choice. Whoever took one tonight was agreeing to break into Loxley.

Alaini reached for the pouch first. "I hardly need a reason to put on a disguise and cause some chaos for the bastards in Loxley."

A ripple of laughter went through the group, easing some of the tension in Renna's body. Apart from Edwine and the youngsters, everyone took one of the amulet bracelets. When her turn came, Renna hesitated, staring at the pouch.

Blood running down her front.

A cracked piece of aurem at her feet.

Her finnikfire extinguished.

Not worthy not worthy not worthy.

Much's voice may as well have been thunder for how it jolted her. "You aren't doing this as the fallen Koravik princess. You are joining this fight as a nameless hooded outlaw like the rest of us."

While some of the others had turned their attention to securing their bracelets or gazing at the Oakheart, Renna's Thorns were looking at her, determination in their eyes. Her friends knew her well. They understood her fears and the vulnerable parts she tried to hide, and they did so without being inside her head every hour of every day. Gods, they'd hardly batted an eye when her past had been revealed.

Renna swallowed against the sudden emotion in her throat and withdrew a bracelet, the smooth stone cool to the touch.

Little Jon produced an acorn the size of Renna's fist, and they took turns carving letters into it. Renna's hands trembled as she made the final stroke. NO TITHE TO TYRANTS: an oath, a promise, a declaration. A sense of purpose began to thrum in her veins as they placed the talisman outside the wards. It remained as they returned to the meadow, the atmosphere shifting from careful apprehension to rowdy relief and excitement. Alaini jumped up on a boulder, raising her glass high, offering up a toast. There under the moon and the Oakheart, bathed in the glow of the fire and the dragonfae flitting around, they all chanted the words: no tithe to tyrants.

CHAPTER 24

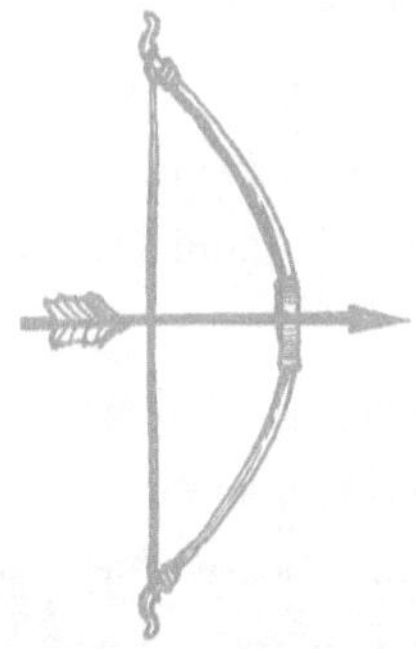

ALL IN ALL, IT TOOK THREE SEPARATE TRIPS TO WENDSVIK TO PROCURE THE DISGUISES FOR THE MASQUERADE, USING THE COIN DRAIC HAD LEFT IN THE HAWTHORN AFTER THEY AGREED TO HIS PLAN.

They had long days of training in archery, hand-to-hand combat, and agility. They'd not caught any more Keepers in the forest, though they had ambushed a few just outside Wendsvik, leaving them tied up, gagged, and relieved of their coffers.

With the increase in tithes there would be a considerable amount of bloodstone siphons in the royal treasury along with coin. Renna sketched maps of the castle from memory, and the crew spent hours studying them. The Mother's Flame was at the base of the castle. The treasury was located one level above it, across from the library. Renna had been to the treasury once when she was younger, but the memory was hazy.

"The vault is charmed to respond to royal blood," Ulrik had said as the two of them entered the small antechamber to the treasury. "You will soon be the key to the Mother's Flame."

Renna had swallowed her questions—she'd wanted to take some of the burden that Ulrik had carried since her parents' death. Her crescent-moon scars wept, her palm slick with blood. Then they were inside the treasury, mounds of aurem coins filling the cavern. Heat had licked at her from the end of the expansive room, fierce shadows on the cavern wall. Something had lurked at the edge of her vision, but she hadn't been able to turn her head.

The memory faded there, distorted as if obscured by fog before shifting back into focus as Ulrik said, "—won't remember, but it is necessary."

"All right there, Hood?"

Renna jumped as Alaini poked her head into her room. Her friend gave a low whistle, looking down. "Your room is much higher up than I realized. How do you not get dizzy?"

Renna shrugged. "I don't look down."

"Got your cloak for you…" Alaini trailed off, eyeing the maps and books covering the floor.

There were pages upon pages detailing the magical properties of each tree, the way to properly brew herbs to soothe menstrual cramps, enhance memory, draw out poison from a wound. Scarlet had been teaching her, as well as Little Jon. Most elixirs had to be meticulously brewed, but Renna enjoyed the challenge of creating something with her hands. She had to be exact to brew a serum that would render clothing resistant to fire, and the required focus did more to soothe her mind than most things.

Study and practice she could control—that was power in and of itself. It kept her from spending her nights full of sleepless anxiety, wondering if she'd ever be deemed worthy to receive magic.

"No, don't stop on my account," Alaini said when Renna made to clear a path. "Here." She tossed the cloak and Renna caught it easily. "You ready for tomorrow?" Alaini asked.

Renna ran her fingers along the cloak's hem, feeling the new stitches. "Are you?"

Alaini puffed up her chest, her tone dripping with sarcasm. "Oh yeah, can't wait to go back. Visit all the people and places I've missed."

Renna smiled weakly. Tomorrow she would be breaking into what used to be her home. Thinking about Nastasia made her hands grow clammy. She knew she couldn't try to talk to her—it was too dangerous—but still…

"Hey." Alaini cut through her spiraling thoughts like a knife through butter. She smiled. "We got your back, Ren."

They began the journey in staggered groups of two or three: Baz and Asher first, then Kaja and Vanya, followed by Little Jon and Much. Scarlet, Alaini, and Renna brought up the rear.

With the tide out, the trade highway spanned the miles of marshy land between the edge of Sherwood and the walls around the kingdom. The road was filled with people from Loxley's annexed villages, coming for the masquerade. The wind whipped the hem of Renna's dress and pulled at her hair. She felt dangerously exposed. The castle loomed high overhead, spires of black and aurem piercing the twilight sky as the throngs of people carried her and her Thorns closer to the checkpoint for entry.

Renna adjusted the mask she'd picked out at the shop in Wendsvik. The fox face was crafted from amber, orange, and white feathers, shifting to darker browns at the ears. The back of her gown had a high stiff collar, but it dipped low in front, revealing more cleavage than she was used to. A thick strip of velvet covered the scars on her throat. Long slits on either side of the skirt allowed her legs to move freely and gave her access to a dagger surreptitiously strapped to her thigh and the other tucked inside her boot. Under her cloak, her arms were bare, lean, and muscled from her time in Sherwood. But most striking was her hair. Scarlet had helped comb red and ginger dyes through the strands, and it haloed around her head and fell to the middle of her back. Renna hardly recognized herself.

Like autumn personified, she'd thought as she'd donned the fox mask.

"I feel like chattel," Alaini hissed beside Renna, adjusting her wolf mask. All around them were masked revelers in various states of inebriation.

"Well, you don't look it, love." Scarlet, in a dark violet gown and a raven mask, eyed Alaini's deep emerald dress that hugged her torso before flaring gently at her hips.

Alaini waved a hand, craning her neck to see ahead on the road. "Obviously. But must we move so slowly? I don't like being stuck in a crowd like this."

"I doubt it will feel much better inside." Even as she said it, Renna recalled the press of bodies during the Fire Feast, the crowded corridors, and the cloying silence of the temple. She touched the charmed amulet on her wrist, taking a steadying breath. The enchantment on each bracelet was set to activate from now until tomorrow. The castle dominated the horizon, the domed oculus already visible. Alaini squeezed her hand but didn't say anything, and Renna was grateful. She didn't know how to explain everything she was feeling and wasn't sure she could speak about it without losing her nerve entirely.

As they neared the entry point, the atmosphere pulled strangely, a sharp twist in Renna's gut making her queasy. An ache built behind her eyes. Scarlet sucked a breath through her teeth, clutching at her side. Renna caught only a glimpse of what had alarmed the other woman before Scarlet tugged her cloak shut. The glamoured wand strapped to her hip had begun flickering in and out of view. With an impressive sleight of hand, Scarlet crouched down under the guise of fixing her boot. The worn leather came up to her knee, and she tucked the wand into it, out of sight.

There was no time to address what had happened. The guard ahead shouted orders, and the line of people split into two. To the left, a guard stood by a large palanquin of bloodstone siphons and aurem coins; to the right was a small tent with a pair of Keepers outside. The tang of copper filled Renna's nose.

They were taking tithes as payment for entrance.

In the pocket of her cloak were the bloodsiphons they'd nicked from the Keepers. Her rationale warred with her upbringing, trying to untangle the knotted threads of who she was and what she believed. A part of her whispered that she was damning herself, but the thought of giving a tithe now made her recoil, so Renna wordlessly paid their fee with the stolen goods. With barely more than a glance at their faces, the guards took the offerings and waved them on. And then they were walking through the archway cut into the thick battlement wall, and into Loxley.

Renna was grateful that her mask obscured the horror that was surely painted on her face as she took in Nottingham as if with new eyes.

Debris blocked doorways and filled alleys. Watermarks stained the stone walls with dark bands of algae. There must have been flooding recently, though some of the waterlines on the walls looked old. No one seemed to mind the large brackish puddles marking the roads; they waltzed through the muck, water soaking their clothes, without a moment's hesitation. The air reeked of dampness and mold, mingling with the usual blood smell and the stink of sweat. There was a bloated corpse discarded in a darkened archway and Renna had to stifle a gag. She itched to confer with her friends but didn't dare use sign language here where anyone could see. Conditions improved marginally as they traveled up toward the castle, but still nothing quite matched her memories of this place. It was as if something had been peeled away. Their newly reinforced cloaks kept out the chill, but Renna crossed her arms over her chest, repressing a shiver.

When they breached the noble sector, the cleanliness was jarring. The three of them spread out, blending into the sea of people. The stone staircase that wound around the outside of the fortress was just ahead. The Hallowed Walk. Renna counted the steps, focusing on keeping her balance, her hand trailing across the grooves on the weathered wall.

One thousand, four hundred and nineteen.

One thousand, four hundred and twenty.

Her nerves hardened as she finally reached the top. She'd never noticed how the main archway yawned open like the mouth of a beast: the thick spikes on the portcullis its teeth, the stench of blood in the air the carrion in its belly.

"Spare aurem for the poor, mum?" Much looked like he'd rolled around in the dirt, every inch the beggar he was pretending to be. He'd torn his shirt in a few places and run his hand through his hair enough that it stuck out at unkempt angles. He held out a dented tin bowl. His quarterstaff was tucked under his elbow as if it was merely a walking cane, stained to look like cheap metal instead of the precious oak it was carved from.

A Keeper stood beside the guards to collect an aurem coin from each guest. Renna kept her eyes down as she handed one over. They accepted it without pause, and Renna was admitted. Grief and nostalgia clung to her like tar, weighing down her limbs. The ball was as decadent as Fire Feast; velvet chaise lounges lined the halls, aurem-infused mead flowed in lavish fountains, Trissaia giving personal Foretellings, and musicians playing brass instruments. Couples danced in extravagant gowns and tailored suits, faces hidden behind brightly painted masks. The elaborate spread of food could feed an entire village in Wendsvik for days: skewers of lamb, roasted pork, and potatoes. There was a selection of hard cheese, oysters, and sweet breads dusted with cinnamon and sugar.

Renna plucked up a scone from a neatly piled platter. They were drier than she remembered and needed honey. Brushing the crumbs from her fingers, she moved farther into the castle, keeping to the outer edges of the festivities. The vise around Renna's lungs loosened with the anonymity the mask gave her. They wouldn't move to the lower levels of the castle until closer to midnight. The distractionists for the evening—Asher, Baz, Vanya, and Kaja—had specific instructions about when to set off their fireworks, coordinated with the time Draic had said the guard would change. Renna just needed to remain inconspicuous until then.

She stilled, realizing where she stood.

The throne room.

Memories of the last time she'd been here swooped down on her like dark shadows, scattering her thoughts and intentions. Unconsciously, her hand went to her throat, pressing against the scars hidden by the choker. The high ceilings seemed to be closing in on her. Why had she never noticed how terrible it felt not to have the open sky above her? She'd slept too long under the canopy of leaves and the stars. And now, returning to *this* felt unnatural. Her hands were cold and she wanted to run.

I shouldn't be here. I shouldn't be here.

But fear rooted her to the spot, frozen in time as she saw over and over the bright blood crawling across the stones, staining the floor with her failure. Her heart kicked at her chest like a horse trying to unseat its rider. And then she heard it: the voice she'd once known as well as her own. The same voice that still whispered in the back of her mind, reminding her of her failings.

Nastasia.

Renna craned her head but couldn't see her. She *needed* to see her. Her legs unstuck themselves, and she began moving toward the dais, creeping close to the darkened edges of the room, searching for purple robes.

Did you know Nastasia's been made a Keeper? Draic's words were a taunt. *She climbed through the ranks at alarming speed after you abdicated.*

A familiar laugh pierced through the noise, hitting her like a punch to the gut. There, no more than thirty paces away, near the musicians playing a festive tune that only added to the horror of what she was seeing, stood her cousin.

Nastasia's robes were not the purple of a Keeper, but rather the deep bloodred of a Trissaia.

A feeling like a poison-tipped arrow pierced Renna's heart and spread to her core as she looked at the collar that adorned Nastasia's neck: blood-aurem that enhanced the powers of Trissaia, just like the one Gisborne had shown her a lifetime ago. A rushing filled her ears. This shouldn't have been possible. Nastasia was only just beginning her tenure as a Keeper. It should be years before being anointed was even a possibility.

And yet there she stood.

Unequivocally collared and ordained.

Nastasia's shoulders were straight back, her head tilted so that she could peer down her nose at the fawning acolytes. The faint smile on her lips twisted something in Renna's chest even as hot anger ran up her spine. She slipped behind a cluster of revelers, keeping her chin tucked, watching from afar.

The aurem they placed under your skin during the ritual simultaneously dampened your true powers and allowed Nastasia to channel her finnikfire to you, Draic had said. Renna had tried so hard to bury those words. Now her neck ached as sharply as if she'd just undergone that damned ritual, her hands itching for fire that no longer coursed through her veins.

There was a flash of gold. Renna's focus went to the aurem bracelet wrapped around Nastasia's wrist. Thoughts of the heist rushed from her mind, replaced by urgent need. An invisible tide pulled at her. The music was far too loud. A man approached Nastasia, whispering something in her ear. A low vibration began in Renna's bones as Nastasia dismissed the others and conversed with the guard. Welded at the center of the collar, perched directly over Nastasia's throat, was a bloodstone.

Even if what Draic had said was true, there was an explanation. Nastasia would have done anything to protect and help Renna succeed, even if it meant deceiving her. There was no way Nastasia had known about the attempt on her life. Surely she believed that Renna was safely living out her exile. Her rise in the church was unrelated.

Renna's chest ached with loss, with the cruel fact that they were so near each other but could not be further apart.

Someone pressed a cool pint of ale into her palms. Alaini stepped in front of her, blocking her path, eyes sharp and assessing. The sounds of the hall crashed over her. Panic and relief struck her simultaneously. If she'd gone any nearer to Nastasia, surely she would have revealed her presence. She followed Alaini's lead, retreating to the edge of the room, her pulse loud in her ears. Alaini made a show of shuffling unsteadily through the crowd as she took a swig from her tankard, simultaneously appearing to belong *with* everyone and not *to* anyone, blending in perfectly.

Renna tried to picture the river, reaching for stillness and calm. But instead of remembering the water washing over her, she felt like she was being tossed around by the tumult of her emotions. She brushed a hand over her thigh, touching the hilt of her dagger. Cool condensation gathered on her mug, and Renna clutched it tighter.

A group of Keepers jostled her, giggling. "I hope the Mother favors me like that one day. Did you see the betrothal ring? Her life is a dream come true."

"You, as favored as Trissaia Nastasia?" The other girl laughed with a nasty cutting tone.

"Come, now, don't be mean."

"Your idea of a dream come true is being married to the high sheriff?"

The floor turned to quicksand, shifting underfoot, inexorably pulling Renna down.

"Have you seen him?"

"*Yes*, every week at the executions. The man is terrifying."

"Bite your tongue, Sasha, before it's removed."

"He is only keeping our city safe and protecting the Mother's Flame."

The girls disappeared into the crowd, their conversation fading. Anger coiled hot in Renna's chest. Draic and Nastasia, betrothed? There was no time to examine the reason behind her reaction right now.

Alaini all but pushed Renna toward the wall. "Don't. I know that look."

"I don't have a look," Renna snapped, eyes scouring the crowd.

Alaini pulled her close as if to dance, her voice dropping even lower. "We must maintain our facades. We don't have all the information. It's possible he… did a switch…like before."

It clicked, then, that Alaini was referring to the weekly executions, not the betrothal. She was indicating that perhaps Draic was swapping out the innocent vedra prisoners and replacing them with actual criminals. Shame sprouted in Renna like thorns, but before she could say anything, Alaini added, "Keep your wits about you, this is a viper's den," and slipped off.

Easier said than done. Renna struggled to keep all the thoughts clamoring for attention tamped down. She kept checking for the moon in the oculus, but time mocked her, slowing to a snail's pace. The heat was too much, and she wanted to rip her cloak off, but she didn't dare for fear of drawing attention to the enhancements they'd made before leaving Sherwood.

The revel was deteriorating to new levels of debauchery; the air was ripe with the smells of alcohol, sweat, and sex. The constant brush of people against her, the way the music increased in speed and volume, was stifling. Renna darted down a lesser-known hallway, desperate for a chance to breathe. She leaned against the wall, savoring the chill of the stones, pressing her palms flat against them to keep them from shaking.

The image of Nastasia in Trissaia robes would not leave her mind.

Alaini was right—she needed to focus. Lethal danger lurked all around them.

After a few slow breaths, Renna's spine straightened with resolve, and she made her way back down the hall. She didn't see the figure materializing from the shadows to grab her until it was too late. She tried to reach for her dagger as she was dragged back into the darkened alcove, but her attacker spun, slamming her back against the wall and pinning her wrist above her head. His other hand clamped over her mouth.

"Do you have a death wish, lishka?" The smooth baritone voice cut through her panic, replacing it with fury. She looked up into Draic's face—masked as a wolf—and made out a flash of white-blond hair as her eyes adjusted to the dim light.

"Get off of me," Renna snarled into his palm. Chagrin licked up her spine at the many missteps she'd already made this evening.

His breath was hot on her face, his eyes flashing. "You're not meant to be sneaking around where your presence would raise questions. A patrol is set to come through here any minute."

A crash echoed through the corridor, followed by footsteps and the sound of armor clanking. Several voices spoke over one another. Draic moved swiftly, pressing her deeper into the shadows. Fingers splayed to fit between the grooves of her ribs, his other hand braced on the wall beside her head, blocking her from view.

Unexpected warmth pooled low in her stomach as he bent his head into the crook of her neck. His breath skated across her collarbone as he traced the column of her throat with the tip of his nose. The fingers on her waist squeezed gently. "If you fancy getting caught and burned for treason, then by all means carry on acting like a statue."

The words, murmured against her skin, were rough and low. Renna slid her arms around him, softening. Her heart beat wildly as she tipped her head back, aware that every breath brushed her chest against his.

"You *can* take direction, then."

She raked her nails down his back harder than was necessary.

Draic sucked in sharply, and too late she recalled the lashings he'd endured. The scars he bore. His fingers closed around her wrists and then her arms were pinned up by her head. His voice was strained. "Behave."

The guards were nearing their alcove, talking loudly over the protests of whomever they were escorting. An apology stuck in her throat and she could only nod her understanding. He released her hands and she let them rest on his shoulders. His thumbs brushed against her hip bones as his knee pressed between her legs. When he dipped his head again his scent, like rain and leather, muddled her senses. She slid one hand to the nape of his neck. She thought maybe his open mouth brushed against the hollow of her throat. Her skin tingled in the wake of his touch. Someone whistled. After what felt like an eternity, the voices faded completely. Draic's hand dropped to the slit in her skirt, gently grazing her outer thigh, moving up, up, up…

His fingers closed around her dagger, and in the space of a breath, he'd disarmed her.

The loss of heat from his body was a shock. With a practiced flip, he gripped the dagger so the blade ran parallel to his forearm. A quick hook, and his elbow rested against her solar plexus. Draic clicked his tongue, tapping the flat part of the dagger over her heart for emphasis. Just like he used to do all those years ago in the sparring ring.

Renna shoved him hard, her cheeks flushed and head unmoored, glancing up and down the corridor to ensure that no one else was wandering toward them. "Must you always be such a bastard?"

He didn't reply, just presented the handle of her dagger. Their fingers briefly tangled on the hilt. A line appeared between his brows and his mouth pulled down before he relinquished the weapon. Renna sheathed the dagger on her thigh, tugging her gown roughly down to cover it once again. She flexed her chilled fingers to encourage warmth.

He was still studying her, arms folded across his chest. He wore a black tunic under a jerkin, his dark cape with red stitching over one shoulder. Renna adjusted her cloak, feeling suddenly bare under his scrutinizing gaze. "Stop looking at me like I'm a problem to solve."

Draic's lips quirked to the side. "Oh, you're a problem, but I wouldn't dream of trying to solve you."

His words had a disarming effect, and she fought to regain her footing, then changed the subject. "What does your betrothed think of your split loyalties?"

"I don't much care."

She'd touched a nerve, if his acerbic tone was any indication, but around him she'd never been able to hold her tongue well. Her laugh sounded hollow and forced. "So it is true? You and Nastasia?"

"The betrothal is an unfortunate necessity if my place at court is to remain secure."

"Yes, I'm sure that makes it much more bearable to take her to bed," Renna snapped.

"Are you insinuating that I would bed someone without desire or consent?"

"Murder and treason are on the table—why draw the line at whoring yourself out for a cause?"

The flash in his eyes said she'd gone too far. He leaned closer, bracing a hand on the wall by her head to block her in once more. "What is it that's *actually* bothering you? That I'm not weak-minded enough to be fooled by Nastasia, while you let her bleed the life from you for years? Is this childish behavior simply self-loathing for being too much of a coward to fight back?"

Heat spread through her chest. "You dare to call me a coward when I am here?"

"We both know you wouldn't be if you weren't so afraid of losing your newfound friends. Even when there is dissent among the people, whispers of *your* name, of—" He cut himself off, chest rising and falling rapidly to match her own ragged breathing. Something shifted in his eyes, and he straightened, his stoicism returning, walling off whatever emotions had briefly evaded his control.

Renna pressed her nails into her palms. "So you just conveniently left out this detail last time we spoke?"

"Corruption works quickly. Not all of us have the luxury of remaining clear of it." His words carried a bite, along with exhaustion. "The betrothal was only arranged after she became a Trissaia, which happened *after* solstice. Ulrik has been bringing her to council meetings and conferring with her on matters of the church."

Objecting to such a prestigious match would raise suspicion, she knew.

Draic studied her with grey eyes. "Where are all your merry maidens?"

"Don't call us that." Renna pushed past him, checking that they were still alone in the corridor before unfastening her cloak and turning it inside out.

Draic eyed her now-purple mantle. A chime rang in the distance, marking midnight, and he transformed back into the high sheriff. Cold. Aloof. But his fingers wrapped around her wrist, over the charmed bracelet there, his thumb pressing the cold stone against her skin, as if assuring himself it was there.

"I believe you have somewhere to be, Priestess."

CHAPTER 25

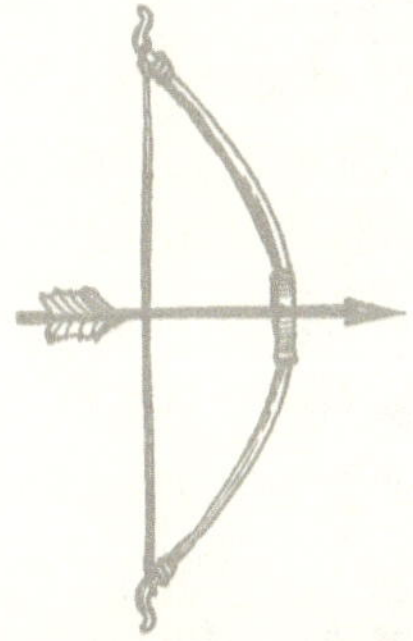

THERE WAS A COMMOTION JUST BEFORE SHE REACHED THE STAIRCASE: A SERIES OF POPPING AND WHIZZING SOUNDS FROM SOMEWHERE NEARBY. The distractionists at work. Guards rushed out of the shadows and up the stairs, spreading through the crowd like spilled ink. Renna kept her head down as she pulled the thick cowl up over her face, seeming like a pious priestess to any onlooker as she took the stairs to the library.

The library and the treasury were located on the same floor. The only level beneath contained the Mother's Flame and the forge, where the aurem mined from the mountain was divided into what would be manufactured (into coins, lanterns, jewelry, building material, and the like) and what would be kept in its raw form (to be burned for fuel or sent to Lord Gisborne for research and development).

The din became muffled, though the revel continued up above. From the corner of her eye, Renna saw Alaini and Scarlet standing near the library doors, cowls in place, and two guards standing opposite by the single entrance to the treasury.

Much came around the bend in the hall, pulling everyone's attention. "Spare aurem for the poor?"

A ripple of unease snaked through the foyer at the disturbance. Renna stayed silent, pressing her lips together tightly, acting as Nastasia would: unwilling to break a Pillar of Truth. She backed up a few steps as Much neared her.

Much waved his bowl in the air. "Too good to speak to a lowly peasant? Not even a word to spare?" He waved his staff, and Renna jumped back to avoid getting hit.

Scarlet peeled away from the library doors. "Bite your tongue."

"*Please.* They won't take me blood no more." He was shrieking now, staggering toward Renna, arms outstretched, tearing at his sleeves to show the pustules marring his skin. Though she knew that the blood sores were merely a reaction to a poultice of herbs Little Jon had made, looking at them in combination with his filthy clothes and frantic begging sent a shudder through Renna.

The guards moved instantly. "You there, stop!"

Much followed Renna as she retreated, drawing the guards away from their post. Alaini and Scarlet scurried to the sides of the hallway, positioning themselves out of the way and behind the guards. Little Jon slipped out from behind a pillar, quarterstaff at the ready.

The guards were too focused on Much to realize they were surrounded. Much reached under the collar of his tunic, yanking up a thick cowl while reaching into his pocket. The glass vial he pulled out was the size of a fist, stoppered with a cork and sealed with wax. A shimmering dark green substance swirled inside.

It had been tedious witchcraft to brew the potion and create the sleeping vapor. Wormwood had to be infused with henbane, mandrake root extract, poppy resin, and moss. They'd moved the boiling cauldron to the willow pond after everyone else had dozed off around the hearthtree. Later, the distilling and separating of the oil and sediment had left everyone a sticky, grumpy mess.

Much spun on his heel toward the guards, now within arm's reach, and threw the vial at their feet. The glass shattered, smoke unfurling around them in a dense cloud.

Hacking coughs filled the air, and Renna pressed her own cowl close to her face, breathing through the soaked material just as Little Jon had instructed. A pinch of camphor, crushed peppermint for alertness, rosemary for remembrance, and pine needles to purify the air. Her nostrils burned and her eyes watered, but when the guards' bodies hit the ground with a thud, she and the others were still conscious.

"Bloody Mother." Much surveyed the guards. "Remind me not to get on your bad side," he said to Little Jon.

"We have only an hour before that wears off. Flip the sand, Scarlet," Little Jon said, dragging one of the limp guards down the hall. Scarlet pulled at a leather thong that hung around her neck and turned the small hourglass upside down to track the time.

Alaini peered at Much's arms. "Those sores are positively gruesome."

"They itch almost as bad as they look," Much replied.

"Help me with his legs."

"Heavy son of a bitch, isn't he?"

"Keep your cowls on," Little Jon instructed as they moved quickly toward the treasury doors. "If someone comes to relieve those guards, I have a few more vials."

It took their combined strength to push open the solid aurem door before they filed into a small inner room, empty except for an aurem pillar that came up to Renna's chest. A single spike rose from the center, rivulets carved into the precious stone.

"What the bloody hell is this?" Alaini hissed. There was a thud followed by, "*Ow.*"

Renna licked her lips, her body tingling. The pillar was a larger version of the ritual daggers that collected blood in siphons. The spike was sharp-edged, allowing the giver to choose a slice or a puncture. Her mind raced, palms sweaty even though her fingers were cold. Would the blood of a fallen royal suffice? Would it cause an alarm to sound? She glanced at the vial of sand around Scarlet's neck. Too many grains had passed through already.

"Truth is in the blood."

The familiar prayer tasted like a lie.

Renna sliced a deep line in her palm. She clenched her fist over the pillar. Her blood ran in a steady drip, filling the carved rivulets. She counted her breaths.

One.

Two.

Three.

On the fourth, the ground rumbled. A deep grinding noise filled the small chamber, and they all moved closer to the center, away from the walls. Renna's pulse skipped as the floor moved, the pillar in the center elongating as they descended into a lower chamber. The moving platform took up nearly the entire floor, leaving only a small ledge by the door above as it came to a halt in the cavernous treasury.

Scarlet's low whistle echoed off the walls as they took in the size of the room, which was carved into the mountain.

"This stretches the entire length of the castle." Much sounded sick.

Blood aurem gems and coins were stacked in large piles, forming rolling hills of gold. Bloodsiphons filled with crimson had been laid out on two large metal pallets—the new offerings that would be thrown into the Mother's Flame at the

Blood Tithe. Normally it would not need to be refilled quite yet. The amount turned Renna's stomach.

A phantom breeze stirred the air, and heat pressed against her back like a caress. Renna turned, holding her hand in front of her face to ward off the blast of hot air. At the far end of the room, a reddish glow pulsed. The treasury opened onto an observation deck for the forge and the Mother's Flame below. The glow of the goddess-blessed flame bathed the walls.

"I don't know if I can use the glamour," Scarlet confessed. The plan had been to use their cloaks for coins while her wand would obscure the pouches they would fill with bloodsiphons. "It's been erratic since we entered the gates."

"We'll improvise. Take however much we know we can keep hidden," Little Jon said.

"I'm always down for a bit of smuggling," Alaini said, though there was an undercurrent of worry in her tone as she began dropping bloodstones into her boots.

They worked without talking, hands and fingers moving swiftly, taking turns glancing above every few minutes to be sure no one came through the door. They undid their cloaks, opening the hidden linings they'd sewn in. The clink of coins made a soft melody as they filled the huge pockets. Edwine had come up with this trick, designing pockets running the full length of the cloaks that they could fill by inserting coins near the shoulder clasps. This way, the cloaks wouldn't be bottom-heavy but would keep their proper shape and fall normally around their bodies. Once their cloaks were filled, they set about securing the ties at the top, being sure to tuck the strings back inside the double hem. Renna's cloak was heavy as she secured it around her shoulders. They'd ended up taking equal amounts of coins and bloodsiphons.

Scarlet held up the glass: only about a fourth of their sand remained.

Renna's attention was pulled to the far end of the room again. The gap in her memory needled at her. There was something that her body was shying away from, a reason her mind was keeping her in the dark. *You will soon be the key to the Mother's Flame.* Ulrik's words turned sinister in her mind. *…won't remember, but it is necessary.*

What wouldn't she remember?

"I need to look at the forge."

Scarlet and Little Jon agreed to wait while Renna, Alaini, and Much picked their way through the stacks of aurem. Sweat beaded on Renna's brow as they neared the far end of the room that opened to the Mother's Flame. The air shivered with the heat. No longer in neat piles, the unprocessed aurem spilled all over the floor, forming larger rocks and crystals. The cavern opened to an observation platform where one could look down at the lower level of the forge. A foreman could watch deep basins be hoisted up on chains, full of aurem ready for the treasury.

With her fragmented memory, Renna knew, rationally, she must have seen the forge from this angle before, but all she could recall was how it looked from the other side when she'd knelt before the Mother's Flame. The hammers, the smelting blocks, the cooling wells—she'd known all these things were necessary, but she'd never given them much thought. How could she when she was so overcome by the Mother's presence and the scent of the incense and the thought of her flaws hanging over her head while she offered up more blood?

Unbidden, the Tomes of Truth came to her: *Let the flames be kept at the heart of the kingdom, resting on a hearth carved directly into the mountain, that nothing shall be below, and in this the Mother is our foundation.* Now, seeing the vast set of tools, the machinery required to shape the aurem, it all felt...less holy. Just a large-scale blacksmith's shop nestled by an enormous fire.

Bloodsiphons rained down in a steady flow as revelers above gave blood and tossed their offerings. This was new. The absence of the Keeper's acting as intermediaries was alarming.

"What's the plan here, Hood?" Alaini whispered.

Everything appeared to be normal.

And yet...

Apprehension siphoned the air from her lungs. She gripped the edge of the half wall along the observation deck. Alongside the chains, were crude handholds carved into the stone. Renna swung over the wall and began to climb down. Her friends whispered furiously after her, but she couldn't even explain to herself what she was doing; she just knew she had to look, had to remember. The handholds were old and crumbling. She was still a ways from the bottom when her foot slipped, sending down a spray of rocks. As she scrambled for purchase, the rough wall tore up her forearms and scraped her wrist. She was falling, only to collide with Much, who was somehow underneath her now. Quick thinking and even quicker wind-walking allowed him to break her fall, though the effort looked like it cost him dearly.

They were still sprawled in a heap when Alaini landed next to them, far more gracefully. The forge floor was deserted, as all those who worked here were enjoying the celebrations. No aurem torches were lit, but the red glow of the Mother's Flame provided enough visibility. Renna couldn't shake the memory of feeling frozen, unable to turn and see the danger that lurked nearby as Ulrik let out a stream of placating words meant to soothe her.

She walked through the rows of equipment until she reached the outer edge of the forge. Much and Alaini trailed behind her. *You won't remember, but it is necessary.* Dizzy and feeling like she had when she'd seen Nastasia upstairs, Renna steadied herself with a few deep breaths.

Picture the roots.

In this place of stone and blood where trees were outlawed, she imagined roots growing from her feet, grounding her, holding her up. Even though it was impossible, she conjured the image of the golden glow of the Velmir existing here beneath her.

You will soon be the key to the Mother's Flame.

Her eyes fluttered open. The pillar in front of her seemed like all the others, ornate designs chiseled into the rock face. But Renna reached her hand out, running it over the cool surface, feeling like she was reliving a memory. Bending to inspect the pillar, she saw it.

A razor-sharp edge jutted out of the pillar, its existence camouflaged by the veins of color swirling through the stone. She brought her hand to the blade, and bright blood oozed from her palm.

The ground shook. The pillar visibly shuddered as it rotated until a doorway appeared, revealing a secret passage—an impossible passage—with a spiral staircase leading *below* the Mother's Flame. Renna cast a glance back at her friends, unable to speak. Did they realize this shouldn't exist? Nothing was below the Mother's Flame. It was the foundation of their whole system of beliefs.

And yet.

The cavern underneath the flame was massive. The stone walls were ice-cold, carved directly into the mountain, but an intense heat emanated from the underside of the hearth holding the Mother's Flame. Renna trembled violently. Everything inside her was screaming *wrong, wrong, wrong.*

Hundreds of people, clothed in beige, covered with grime and red mist, moved through the room in absolute silence, strange tools in their hands. There were *children* in the crowd. They all carried buckets of more blood toward the center of the room. Something pulsed there, but every time Renna tried to look, her vision smeared and she found herself focusing elsewhere.

The air smelled of rotting meat.

A noise like the cracking of bones came from above, and then blood—thick and crimson—rained down from the Mother's Flame, splattering to the floor in a sickening, wet cacophony. Revulsion churned through Renna as maroon droplets stained the faces of the people filling the cavern.

She braced herself against the wall to remain upright when she saw a familiar face in the crowd.

"Yana?" It came out choked and ragged, shattering the silence of the cavern. But no one even looked her way. Alaini's voice was laced with warning behind her: they were out of time, they had to go. But Yana was right there, and Renna could not turn away. She took the stairs two at a time, pulse jumping. No one paid her any mind as she wove through the crowd, unease a tight noose around her neck. She spun Yana around by the shoulders, blinking against the burn of tears, taking in the flecks of blood—a mixture of dried and wet—all over her face. Renna's heart wrenched.

Recognition flashed in Yana's eyes, and she shook herself as if waking from a stupor. A soft pained moan slipped past the woman's cracked lips, and she trembled like a leaf in a strong breeze.

"What are you doing here? What is—" Renna choked on the emotion clogging her throat, still unable to look at the hideous thing in the center of the room. Yana shook her head, the movement stilted and unnatural. Her eyes were wide and darted around the room as if in panic, and she clung to Renna's cloak. Her lips moved wordlessly, allowing Renna a glimpse of the brutalized muscle that was her torn-out tongue.

"Hood." Another warning, louder this time.

Renna took her shame and horror and shoved them down deep, gave them to the roots. There was no time for those feelings now. She gripped Yana's hands, tugging her toward the stairs. "You must come with me. Now." She half dragged, half carried Yana up the steps, unable to look at all the others she was leaving behind. *I'll come back, I'll come back*, she repeated to herself. No one came after them or made any sign that they noticed them at all.

"I couldn't leave her." Renna was breathing raggedly as Much reached down to help pull the cook up through the secret door.

Alaini replied without hesitation "We'd never ask you to."

Renna cast one last look over her shoulder, then followed her friends. The scrape of stone reverberated in her bones as the pillar shifted back in place, sealing off the room again.

With Yana in tow, it took longer to rejoin Scarlet and Little Jon at the moving platform. "I'll explain later," she said. They piled onto the platform, and Renna hurriedly let her still bleeding palm drip onto the offering site to make it rise.

Little Jon eyed Yana. "Do you have a plan for how to keep her from being noticed?"

The platform rose, and Renna chewed her lip. "It's still in the early stages."

Little Jon grunted, helping to hold Yana upright. She was so frail that it seemed she was spending all her energy on simply remaining conscious.

Much fidgeted with his quarterstaff. "How likely is it that those guards have awoken?"

They all looked at each other, but no one answered. The last of the sand was already gathered in the base of Scarlet's glass. The guards would be waking up any moment, if they hadn't already.

Much took a fortifying breath. "Right."

Once they were back in the small room above the vault, Little Jon passed Yana to Much to help the others slowly pry the door open, peering out into the hall before pulling it wide. The guards were stirring, but not fully awake. Alaini swept through the doorway; after a moment, they heard two dull thuds. Alaini reappeared from around the pillar, flipping her dagger idly. "I bought us a few more minutes."

"Tell me you didn't get blood on their cloaks," said Scarlet.

"I just hit them on the head with the hilt," Alaini said, pulling a cloak off one of the guards for Yana.

There was no sign of other guards as they reached the upper level of the castle, but the last modicum of decorum in the guests had deteriorated in the last hour, and the revelry had spilled down from the main floor to the rest of the castle. Lascivious laughter bounced off the walls, the smell of mead stung Renna's nostrils, and there were no fewer than five couples in various stages of undress. Renna's cheeks warmed, and she averted her eyes from the chaise where two noblemen were tangled in each other's arms, hands skating over bare skin and under britches. Yana's fingers twitched in the crook of her elbow. At the sound of armored boots striking the ground, Renna steered Yana behind a pillar, the others quickly following her lead. Her pulse ticked in her throat. She wiped her palm on her hip.

"My good nobles," someone yelled from the floor above, his voice spilling from a balcony that opened to the night sky. Lord Gisborne.

The crowd moved on an invisible current toward the center of the room, necks craning to get a look above. It seemed Gisborne had not changed, always droning on when she'd rather he shut up.

Gisborne began to speak of *a betrothal of two great houses* and *a blood match if there ever was one* and *what a blessed union of church and might*. Renna tried to block out the names as she and her friends crept along the stairs, but it was impossible.

High Sheriff Garen Draic. Trissaia Nastasia Bogdanik.

"The Mother has blessed us, sending us Truth and Light at this dark time to show Her favor for the recent coronation of King Ulrik."

Renna couldn't take a full breath, her lungs constricting like there was a vise around her chest. Her palm throbbed where she'd cut herself. One more set of stairs, and they'd be out.

"King Ulrik has seen that it is the Mother's will that Nastasia Bogdanik be elevated to the role of Head Trissaia."

CHAPTER 26

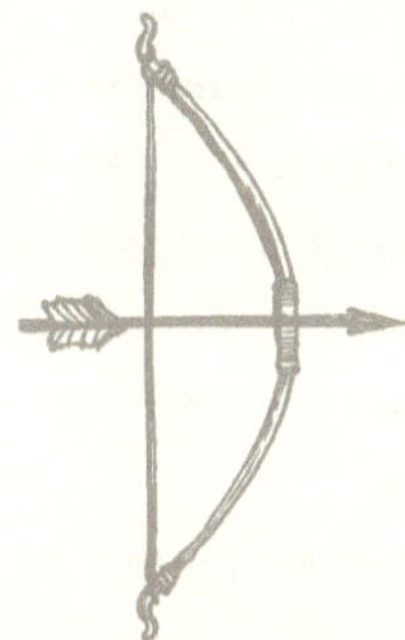

The crowd's cheers were drowned out by the ringing in Renna's ears. Nastasia was to be the Head Triss.

Ulrik had been Head Trissaia for decades, since before Renna's parents had died. The role was one that required years of tutelage and obedience. Nastasia had shared that it was her deepest desire to attain the role. *Think of it, Ren. To be the voice of the Mother Herself, helping guide our people to greatness, crown and church in harmony.*

Renna missed a step, her shin striking the sharp edge of the stairs painfully. Little Jon's hand closed around her upper arm, helping to steady her as they all crept up the final steps, but it was as if the floor had dropped out from under her. For there they stood: Nastasia and Draic, Ulrik and Gisborne. None of them wore masks as they stood on a raised platform by the railing. A yell built in Renna's throat, choking her, fighting for release as she moved through the room. Nastasia had never liked being the center of attention, but her face was split with a wide smile as she waved to the crowd like she'd been born to do it. Draic stood still as stone, all sharp edges and hard lines in his black jacket. His icy-blond hair was swept back, the lock that tended to fall over his forehead pushed back into place. With his mouth pressed into a harsh line and his expression shuttered, every inch of him emanated cold, calculated control.

His grey eyes snapped to hers, piercing Renna like an arrow a moment before guards burst up the stairs toward the crowd, armor clanking loudly.

Time slowed as Ulrik turned toward the commotion, head cocked to the side, his brow furrowed. Renna's blood chilled. She knew that look. Did the guards feel any pain as Ulrik connected to their minds? A silent conversation passed between them, tension snaking through the room. Metal rang in the air as the royal guards unsheathed their swords and moved to block the exit. Renna and her friends needed another way out, and they needed to run.

But a searing pain dragged across the base of Renna's skull, sharp as talons. This was different from the mettlemancy she'd grown accustomed to; it felt desperate, angry, like a wild swipe from an animal backed into a corner. Her knees buckled as images flashed through her mind, all tinged red in a haze of anger and bloodlust. She was dimly aware that none of her friends were cowering or gripping their heads. Then the sensation stopped abruptly, the connection severed. Renna gagged, drenched in cold sweat.

Shouts filled the air, commanding that no one move on order of the high sheriff. Little Jon yanked her up by the wrist, and that was when she realized her bracelet was missing, the one warded to keep her mind shielded. She recalled the sensation of something snagging and realized she'd lost it while climbing down below the forge.

"Vedra in the castle! No one leaves until the witches are found."

Someone shrieked as a guard ripped away their mask. Pandemonium was spreading like wildfire. Nastasia and Ulrik were ushered swiftly from the dais. Draic was bellowing orders. Armor and purple and red robes swept in from the edges of the party like hunting dogs released.

Renna tried to think, to find a way out of the absolute shit storm they were now in. If the guards took off her mask… The exit was barricaded. There were too many people; they'd never make it to one of the tunnels before being stopped. Shit, shit, shit. She needed her bow—there was a large tapestry on the wall that she could release with a precise arrow to the ropes. A nobleman was drunkenly refusing to take his mask off and suffered a sharp blow to the temple.

Yana whimpered in terror, silent tears making tracks down her cheeks.

Time snapped back into place.

"The kitchens, quickly," Renna hissed as she led them in a zigzag pattern through the crowd, scanning for guards, shoving passed dazed revelers. She would have laughed at the affronted expressions on their faces—who would dare to ruin their precious party?—were the situation not becoming increasingly dire. Renna gripped Little Jon's arm. "You have more vials? We need to buy some time."

They pulled out two more stoppered vials of vapor. With an expert wind-up, they launched one in the opposite direction. There were cries of alarm and a tinkle of glass, then a plume of green smoke and bodies slumping to the ground. Guards surged to the impacted area.

She picked up her pace, urging the others to hurry as she led them to a cramped servants' entrance to the kitchens.

The smell of meats and scones and kvass was overwhelming, the air sticky with heat and sweat. The kitchen was a long room lined with hearths, tables for preparation down the middle and barrels of fish, flour, and salt in the corners. Slabs of dried meat hung from the ceiling. Renna shoved the image of skewered boar from her mind. No, that would not be their fate. They were not dying today. Twenty or so kitchen staff shrank back as they burst in. A few swore, and one young man brandished a silver ladle dripping with brown sauce.

"The windows." Renna pointed, and Alaini broke into a run toward the far end of the room. She and Much began to muscle a heavy barrel in front of the door, but someone ducked in after them before they could block it. Little Jon turned on instinct, arm cocked to land a blow as Renna cried out, "Don't!"

But she needn't have. Priestess Briar dodged the attack like it was second nature. Little Jon glared at her, but to her credit, the woman didn't cower. "Are you going to accept my help, or would you rather burn for treason? Hurry up, then," the priestess ordered, shoving the barrel against the door. Satisfied, she swept into the room and called to Alaini, who had reached the glass panes. "Not that one, unless you fancy falling to your death at the bottom of a ditch. The far right."

Alaini shattered the indicated window with a swift kick. A kitchen maid whimpered, and another gasped. Several onlookers uttered Yana's name as they hurried across the room. Little Jon retrieved coiled ropes from their pack, handing them out. Much fussed in his cloak, pulling out a few small bags of coin and tossed them to those nearest; the workers gave him looks of awe, scrutiny, and nerves as they quickly tucked them out of sight.

They were all gathered at the broken window now, the cold air whipping in, scattering flour from an open sack. Renna cast a glance over her shoulder, waiting for the door to fly open, for them to be discovered. That barrel wouldn't hold anyone off from more than a moment or two. Alaini pulled out what looked like a jumble of wood, but with a few quick snaps, she assembled a small crossbow. Little Jon handed her the grappling hook tied to the end of one of the ropes, which she fastened to a small bolt pulled from a holster on her thigh. They'd brought all the ropes as a precaution, but Renna realized she'd been foolish to think they would be able to walk out of the castle the same way they'd come in.

Alaini took her shot, and the rope whizzed out the window, followed by a dull sound of impact.

Little Jon secured the other end of the rope to the metal grate in front of one of the fires. Alaini jerked her chin. "Hood—up you go."

The crisp night air hit Renna's cheeks as she stepped up on the table to reach the window, ducking to avoid the sharp edges of the glass. The far end of the rope was now hooked to a barred window on a lower level of the castle. It was hardly an ideal option, as there was little to no room for them to land on the other side, below the window, the roof ran at a steep angle to another balcony below. Renna tried to imagine she was looking at the training rig in Loxley. Renna wished she had her bow to slide across the tether, but instead she slung her cloak over the rope, then wound the fabric around each hand a few times.

A boom filled the kitchen as someone or something landed heavily against the door.

"Don't look down," Alaini said.

Renna jumped out the window.

Her shoulders screamed in protest at the sharp drop, and her palms burned. The cloak slid across the rope in jerky spurts, each one loosening her grip a little. She struck the wall and rolled on the narrow ledge, fighting for balance. Her shoulders and knees would be bruised tomorrow. Panting, she motioned for Scarlet to come next. The sounds in the castle were muted, but they were far from out of danger.

Renna caught Scarlet, saving her from the harsh landing. The roof had the same pitch as the fallen tree trunk that they raced across back in Sherwood, albeit much higher off the ground and without a net below to catch them. She fervently hoped that Asher, Baz, Kaja, and Vanya had gotten out before the castle doors had been sealed. If not…she couldn't think about it now. They were fine. And if they weren't fine, they were capable. She couldn't afford to believe otherwise.

The others followed like shadows, Little Jon with Yana strapped to their back, the woman holding on tightly. Much secured a rope ladder to the balcony and tossed it down the wall. It swayed and creaked under their weight. As Renna dropped onto solid ground, an arrow whizzed past her ear. She threw her back against the wall. An archer was leaned out a slot window above. The shouts inside the castle grew louder. Alaini shot a bolt in return, but the opening was too narrow, and it clanged off the stones.

"Hurry!" Renna's voice was hoarse, and panic raced through her veins.

A horned owl with dark brown and black feathers soared overhead before diving sharply. It was just like one she used to watch out her window. Renna blinked hard.

"Follow her," Little Jon barked, jumping down past the last few rungs of the ladder.

"Her?" Renna's confusion was echoed by Much and Alaini.

Another arrow struck the ground. They ran across the small courtyard, their footfalls and breathing heavy. Renna wished they'd spent time crafting an additional collapsible crossbow. They weren't as powerful as regular bows, but right now one could mean the difference between life and death. They were too exposed. She tried to get her bearings, searching for anything familiar, anything to get them out of this alive. Adrenaline and panic scrambled her memory, despite all the time she'd spent studying her rudimentary maps.

The archway they passed under had a particular pattern on the stones, one she'd seen countless times as she'd left training with her head tipped back to stanch a bloody nose courtesy of Draic. They were near the stables. Her mind reoriented, a plan crystalizing in the chaos.

"Wait!" Renna veered left, though the others had gone right. There was an old supply room where Devana used to store her extra weapons that she didn't want common soldiers using. It was known to few people besides Renna, Nastasia, and Draic. But it seemed that since the weapon master's retirement, no one had touched it. Renna shoved the door open and was greeted by the sight of several longbows and three full quivers. She let out a triumphant noise.

The others were where she'd left them, the horned owl somehow managing to look scolding. Renna tossed the extra bows to her friends. The quiver on her back felt like a shield as they ran. Four more archers shot at them from above, but they sent their own arrows back. They followed the owl down a narrow section of the castle's battlements, then wound up a staircase to the top of a turret. It was near where the royal ravens and carrier pigeons were kept, but…Renna's heart stuttered. The birds were kept on the less inhabitable side of the mountain that faced out toward the expansive ocean. It was mostly sharp rocks and steep cliff below the castle here, apart from what was directly beneath them: a knoll butted up against the stone wall next to a stretch of flat ground and the drainage pipe for sewage.

It was a dead end.

"Where the bloody hell are we supposed to go now?" Alaini was holding a stitch in her side. Much cursed, wiping the bird poop he'd stepped in onto the stones. Little Jon didn't answer, just leaned over the side of the outlook. The owl dropped to the wall, looking suddenly exhausted.

"There." They all followed Little Jon's gaze. It was so subtle, so perfectly camouflaged against the landscape, that one would miss it if they didn't know to look for it. Strange stones marked a haphazard trail that led down the entire side of the mountain.

Renna suddenly remembered flashes of her hurried escape from the castle the night she'd straddled life and death. That knoll was where she and the priestess had emerged from the tunnel.

Alaini shot a grappling hook arrow once more, sinking it into the ground. "She'll cut the rope once we are down," Little Jon explained, gesturing to the owl.

"I have so many questions." Alaini shook her head.

Renna's hands sustained more burns from gripping her cloak, and her stomach lurched at the steep drop. But soon they were all on the ground, and the rope was indeed being tossed down. Someone leaned over, only a smudge of a purple robe against the night sky.

The knoll was made of rock and aurem, a faint outline of the tunnel door disappearing seamlessly into the mountainside. They followed the trail carefully. The ground was broken sheets of shale and gravel where nothing grew. Far below them, the tide was blessedly still out, leaving the marshland surrounding all of Loxley exposed. The rocks slid underfoot, and it took them a long time to pick their way down, stopping often for Yana to catch her breath. The cook's fragile state was the only thing keeping Renna from spiraling out of control herself. She kept seeing flashes of that night she had escaped, clearer now. Briar had all but carried her down this path; she'd been so groggy from the moonshade Draic had slipped her, besides being in shock and dizzy from blood loss. If they were to veer left here, she'd find the spot where Kit and Alita had been, ready to take her to Sherwood.

This time, they went to the right. The rocky trail eventually connected to worn-down roads that wound through Nottingham. When the rest of their companions emerged from an alley and joined up with them, they were unscathed, apart from Asher's singed eyebrows. Relief washed through Renna. The twins took turns carrying Yana as they hurried through the streets. No alarm had been sounded down here yet; the palace guards must have thought they were hiding up on the battlements somewhere. Had Briar been discovered? Renna recalled those horrible talons in her mind, the distance between them and the castle doing little to ease the tension in her chest.

It was the middle of the night now, the hours when nothing good happened. Most of the citizens had retired to bed, and the streets were empty. The apartments got progressively worse for wear the lower they went, towering high and precarious, crowded so tightly together that it felt hard to take a full breath. The smell of the sewer seemed to have settled here. Everything was rusted, broken, or damaged. Renna blinked back tears, fiercely grateful when Scarlet whistled a tune, reminding her of the last piece of their mission, signaling that it was time.

Wordlessly, they fanned out through the deserted street. Renna fumbled inside her cloak, searching for the first of the small strings Edwine and Scarlet had sewn in. Tugging with quick sharp movements, Renna pulled it free. The stitches drew zigzags across her shoulders and back as they unraveled. Coins rained down through the cloak and out the now-open hem, clinking against the stones. The sound echoed through the streets as they all released the aurem from their cloaks' linings.

The coins flashed in the moonlight, winking up at her. At each street, she pulled another cord, releasing more stolen coins. Renna's cloak got lighter, but the night's events weighed heavy on her heart.

At least in the morning, the citizens of Nottingham would wake to find a trail of aurem left by hooded, nameless outlaws.

PART
THREE

CHAPTER 27

THE WHIP CRACKED, SPLITTING OPEN GAREN'S BACK, ROBBING HIM OF BREATH AND VISION. His tattered shirt was soaked with blood, sticking to the raw strips of skin. The pain was all-consuming.

Then the mental talons struck.

How is it possible that she lives?! Ulrik screamed through their mental connection. The sensation was akin to white-hot pokers skewering beneath his fingernails, fire running through his veins. Garen slumped forward with a moan, unable to form words, ropes of blood and saliva dripping from his mouth.

Pain is temporary. The pain will end. The mountain around my mind will stand.

The mantra swam in his torment-addled mind. He was distantly aware of Kirin and Ilya among the guards who stood watch around the room, of Nastasia and Gisborne next to the king. Ulrik ripped through his memories to find the night of the Blood Tithe, when Renna had been forced to abdicate.

Garen let him.

Let him see the details he had carefully shaped: his blade cutting into Renna's neck, blood gushing over his hands, the light in her eyes dimming. The sound of her body hitting the floor, the rioting outside the door, the command he'd given to a lower officer to burn the corpse.

What Ulrik could not see was what lay behind those memories: the massive mountains built up high; the foxhole leading to a hidden lair with vast winding tunnels that stretched on indefinitely. Behind those mountains in his mind were the memories he'd hidden away: the trace amount of moonshade he'd brushed onto Renna's mouth to mimic death, the revulsion in his gut at the abject terror in her eyes; removing the sliver of aurem; the false commotion that had called him away; the vedra magic that even now pulsed through his tattoos, lending him the strength to resist the mental ravaging; his training in Wendsvik; his desire to kill the man in front of him.

His secrets were guarded. He took the punishment he was given, letting anger alchemize it into a weapon for him to use later. Garen keeled over and coughed, splattering blood on the ground. Then he blinked for too long and slipped out of consciousness.

When he came to, Ulrik was muttering to Gisborne and Nastasia. Every nerve was on fire, and Garen could understand only fragments: "…in my own castle…not leave rot unattended…let the Keepers…the claim to the throne…root her out, Nastasia."

The king called for his next victim: the guard from Garen's false memories, the one who'd supposedly been tasked with the removal of the princess's body. By now, Garen was adept at choosing who would take the fall so another could live. Kirin had done his job well, learning all the secrets of the red clerics around them, and today Garen had picked the guard with a predilection for children. He, Ilya, and Kirin had not hesitated for a moment as they'd spun the false memories and planted them in the guard's subconscious.

He was dragged before the king, eyes wide with terror as he looked at Garen on the floor, beaten and bleeding. Garen's breath was shallow and painful, and dark spots filled the edges of his vision, but he made himself watch as Ulrik delved into the guard's mind and saw the mettlecast memory they wanted him to see:

The guard came to dispose of the body but found a faint heartbeat. It occurred to him that he could get some coin in exchange for the live princess. He knew a few of the rebels, after all; he frequently took bribes to look the other way. It was the king's own fault, really—if he wanted absolute loyalty, he should've paid the clerics more. It was easy to find someone on the brink of death whom he could burn, then pass off the remains as the princess's body.

Ulrik released his mental hold and let the man topple to the floor. Blood leaked from one ear. "High Sheriff, you've received your punishment for what happened on your watch. Now you will punish this disappointment."

Garen called his finnikfire, despite the fresh agony pulsing through him. *Pain is temporary. The pain will end. The mountain around my mind will stand.*

The stench of burning flesh lingered in the throne room for days.

CHAPTER 28

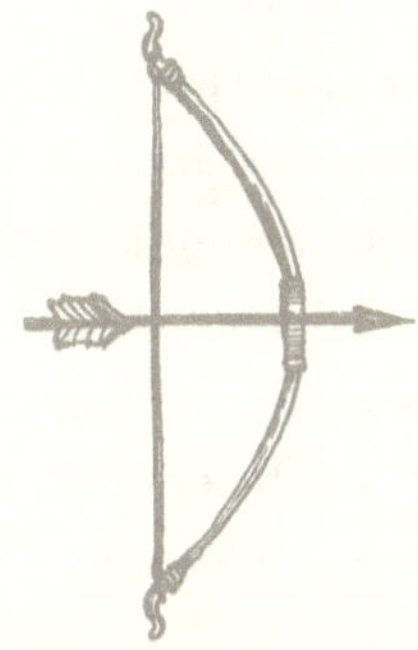

"SOOO…ARE WE GOING TO ADDRESS THE FACT THAT THE PRIESTESS TURNED INTO AN OWL LAST NIGHT?" ALAINI ASKED AS THEY HUDDLED AROUND THE HEARTHTREE EARLY THE NEXT MORNING. Renna had barely been able to sleep after they'd returned to Rowan Reach the night before, and she'd found Little Jon, Much, Scarlet, and Alaini congregated under the moss-covered tree.

"Briar is what's called a wyldling," Little Jon explained. "She's a witch who can shift into an animal form. Historically, druidhen carry the trait, but it's occasionally seen in witches."

In the chaos of the escape, Renna had not been able to comprehend what she'd seen, but now the explanation seemed obvious.

Little Jon's face was grave. "Something was off about the king."

A lump lodged in her throat, and she couldn't speak aloud her fear that Ulrik had forced his way into her mind. The memory of the phantom talons clawing at her. What had he seen? Her fingers brushed the spot where the charmed bracelet should have been. She couldn't bring herself to look her friends in the eye.

"The whole kingdom felt off. What was that under the Mother's Flame?" Alaini asked.

Renna shuddered. "I couldn't focus on whatever was in the center of the room. Every time I tried, I was suddenly looking somewhere else."

Much glanced toward the tree house where they'd put Yana. The woman had been in shock when they'd entered the wards, and Little Jon had given her a sleeping draught. "Do you think she knows anything?" he asked Renna. "How do you know her, exactly?"

Renna stared at the ground, her voice cracking as she spoke. "She was the cook in the palace. She…when Draic returned to Loxley, he…when he put those Keepers to death, Yana called a storm."

The memory played over in her mind: Yana's outstretched hands, the wind picking up speed as storm clouds rushed in. Ulrik demanding that Renna prove herself by honoring the laws she was meant to uphold. The fear that had frozen her. The knowledge that if she did not obey, she too would be sentenced to the pyre. The way she'd told herself that it was a mercy. *Better to be Silenced than to burn.*

Shame sprouted through her chest like vines, twining tightly around her ribs.

"I gave the order for her to be Silenced."

No one spoke.

Then Much said quietly, "You did what you had to do in order to survive." The words did nothing to assuage Renna's guilt and self-loathing.

They began a rotating watch outside the wards for red clerics as well as word from Draic, Briar, or anyone else working with the Falsehoods.

The afternoon following their return, Renna gathered parchment and a stick of charcoal to her chest and approached the log Yana sat on. She would beg forgiveness and see what Yana knew of the room beneath the Mother's Flame. Everything in her upbringing was demanding that she put her questions aside, that she stay silent. But silence could cut and harm as surely as any blade. Silence slowly turned on itself and its wielder.

Yana eyed her warily.

An apology was not enough, would never be enough, but if she did not say something, the shame would eat her alive. Renna cleared her throat, wincing against the pain that had returned following the ball. "Yana, I…I'm so sorry. I never should have—"

Yana stood, her whole body trembling, her eyes hard and brimming with tears. Her gaze scorched like finnikfire, burning away Renna's carefully crafted words. The woman turned on her heel, leaving Renna to sink deeper into her guilt.

The next morning, Renna didn't get out of bed. Her disastrous interaction with Yana was seared into her mind, and her throat had hurt so much when she'd awoken that she could not speak without pain. Her state did nothing to deter Alaini.

"Don't think for one second that you can get away with staying in bed just 'cause you've lost your voice." They both knew it was so much more than that, but

Alaini was like sunshine—you could count on her to rise after the darkness and pull others into her warmth. Her friend called out to Much, asking him to make a cup of honey tea. The sound of the pot clanging as he set to brewing it reached them. Alaini tugged on Renna's arm. "Up."

I'm really not in the mood today, Renna signed, hoping Alaini would take pity on her and leave her be.

You don't have to be happy, Alaini signed back, *but come be with us. Better to be miserable with friends than miserable and alone.*

And how could one refuse the sun?

Nine days passed. Nine days of the Thorns trying to coax some life into Yana's eyes, of trying to convince her to eat more than tea and broth, of waiting for any word from Draic or Briar. Renna gave Yana space, letting the others tend to her; Asher, of all people, was surprisingly tender toward the woman. Renna turned her focus to what she could control. She pulled every book off the shelf in their library, searching for clues to explain what they'd found under the Mother's Flame. But it felt like she'd been blindfolded and commanded to find the Spine of Kaerenthal on the other side of the forest. She was feeling sorry for herself, sitting cross-legged in the library and leafing through an old book Scarlet had picked up on their last trip to Wendsvik, when her eyes snagged on a faded passage:

Blood mages once roamed Dravmir but have now dwindled in number (see also: Great Culling, morglak, silmorra). The highest level of blood mage is a sangeserre, one able to exert control over someone else's mind. The term translates to blood talons, *both for how the intrusion feels to the victim and the steep price of blood that the wielder must pay.*

Past lessons with the Keepers flashed through Renna's mind, all boiling down to the fact that using blood for anything other than an offering to the Mother was an abomination. Heart pounding erratically, she read the lines again. Blood talons—that was how it had felt when Ulrik had reached into to her mind in the castle. She gripped the roots of her hair tightly, focusing on the pain to keep from spiraling, but…the pieces fit together.

Ulrik was not simply a mettlemancer but a sangeserre.

The thought bubbled like acid in her gut. Her eyes burned as she pictured how her cousin had looked at the ball, the cold and calculating look on her face. A heady mixture of outrage and relief surged through her. Ulrik had to be controlling Nastasia.

Plans to save her cousin were rippling through her mind when Much stuck his head around the corner. "Ren, come quick. Yana told Little Jon everything she knows."

She hastily marked the passage, tucking the book under her arm as she followed Much. The other Thorns were waiting at the edge of the hearthtree. Yana was nowhere to be seen, and Renna relaxed a little. Little Jon held a few sheets of parchment full of charcoal scribbles. They'd asked the woman questions, and she'd written down her responses.

"After Yana was Silenced, she was told that now she would become part of something bigger than herself. That she had a great opportunity to please the Mother as an Acolyte to the Flame."

Renna had never heard that term before, and by the looks on her friends' faces, neither had they. Little Jon continued, handing the parchment around for them to look over. "Acolytes to the Flame are sequestered in Keeper's Keep, only able to travel to and from the cavern you lot saw through an underground tunnel."

Renna held up a page so Much could read along with her. The description of the terrible living conditions the Acolytes were subjected to made her blood run cold. Every Acolyte was Silenced and kept within the confines of the Keep. The shock and shame of just how little she'd understood of what was happening in her kingdom was as intense now as the first time she'd felt it. Renna doubted it would ever become less painful. To be honest, she wasn't sure she wanted it to. She needed to hold on to this feeling, to bear witness to the suffering her actions and inactions had caused.

There was a ripple in the air, and they turned as Briar burst through the wards, covered in grime and stained with blood, her eyes wide. She clutched a trembling child to her chest, their face buried in her cloak. "I didn't know where else to bring them all."

"All?" Little Jon echoed.

"There are a dozen of them—vedra sympathizers who were meant to be put to death. Kirin is waiting outside with them."

The outlaws leapt into action. The familiar name sent a little shock wave through Renna—Kirin was one of Draic's friends—as she eased the child from Briar's arms. The others quickly slipped through the Thorne Crown to bring in the wounded. The child was shaking, but from cold, shock, or fear, Renna couldn't say. She called for Edwine, wrapping the child up in a thick blanket by the fire. The older woman rushed over, armed with a scone and a mug of hot tea, already singing in a soft tone as she sat down to tend to the child. The sight reminded Renna painfully of Marian, and she turned her attention back to the chaos near the edge of the camp.

Kirin had already come through the wards, blindfold discarded to reveal his striking features. She'd been so distracted by Garen's apparent return from the dead, and then the horror of watching people burn, that Renna had not gotten a good look at him back in Loxley. One eye was framed by a white birthmark, stark against his otherwise brown complexion; it spanned diagonally from one brow to the opposite cheek, fading at the ends into scattered freckles. As she neared, she could see that one eye was green, the other blue, and there was another smattering of white skin along his neck.

"I am Kirin, my lady." His voice was gruff as he watched her approach.

"Renna is fine. I'm no longer a lady."

Kirin merely dipped his chin as men, women, and children staggered into Rowan Reach, tightly holding hands as they were led through the wards. Each was more ragged than the last; telltale stains of dried blood down a few chins spoke of tongues removed. Kirin hesitated, then explained, "It would have aroused too much suspicion if they'd all been rescued before they were Silenced."

An awful, knowing stillness followed his words. Bile rose in Renna's throat. Someone had made a call to wait, to stay their hand until enough had suffered.

"Is Garen—"

"He's alive, my lady," Kirin said. "And the Falsehoods inside the castle remain secret." He hurried off, leaving Renna with a million unanswered questions.

She was swept up in the commotion for the next hour. Her healing skills were nowhere near those of Little Jon or Scarlet, but she could stitch just fine. She pushed up her sleeves, splashed Little Jon's sterilizing solution on her hands, and went from person to person, carefully suturing skin. After a while, her back ached from hunching over, and her eyes burned from exertion. She tended to a woman who had been spared Silencing, though her wrists were badly chafed from shackles, her face was swollen with bruises around her jaw and cheekbones, and she had a nasty cut along her forearm, most likely from a dagger.

"What happened?" Renna asked gently as she worked.

The woman whimpered from the pain but answered after a few beats. "The clerics just started rounding us up, kicking down doors in Nottingham in the middle of the night. They claimed we were aiding the rebel cause. I never saw a witch in my life, I swear it. But they didn't care, just dragged us up to the dungeons, said we'd burn for our crimes. They knocked me out cold. When I woke, that one was pulling us all out of the cells." She nodded toward Kirin.

Hours later, Renna felt like an exposed nerve, desperate to exchange information with the others. They gathered in a small group: Little Jon, Alaini, Scarlet, Much, Renna, Kirin, and Briar. The priestess began to fill in the gaps of what had transpired on the night of the ball.

"Once the treasury guards woke up, they ran straight to the throne room to inform the king that the vault had been breached. They didn't know how long they'd been unconscious, only that gold and bloodsiphons were missing. Ulrik used his mettlemancy and found Renna in the crowd."

The confirmation swept through her in an icy wave as the others looked at her. "Actually, I don't think it was mettlemancy. I think…I think Ulrik is a sangeserre. Someone who can not only read minds but control them."

"Is that possible?" Much asked.

Renna retrieved the book and opened to the marked passage. Alaini squeezed Renna's shoulder, concern etched on her face.

Little Jon read the passage once, twice. "Sherwood Forest is one of the largest sources of Velmir. That amount of concentrated power allowed for thinning areas into other realms filled with olden creatures, fae, and magics we don't fully comprehend. I would wager that this vein of magic is a remnant from another world."

Nastasia's face rose in Renna's mind, and she shuddered again at the implications of mind control.

"Shit." Kirin ran a hand over his face. "Unfortunately, this fits with something the Falsehoods have suspected for a long time: that there's a large-scale compulsion spell at work in Loxley."

Information was guarded even among allies, it seemed, for the warmth drained from Briar's face at Kirin's revelation. Gathering her composure, the priestess said, "We know there's something that interferes with other types of magic inside the walls. Perhaps that's part of the compulsion enchantment?"

Renna caught Scarlet's eyes, recalling the way she'd struggled with her glamour once they were inside Loxley.

"We don't know much about the compulsion beyond its existence, but we've received orders to find a way to disrupt and dispel it." Kirin's dual-tone eyes flicked from Little Jon to Briar. "Rumor is that the druidhen know how to break that sort of enchantment."

"The type of magic you speak of *does* exist…" Briar trailed off, deferring to Little Jon.

They sighed. "It's not knowledge I possess. I would need to speak with the druidhen matriarch…but I can't guarantee she'll be able or willing to help."

Briar's face flickered with sorrow momentarily. A thousand words were spoken in the way the atmosphere between them softened. An echo of how it used to be shone in their held gazes. "Perhaps we could try mistletoe and rowan berries instead of the fern? It takes longer to brew and is less potent, but…"

Little Jon nodded. "Better than nothing."

The knot of dread that had lurked in Renna's throat since she'd realized she'd lost the charmed bracelet was threatening to choke her now. "Do we know what Ulrik learned when he looked into my mind?"

Kirin shook his head. "Beyond the fact that you still live? No. The king was livid when he discovered you had escaped. He whipped Garen for letting it happen on his watch, then made him execute the officer we blamed for your escape."

Images of chains, blood, and knives filled Renna's vision. Of Ulrik ripping into Draic's mind, pulling out all the plans, deceptions, and lies before gutting him. A copper taste filled her mouth. She'd bitten the inside of her lip.

Her fear must have been evident on her face because Kirin went on. "He doesn't suspect Garen's ties to the Falsehoods, but he has lost faith that his high sheriff can implement all his plans. As such, he's been giving the high-level Trissaia more responsibility and keeping his secrets more well guarded."

"At the very least, Ulrik knows you're involved with the rebels." Briar pulled out a thin sheet of vellum. On it was a sketch of hooded figures with large bold words:

DANGEROUS OUTLAWS ON THE LOOSE: THE ROBBING HOODS.

Vedra sympathizers in league with the False Queen.

One thousand aurem reward for information leading to their capture.

The False Queen.

The bitter irony of how much time she'd spent fighting not to become the next Almost Queen, only to earn a much more damning title, was not lost on her.

Much gently shook her shoulder. "This changes nothing for me."

"Same here," Alaini added, and Little Jon and Scarlet nodded in agreement.

Despite their reassurances, Renna knew her involvement had indeed put a much larger target on her friends, just like she'd feared it would. Again, she remembered her Foretelling: she'd bring destruction to her kingdom, to the people she cared about most. In surrendering to her vedra instincts, had she doomed them all, regardless of the fact that she hadn't taken the throne? She could not rescind her choices now. And would she truly want to? Renna could still feel the weight of the trembling child she'd held an hour ago. She saw the faces of those trapped below the Mother's Flame, the scars along Much's arms that mirrored her own tithes. The Velmir pulsed steadily around her. *In a world where you have no magic, you must make your own.*

"There'll be more people who need refuge," Briar was saying.

"Rowan Reach will take them in," Little Jon replied.

Renna addressed the two spies. "Tell Draic he needs to go to Keeper's Keep. He must follow those who are Silenced and look beneath the Flame." Draic had said that for their safety, they should each only know what was necessary, and Kirin didn't bat an eye at receiving an obscure message to deliver to his commander and friend.

"There's one more thing," Kirin said. "We know the king is expecting the Blood Tithe from Wendsvik. We need to intercept the delivery."

Renna lifted her chin, looking at her friends. What she saw in their faces reflected her own: acceptance of a reality they hadn't chosen but would meet just the same.

Her Thorns. The Robbing Hoods.

"Let's bleed 'em dry."

The Thorns snuck through the forest: Little Jon with their quarterstaff carved from oak, etched with runes and embedded with crystals; Renna and Much each armed with a bow and a short sword; Scarlet with her green-gemmed sword and dagger; Alaini with her new bow, which was truly a work of art. Unfolding from a long-necked mandolin with extra strings, it could play a tune or send an arrow on its way.

The snapping of branches pulled them all to attention. Little Jon stood with tension rippling off their broad shoulders. With a small movement of their fingers, they signed, *Up ahead. To the left.*

A heavy drag across the leaves accompanied more snaps and some heavy breathing, but Renna and the others glided over stones and gnarled roots, silent and one with the forest. Renna pulled back her bowstring, arrow pointed in the direction Little Jon had indicated. Between the trees were flashes of the deep purple robes of Keepers and the red of a Trissaia. Four of them hefted a metal palanquin through the dense forest, the Trissaia walking out front, leading the way. A thick metal collar adorned her neck. Renna's hackles rose. These Keepers of the Truth represented all the lies she'd been fed, all the pain the crown had inflicted, all the betrayal she still carried with her like a wound that refused to heal. By their own laws and beliefs, this place was poisonous and wicked.

And yet here they were.

Hot rage spread through her like wildfire, licking her bones, swirling in her gut, and roaring in her skull. All she could think of was how sweet it would be to pull screams from them as they suffered like she had suffered. The logical part of her brain retreated, an animal taking its place.

There was a small overhang where the trail sloped lower, crossing beneath the unearthed roots of a tree on higher ground. The unseen Thorns spread out like mist until they surrounded the five travelers below. A whisper of movement stirred at Renna's heels: Kit, ears flat, teeth exposed, gaze locked on the unsuspecting Keepers. The fox darted down to cut in front of them.

There was a scream and a curse. One priestess kicked at Kit. "I thought it was the bloody Night Watchman."

"I told you to stop speaking of that Falsehood." The Trissaia narrowed her eyes at Kit, who merely swished his tail twice. "Filthy, nasty oversized rodent."

Renna sent an arrow flying toward the woman's feet. "Didn't your mother ever teach you any manners?"

The Trissaia flinched, mouth open as she tugged at her robe, which was now pinned to the ground. Little Jon landed on the path in a semi-crouch, quarterstaff at the ready. The trees seemed to vibrate with anticipation. Someone whimpered. An angry vein bulged in the woman's forehead. Her face was riddled with pox scars.

A dagger moved through the air, expertly thrown. One priestess dropped the front of the palanquin with a yelp, yanking her hand away from the blade. The heavy thud of metal shook the forest floor, and then Scarlet leapt down gracefully. "Pray, what brings you to the forest? You're a long way from the Mother's Flame."

"Do not speak to them," Pox Face hissed to her companions, who were struggling to hoist the palanquin back up. She turned her narrowed eyes back to the outlaws. "I'll give you one chance to stop delaying us and let us go about our business."

Alaini gave a mock gasp from her perch across from Renna, strumming a cheerful tune on her mandolin. The leaves shivered. "Delaying you? I was under the impression we were ambushing you."

Scarlet retrieved her dagger and began flipping it. "Semantics, love."

"You have no authority here among the trees. State your purpose, and perhaps we'll let you go," Little Jon said.

"I command that you vagabonds stand down and be grateful we're letting you keep your tongues." Pox Face's voice had taken on a distorted tone.

Then something strange happened; Renna found she could not pull her eyes from the aurem collar the woman wore. As if roots had sprung up from the ground and grown around Renna's legs, she stood frozen as her arms lowered the bow. Her mouth suddenly felt like it was filled with sand. A scream was lodged in her throat.

Little Jon kept speaking, completely unaffected. "As I said, you have no authority here among the trees."

In a blur of movement, Little Jon struck Pox Face squarely in the solar plexus. Renna could practically hear the air leave the woman's lungs as she sprawled on the ground. The two priestesses in the rear dropped the palanquin and produced thin rapiers from their robes. Scarlet launched into a dance with them, drawing her green-gemmed sword, baiting her opponents into making frantic jabs and slashes. She twirled between them, her hair whipping through the air. Much took one priestess by surprise, wind-walking behind her to kick the backs of her knees. Alaini's music swirled around the battle; flowers bent toward her, and vines began to burst from the dirt, snaking around the fallen priestess and binding her before she could retaliate.

The Keeper who'd been afraid of the Night Watchman was frantically trying to get away from the palanquin, her robes caught underneath its weight. Stopping her from escaping would be simple, but Renna still could not move; the Trissaia had a hold on her mind. This wasn't mettlemancy or the talons of a sangeserre. The command was weighted, dragging her down.

She was back in the training grounds, the tang of a storm in the air, an angry crowd calling for blood.

Yana weeping as Renna gave the command that she be Silenced.

Draic's dagger flashing.

She was weak, *so* weak.

A priestess sliced Scarlet's leg, her blade coming away dark and wet. Much yelled at Renna, but she couldn't hear his words over the roaring in her ears.

Razor-sharp teeth latched onto the meaty part of her calf, and Renna's body jolted, adrenaline shooting through her. Kit was weaving around her legs where the invisible roots had grown.

Suddenly her body and mind were hers again, and she pulled back her bowstring, taking aim at one of the priestesses fighting with Scarlet. The hiss of the arrow was followed by a low thunk as it lodged itself into her shoulder. Her scream was high-pitched. Two more arrows in quick succession pinned the whimpering priestess to the ground, tangled in her robes. Alaini sent ropes of vines to bind her. Little Jon was wrestling Pox Face now, their hands clamped around her mouth, holding her tightly to their chest as she kicked in protest.

"Get me something to gag her with," Little Jon called out, arms locked tightly around the thrashing woman. Renna leapt off the overhang, finally joining them on the path. She found a cowl in an unconscious priestess's robes, but she wasn't fast enough.

Pox Face bit Little Jon's hand, then screamed to her companions, "The Mother will greet the righteous at her gates." Her voice again took on a distorted quality. "Do your duty." Her garish smile was stained red as she bit down.

There was an audible crunch, a dribble of saliva, and then she swallowed. Her eyes bulged, the tendons on her neck straining against her golden collar. With a horrifying slowness, every priestess began foaming at the mouth, choking.

Dying.

And with them, all the answers the Thorns hoped to find.

The poison in their false teeth worked quickly, and their faces soon turned purple, leaving the outlaws with five robed corpses and a locked palanquin.

Alaini, practically vibrating with adrenaline, rounded on Renna. "What the fuck happened up there, Hood?"

Renna flinched, shame and anger filling her mouth with a bitter taste.

"Easy," Little Jon cautioned. They were all looking at her, worry and apprehension clear on their faces. Renna's eyes dropped to Scarlet's injured leg. She'd just stood there and let her friend be wounded.

"I'm sorry, I don't know…I couldn't…she spoke that command, and I lost control over my body." There was a heavy silence. Alaini looked away, rage reined in but not gone. The anger felt good, a blade to press to the wound that had scabbed over and burned with irritation.

Renna knew she should be blamed. She thought about Ulrik's mental talons at the masquerade. They should be angry at her for *something*.

Little Jon sighed heavily. "I think you should stay in Rowan Reach until we sort out why it affected you."

Self-loathing scraped through her, and Renna blinked away the burn behind her eyes. They were right, of course. She was lucky no one was more badly hurt. But the feeling of failing, of being found unworthy, was like quicksand beneath her, dragging her under.

"We need to focus on the elixir anyway. You can help with that," Scarlet added, more gently than Renna deserved. They'd been making small batches of elixir to soak aurem in to imbue it with the ability to dissipate compulsion spells. It was meticulous work, and it had been going slowly. They were meant to sneak into Loxley in three nights time to distribute the first round. And they still would, but without Renna. She tried to ignore the sting of being left out.

It's your own fault. You are too weak.

Hauling the palanquin back to Rowan Reach took much longer than anticipated, and by the time they stumbled through the wards, Renna was slick with sweat and aching all over. All she wanted to do was curl up in bed, but their return drew attention and a small group gathered around the locked chest.

Sif signed hello, sidling over until her arm brushed against Renna's.

Little Jon ran their hands over the metal box. It was completely sealed. It came up nearly to Renna's hips even while on the ground, the red-gold material that had once been a sacred sight to her now churning her stomach. Still stewing in her own shame, Renna peered closer at the palanquin. There was a faint interruption in the metal's pattern outlining a small square about the width of two hands.

Alaini inserted the point of her dagger, trying to find purchase. It finally caught, and she pried the lid off and immediately covered her nose. "Why is it always blood with these people?"

A wrongness filled the air, along with a distinct metallic smell.

Before she could get a good look, Sif gripped Renna's arm so hard she was sure there would be marks. The young girl tugged at her, trying to pull her away, signing frantically with her free hand. Renna could comprehend only half of the gestures: *don't make me* and *how can you* and *evil.* Her attempts to soothe Sif failed, and Edwine intervened, pulling the sobbing child away.

Unsettled, Renna turned to the palanquin.

A shudder built in the ground, and it took Renna a minute to realize it was her who was trembling. A ringing filled her ears. She couldn't make sense of what she was seeing, what it meant. They'd expected bloodsiphons or aurem coins. But this…

The entire vessel was filled with thick crystal-like clots of blood.

CHAPTER 29

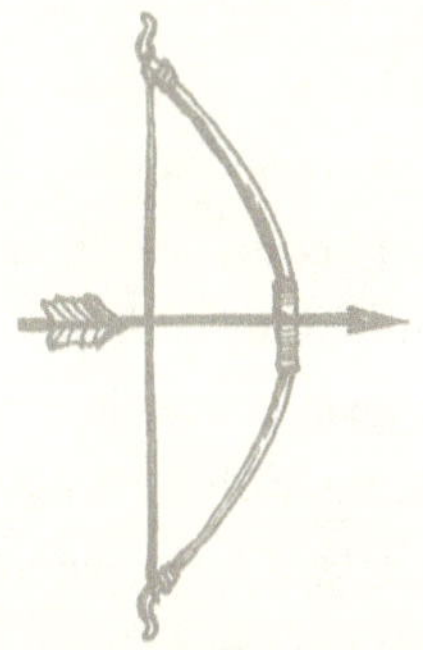

Renna had a sneaking suspicion that Little Jon only invited her to go with them to confer with the Druidhen Matriarch as a peace offering because she was not allowed on the missions into Loxley. In preparation for the ride, Renna spent the morning brushing down Alita, the repetitive motion helping to calm her mind. After she'd run her fingers through the patches of swirled hair behind the mare's front legs, Renna wove intricate braids into her mane.

Winter was thawing outside the wards, and life was returning to Sherwood. A few songbirds sang back and forth as Renna and Little Jon rode through the woods. Spring equinox would arrive before too long. As they crossed a shallow river, Renna shivered, remembering the beast that had hunted her on the night she'd escaped the castle.

"Do you know of a creature in the forest that won't cross a river?"

"There is the morglak. It's a mix between an ogre, a boar, and a wildcat. A foul and cunning beast to be sure, but they do fear water. Most likely a trait carried over from whatever demon realm spawned them." They cut her a look. "Have you encountered one?"

Renna hadn't gotten a good look at the beast in the pitch darkness, save for its massive size, long teeth, and tusks, but the description fit. "The first night I entered the woods. I thought I was done for, that all the horrible tales I'd been told were true and I was going die. Then Kit showed up and led us across the river."

Little Jon smiled faintly. "The forest has fearsome monsters and wonderous, beautiful creatures. Loxley would have you believe that it's only the former, but the forest is the same as magic, Ren. There is light and dark in both, and neither can exist without the other."

Renna considered their words. "Growing up, everything was divided into light and dark, good and evil."

Little Jon hummed in agreement. "I think that's common. Mind you, Loxley takes it to an extreme. But just because it's common doesn't make it right or true. You cannot have the light without the darkness."

They fell back into companionable silence for a time, and then Little Jon began to share tales of growing up with the druidhen. Once, a young druid girl had shifted into a raven in the middle of lunch, knocking over buckets of fresh-picked cherries as she did. Renna hung on every word, amazed at how different two life paths could be. She couldn't imagine growing up being accepted for who you were, being taught to have interest in the way other people live and to treat magic with honor and respect. Though it was on both of their minds, she and Little Jon did not discuss the strange clotted blood they'd taken off the Keepers. The outlaws had talked about it endlessly, and they were no closer to understanding what it was. Sif still refused to go near the chest. It was almost a relief to not talk about it.

The silvery mist began as a trickle across the ground, eventually obscuring the forest floor completely, pluming around the horses' hooves as they walked. They must have been getting close. Little Jon had sent a messenger bird a few nights back, asking the druidhen matriarch to meet them at the Misty Meadows, a place outside the wards that the druidhen still frequented and treated with reverence.

The meadow unfurled before them, cloaked in heavy mist, the tops of wildflowers peeking through. They dismounted and waited only a few minutes before something soared overhead. Renna gasped as a vast winged animal landed mere paces from them. It had the head of an eagle and the body of a lion. The name floated to the front of her mind, and she recalled a folk tale she'd read in Rowan Reach: a griffon.

Renna blinked, and where the griffon had been a moment ago, there now stood a woman. She was tall and muscled, her hair woven with feathers, tiny crystals, and acorns. Her eyes shone like a lion's, her face weathered and wise-looking, her skin the color of mahogany, as if she'd been born from the forest. She held a gnarled staff with a griffon carved atop it.

The matriarch of the druidhen moved as if to cup Little Jon's face, then stilled, seeming to think better of it.

"Hello, Mother," Little Jon said.

A jolt ran through Renna. Little Jon's *mother* was the leader of the druidhen.

"This is Renna, Mum. Ren, this is my mother, Myrryn Bjonir."

"My dearest," Myrryn said, and then her eyes slid over to Renna. "And a Truth Sayer."

Renna stiffened. It wasn't possible that she recognized Renna as the fallen queen. Behind her, Alita huffed. "I am no Trissaia," Renna said.

The druid cocked her head, eyes sparkling, assessing, like she was reading something they could not see. Then she dipped her chin. "My mistake." She turned her attention back to Little Jon, taking a few steps closer. The mist moved around her like rippling water. "It has been some time."

"You know the way through the wards."

Hurt flickered across Myrryn's face, but she rolled her shoulders back. There was an undercurrent of things unsaid, both small and large hurts given and received.

Myrryn said, "You want to know about the Flowering Fern. Dare I ask what trouble you have gotten yourself into?"

"Would it make a difference if you knew?"

The two druids stared at one another as crickets chirped nearby. The air smelled of pine and rain. Renna rubbed her sweaty palms on her pants. Myrryn's shoulders dropped a half inch. "I suppose not. The magical properties of the fern aren't entirely known, but I trust that if you are asking, it will serve your purpose."

She addressed them both. "The quest to find the fern will be more emotionally than physically challenging. The Flowering Fern is heavily guarded by wood wraiths. You will each have to confront inner demons. They'll attempt to turn your focus away from the path, but you cannot allow that. The wood wraiths will play tricks on your mind to lure you away from the flower and toward your death."

Renna looked at Little Jon, but their face was unreadable.

"You'll want to follow the whisps. Stop your ears up with beeswax, Jon. And whatever you do, don't look away from the path."

Renna's mind scrambled to understand all the unfamiliar terms. Feeling out of her depth, she asked, "How do we find the path?"

"Draw the rune for guidance on your palm in charcoal when the moon is full. Travel east within the wards toward the foothills of the Spine. Take an offering to leave where you find the fern. If you are found worthy, the whisps will appear and lead the way."

If they were found worthy.

Little Jon nodded, satisfied. They stood in awkward silence. "Thank you, Mother."

"Before you go…" Myrryn blurted when Little Jon made to turn away. The matriarch stretched her hand out toward them. She licked her lips. "Please, tell me. What is it for?"

Little Jon cast Renna a sidelong glance. "Something evil is brewing in Loxley. We think there's a curse or a compulsion of some kind at work. We mean to break it."

Myrryn took a steadying breath, eyes fluttering shut.

"I know what you're going to say, but it won't change my mind," Little Jon ground out.

"You cannot possibly know what I mean to say."

"You've said it a hundred times. 'Druidhen do not concern themselves with the ways of mortals and witches.' Right? I should keep to the forest and let the world burn."

"You think me so callous, Jon, but—"

"I really don't, Mother. I'm just…disappointed."

It was a well-worn conversation. A dance that had been done until both parties were blistered and exhausted. The Misty Meadow was charged, the smell of salt in the air. Renna could feel Little Jon's staff pulsing with magic, answering the vibration of their mother's.

"Jon. Please. You cannot fully understand what it is you ask of us, what you ask of me. You are free to live how you choose, but you cannot fault me for wanting you to be safe."

"There's no hiding from the evil that's growing, no matter how deep into Sherwood you go."

Myrryn looked away, her chest lifting with a shuddering breath as she tried to regain composure. Renna shifted closer to Little Jon. They worked their jaw, battling internally.

"Tell Ma hello for me." They turned away, pulling Renna along.

"Little Jon, wait. There is an old enchantment. It's not been cast for hundreds of years, but it could break even the strongest of compulsions."

Renna and Little Jon exchanged guarded glances as Myrryn took parchment from her robes and began to impart her wisdom. The instructions were detailed and lengthy by the time she sent them off, armed with a spell for petrification, and hope.

CHAPTER 30

Keeper's Keep smelled of blood and incense. Garen couldn't think of a less pleasant combination. Aside from the putrid stench, it was what the smells represented—the lies those in power told in the name of the Mother—that offended his senses more than anything he'd experienced on the battlefield or while doling out punishments as the high sheriff.

The hour was late or early, depending on how one looked at it; the corridors were mostly abandoned, the castle's residents asleep or at prayer. Garen's ink-black cloak allowed him to melt into the shadows. The lines of his tattoo pulsed with magic, cloaking him in obscurity. He checked his mettlemantic shields, ensuring that the carefully constructed facade was all anyone would see if they brushed lightly against his mind.

The king's behavior had become erratic since the ball. Everyone was under scrutiny. There had been more executions in the last fortnight than during the previous month. Garen and his fellow spies had been working tirelessly to smuggle as many innocent people out of the city as they could. Loathe as he was to remain inside the city walls, he could not risk visiting Sherwood just yet. He'd sent Briar and Kirin with a group of men, women, and children who needed a place to stay. Garen had not been able to shake the memory of the small child he'd carried in his arms. She'd trembled with fear so violently that it had taken several minutes to coax her to release her grip on him and go with Briar.

Tonight was the first chance he'd had to slip away to act on Renna's intel, if it could be called that. He scowled, picking his way along the darkened corridor. When Kirin had returned and delivered her message to go to the Keep, follow the Silenced, and look beneath the flame, Garen had wanted to ride out to Sherwood and drag her back to the castle for a lesson in espionage. (Of course, that would have been a perfect example of what *not* to do as a spy.) It was his own damn fault that she'd been so vague; he'd been the one to suggest that the less information passed between them, the safer it would be for everyone. Which, technically speaking, was true, but Garen didn't want things kept from *him*.

The layout of the residential wing of the Keep reminded him of the lower levels of Nottingham: small living spaces stacked on top of one another to cram in as many people as possible. As he rounded a corner and descended to a lower level, the smell of unwashed bodies stung his nose. Inside the rooms were rows of occupied beds, purple robes hung on hooks, flickering aurem lanterns.

What do you want me to find, lishka?

He was about to turn back when something caught his eye. Like the entrance of the room where he'd taken Renna all those months ago, the seam in the stone was so meticulous, following the pattern of the rock so perfectly, that it was nearly invisible. Garen ran his fingers along it, unsuccessfully searching for a catch or a release mechanism.

From his robes he pulled a vial the length of his ring finger. The blood inside had a congealed quality to it—the stasis charm was wearing off, he'd need to have Briar make him another soon—but it would suffice. When one single drop touched the seam, the stone shifted. The air in the passage was significantly colder, the floor sloping down at a steep angle, the low ceiling forcing him to crouch. When it finally leveled out, it opened to reveal another residential floor.

But unlike the previous ones, it could have been midday for how many people were roaming about.

Garen had felt this way before: on the precipice of discovering something he did not want to know, something that would rip the ground out from under him, leaving him in a free fall of terror. It was the same sense of foreboding that had overtaken him when his troop had been captured by the Falsehoods, and again when he'd realized they were not the inhuman, vile creatures he'd been taught to hate, to eradicate. Instead, they'd offered him the truth—the real truth, not the doctrine the crown used as a means of control.

The Trissaia were no different from the vedra they so vehemently opposed.

Magic simply *was*. It was the wielder who used it for good or for ill. The burning shame that followed the realization had nearly killed him; he could not bear to think of what he'd done, the people he'd slain, the monster he'd allowed himself to become—

Once you knew the truth, you made a different choice. Sindri's words from so long ago still echoed through his mind like a second heartbeat. The distance from his familiar was uncomfortable, like an itch on his back that he couldn't reach, but Sindri's presence in the forest allowed him to have quicker contact with the Falsehoods and keep an eye on Sherwood. More important to Garen, though, was that Sindri was safer away from Loxley. Just three nights ago he'd walked past someone auctioning off fresh fox furs in the noble sector. His hatred for this place had only hardened more.

Garen exhaled slowly, bringing his focus back to his surroundings. The wing stretched some fifty feet, an archway carved out of the stone at the other end. Light emanated from beyond it, and a steady stream of people entered and exited. No one spoke. There were no purple Keeper robes; everyone wore dull beige. Some were sprayed with blood, and all were covered with a layer of dirt. At the center of the hall was a large well of dark crimson liquid.

A crash filled the air, jolting Garen. Two people had collided, sending their tools flying—a pickax and a small shovel. But no one around them paid them any mind, as if they hadn't heard the noise.

Keeping to the edge of the room, Garen moved toward the archway, unease scratching at his throat. The tunnel before him was wide enough for five men across. Garen wove through the slow tide of people. Fear hung heavy in the putrid air. The tunnel took the better part of an hour to traverse, winding around and delving deeper into the mountain.

When he'd first defected from Loxley, when his doubt and shame and anger had begun to feel like a vise around his lungs, Garen had stayed sane by focusing on what he could fix around him. He needed a way to have control, a way to be proactive.

It had started small: the weapons unit of the Falsehoods was a jumbled mess. He'd catalogued and organized everything that first week. One of the higher-up officers was missing information about Loxley's initial production of aurem. Garen didn't sleep for several days straight, poring over tomes and parchments, reading nearly illegible accounts until he found the necessary intel. Bringing down Loxley soon became an obsession. He'd climbed in the ranks quickly, making himself invaluable to the Falsehoods, and volunteered to be sent back as a spy.

His most recent contact with Sindri had buoyed him after his punishment from Ulrik. The Falsehoods had confirmed through their network of spies that Loxley was under some type of compulsion spell. But how could someone hold that kind of power over an entire kingdom? Garen felt the familiar pull to solve the puzzle as he went deeper into the mountain.

Abruptly, the tunnel opened, and a blast of heat from above made him blink rapidly.

He was in a cavern beneath the Mother's Flame.

The fire stretched across the ceiling, barely visible through the lines of grated aurem that made up the hearth. Squinting, he could make out the angle at which each slate had been placed, making it possible to see up and out, but from above, the room below was obscured. Blood dripped through the thin gaps.

A terrible scraping sound shook the chamber. No one acknowledged it, and the strange behavior raised the hair on his neck. Shadows lengthened down the stairwell on the far side. Pressing tight against the stone wall, Garen snuck toward where the rock jutted out, providing a small spot of coverage. Magic rippled over his skin, emanating from his tattoo, the names of each rune echoing like a prayer in his mind: uruz for vitality; thurisaz for strength; eihwaz for resilience; laguz for healing; lauma for stealth.

King Ulrik emerged at the base of the stairs, looking exhausted. Several sets of hands trembled among the prisoners, but no one looked toward their king, as if they knew better than to acknowledge what was happening or draw any attention to themselves. Garen couldn't concentrate on the center of the room, like there was something actively forcing him to look away.

But Ulrik walked with purpose toward the middle, unaffected, and then disappeared.

Garen snuck around, trying to get a better line of sight, and he was just able to make out some of Ulrik's profile. His head throbbed angrily, but he strained to hear what the king was doing. There was the wet sound of blood dripping from above, a hiss as Ulrik dragged a dagger across his palm, and then Garen saw movement as he knelt, hands pressed to the ground.

Deep dread, a kind of animalistic self-preservation, kicked in. The atmosphere in the room reminded Garen of the kingdom's war camps, the terror and grief that hung on each malnourished frame. A voice rumbled through the cavern, neither masculine nor feminine. Garen's hackles rose at its otherworldly quality even though the words were unfamiliar. He forced himself to breathe.

Once in a library in Wendsvik, he'd read about eldritch entities from another realm, a place of demons and monsters that the human mind could not comprehend. When he'd asked Sindri if such a place existed, his familiar had gone quiet. When he'd finally responded, Garen had heard real fear in the fox's words for the first time.

My kind comes from another realm where fae and humans lived beside one another and magic was wild and rampant. Where winged stallions crossed the sky, the woods were alive with magic, and it was more common to see foxes with many tails than one. But where there is good, there is evil, and those who would take advantage of powers they should not tamper with. Opening one realm to another leaves opportunities for monsters to slip through and enter the hearts of evil and greedy men.

Garen's core trembled as if he was straining under a massive weight. He pulled his magic around him like a cloak, desperate to remain undetected.

Ulrik spoke. "She will be handled, I assure you."

This time the creature spoke in the common tongue. "You have made such assurances before."

The king stammered, so at odds with the calculating monarch Garen was used to seeing. He could not catch what Ulrik said before the creature cut him off.

"You lie. The druidhen would do no such thing."

"I have seen it! I swear to you. It will be ready soon."

"You are running out of things to bargain."

"Strike years from our original deal. Two centuries is more than enough—"

"You are halfway through your time. Your life is already forfeit and therefore holds no real value."

A sickening silence followed. Garen did not move, his mind spinning. What sort of bargain had the king made with this creature? Had he simply wanted a longer life? It was clear he was desperate, worried about upholding the terms of the deal. Garen's skin crawled at the implications.

"Gisborne." The creature said the king consort's name as if it could taste him.

"W-what?"

"If you cannot fulfill your promise by the next full moon, you shall give Gisborne to me." *"No."* The king sounded anguished.

"Your wager means nothing to me if it doesn't mean something to you. Don't look so horrified. I have no use for him dead. But his knowledge of metallurgy fascinates me, and I quite like the idea of a new pet."

Garen stole a glance at the center of the room, squinting through the pain it brought. A soft whimper came from the king. Light refracted, bending around whatever cloaked the creature. Nausea churned in his gut. Garen looked away, brow sweating. Whatever was there was more powerful than anything he'd ever encountered. The two were speaking in hushed tones now, and there was no way to get closer without revealing his position. Garen clenched his jaw so hard it hurt, swallowing down his frustration as he sat there for several more tense minutes, unable to hear what was happening.

He replayed everything over in his head, committing it to memory so he could report it back to Sindri. The Falsehoods had to be informed; their extensive academic team could surely figure out what this entity was. Perhaps this was the source of the compulsion spell. And then there was the matter of Ulrik himself; it appeared he had lived for much longer than people believed.

Garen's muscles were cramped from crouching. It reminded him of hiding in the trenches, and he shoved the memory aside. Instead, he watched the workers, all of them still behaving as if nothing was happening, though they kept their gazes averted and he could see more than one trembling. Those who worked close to the center of the room seemed to be scrutinizing…something. The others brought them buckets of blood along with large brushes.

Finally, the king dragged himself back up the steps, vanishing as if he'd never been there.

Garen ran through the tunnels, back up through Keeper's Keep, and outside, where the sky was lightening. Even after he'd retched bile onto the cobblestones, he could not shake his revulsion.

CHAPTER 31

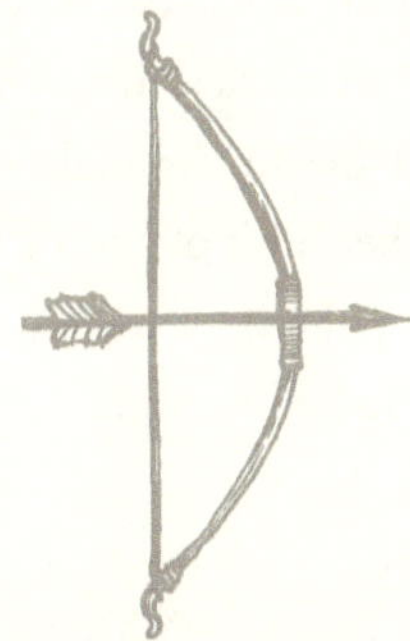

IT WAS JUST THE Thorns HUDDLED AROUND THE FIRE AS THE FULL MOON ROSE, WEARING THEIR CLOAKS AND READY TO GO IN SEARCH OF THE Flowering Fern.

They took turns with a stick of charcoal, drawing the rune algiz onto their open palms for guidance. It looked like a diamond with long tails. Renna sketched the rune over the crescent moon scar on her palm. Then Little Jon handed each of them a small tin of beeswax to put in their ears to block out the voices of the wood wraiths. The effect felt like slipping underwater, different from the oppressive silence back in the castle. This felt strangely freeing. The wax left a sticky residue on Renna's fingers. She swiped them in the dirt, rolling her fingers together until the excess gum clumped into small beads that she brushed off on her trousers.

They set out, Little Jon in the lead, Much and Renna a few paces behind them, Scarlet and Alaini bringing up the rear. Little Jon carried a small lantern that held a flickering candle and used their quarterstaff as a walking stick. The forest stretched east, butting up against the Spine of Kaerenthal, which stood against the night sky like sharp teeth, an onyx battlement built for giants. It was strange not to hear the leaves crunching beneath their feet. Every so often Little Jon would twist to sign something—*the ground is marshy here* or *keep your eyes open for whisps*.

The whisps, Renna had learned, were descended from the fae and had nearly been wiped out during the Great Culling. They were like tiny fireflies and could lead travelers to what they sought. Renna was certain she'd seen some that first night in Sherwood.

For hours they picked their way through lush ferns in the dark forest. (Alaini gave up signaling each fern they passed after the fifth time Little Jon said they were not the magical kind). Occasionally a flicker of blue light swept around them, pulling them one way or the other, nudging them down a different path. Little Jon followed each time without hesitation. Renna wondered what it was like to grow up without being indoctrinated with lies, to see magic and just be able to marvel at it rather than worrying that witnessing it might end with you being burned at the stake. The whisps reminded her a bit of the Fire Feast, where there were always dancers with flames—the way the light traced patterns across the inky sky only to fade a moment later, leaving an impression of light behind, as if you'd pressed hard on your closed eyelids.

Renna preferred the whisps.

Just when she began to wonder if the beeswax was strictly necessary, an unexpected chill fell over her. The hairs on her neck prickled, and pressure swelled around her ears. Little Jon halted, still as a deer scenting a wolf.

They signed, *Form a single-file line. Don't let go of each other. Don't look off the path until we are allowed into the Flowering Fern's grove.*

Everyone obeyed, falling into a line, each holding the shoulder of the one in front of them. The sky, impossibly, darkened even more. Something brushed against Renna's leg, then her arm. She tested the ground with her feet carefully before taking each step as the path narrowed, twisting sinuously now. Out of the corner of her eye, the trees bent over them like vultures. Renna's mind was screaming with every childhood story about wicked forests: demons would find you in your sleep and sit on your chest, slowly suffocating you; a witch would curse you and you'd be unmade, unraveling into blood and bone and gristle.

Renna focused on the curls at the nape of Much's neck. The skin around her knuckles stretched tight as she gripped Much's shoulder to keep from slipping. She couldn't hear anything, but she could sense a presence swirling around her body, searching for a crack to slip through, looking for a weakness in her armor. It felt like thick cobwebs draping over her, clinging to her face before slipping away.

Despite their precautions, something was whispering to her, urging her to remove the beeswax, to listen to the words and the truth they held. She was wicked like this forest, so why shouldn't she? Her chest was heavy with guilt, as if a demon really was upon her, claws wrapped around her ribs, tugging to get in. It was hard to breathe. Rotten roots snagged her boots, and thorns bit into her ankles.

Listen to me, listen to me, listen, LISTEN.

Wind whipped at her face, stinging her cheeks. She tasted salt.

LISTEN TO ME, DAUGTHER OF LOXLEY.

FAILED QUEEN.

UNWORTHY WITCH, UNSTOP YOUR EARS.

YOU HAVE NO POWER HERE.

Darkness searched for a way in, viscous and thick like tar. Alaini was gripping her shoulder so tightly she'd have a bruise in the morning. Would she make it to morning? Her palm was slick, the rune she'd drawn surely smudged.

The rune. Algiz. For guidance and protection. To keep her on her true path.

Biting her tongue to keep from screaming, Renna used her free hand to trace the rune in the air, if only for a focal point, to keep her head from turning, to keep her from looking, from ripping out the wax in her ears that felt like they were bleeding. Much's head twitched as if he too was fighting not to look. Renna drew the rune on his back; she could bolster him even if she was doomed to fail. His shoulders shook with sobs she could not hear as she wrote the rune again, again, searing it into his skin.

Draic's offer flashed in her mind: the tattoo that would help her resist mind magic. Her powers had been taken, but that didn't mean she was powerless, did it? She'd discovered how to muddle a few herbs and plants to create a mild-flavored paste that soothed the scarring on the stub of Yana's tongue. She'd been brewing the elixir to break the spell wrapped around Loxley. She'd learned to calm her mind when it turned against her. Renna had pored over every grimoire and spell book she could get her hands on, spent all her own allotted coin on healing scrolls and spells to bring back to Sherwood. Now she riffled through them in her mind, whispering old enchantments she'd learned, trying to infuse her will and intention into each flick of her tongue, the shape of her lips.

Ahead, there was a faint light glowing, haloing Much and Little Jon in hues of brilliant gold, red, and purple. The shadowy wraiths at the edge of her vision wavered. The muscles in her neck relaxed slightly, no longer resisting an incessant pull. Renna sucked in a breath, and it was like her head had broken through water. The darkness was receding, and the pressure on her skull was lifting.

The grove shimmered like a bubble forming around them, a large boulder off to one side with the blooming fern in the center. The enchantment surrounding them buzzed pleasantly on Renna's skin. At the signal from Little Jon, they all unstopped their ears. Much's mouth was clamped tight, and he looked pale. Renna wondered what awful things the wood wraiths had said to him.

The Flowering Fern was so beautiful it was nearly painful to look at, conjuring reverence and awe the same way the Oakheart did. Huge long petals spilled wide in shades of purple, red, orange, and gold, vibrant and alive. The heady floral scent was intoxicating. The fern leaves reached up and out; warmth emanated from them. They were not of this world—they *couldn't* be—and yet here they were. The flowers tipped toward the moon, drinking in the ethereal light.

"Well done." Alaini laughed shakily, clapping Little Jon on the back.

The boulder shuddered.

A low rumble shook the ground as the thing they'd all mistaken for a boulder began to rise. It moved with agitation, a hibernating animal being awoken too soon. Fear speared through Renna. She'd not seen it clearly before, but there was no mistaking the hulking mass and razor-sharp tusks as the beast unfurled to tower over them.

The morglak's eyes were pitch black rimmed with red as the lids peeled back against bone. Its horrible snout was reminiscent of a boar, just like Little Jon had said. Tusks jutted from its hideous mouth. Its leathery, patchy skin seemed to pull in the light around it.

Little Jon's fingers flicked. *Don't move. It craves the chase.*

Renna couldn't have moved even if she'd wanted to, for the beast opened its mouth, gnashing its rotten teeth. Its grating voice, like the sound of bones being ground together, seemed to emanate from its chest rather than its mouth, ricocheting around the grove.

"WHO DARES TO ENTER HERE?"

Little Jon raised their voice, still as a statue. "We seek the Flowering Fern and nothing else. The spirits of the woods who protect this grove have allowed us to enter."

The beast threw its head back in an unsettling mimicry of laughter. "YOU THINK TO USE THE OLD LAWS OF THE DRUIDHEN ON ME? I OBEY NO LAWS." The beast dropped down onto all fours, its claws ripping up the ground. "YOUR DRUIDHEN MAGIC IS WHAT KEEPS ME LOCKED IN HERE, AS I CANNOT SURVIVE WITHIN THE WARDS YOU CAST. AND IT HAS BEEN A LONG TIME SINCE SUCH FOOD HAS WANDERED IN."

The morglak prowled before them. Its breath reeked of rotting flesh and mildew. Renna took in the grove, seeing what she'd not noticed before: the bones of small animals that littered the ground, all picked clean.

"A bargain, then, for your safe passage out of the wards," Little Jon said.

Renna fervently prayed they knew what they were doing. The morglak's tongue flicked out, mottled purple and forked in the middle. The ghastly thing flitted in the air as if trying to taste them. Much squeezed Renna's hand, crushing the small bones together.

"I DO NOT BELIEVE YOU."

"I swear it. You will pass through in peace if you let us go about our business. On my word."

The cracked lips peeled back, exposing a second row of teeth. "ON YOUR BLOOD, DRUID."

Renna's heart was in her throat. Surely the creature meant an offering, not a full sacrifice. She was farthest from the thing, angled in such a way that she could sign to Little Jon, her hand hidden from the monster's sight.

Or so she thought.

The morglak lunged, a streak of darkness shooting toward her, pinning her flat to the ground. Something snapped in her side, eliciting bright stars of pain in her vision. Each breath hurt. She'd broken a rib. The saliva that hit her face burned like acid, and she screamed.

"STOP PLOTTING AMONGST YOURSELVES."

A seismic wave rolled through the grove as Little Jon spun their staff overhead. Light exploded from the crystal, and the morglak's body whipped back as if struck, even though the staff had not touched it. Sweat shone on the druid's face, but still they brandished the staff at the beast. "If you harm her, you will die in this grove before the sun rises."

The morglak crouched, snarling, but did not move to attack again. "I DEMAND BLOOD."

"Then you shall have it and be gone," Little Jon said.

Pulling a dagger from their hip, Little Jon held up the palm that did not carry the rune and made a clean cut. The morglak shuddered as the tang of cooper filled the air and red blood bloomed. In a strange echo of giving a tithe, Little Jon knelt, eyes never leaving the creature, and placed their palm to the dirt. Renna did not think the two so different now: giving blood to a flame or to a monster.

The morglak inhaled deeply, then buried its snout in the bloodied earth, drinking deeply. Its eyes were glassy, almost intoxicated. "YOU MADE AN OATH."

Little Jon's hand was trembling as they reached into their pocket for the charcoal, then stepped right up to the beast. Renna tried to decipher each rune they drew on its chest, but they were laid over one another, forging a sigil she didn't know how to interpret. Finally, Little Jon said, "You have your blood and your way out. Begone from this place."

The morglak bared its teeth once more, eyeing them all, before slinking out of the grove.

"What in the absolute bloody fuck was that?" Alaini breathed.

"A creature from before the Culling." Little Jon leaned heavily on their staff, whatever magic they'd done clearly taking a toll.

Renna held one hand against her rib, looking at the druid. "Thank you."

"You all right, Ren?" Much's brow was pinched as he knelt beside her.

Every sip of air brought a sharp pain to her lung. She was trembling, and her body was coursing with adrenaline. A strange hush fell over the grove, which now had the look of an abandoned graveyard. Renna nodded, desperate to leave this place. "I'm fine. Let's get the flower and be done with it."

Little Jon pulled out a golden sickle, the one they'd used on winter solstice, and cut one bloom, so carefully it felt almost intimate to watch. Renna had not understood when Little Jon had told them that they must take only one and not disturb the others. Now, kneeling before the fern, it made sense.

One was more than one person deserved in a lifetime.

Then each of them pulled their offering out and dug a hole in the dirt to bury it. Alaini, a string from her lute; Scarlet, a small piece of stone that matched the hilt of her sword; Little Jon, a bright purple crystal; Renna, the owl pendant; Much, the token Draic had given him to escape Loxley. As they raked the dank soil over their precious possessions, the fern shone brighter, as if gaining power. The intensity of the blaze became too much, and they all shielded their eyes.

When they opened them, they were in an ordinary grove under the moonlight, the fern hidden from their realm once more.

Renna's nerves were on edge as she bent over a simmering cauldron, shoulders aching from the constant stirring, waiting for her friends to reenter the wards. While they ambushed more Trissaian palanquins, Keepers on horseback, and carriages filled with wealthy nobles on the highway road, Renna and the others who remained at the camp took turns tending to the potions. This mixture required continuous stirring for three nights, and they were now on the final evening.

The table was covered in supplies: mistletoe that had been plucked clean, the muddler full of rowan berry pulp, and a large glass jar of fern flower crushed to a shimmery powder. Each batch needed only the smallest dash of the fern dust. The heat from the fire and fumes from the elixir had given Renna's hair a life of its own, and she was sure she had smudges of red across her face where she'd brushed back stray strands, her fingers stained with the juice of the rowan berries. She'd already watched the cauldrons for more than her allotted time, but she'd sent Edwine away when the woman had tried to take over, despite the soreness the movement caused her still healing rib. She was too restless while her friends were outside the wards. A healing poultice from Little Jon had helped the bruising and swelling go down immensely, and breathing was getting easier. It put the balm she used back in Loxley to shame. She still moved in a guarded way, sudden movement causing sharp pain. Renna continued to stir the murky red substance until finally it changed to a vibrant, luminescent pink. She set the cauldron aside to cool just as the wards shivered.

Alaini, Scarlet, Much, and Little Jon stumbled into camp, dropping heavy bags that clinked with coins. Though tired and muddy, they were all whole. One sack bore blood splatters. The stolen aurem would be placed in the cooling elixir, while the coins now sufficiently infused with the previous batch would be put in sacks to go back into Loxley.

Alaini slumped down on a nearby log, resting her head in her hand. Scarlet was dabbing a small cut above Much's eyebrow. When he was finished, Much pulled out a folded piece of vellum and spread it on the table for Renna to see.

WANTED FOR AIDING THE ROBBING HOODS

THE OUTLAW WITCH & FALSE QUEEN

RENNA HOOD

The reward for information on her whereabouts was listed below two sketches of her: one with a cowl over her face, the other without. Much tapped the cowled face. "This could be *me*."

Scarlet cocked her head. "You think you and Renna have the same eyes? How precious."

"No one's got eyes like Hood," Alaini added.

"Do you mean murderous?" Little Jon called.

"Unhinged, but in a seductive way?"

"Like you'd better pray to all the gods that she's on your side when they change from green to gold?"

"What?"

"That's hazel eyes for you. Are they green, brown, gold? Witchcraft," Alaini hissed, wiggling her fingers in mock horror. Weak laughter ran through the group.

"I'm serious," said Much.

Alaini looked between him and Renna, holding her hands over the lower halves of their faces. Her brows inched toward her hairline. "Huh."

Much's eyes glinted, and Renna's heart sank at the familiar expression. "No," she said firmly.

"What?"

"That looks says, 'I've got a foolish idea that could get me killed.'"

Much waved the warrant. "I'm just saying we could use their desire to capture Ren to our advantage, even if she can't leave the wards yet."

"You are not posing as me."

"You do have the same build…" Alaini held up her hands in defense as Renna scowled at her.

"Look, your name and face are giving the people of Loxley hope, and it's making the king nervous." Much sighed, speaking more gently. "All I'm proposing is that we let them think you're still running around, causing chaos. I can use your arrow-splitting move—they love that. It won't be any more dangerous than what we are already doing. Besides, it's my choice, isn't it?"

There was no good argument against that. Renna kept quiet as they began planning, her mind turning over an idea that had been forming since they'd found the fern. Briar was expected in the morning. Renna would send the priestess back with a message for Draic. Submitting to a painful tattoo ritual would keep her mind safe, which would mean there'd be no reason for her to remain behind any longer. No reason for her friends to take unnecessary risks by pretending to be her.

That night, the sound of the stolen aurem coins hitting the bottom of the cauldron felt more holy than the clink of bloodstone siphons falling into the Flame ever had.

CHAPTER 32

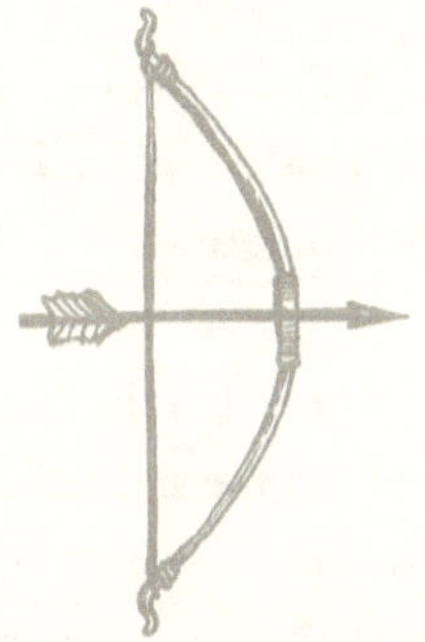

RENNA SAT IN A TREE JUST OUTSIDE THE WARDS AS NIGHT BLED INTO DAWN, WAITING. A way off, Alita nosed at the ground, though it was apparent from the huffing and head tossing every few moments that the grazing options outside the wards were not up to her standards. They'd been out there for a few hours now. When Renna had awoken from yet another nightmare—phantom talons digging into her brain, her friends trapped under the Mother's Flame, Nastasia calling for her execution while Garen was tortured—she knew it was futile to attempt to go back to sleep. She wasn't the only one who was having trouble keeping demons away. In the past few weeks, they'd taken in upward of four dozen people looking for refuge after fleeing Loxley. People weeping in their sleep or staring off into space with haunted expressions was common. The way the crew in Rowan Reach seemed to know how to handle the changing current of emotion in the camp was simultaneously inspiring and heartbreaking. They knew suffering and pain intimately enough to know how to offer space for healing and grief.

They had been working tirelessly on a petrification spell that Myrryn had shared with them in parting. They gently cut away small branches, strips of bark, and acorns from specific trees: oak would be the anchor, due to its strength against deceptions and the way it allowed people to see the truth. Then there was hawthorn, which naturally warded against malevolent spirits (and thus created a perfect boundary around Rowan Reach); birch for purification and counteracting existing curses and spells; rowan to shield against dark enchantments and to aid with truth-seeing. Yew would help with transmuting the wood and acorns into stone, while willow and elm would stabilize the spell. Each individual ingredient needed to be carved with runes and sigils and imbued with tinctures of willow and birch, rowan, and yew. A powdered mixture of fern flower, yew, and rowan wood would seal the grain in the wood before it was buried in the grove of the Oakheart by moonlight. It would take months buried under the soil for the wood and acorns to turn to stone, but when the alchemical process was done, they would be able to disrupt even the strongest compulsion spells. The petrified wood, along with the potion-infused coins they were scattering through Loxley every few nights, would give them a fighting chance.

A twig snapped, leaves rustled, and the Night Watchman materialized from the trees. Renna's body reacted to the sight of him, her pulse picking up. Draic approached slowly and spoke in a hushed tone to Alita, who sniffed his hand before nuzzling him. He chuckled softly, whispering something too low for Renna to hear, petting Alita's neck. From the pack slung on his back, Draic pulled out an apple, which he fed to the mare. The interaction plucked at Renna's heart, a strange warmth swirling behind her ribs.

Renna landed in a silent crouch, but even still, Draic was unfazed when she approached. Neither of them spoke as she came to stand on Alita's other side. His gaze unnerved her. The moment they'd shared in the hallway in the castle suddenly came rushing back: the feel of his stubble on her cheek, his hand splayed on her back to pull her into him, how her breath had caught and her mind had gone still for a moment. Heat rushed to her cheeks now.

When Draic finally spoke, his voice had the same gentleness that his hands did as he stroked Alita. "I got your message."

In the weak light he looked ghostly, all the color drained from his skin. There was a stiffness in his shoulders as he moved—lingering effects of the punishment he'd borne, no doubt. The dark circles under his eyes looked like bruises. All at once, they were children in the stables, him standing before her with a black eye and saying, "She should not have said that about your parents," her realizing that perhaps she did not know the boy in front of her at all.

A fierce need to understand what had happened before he'd found her in the stables overtook her. "Did your grandmother hit you that day?"

Draic's hands stilled.

"After she said—"

"I remember." He resumed his ministrations to Alita, eyes down. "Does it matter?"

"How could it not?"

A muscle feathered in his jaw. He ran Alita's mane through his fingers. Renna waited.

"I'm surprised you remember. It was not the first or the last time that Devana struck me."

Devana. Not even *Grandmother*, then. Renna picked a small burr from Alita's coat, trying to sift through her feelings. Grief for young Garen, for her younger self, for the roles they'd been born into. Anger at who he'd been forced to become to survive. Her throat itched. *I apologize for the way in which I had to save your life.* The forest seemed to hold its breath, stillness falling over them both, the moment fragile. As if they were both thinking about the dark room that smelled of blood and moonshade. The words *I'm sorry* hung on her tongue.

As if he could sense it, Draic cut her a quick look. "Don't. Please. You need not feel sorry for me."

"You do not get to control how I feel," she snapped, trying to hide the sting of embarrassment.

His lip twitched, the ghost of a smile. "I would never dream of it, lishka. I only meant that we are at a large imbalance for who owes whom an apology. And I do not think I could take it growing even more one-sided."

Renna continued to pick at Alita's coat though there was nothing there now, needing somewhere to look besides his face. Emotion clogged her throat like a too-tight collar; she was unused to this earnest, sincere version of him. It was like the familiar sensation of removing her hand from a sturdy tree trunk when climbing high, balancing on a thin limb: exhilarating and dangerous, knowing the fall could break her. She risked a glance at him, the intensity of his expression stirring something inside her.

Renna imagined letting go of the tree. "Though it's better than last time, I still do not think that counts as an apology."

Some of the tension in the air eased. "I am sorry."

Renna raised a brow, trying for an unaffected expression even as the words speared through her. "You *can* learn, then."

"If properly motivated." Draic pulled out a thin pair of leather gloves and held them out to her. They were a rich black and so thin they felt like part of her skin when she tried them on. Renna flexed her hands, the expert stitching across the knuckles allowing for fluid movement. "They're dragonhide," he said.

Renna balked. The great beasts of old were all gone. The only ways to obtain something made from the precious material were to inherit it or procure it for a sum so large even a king would hesitate. She'd only ever seen one person wear such a precious leather; Devana had prized her dragonhide gloves more than anything.

"Can't have your cold hands impeding your combat skills," Draic said.

The heat in her face spread across her collarbone and down into her stomach at his casual observation. The usual chill in her fingertips had indeed subsided. "Thank you."

Draic shrugged. "Consider them a late birthday gift."

Renna started. She'd completely forgotten; she'd turned twenty-four shortly after the masquerade. She hadn't even marked the day.

Alita chose that moment to chuff, stomping her foot impatiently. Renna cleared her throat, gently prying off the gloves and stammering that they should get going. The location of Rowan Reach was too important to reveal, but he could ride astride Alita and be led in as long as he was blindfolded. Draic did as she instructed, climbing onto Alita's bare back—the horse loved being without the saddle, and Renna had indulged her this morning—and taking the proffered strip of fabric. But before putting it over his eyes, he reached down to offer her a hand up.

Renna hesitated. She'd assumed she'd guide Alita on foot and said as much.

"The choice is yours, but the ritual is extremely taxing. It will take the better part of the day, and you'll want to save your strength."

His outstretched hand felt like a challenge and a peace offering at once. His calloused palm was rough against hers as she took it. He hauled her up and Renna said a silent thanks for Little Jon's poultice as the movement only brought a dull pain. Alita tossed her head as the two of them shifted to accommodate each other. His thighs braced her hips, the heat of his chest against her back. She handed the blindfold over her shoulder, ignoring how close she was to him. Even sitting, he was much taller than her. She could easily tuck herself under his chin if she wanted—which she didn't, obviously. It was merely an observation.

Draic's large hands wrapped around her waist to keep balance, and Renna steeled her focus, pressing her heels gently into Alita's belly. The gentle trot rocked and swayed the two of them. Renna twined her hands through Alita's mane to offer direction as they wound their way toward the hawthorns and the wards beyond. Their bodies pressed firmly against each other as they moved with the Nozdravian. Draic's fingers flexed against her waist as he leaned forward, head bowed slightly.

Renna needed to focus on something else. "Tell me about the ritual. Does it matter where we do it? The tattoo, that is." Bleeding Mother. She was grateful he could not see her face.

"For this specific type of mental protection, it needs to be on your torso—both sides if you can handle it—and two limbs."

Her heart sank a bit. Her chest was out of the question for modesty's sake. Only Nastasia had ever seen the extent of the scars on her back, but Renna had already made her decision: no one would ever again enter her mind without her permission. She would not be the weak link among her friends and crew. And it wasn't as if Draic didn't have scars of his own.

"You have them on both sides of your torso," she said, hoping he'd taken her silence for contemplation instead of nerves. His cheek brushed against her hair as he nodded. Renna recalled the swirls along his shoulders that trailed down both arms. Not for the first time, she found herself wondering what the full piece looked like. "How do you decide on the design?"

"I don't. The soot that's used to create the ink comes from a firebird's ashes. The bone needle is crafted from the antler of a peryton." At her silence, he clarified, "A beast with the body of a stag but the face and wings of an owl. I'll be inscribing runes into your skin, but the magic interacts uniquely with each person. We won't know what the design is until we are finished. Because of the enchantments set in the bone, the pain is…intense."

"I can handle pain."

They reached the tree with the familiar knot, and Renna leaned to place her hand on the trunk, whispering the required words before urging Alita to follow the path that led to the wall of hawthorns. Neither of them spoke. Draic was taking even breaths, and she wondered for a moment if he despised being blindfolded as much as she did. She thought back to how he'd struggled to remain composed when she'd left him in the forest and he'd thought she was out of sight.

The wards shivered against Renna's skin in recognition. When the time came, she swung down and drew the appropriate runes into the dirt, and the trees opened onto Rowan Reach.

They set up for the ritual in one of the unused tree houses built straight into an oak that had been hollowed out by lightning. The tree cocooned them. Inside was a soft cot, an oversized cushion to sit on, one window, and the green canopy overhead. Birds sang outside, and sunlight began to spill through the window.

Draic spread open a leather bundle, his long fingers moving deftly. Nestled inside were several small cloths, jars of black and silver ink, and a sharpened bone shard the length of Renna's hand with a small, wicked-looking thorn attached to one end. Anticipation and nerves danced along her skin, and she rubbed at her upper arm. Draic's eyes flicked up to track the movement.

Ever since she'd decided that she would get the tattoo, her mind had been cycling through memories of midnight trysts and morning blood tithes, for those were the primary reasons she'd disrobed in front of someone else as an adult. Of course, the tithes were all with Nastasia, the only one who had ever seen the full extent of her scars. Now she recalled the last occasion on which she'd traded passionate kisses in a darkened room. The nobleman in question had danced with her at a Fire Feast. He'd been respectful to a fault, and Renna had dragged him away from the crowd with pleas of *kiss me*. His caresses through her gown had been delicious, making an aching need build between her legs as he undid the lacings. There'd been a rustling sigh of fabric dropping, and the air had kissed her shoulders and back, and then he'd reached for her. Desire to touch her bare skin plain on his face, but she was half naked with nothing between them, and he'd feel her scars, and no, no, no.

Seized with frantic fear, she'd slapped him.

Would it be more humiliating to warn Draic about her scars or let him discover them himself? And why should she worry, anyway? He had been to war, had seen horrors before. But now everything was set, and still Renna could not bring herself to say anything. Draic turned away to give her privacy as she pulled off her tunic. The air prickled her exposed skin. She clutched the fabric to her bare chest and lowered herself face down onto the cot, folding her arms underneath her chin. "Ready."

Clothing rustled as Draic sat on the cushion beside the cot. Too long passed without him saying anything, and she envisioned repulsion on his face, or worse, mockery. Renna peered back at him. His expression was blank, but the muscle in his jaw was jumping as if he was biting back words. Draic gathered her hair, wrapping it around his palm to hold it aside. One finger trailed along the scarred skin. Shame rose in the wake of his touch.

"How did you get these?" His voice was low and rough. "Who did this to you?"

"It's not what it looks like."

"Really? Because it *looks* like someone tortured—"

"*It was my choice*," Renna snapped.

Her whole body was vibrating, a storm building behind her ribs. Tears burned at the back of her throat as she looked away, humiliated by the righteous anger she'd glimpsed on his face. This was somehow worse than if he'd mocked her or flinched at the sight. She did not deserve his sympathy. Her back was a representation of just how much she had failed. Despite her best efforts, she'd still come up short; she hadn't been who her people had needed her to be. She wished for this moment to be over, for the impending pain to begin so she could focus on that instead of this maelstrom of shame and self-consciousness swirling through her.

Then Draic was kneeling by her side, cupping the back of her neck gently but insistent. His thumb swiped once along her jaw, resting behind her ear. His eyes burned silver in the light. This close, she could make out the strokes of blue amidst the grey. "I do not care what lie someone fed to you as the truth. *That* was never a choice."

Renna blinked rapidly, unable to respond.

Draic began to prepare the tools, and when he spoke again, the careful, controlled tone to his voice was back. "We can't stop the ritual once we begin, or else the protective magic won't take hold. But there are some ways we can"—he cleared his throat—"give you a reprieve without stopping the process. Bend the magic a bit."

There was something unsaid in his words. "What ways?"

"Mettlemancy cultivates the same intention that the spell demands in order to keep the protective enchantments building."

"So if I want the pain to stop, I have to let you into my mind?"

"As I said, this is a demanding magical ritual, so if you're not comfortable with all aspects before we begin, then maybe we should—"

"No." Renna cast him another look over her shoulder, her expression firm. "We're doing it. I can accept all aspects."

Draic reached into his satchel. "Take this, then."

Renna took the proffered flask, unscrewed the top, and sniffed. The overwhelming scent set her coughing. "*Bloody Mother*, Draic." The liquor burned even more going down her throat, coating her stomach like flames. She sucked in a breath and blew it out, half expecting to see smoke come from her mouth, and settled back into position.

At the first drag of the needle against her skin, her mind hurtled back to her room in Loxley. Nastasia stood over her, making careful slices, Renna's back slick with warm blood as she tried to keep her tears silent.

I am not there. Renna forced her eyes open, staring at the trees through the window. *Sherwood. I am in Sherwood.*

"Breathe, lishka," Draic said gently, as if he could sense the riot in her mind. Renna exhaled through her teeth. "Good."

She tried to keep her focus away from the scraping sensation and the way her nerves flinched. The pressure of the needle paused briefly as Draic dipped it into one of the jars, then resumed as he started to etch another rune. Her back began to burn, an ache spreading across her shoulders and down her spine. Renna pressed her forehead into her palms, wiggling her toes. Draic dabbed a cloth over the fresh tattoo before the needle sank into her skin again. Each stroke added kindling to the fire running through her veins. Every few moments, he wiped away the blood that welled up, the sensation like sandpaper dragging against her skin. Renna focused on the spot on her ribs where Draic braced his free hand while he inked another rune, trying to picture the indentation each finger was making on her skin as the heat built at the back of her skull. A curse slipped between her clenched teeth, and she reached for the flask again.

"What runes are you drawing?" Talking was good; talking was distracting.

"That last one was algiz, for physical protection. Next we'll do ansuz, which is for mental fortitude, clarity, and truth. Those, bound with the eihwaz rune, will ward off the powers of a sangeserre, helping with your mettle shields. We'll add a few that will help to accelerate healing, as well."

"Are those the same ones you have?"

Draic lifted the needle, then set it down a breath away from where it had just been. "Among others. The man who gave me mine added a few specific ones to help with the things he knew I'd struggle with when I returned."

The needle pulled across her skin. Focusing on the conversation, Renna could let the sharp, clawing nails against her back fade into the background. "Like having to endure a ball?" Draic chuckled, and the reaction swelled something in her chest. "Like having to deal with arrogant fallen royalty who are shite with a knife?"

"Like having to appear unaffected by the things I'd have to do for my deception to be believed."

The honesty of his answer stunned her momentarily. "I'm sorry."

He fell quiet, concentrating. Her stomach flipped as he went over a tender spot between her shoulder blades. "You needn't be," he said, "Loxley honed me into a weapon long ago, and I make no apologies for turning that against them now. What I mean is, I must keep my loathing for them hidden. I must accept their accolades and their company as if I'm not thinking about how it would feel to watch the life drain from their eyes the entire time."

A shiver prickled up and over her arms.

"Don't mistake me for a hero, lishka. Everything I do now is to exact retribution on the ones who took away my freedom of choice."

He answered her questions about how he'd learned to perform the ritual in a low, matter-of-fact tone, the same way he spoke about how to handle a weapon. Among the Falsehoods the tattoos were widespread, harnessing the combined magics of witches, druidhen, and olden creatures. He'd observed many sessions and practiced the runes on his own. He'd given Kirin and Ilya their tattoos— under supervision, he added, as if Renna was going to run off and start stabbing everyone with ink. The supplies were hard to come by, though, especially now that he was in Loxley most of the time, and Renna got the impression that he was bending some rules by using them on her.

The pain went beyond that of her practice sessions with Nastasia, beyond the smarting ache of sparring. This gripped her soul, her mind, and her blood. She could no longer speak; she could only focus on each breath in and out. Nausea rolled through her, and sweat beaded her brow. Her fingers were clasped together so tightly they went numb. At one point she thought she heard Alaini speaking to Draic, but she was tunneled so deep inside her mind that she couldn't be sure. She took another drag from the flask and wiped her mouth on the back of her hand. Draic murmured in thanks, and something cool and damp was draped across her skin. A whimpering sigh escaped her as more strips of wet cloth soothed the burn, giving her mind a moment to surface from the intense sea of pain. But all too soon, the cold did little to dull the sensation. Like a wave gathering speed, it swelled to a crest, and Renna thought she might pass out.

The pain of mettlemancy would be a reprieve from this. All she could hear was her ragged breathing; her vision was spotted, and a moan slipped past her lips. Pressure squeezed her bones, threatening to crush her, or perhaps rip her apart. Panic gripped her. *I can't do this. I can't do this. I can't—*

Her whole body shook, every nerve on fire. His name came out as a plea. "Garen."

His fingers stilled for a half a breath. "Are you sure?"

"Please." Her voice broke on the word. "It's too much. I— Do it."

He cupped the back of her neck, fingers tangled in her damp hair. The roaring in her ears dulled, and the fire in her veins temporarily died down to embers. The sharp edges in her mind softened.

Relief washed over her.

Renna stood in a meadow bathed in soft light, a lake with glistening, calm waters at its edge. Trees lined the edge of the meadow, and a large mountain range circled them. Vaguely, she could feel the press of fingers at the back of her head, grounding her in her mind. She looked around the mental scene and saw Garen a few paces away, hands clasped behind his back. Here in her mind, he wasn't dressed in his usual Night Watchman leathers or the finery he'd had on at the ball. He was still in all black, but his loose tunic and pants seemed to smooth out his harsh lines. The realization of what was missing struck her.

"Why doesn't this…" Hurt? The word floated between them, unsaid.

Garen searched her face, his expression regretful. "Mettlemancy isn't inherently painful. There's only discomfort if the wielder intends for there to be."

Grief bloomed behind her ribs. A memory shifted at the edge of the meadow: Ulrik explaining that the reason for her pain during mental connections was because of the flaws in her blood. The pain was her fault, so she must work harder to win the Mother's favor, mustn't she? The memory stung less, though, here in this place.

"Where are we?" she asked.

"I thought it might be easier if we were in a neutral place." He looked back at her and held her gaze for a moment. "I don't need to be anywhere in your mind that you don't wish me to be, Ren. Take however long you need."

Exhaustion and gratitude hung on her shoulders, but she was concerned about the mental toll the connection would have on him. Nastasia and Ulrik had only been able to sustain mettlemancy for the lesser part of an hour at most.

A smirk tugged at the corner of Garen's mouth as if her doubt amused him. "Take the time you need, lishka. When you're ready, we'll keep going."

In the time it took for her to blink, she was lying on the soft grass. Here in the mettlemantic connection, she couldn't feel the bone-deep exhaustion that her body was experiencing, but her mind was weary. A dull ache settled behind her eyes, and she allowed herself to close them.

When her eyes fluttered open, every part of her felt refreshed and peaceful. Garen sat a few paces away, his face unreadable as always as he looked off into the middle distance.

"How long has it been?"

Garen turned to her but didn't answer her question. "Ready?"

Renna nodded, her awareness shifting to the feel of his fingers at the base of her neck, a soft tug pulling her back into her physical body.

The mettlemancy slipped away like a running river.

She was back on the cot, a cool towel draped between her shoulder blades. One of Garen's hands was still tangled in her hair as he gripped the back of her neck, the other resting on the small of her back. Pain seeped into her, but it was softer than before as they resumed.

Time stretched on, the pain clouding her sense of reality. All she knew was the burn of the bone shard, the sting of every wipe, the spark of each nerve. No inch of her back was left untouched, nor were her upper arms or shoulders. Seven more times she had to ask Garen to use mettlemancy. Each time, he wordlessly paused, his fingers sliding into her hair, holding her steady as he gave her the reprieve she desperately needed. Each time, they sat in silence in the meadow of her mind, the glassy surface of the lake and his stoic presence calming her.

When the tattoo was finally complete, Garen wiped a soothing balm onto her skin from her shoulders to her hips. She didn't lift her head, fatigue making her body heavy. The pain was dulling now. "What is it?"

"It's…a winged stallion. Your scars make it look like it's gathering a storm."

Renna pulled herself up to sit, clutching her tunic to her chest. Her mind was addled, her hair falling into her eyes. Garen still knelt at her side and pushed an errant lock away from her forehead. She swayed forward, unsteady, but Garen supported her with gentle hands, careful not to touch any tender skin. "Show me."

The touch of his mettlemancy was now familiar. She sank back into the meadow, her muscles sighing with relief. The image of herself played behind her eyelids.

A Nozdravian, muscled and midnight black like Alita, with wings sprouting from just behind the shoulders was etched across her skin. Swirls of black, grey, and silver covered her back and curled around her shoulders and the tops of her arms. Her scars, though…Gold painted each raised mark like lightning dancing across her skin. The effect was so beautiful that emotion caught in Renna's throat.

The image faded, and Renna was back in her body. Reality seeped back in slowly. Her forehead was pressed against something hard and warm, her back pulsing with its own heartbeat. She'd slid off the cot, her legs on either side of Garen's hips as she leaned against his chest, fingers tangled in his shirt. Renna pushed back, mortification beginning to clear her mind, but his hands tightened, holding her firmly in place on his lap.

"Lishka." The nickname on his lips, said more gruffly than usual, sent a flutter through her core. Garen shifted her with him as he leaned over, pulling something from his pack. That was when she realized her shirt had dropped to pool in their laps and the thin material of his tunic was the only thing separating her bare chest from his. Her face warmed.

Garen kept his eyes fixed over her head as he instructed her to raise her arms and helped dress her in the loose shirt. His movements were gentle, almost reverent. It did nothing to help soothe the sting of tears still burning her nose. Once she was fully covered, Garen sat back on his heels, though his hands remained on her hips. The increased space between them cleared her head slightly, but she mourned the lack of warmth.

The sky outside the window was dark. His tunic was huge on her, hanging off her shoulders. Renna felt like they were still in that meadow of her mind, just the two of them, safe and protected. She wasn't ready for that to end, to leave this tree house and go back to everyone in camp. Garen's face was tilted up to her, moonlight now spilling through the window painted the long column of his neck, the curve of his lips, the sharp line of his nose. Renna spread her fingers wide, palm pressed over his heart. She kept her eyes down as she traced the line of his collarbone. His hand slid up to the nape of her neck, fingers pushing into her hair again. The touch was something she was coming to crave. She thought about the golden scars on her back, and a tear slipped down her cheek, but with a quick swipe of his thumb, Garen caught it. His fingers brushed against her throat, tracing the scars there—one from Ulrik, one from him. She shivered, aware of the tingle of magic that caressed her neck, the same magic that coursed over her back. These too then, she realized, would be painted gold.

"Tell me something true," she said.

"I wept like a babe when I received mine."

Renna's laugh was more a breathy sigh, her fingers still playing with the fabric of his shirt. "Really?"

His mouth pulled into a sad smile, and it was so beautiful it hurt. "Where's the fun in a lie when it's the truth that's outlawed?"

CHAPTER 33

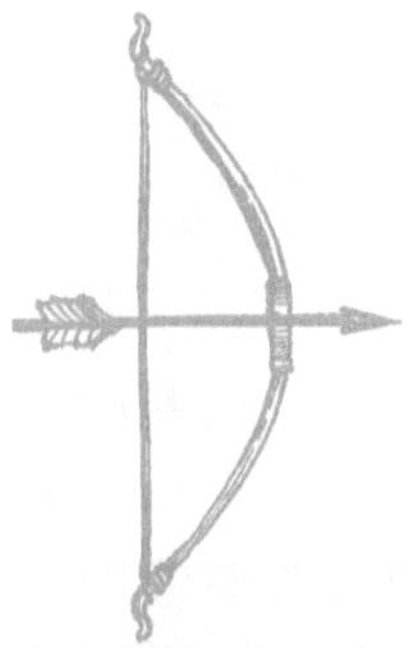

RENNA SAT UNDER THE WILLOW NEXT TO THE POND. Moisture clung to the air here, another pocket of magic inside Rowan Reach, an ecosystem all its own. Dragonfae flitted around; sparrows dove back and forth. Lily pads and lotus flowers floated on top of the glassy water. Almost a fortnight had passed since she'd gotten the tattoo. In the days that followed, the healing of her rib had accelerated, and no longer bothered her. She'd noticed an increase in her stamina and speed, too. Even after long nights spent looking through the books from the library, she'd wake refreshed, ready to spar and go with her Thorns to villages at the edge of Sherwood and Wendsvik. Most of these smaller establishments were loyal to Loxley, paying the tithe and worshipping the Mother, and so the Thorns had begun delivering a steady supply of the elixir-infused coins to them. Renna was pleased to find that when they encountered Keepers or Trissaia on the road, she felt no obligation to heed their words.

Garen had warned her against thinking the tattoo could do all the work for her and had given her strict instructions on how to practice mettleshielding. Renna had been spending an hour each day doing so by the serene pond. Today it was proving more difficult than usual to concentrate, though. They'd received word from Briar that Garen was finishing up business at the battlefront and that they should expect him to stop by Rowan Reach before returning to Loxley.

Everyone seemed a bit on edge, wondering what news the Night Watchman would bring. They knew from their escapades that unrest was catching. Riots had broken out between neighboring cities, those who adhered to the Truth fighting those who were vehemently opposed to it. War seemed to be spreading out from the battlefront, eliciting distrust among the people. Rebels left scrawled messages invoking the False Queen, praising the Night Watchman or the Robbing Hoods. At least now Renna could ride out herself instead of leaving Much to pretend to be her.

They were meant to return to Loxley soon. The first batch of petrified acorns was nearly ready. Renna was itching to visit the castle again; her concern for Nastasia had become a constant distraction since she'd learned that Ulrik had the ability to control minds.

Alita lay beside her, her ears twitched back as if reading Renna's thoughts. Renna closed her eyes, bringing her attention to her breath, to the light breeze on her back, where she now felt the gentle pulse of magic. Dropping into herself, cocooning her mind, she thought of roots sinking into the ground. She pictured ivy growing and spreading, the verdant vine covering a vast mountain, each leaf unfurling to shield the rock face.

The mountains of my mind surround the forest of my soul. Deep at the heart, an oak tree grows. Only the branches and crown can be seen, but far below are the roots, anchoring deep. Even when storms rage, this tree remains safe. As above, so below. These roots are anchored deep. This tree remains safe.

A breeze rustled the leaves above, starlight winking through the gaps in the treetops as Renna sifted through the foliage on the ground until she found another acorn. She brushed it off, turning it between her fingers. Dirt was caked under her nails; she'd gathered an acorn for each member of their crew and tucked them away in a small pouch.

Renna wiped her forehead with the back of her hand, debating for only a moment before pulling out a small blade. She cut off a newer branch that was near the base of the nearest tree with precision, the width no thicker than two fingers. Under the canopy of an oak, she began to carve. Alaini could've done it better, but Renna felt like she needed to make it with her own hands.

No short amount of time later, after several nicks on her fingers and an abundance of curses, Renna had two wooden rings. They were crudely shaped, but would do well enough. Her mouth pulled into the beginnings of a smile as she shaved a bit more wood away from the larger one, shaping a flat spot where she etched a small fox on the inside before adding it to the pouch with the acorns. Feeling a little smug, she tipped her head back against the oak and shook out the tension in her hands. Morning was well on its way, and exhaustion was slipping over her like a blanket. She'd planned to wait for Little Jon and Scarlet's help with the enchantments, but there was something compelling her to do them now.

Renna placed her hands over her bundle of acorns and closed her eyes. Her mettle shield was easy to conjure: *The mountains of my mind surround the forest of my soul. Deep at the heart, an oak tree grows.* The oak was firm against her back, grounding her. The Velmir rippled around her. She thought of Little Jon, Alaini, Scarlet, Much, Briar, Garen…

A charged, swirling vortex began to build in her center, spiraling up the column of her spine like a brewing storm that crackled with lightning and rumbled with thunder. An underground river swelled before her, rushing and loud and powerful, unwieldy like the one she'd fallen into when she'd first met Little Jon. There were threads of power in the river, magic waiting to be cultivated. Renna submerged her hands, plucked out only the things she needed, and wove them into the enchantments, moving purely on an instinct. Was this what Little Jon felt when they performed magic? Was it the same for Scarlet? Light danced before her eyes, forming interconnected paths, weaving patterns that she knew were visual representations of her thoughts. Renna's lips formed the incantation as her fingers drew sigils in the water and the air over and over.

The forest speaks, and so must we.
Make us one with the bark,
with these acorns we mark.
Lend us your connection,
the roots that spread in all direction.

Warmth buzzed in her hands, the magic simmering. Renna realized it was time to turn back, return to the surface. She knew in her bones that the enchantment was complete; she felt a sense of wholeness that she couldn't define but was sure of all the same.

But curiosity nudged at her. An image of an ancient well unfurled in the golden river of power, a palpable vibration emanating from it. Renna drew nearer, the energy dancing over her limbs and seeping into her middle. Roots tangled around the stones that made up the well, ivy crawling across the surface, and inside were narrow spiraling steps leading down into the darkness. There was a tugging sensation behind her breastbone. Time was meaningless, and she couldn't tell if seconds or hours passed as she walked deeper and deeper into the darkness. It cloaked her like an old friend, with a comforting weight of truly *knowing* her.

As she descended, images began to flit in and out of her vision. The walls around her were suddenly gone as she descended the stairs. The smell of damp earth greeted her. She could sense the labyrinth of roots surrounding her, calling to her, welcoming her home. The air thinned and cooled significantly, and the smell of fresh earth turned sour and decayed. She stood poised to take the next step, but an invisible hand gripped her by the throat. Pressure squeezed her lungs, and panic clawed at the back of her skull. But she couldn't turn around, couldn't move, couldn't breathe.

Too far, too far, too far, her mind raged. *The darkness in you will destroy this kingdom if you let it.*

Her body sank into the maw of the darkness that now roiled with something sinister. Her screams were locked inside her; she was helpless to do anything.

Too far, Ren, she scolded herself.

Ren. Come back.

Come back.

Lishka, come back.

The name struck Renna like lightning, thundering through her body and yanking up.

She sucked in a ragged breath like she'd been drowning. Grey eyes filled her vision as pins and needles exploded over her skin. Her hands were clenched into fists around the pouch of acorns, and the trunk of the oak dug into her back painfully. Cold sweat covered her body. Large hands gripped her shoulders. Garen knelt in front of her, his face close. Too close—she could feel his breath, tinged with mint, wafting over her cheeks.

You're safe. The words were a balm on her mind. But terror still clutched her, and her heart beat painfully against her ribs. "You're safe," Garen said, aloud this time, eyes locked on hers. He clenched his jaw. "You went too far, Ren. Why didn't you have a tether?"

Renna blinked. How was he here? How had he found her? "A…what?"

Garen sat back on his heels, putting a bit of space between them. "A tether."

Now that the world was settling back into place, Renna could see the tension in his face and the fire in his eyes. He was furious. Garen continued, "You are inexperienced. You cannot cast enchantments on your own, especially without a tether—someone to keep you grounded, keep you from going too far."

Ire flamed up in her chest, and her grip tightened on her newly charmed possessions. "Inexperienced? You should be thanking me for figuring out a way to keep us all safe."

"Are you so foolish that you think you can do everything on your own?" Garen snapped, matching her tone. "How about 'Thank you, Garen, for making sure I didn't die just now.'"

Renna's arms shook, and she pressed them against her thighs to steady them. "I don't need you to rescue me," she hissed, shoving aside the unease in her stomach that told her Garen had indeed just rescued her.

Garen scoffed. "Right, well, next time you're so wrapped up in an enchantment that the life is being sucked out of you, I'll just mind my own damn business, yeah?"

"I had everything under control." The lie felt like ash in her mouth. She shoved the pouch at his chest. "And it was entirely worth it, because now we have these."

Garen's look was skeptical, but he placed his hand over hers and took the pouch. She ignored the heat left by his touch and watched as he opened the pouch. "These are just acorns."

"The trees communicate with each other—Little Jon is so attuned to them that they can hear them nearly all the time. I charmed the acorns to expand the net of communication to us as well."

Garen narrowed his eyes. "Go on…"

Her chest swelled with pride when he didn't immediately dismiss her idea. "So when there's something wrong, we can warn each other," she continued. "When the trees are telling each other there's danger, we will know as well. Here," Renna said, fishing around in the bag until she felt the larger ring. "This one is for you."

Garen raised his eyes to hers, and heat crept into her face. His lips twitched into a smirk, and he arched a single brow as she rushed to explain.

"Obviously you can't walk around Loxley with an acorn in your pocket. And I don't trust you to move it between the pockets of all your ridiculous clothes and uniforms, but we must be able to reach each other. We'll coat it in metal, the same as Much's staff, and that way you can wear it and no one will question it."

"Yes, we can't have my fashion choices be the downfall of this rebellion." Garen took the ring from her, turning it over, still smirking. He ran his thumb over the tiny fox she'd carved into the inside of the ring.

"I thought you could pass it off as a family signet ring or something." Embarrassment itched between her shoulder blades. *Bleeding Mother, damn him*, she cursed inside her head, feeling incredibly foolish with his gaze heavy on her. "If you don't want it—"

She made to snatch it away, but Garen closed his fist around it and pulled it out of her reach. "Don't make assumptions about my wants, lishka." His words had the effect of a warm fire roaring to life on a cold day. A shiver ran under her collar. Her heart picked up, and her tongue felt heavy in her mouth, rendering her unable to quip back. "What method of communication do you plan to employ?"

"I found a pamphlet on coded tapping. Apparently it's an old military tactic used in Wendsvik. Have you heard of it?"

There was a ghost of a smile on his lips. "I've heard of it. The Falsehoods use it quite often." He slipped the ring onto the fourth finger on his right hand, flexing it a few times as if testing the feel of it. "It's a good bit of magic, Ren."

Garen shifted to sit beside her, leaning against the oak. He sighed heavily, and Renna felt the bone-deep weariness of it. A few drops of blood stained his cloak. His or someone else's? Had he been forced to torture someone today? If so, was it someone he thought deserved it? The fierce desire to take away his pain, as he'd done for her during the tattoo ritual, surprised her. What was she to say, that it would be all right? None of this was all right, and suggesting otherwise would be like coating dung with honey. Renna could not undo the horrors happening around them.

But maybe it wasn't about fixing anything. Maybe it was about sitting in the darkness together.

They stayed like that, staring into the middle distance, for quite some time. Renna was reminded of how they'd rested in the meadow in her mind. Eventually the rigid line of his shoulders softened, and he tipped his head back, exposing the long column of his neck. Dark lashes splayed across his white skin, eyes flitting behind closed lids as if his mind was still racing, searching for a threat.

Renna pulled a dagger from her boot, gestured to the one strapped to his thigh, and suggested what she liked to do to quiet her mind when it felt full of darkness. "Want to spar?"

Garen's face relaxed a bit as he eyed her weapon, one eyebrow lifted. "There is little room for error in a knife fight. It's a close-range weapon with high stakes. And judging by our reintroduction in the woods, I'd wager you struggle with some of the more…intimate aspects of wielding it."

Renna shoved his shoulder. "I had you by the throat. Or do you need reminding?"

Garen flipped his knife with expert ease. "I promise I'll be gentle the first time."

His words conjured images of tangled silken sheets and soft murmurs, and something swooped low in her belly as they both took their opening stance.

They moved, jabbing and parrying like a dance, and Renna began to find stillness in herself. She executed a thrust that he sidestepped, cutting down from above. Renna slipped his attack and answered with two quick blows, the sound of metal on metal ringing out. The edge of his knife moved in a pattern, too quick and complicated to follow, disorienting her.

But there—an opening on his right side, a mirror of how she'd disarmed him that first day in the forest. Her feet took her in another half circle, and she thrust forward, but at the last second, Garen pivoted. He captured her free arm with his, looping up and around her forearm to grasp her triceps, locking her outstretched arm in a bind. One foot behind her knee and a sharp twist of his hips threw her onto her back, and he pinned her in seconds.

Laughter danced in his eyes, like moonlight reflected on the river, as he looked down at her. "In truth? I *let* you win that day."

The scoff that came out of her was wounded pride and disbelief and the desire to shut him up. She sprung up, and they began again, circling each other, answering thrusts with jabs.

"Eyes on me, Ren. Don't watch the blade."

Renna feinted to the right with a thrust. Garen moved to block her and she parried to attack the opening now on his left. She gasped as he anticipated the move, grabbing her wrist and twisting her into another bind, pulling her until her back was against his chest. His lips brushed the side of her ear, sending a shiver through her. "The way you engage my blade tells me exactly what you intend to do. I don't need to read your mind to see your plan two steps ahead."

He let go of her wrist, but for a heartbeat, neither of them moved. Magic pulsed through her tattoo, tingling in her veins. "And if you *were* to attempt to read my mind? I doubt any enemy would give me the courtesy of staying out."

There was a light caress against her mind, asking permission. She nodded her consent.

"All right. Try to keep me out, lishka."

Renna built up her mental walls. *The mountains of my mind surround the forest of my soul. Deep at the heart, an oak tree grows. Only the branches and crown can be seen, but far below are the roots, anchoring deep.*

They continued to spar—physically and mentally—Garen testing her mettle shields. She did as he'd taught her, only allowing him to see what she intentionally revealed. The effort was demanding, and sweat beaded on her forehead. She didn't have the skill to conjure a mindscape like he did, so they stood in an empty white space. *Even when storms rage, this tree remains safe. For as above, so below. These roots are anchored deep, and I give all my fears and my secrets to the roots.*

"Impressive," Garen said, after what felt like hours. "This type of shielding will keep you from inadvertently shouting out your moves to them. You are well trained—"

"High praise."

"*But* you still fight based on practiced concepts rather than experience. Every move you make is a response to what I do, because I am two moves ahead of you. Since you grew up royal, your other sparring partners probably held back. Think of it as a game of chess. You are waging war on two planes at once, playing your opponent and the board. Just then? You kept your elbow slightly bent as you attacked, which told me you did not really mean it."

Renna lunged to strike. Garen's blade blurred in a flurry of perfectly executed moves, and Renna was once again flat on her back. He had both her wrists pinned overhead with one hand. Adrenaline and his nearness made her insides feel fizzy and bubbly, like she was an elixir he was brewing. The mindscape shuddered but held. Even though she was pinned, it tasted like a victory. The feeling was heady, like the rushing of the river, the magic in her veins coursing through her, answering her call.

This tree remains safe.

Garen looked down at her, grinning, and it gave him a boyish quality. The harsh masks of the high sheriff and the Night Watchman were gone. She could feel the ring she'd given him against her wrist. Even though his body covered hers, he held the bulk of his weight on his forearm. The thought that he was still trying to maintain a proper distance riled her. Renna shifted under him, brushing their chests together. Garen's tongue darted out to wet his bottom lip. One finger traced the gold scars on her neck, leaving a trail of warmth in its wake. She tilted her chin just so, baring the column of her throat to him.

His eyes flicked up to hers as he continued tracing the tattooed scars almost reverently. "Have you noticed anything unusual?"

She was having a hard time focusing on what they were talking about. His touch was eliciting full-body chills. "Should I have?"

"I first noticed the connection with my familiar shortly after I got my tattoo."

Renna made a noise that she hoped sounded interested in what he was saying, but he'd shifted as he spoke, and now his hips pressed her more firmly into the ground. Renna's eyes fluttered closed. The pads of his fingers gently brushed over the golden tattoo—yes, that felt better than calling it a scar. She was quickly losing the thread of the conversation.

With barely a whisper, he asked, "Does it still hurt?"

"I don't feel any pain right now."

The backs of his fingers stroked the tattoo. "But sometimes?"

If she spoke, the moment would break. She could only nod once. He let go of her wrists, turning her left palm face up, looking at the two crescent moon scars. The caress of his mouth on her skin sent heat shooting through her and every thought in her head eddied away. It was hardly more than a brush of his lips, but it pierced something deep in her heart. Garen's eyes had darkened, and he studied her face, watching her reaction. He dipped his head—slowly, so slowly, giving her plenty of time to push him away, to stop him.

She did not want him to stop.

Garen dropped his lips to her throat. "Forgive me, Ren."

I forgave you some time ago, she wanted to say. Her hands slid to his shoulders as she arched up into him. Renna felt like she'd sunk into a hot bath, every muscle melting under his touch, tension washing away. His fingers at the nape of her neck and along her jaw moved as if drawing runes, casting a spell. He kissed her neck, lower this time. Want surged through her. She hooked a leg behind his knee, pressing their hips together. His hands roved, flexing on her waist to pull her closer. He kissed across her collarbones, the hollow of her throat. Desire, intense and devastating, bloomed behind her ribs and speared through her core.

More. She wanted—*needed*—more of him.

The realization terrified her. "Wait—"

Immediately, Garen pulled away. The loss of his body on hers felt like the tide ripping out. Renna wanted to unsay it, she'd not meant for him to stop, only that she needed a moment to adjust to the enormity of how his touch made her feel. She could still feel his lips on her throat. His hair was mussed from her fingers. But without his weight grounding her, doubt robbed her of her voice. His hand was a tight fist against his thigh—the thigh that moments before had been deliciously pressed between her legs.

"I—" he started, working his jaw.

Twigs cracked underfoot, jolting them both, as Little Jon appeared around the trees. Renna wasn't sure if she should curse or bless her friend for their timing.

They had the courtesy to ignore the palpable tension they'd walked into. "Ah. Good, you found her. Did he tell you?"

Renna looked at Garen. "Tell me what?"

He rubbed the back of his neck, stalling before answering. "It's Nastasia. She's been working closely with Ulrik. She says she knows you best…so she's offered to spearhead the hunt for you."

Garen's words shouldn't have hit her in the gut as they did. He had always been upfront about the fact that he believed Nastasia was complicit with Ulrik. But now that his mouth had been on her body, now that the desire she'd been resisting had been stoked, the reminder felt like a blade.

If the Falsehood didn't know about Nastasia, it was because she loved the church and was faithful to the Mother first. But that did not mean she knew about Ulrik's treachery. There were other explanations. Ulrik was a sangeserre, after all. Maybe Nastasia was being forced. Or perhaps she had offered to hunt for Renna to try and protect her. Renna offered all these arguments up, looking between Garen and Little Jon, but they merely watched her with aggravating pity and resignation. Surely Garen of all people should understand that this news didn't prove anything about her cousin's loyalties.

Her next words were laced with more poison than she intended. "You commit any number of horrors to maintain your cover, High Sheriff."

Garen stiffened, his expression shuttered, and she was left feeling bereft as he disappeared behind his cold and aloof mask. It wasn't fair to throw this in his face, not after his fervent apologies, not when she'd forgiven him.

He turned away and addressed Little Jon. "The Falsehood astrologers have determined that before this time next year, there will be another Endless Tide. That is when they plan to strike Loxley."

A siege on Loxley within a year. Thoughts tumbled through Renna's brain in a rush. She had to get Nastasia out from under Ulrik's control before then. Had Garen already informed the Falsehoods that she did not want the crown? What kind of fate was she leaving her people to if she did not take it? The words of her Foretelling shook her bones.

Garen continued, "Disrupting the spell that has a hold over Loxley is crucial groundwork for a successful siege. We must loosen Loxley's hold over its people if we are truly going to liberate them."

Little Jon said, "The first batch of petrified wood is nearly ready. Renna and the others have been planning out the route we'll take once we're inside the walls."

Garen nodded, still refusing to look at her, and her heart wrenched painfully. She fought to keep her voice unaffected. "Does Ulrik know another Endless Tide is coming?"

"He hasn't mentioned any such thing to me. But he's becoming more secretive, trusting the Trissaia to enforce the laws more than us. Since Loxley knew about the tide all those years ago, we must assume that the church has its own astrologers who have apprised them of the situation."

Little Jon shook their head. "I don't like this. We are nearing the Blood Moon, which means an increase in chaotic power that can be harnessed with dark magic. Loxley will be more dangerous than ever."

"I've heard whispers about the Blood Moon from the Keepers who are closest with Nastasia. We all need to be on our guard."

Later, Renna would look back on that moment and wish she'd dismissed the idea that began to take root in her mind. It might have saved them all from the grief that was to follow.

Or perhaps the suffering was inevitable.

CHAPTER 34

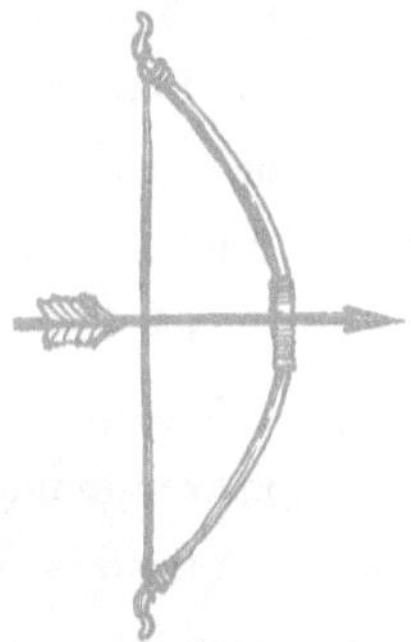

THE AUREM COINS CLINKED AS RENNA RODE ALITA TOWARD HER FORMER KINGDOM, FLANKED BY HER THORNS. As this was their second trip in the last fortnight, Scarlet had painted their faces with her newest concoction: illusion powder. She'd mixed crushed rose petals and chamomile flowers, finely ground mugwort, a pinch of salt, and beeswax into a thin paste that blurred the specific appearance of the wearer. It could not fool someone studying them directly, but anyone who merely glanced at them would have a hard time recalling any distinguishing features and would be left with the impression that they'd seen no one of note. The feel of the paste on Renna's skin was slimy and a bit itchy, reminding her of how much she'd hated having her face done up for revels and the Fire Feast. But the warrants out for the Robbing Hoods had increased significantly over the last month. The king was getting desperate for their capture, so Renna ignored the discomfort, focusing on the task ahead.

The tide was low, leaving a marshy expanse of grasses exposed. They had only a few precious hours to complete their task. The bag of enchanted wood was heavy against Renna's thigh. They'd all agreed that the petrified items should be saved for higher up in the kingdom. Once Renna had dispersed the coins in her other pouch, she was to take the tunnels to distribute the petrified wood. She and her friends would meet back outside the walls before the tide came in and return to Sherwood before the kingdom awoke.

They hid the horses in a shallow cave off the side of the mountain where Renna and Nastasia had once spent an afternoon during low tide searching for mussels and clams. Using an arrow fixed to a grappling hook, they all scaled the wall around the city, avoiding the guards who patrolled the front gate. Renna's heart pounded as she slipped through the quiet streets, the hair on her neck prickling. Signs with crossed-out acorns hung on every corner, nailed next to poor drawings of the Thorns' faces. Renna tossed the elixir-infused coins on each doorstep, jamming others under windowsills. The aurem would help ward off compulsion spells for only a few days at most. It was like scooping handfuls of water from the sea, hoping to hold back the tide.

But there were signs that the coins were working their magic: the phrases NO TITHE TO TYRANTS and WHAT HAPPENED TO THE FALSE QUEEN? were scrawled on alley walls amidst the proclamations reminding citizens of the punishment for harboring vedra or refusing to tithe. A beaten-down church on the corner was the most kept-up building here in the slums. Renna pierced a light sackcloth of coins with an arrow and lined up her shot. The purse went flying through the bell tower window to be found by Keepers at the next silent hour. Quickly, like a shadow moving through the night, she left coins in her wake for the poorest citizens of Loxley as she moved toward the tunnel entrance outside of Nottingham. She wondered if this was the same type of exhilaration Garen had when he donned the Night Watchman mask, and a twinge of guilt struck her. Garen and her friends would scold her if they discovered the detour she was planning. *I'll be back in time,* she assured herself. *No one need know.*

It was easier to spot the hidden doorway now that she knew what to look for. The world went dark and quiet, her breath loud in her ears, as she entered the tunnel. She crept through the narrow passageway, up, up, up. Her back ached from crouching. Did Nastasia still use these tunnels? Her heart kicked a little harder at the thought of running into her here in the darkness.

As Renna climbed, she fortified her mettle shields, crafting a mindscape like Garen had taught her. Magic rippled over her skin, the runes breathing protection and strength into her. Peace pooled in her veins. She pulled a smooth stone the size of her fist from her pouch. The petrified wood was a swirl of browns, gold, and amber, the striations from the tree making dazzling patterns in the stone. It vibrated gently, as if emitting an unheard song. At each new level, Renna left a piece of petrified wood, keeping her thoughts attuned to the intention of the spell.

Soon only two stones remained. She needed to return soon, before the tide sealed off the island. One of the stones had a streak of green through it; there must have been a living vein inside the wood, an offshoot that was about to sprout when they'd cast the spell. Renna felt along the cool wall, fingers searching for a familiar marker. Yes, she was near the private alcove in the temple where she and Nastasia had slipped away from the red clerics so often. When she reached the stairs that would take her through the trapdoor, Renna used her hands to scrape a shallow hole in the dirt and nestle the precious stone inside.

Her next stop proved trickier to find, and she took three wrong turns before she found herself in the tunnel that ran along the back side of a few of the residential rooms in the palace. Renna and Nastasia had been sneaking around one day when they were much younger and had overheard a maid cleaning the bedchamber on the other side of the wall. Nastasia's eyes had glittered with mischief in the darkness. If the tunnels ran behind the rooms, perhaps there were doors that opened into the vast network. Perhaps they'd be able to find a secret passageway between their rooms so they wouldn't be chastened by Marian or the clerics for staying up too late. For months they'd listened, ears pressed to the chilly tunnel walls, trying to determine which rooms lay on the other side. They'd even mapped it out, writing down the name of each occupant to keep track.

Now, Renna traced the words she and her cousin had painstakingly carved into the tunnel wall. Her heart panged with nostalgia and grief. *Gross Gisborne. Silly Stasi. Rebel Ren.*

Tears stung her eyes, and she wiped them away with her forearm. This wasn't the time to fall apart. Breathing in through her nose and out through her mouth, she steeled her nerves. Renna could not help Nastasia escape yet—her cousin was too ensnared in whatever Ulrik was planning—but she could at least give her a fighting chance. She crouched in the tunnel outside of Nastasia's chambers. "Please, let this break whatever hold he has on you. I promise I'll come back for you, Stasi."

She couldn't be sure how long she stayed there, frozen between two different times, two versions of herself, before a scraping sound indicated the bedchamber door opening on the other side of the wall. Adrenaline shot through Renna, and her muscles tensed to run, but then she recognized one of the voices and stayed rooted to the spot.

"—though I'm hardly surprised," Nastasia said. "Don't just stand there. Shut the door."

Renna pressed her ear to the wall, straining to catch every word. The second person said something in reply, the cadence reminding Renna of how the maids used to bow and scrape around her. A servant, then. Maybe a lower-level priestess.

"I think this calls for a toast," Nastasia said, her voice louder.

Renna could see the scene in her mind's eye: her cousin crossing to the drink cart just on the other side of the tunnel wall, selecting the mead. In the silence that followed, she imagined the clink of glasses. Perhaps Nastasia had sprawled on the chaise lounge and lit the aurem in the hearth with a simple twitch of her fingers.

"The king is very pleased with you, my lady," a high, feminine voice said. "You think the plan will work?"

"I know Renna better than anyone. She's desperate for love and approval, which she's obviously been getting from the outlaws. But that will only last if she keeps them at arm's length. When they get close, they'll see her for who she really is. And if they're smart, they'll stay away from her."

The other speaker hesitated, and there was apprehension in her voice when she asked, "Why's that?"

Nastasia let out a cutting laugh. "You'd have me break an oath of silence? Hardly. Take what happened at her crucible and extrapolate from there."

The words scorched through Renna like a ball of finnikfire, eating away at the carefully constructed facade she'd built after her Foretelling. Nastasia spoke of Renna's deepest fears and shames as casually as a butcher explaining different cuts of meat.

She's just keeping up a ruse, she thought desperately, even as she felt the tunnel closing in on her. She should leave now. She'd done what she intended to do and was due to meet the others by the horses in a matter of minutes. Her detour had already made her later than was wise.

"Do you miss her?" the other woman asked.

The silence was damning. Renna's heart twisted viciously, and she pressed the heel of her palm to her sternum as if to keep it from cracking.

Nastasia's voice hardened into something unrecognizable. "Would you miss a thorn in your shoe? I was always left to clean up her messes. She never took any of it seriously. Do you recall her old governess, that vedra sympathizer? If I hadn't taken matters into my own hands, Renna would have been burned alive for not turning her in the moment she discovered the woman's treason."

"You were the one who turned the governess in?"

"Of course it was me," Nastasia snapped "As I said, I know Renna better than anyone—probably better than she knows herself, which is saying something, given how self-absorbed she could be."

Renna was distantly aware of shuffling on the other side of the wall—the thuds of glasses being set down, the scrape of the door opening and closing again—but everything was drowned out by the roaring of her mind. Her limbs felt suddenly foreign, disconnected from her. Garen's face flashed in her mind, the grim look of pity when she'd vehemently denied the possibility that her cousin was lost to her. Had she ever truly *had* her? Nastasia had been the one to turn Marian in all those years ago.

The magic on Renna's back rippled as if disturbed.

Her shields had been in place since they'd approached Loxley, and she'd reinforced them before she'd entered the tunnels, since Garen had been annoyingly insistent with his warnings: Y*ou cannot rely only on the magic, Ren. You must shield your mind.* Now that persistence was the only reason she didn't shatter when a cold grip latched on to the nape of her neck as someone tried to slip into her mind.

Her breath caught in her lungs as she threw all her energy into bolstering her mettle shields. The mountains grew taller, the ivy sprawled, the trees in the forest reached higher and farther. The probing felt like icy needles against her skull. Glass shattered on the other side of the wall.

"Where are you, Ren?"

Renna scrambled backward, away from the wall, gravel biting into her palms. Then she was up and running back through the tunnels, but even so, she could hear the peals of bells ringing, calling for red clerics.

Mercifully, it seemed her cousin did not know where the tunnels let out, but once Renna reentered Nottingham proper, the red clerics were on her scent. Dirty rainwater splashed around her feet as she pounded through the streets. Renna turned down an alley, jumping over a pile of refuse. Higher—she needed to get higher. Her gaze snagged on a drainpipe on the building before the alley opened onto another street. Arms pumping, Renna dashed toward it. She sent up a silent prayer of thanks for dragonhide gloves as she easily gripped the metal and began hoisting herself up. Guards arrived at the entrance to the alley as her boot slipped, and she barely stopped her face from smashing into the building.

She crested the roof and boosted herself over the edge, lungs burning. All the training sessions in Rowan Reach had conditioned her muscles well, and she raced along the rooftop. Shouts from below sounded closer, and the clanging told her the guards were attempting to climb up after her. Renna leapt across the gap between buildings, rolling to soften the impact on her knees. Her cloak caught on her leg, and she swore under her breath as she got to her feet.

Storm clouds darkened the sky. The stench of piss and sweat hung heavy in the air, and Renna gagged against her cowl as she searched the skyline. She nocked an arrow as she ran, throwing looks over her shoulder. When the first guard crested the roof, she twisted around and took aim. The arrow caught the guard in the shoulder, and he tumbled out of sight.

The rain began to fall harder as she cut across the expanse of rooftops in erratic patterns. Her cloak grew heavy as it got wetter, but she didn't dare cast it aside—it was one of the reversible ones with a purple lining and hidden pockets for coins, precious details they did not want Loxley to get their hands on. As she scrambled up a steep roof, some of the tiles cracked, and a large section slid off to shatter on the street below. Renna jerked her attention away from the sheer drop.

A shout went up from below, and she barely dodged the first arrow that came streaking through the darkness. One building over had a flat roof with a terrace that had been tended at one point but had since been forgotten. Rags were tossed about in the brewing storm, caught up in debris and tangled around an old canopy.

A hot stinging pain sliced her calf, just above where her boot stopped. Shit. The sound of more arrows striking the roof joined the patter of the rain. Gritting her teeth, Renna ran in a half crouch down the incline of the roof.

Don't look down. She jumped, arms wheeling for more momentum. It was more of a crash than a landing, and she could picture the new bruises blooming. She blinked away the daze, struggling to her feet. The pain in her calf was dulled by the adrenaline coursing through her, but she was still limping, cradling the shoulder she'd hit on impact.

The charmed acorn in her pocket warmed and began to pulse rhythmically. Little Jon or Alaini, perhaps. *Where—are—you?*

She tapped back, *Delayed.*

The soldiers were shouting below, arrows still sailing up at her. She couldn't outrun them like this forever. If she could just find somewhere to hide for a moment, get them off her tail. Something like panic began to curl in her middle.

Would you miss a thorn in your shoe?

The storm was building too quickly; the tide had to be nearly in, the causeway all but sealed off. If she tried to make it to the rendezvous point now, she would surely be caught. *Great work, Ren,* she thought scathingly. Why could she never leave well enough alone? She tapped on the acorn quickly, telling the others to go without her. She'd wait until the tide went out again hours from now.

A small patrol of guards was running back in the direction she'd come from. When they turned the corner, Renna backed up a few paces to get a running start. She landed nimbly on the roof of the next building, crossing quickly to the far side. Below, a group of youths huddled under the overhang for shelter from the rain. They locked eyes with her, and Renna brought a finger to her mouth. She was looking for the best place to jump to the other side of the alley when a single guard burst from a doorway nearby. He prowled up and down the street, head swiveling.

Shit.

The smallest youth, a boy in clothes two sizes too big for his little frame, darted out into the rain, drawing the guard's attention. He delivered a swift kick to the guard's shin, then turned and ran down the alley. The guard hopped on his other leg, swearing, and chased after the child.

Away from Renna.

She didn't waste the opportunity. When she landed on the opposite rooftop, she reached into her pocket and flung a handful of coins toward the boy's friends. A bell began clanging incessantly—a storm warning. Citizens were to heed the bells and get inside until it passed. Rainwater was rushing quickly through the streets, thunder growling in the distance. *Shit, shit, shit.*

Her ring turned warm. The heat came in tiny bursts.

Empty—church—three—down.

Relief burned through her, and she ran, grateful to not have to think. The building was in poor shape, evidence of the unrest in the lower levels of the city drawn across the stone. Many of the windows were smashed. Renna shimmied down a drainpipe, completely soaked, and dropped to the ground, ignoring the pain in her leg. She slipped into the church and slumped against the wall, pressing herself into the corner.

No longer running, her focus crumbled. A choked sob ripped from her, and she clamped her hand over her mouth. Nastasia. She'd known. The whole time, the whole time—

I know Renna better than she knows herself, which is saying something, given how self-absorbed she can be. That vedra sympathizer.

Of course it was me. It was me. It was me.

Would you miss a thorn in your shoe?

Desperate. Weak. Unworthy.

They'll leave her if they know what's best.

Renna's ragged gasp was drowned out by the noise of the storm. Everything she'd tried to tamp down was finally too much. She buried her face in her knees, curling up tight, biting back another sob. Her fingertips tingled, and tiny needles pricked the back of her skull. It was so loud in her head, so loud and so dark.

How could she have been so naïve?

Renna's skin was too tight, and she dug her nails in, as if peeling it off it might offer a release. She had to calm down, but the thought just brought on more panic. Feelings were spilling out of her too quickly, and there was nothing she could do to stop them. Darkness pressed in, holding her hostage. The panic pinned her. Her sternum felt like she'd taken a hit with a battering ram. She clutched her chest and sucked in a shuddering breath.

Her whole life had been built on lies. She'd thought Nastasia's love was real, but it had always been tainted with cruelty and disdain. Her cousin's words washed all her memories in a new ugly hue: the long-suffering sighs, the eye rolls, the jests that sometimes hit too close to the mark. And Renna, so desperate for affection and love, had still managed to convince herself there was something precious and real between the two of them. Would her Thorns turn on her the same way? Did they too harbor resentments against her? Even if by some miracle they didn't, she was being selfish by staying near them. All she would bring into their lives was ruin and destruction.

Lightning flashed as the door opened, illuminating the high sheriff's uniform as he swept in. And for once, Renna did not try to hide the way she was shattering. *Let him see.*

Garen's stoic mask cracked. He barred the door shut and was kneeling beside her in an instant, hands running over her arms as if checking for the source of her pain. She squeezed her eyes shut, shaking her head. Except the arrow graze on her leg, she was physically whole. Strong arms encircled her, pulling her to his chest, cupping the back of her head.

"You're safe. You're safe. I've got you. This is a wave, just a wave. It will pass. Breathe, Ren."

He whispered the words against her skin. "Even when storms rage, the tree remains safe. Let the storm rage. You are safe."

Heaving sobs wracked her body, but the familiar lines of the mantra acted like a rope thrown to her as she was tossed by the sea. A dam inside her had broken under the unyielding pressure of torrential waters. Somewhere above them a window shattered, and the howl of the wind pitched higher. Garen did not let go, did not loosen his grip. His embrace was the only thing keeping her from flying out of her skin, keeping her tethered to reality.

Just a wave, just a wave, just a wave.

Garen inhaled exaggeratedly through his nose, exhaled through his mouth. Renna fought to match his breathing. Every few breaths, her panic bubbled up again, another wave crashing over her head and sending her spinning. And each time, he deliberately slowed his breathing, squeezing her arms in an alternating rhythm.

And though it felt like it would never end, it did. Her sobs slowly subsided, every muscle wrung out as she clung to him. A pounding filled her skull, but she was slipping back into her body, and the dark thoughts lashing her mind began to quiet. Garen murmured something, shifted her weight. Then he was carrying her, cradled against his broad chest, up the stairs. He deposited her on the solitary fainting chaise in the corner, the velvet fabric worn and dull. Renna shivered violently. Garen quickly undid the catch of her soaked cloak, putting his own drier one around her shoulders before moving to check the perimeter of the room. The smell of vetiver and musk and pine filled her nose.

Renna shifted, hissing at the pain that shot through her calf. Garen swooped down, assessing her leg with the intensity of a surgeon on the battlefield. The wound was a mess—the blood had started to congeal, and there were bits of cloth and dirt stuck in the gash.

The way Garen moved through the room reminded Renna of Edwine fussing whenever someone was hurt. His boots left prints in the dust collected on the floor. He closed all the internal storm barriers except one, latching them tight. Renna sank deeper into the cushions as Garen took one of the collection bowls and stuck it out into the rain to gather water. With a wave of his hand, he lit the aurem stones in the metal brazier. He rifled through a cupboard, tossing aside copies of the Tomes of Truth until he found what he was looking for: a few strips of clean cloth, an old bottle of questionable liquor, and a thin smock dress that had most likely been discarded by a priestess in favor of her robes. Next, he retrieved the collection bowl, now filled with rainwater, and set it atop the brazier burning with red finnikfire.

"Do you need help getting your clothes off?" he asked without a trace of humor. Her face burned hotter than the brazier as she stared up at him in confusion. He held out the dry dress, keeping his tone even. "You're wet, lishka. The tide is in, and with the storm outside, you're not getting back to Sherwood tonight." Garen nodded to the pile of cloths and the collection bowl. "That water should be warm now. I'm going to check that everything is secure downstairs. I'll be right back."

Not trusting her voice, Renna accepted the dress. Garen lingered for a moment, clearly unsure whether he should leave her. Apparently satisfied that she would not fall apart, he disappeared down the stairs.

Renna shivered as she stripped her wet clothes from her body, each article hitting the floor with a *thwack*. Steam wafted from the collection bowl as she dipped a cloth in, and she bit back a whimper as she wiped the hot towel down her neck and over her shoulders. She washed away the sweat and dirt and blood until her skin was clean, even though her insides still felt trampled.

Would you miss a thorn in your shoe?

Renna pulled the dress over her head—it was clearly meant for someone taller and hung nearly to her toes. She was using a dry bit of cloth to scrunch the extra moisture from her curls when Garen emerged from the stairs. Several small vials were secured in a holster at his hip, and he pulled one out. Kneeling in front of the chaise, he touched the outside of her knee on her injured leg. The heat of his hand seeped through the thin fabric of the dress.

"May I?" When she nodded, he lifted the hem just enough to get a look at her calf. "This will sting," he warned, dumping the cleansing solution on a fresh rag before holding it to the wound. But the sting lessened quickly, and soon he was wrapping a fresh bandage tight to keep pressure on her leg. He worked methodically, lips pursed in concentration, long fingers deftly tying off the knot before pulling the hem of her dress back down.

Garen caught her staring. The moment pulled taut between them, an arrow nocked with undeniable aim.

"How did you know where I was?" Her voice was raspy from crying.

"Half the city guard is looking for a hooded outlaw witch right now."

Renna bit the inside of her cheek, looking away, hearing Nastasia's taunt of *Where are you, Ren?* She folded herself into the corner of the cushions, pulling her knees to her chest. Garen took a seat at the edge of the chaise, face unreadable. He had not balked at her tears or minimized her pain. Maybe it was the small attic of the church that made her want to speak her secrets aloud, like the walls would keep them safe and hidden. Or perhaps it the nearness of him, the sharp pang of want that struck her in the solar plexus. But whatever the reason, Renna found herself thinking back to when he'd seen the marks on her back.

"You asked where I got my scars. It was right after my Foretelling. I was worried about what had been said: 'There is darkness inside you, Rennavera Koravik, that will destroy this kingdom and its people if you let it. Vedra blood runs in your veins. Only the Mother's Truth can cure you of this darkness. Obey the Light, and if you are found worthy, your finnikfire will be a beacon to your people. Do not let the darkness inside you snuff out the light.'"

Grief thickened in her throat. Garen didn't rush her, content to let her dig through the memory as if she was searching for roots in the dirt. "Stasi was the one who suggested doing extra tithes. She said it would be a way to prepare…to make sure I was ready for the throne."

After not speaking about it for so long, there was a relief in unburdening herself. It was like a knot was untangling behind her ribs as she told him how the first month had been the hardest. Her back had constantly wept, staining her clothes a rusty red until she'd begun dressing in darker colors. That was when her headaches had begun in earnest, when she'd found she had less energy for sparring and had begun spending more time on horseback than walking.

"But as I said, it was my choice." Renna picked at a thread in the cushion underneath her. It was silent for so long that she finally looked up. Garen was leaning forward, his elbows on his knees, his jaw tight, a line between his brows. His voice rumbled low like the thunder.

"Listen to me. That wasn't a *choice*, Ren. She betrayed your trust, and she used you."

It was all still too raw, and her mind struggled to reject the words, searching for a way to protect herself, to take the focus off her own pain. "And what of you? You returned to Loxley nearly beaten to death, your injuries clearly recent. You were tortured by your supposed allies."

Garen blew out a heavy breath. "We had to make it seem like I'd been a prisoner the entire time I was gone. You would not have believed me if my wounds showed that the torture had stopped within that first year. Nothing was done to me that I didn't have full and explicit knowledge of beforehand. I knew where every mark and cut would be and why it was being done. Kirin…well, I begged him to be the one to do it. I think it may haunt him more than it haunts me."

Renna's eyes dipped to his hand, to his still-healing nail beds. Grief and horror lodged in her throat, unable to comprehend such a thing. Instinctively she curled her fingers around his. She recalled how he'd looked that first day: his arm in a sling, bruises on his face, lacerations on the skin not covered by clothes. Her brows pinched together. The Night Watchman had been seen in perfect condition before Garen's return.

Easily reading the expression on her face, Garen explained, "Remember the tattoo accelerates healing. We couldn't risk someone spotting the Night Watchman with injuries that would match mine when I returned. So Kirin broke my arm only a few hours before we made our entrance."

Renna flinched. She couldn't fathom doing that to someone she cared about—she was still struggling with the injuries she'd dealt to her enemies. Kirin's kind face flashed in her mind, and she felt a surge of empathy for him and the man in front of her.

"So hear me when I say that yours was not a choice."

Renna hated how her chin quivered. She wanted to believe him—*ached* to believe him. *When they get close, they'll see her for who she really is.* A visceral need to be seen for who she truly was, stripped of her armor, the shadows of her soul exposed, swept through her. Like flaying open a nerve, she finally spoke aloud the fear she guarded most closely, the insidious whisper that infiltrated her nightmares. The heavy truth rushed out of her:

"What if everything they did was because of the threat I represent to the kingdom? Even if I didn't choose it, I deserved it because of my Foretelling."

"*Fuck* the Foretelling," Garen spat vehemently. "If there is one thing I know, it is that the Trissaia will twist the truth into a weapon at every turn. Exactly who or what are you supposedly destroying? Because the way I see it, the only thing you might destroy is everything that is wrong with this kingdom. You get to choose what you believe."

"There have been things done in my name that I can never atone for. Things I should have known were wrong, should have put a stop to—"

Garen cradled her face in his hands, his eyes fierce. "There is blood on your hands, yes. As there is on mine. You have made mistakes. But you know better now and can choose differently. But their choices? Their *failings* are not yours to carry, Ren. The people who should've had your best interests at heart—and who claimed they did—were the ones who abused you the most. You never should have been put in those positions. Their failings are not yours, Ren."

Her hands had found his shoulders for support, his words and his nearness spinning a kind of spell over her. He brushed the tears from her cheeks, his eyes searching her face, taking in every detail. He ran his hands down her arms, rubbing warmth into them before giving them a gentle squeeze. "You should get some rest."

A wave of anxiety ran through her when he shifted as if to stand. Her fingers closed around his tunic. "Wait."

Garen stilled immediately, watching her with a carefully neutral expression. "Stay. Please."

Thunder cracked the sky, and wind tore at the building, searching for a way in. The chaise creaked as they shifted to lie down, her back to his chest, his back facing the stairs. With their bodies lined up, he draped an arm around her waist, pulling her to him, and Renna's muscles relaxed. His scruff tickled the shell of her ear.

"You were right," she finally whispered. "About Nastasia."

Garen didn't say anything, but he pulled her closer at the confession, tucking her head under his chin. She did fit there perfectly, she thought sleepily. A yawn overtook her. The warmth of his body seeped into her. Exhausted, every muscle wrung out, Renna fell into a dreamless sleep.

CHAPTER 35

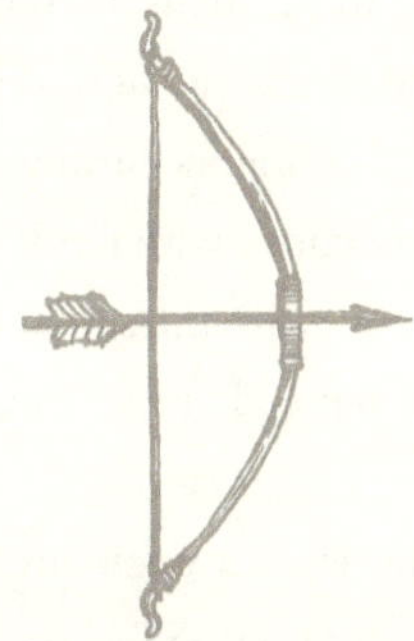

OUTSIDE THE WIND STILL HOWLED, BUT AUREM STONES COULD BURN ENDLESSLY, AND THE RED FIRE WAS JUST AS BRIGHT WHEN RENNA WOKE AS IT HAD BEEN WHEN GAREN HAD FIRST LIT IT, SO SHE HAD NO REFERENCE FOR HOW LONG SHE'D BEEN ASLEEP. She was drained from the panic and the crying, but she also felt oddly…refreshed. Like finally acknowledging all the pain and fear and hurt had made the load a bit more bearable.

Garen's calf was currently tucked between her ankles, his forearm banded across her chest. She was sure that if he woke, he'd be able to feel just how wildly her heart was beating. *What does your betrothed think of your split loyalties?* she'd once teased him. *I don't much care*, had been his reply. At the time she'd meant his role as Night Watchman, but Renna imagined the question now in the context of how he was curled around her, his body shielding hers.

She was under no illusion that Garen felt anything other than contempt for her cousin, and she very much doubted that Nastasia had any romantic feelings for him, either. Not that Renna owed Nastasia any loyalty, she supposed bitterly. While so many things in her life felt like lies right now, this pull she felt to Garen was not one of them.

There were the other words he'd said too—that he would not bed someone without full desire or consent. Her thoughts turned to the day they'd sparred in the woods, when he'd trailed kisses over her scars, earnestly asking for forgiveness. Renna turned each moment over carefully, cataloguing each touch and look. There'd been something he'd said about her tattoo as well—he'd asked if she'd noticed anything unusual. She'd been so wrapped up in how his touch felt that she'd not registered the question until now.

"I don't need mettlemancy to hear your mind spinning, lishka." Garen's voice was gravelly from sleep.

It felt simple to ask while in his arms, facing away from him. "What did you mean about your tattoo and your connection to your familiar?"

There was a long silence, his fingers curling and uncurling against her arm in an absent-minded way. "Connections with familiars are very personal in nature. It seems no two people's experiences are the same. But usually they're brought on by highly charged emotional moments. For me it was tied to the tattoo ritual."

"What did you notice?"

His chest lifted her as he took a deep breath. "Dreams, mostly, to start. I began to have these…dreams that didn't feel like my own."

Renna thought back to the dream she'd had when she'd first entered Sherwood, the one about watching the men in the caravan start a fire. The hair on her arms prickled. "Like you were seeing someone else's dreams?"

"Yes, sometimes. Then it grew into something I could control, enter even while I was awake. I picture a golden river, and when my familiar and I are both in the water, we can communicate." Garen shifted, reaching between their bodies for a moment, then held out his pendant necklace to her. "It helps me to have something to physically focus on that connects us when we're far apart."

She watched the finnikfire bounce off each edge of the stone. "A fox eye?"

Garen hummed in agreement, tucking the necklace back under his tunic. But instead of pulling her close again, he tucked his arm behind his head, angling away slightly to give her more space on the chaise. There was something incredibly intimate about the words he had shared, and the distance now made her heart squeeze with want and desire. An ache was building between her legs, and she twisted to look at him. There was a faint scar above his left eyebrow, a few more on his neck.

"May I see your tattoo?"

He shifted to sit and turned so that his back was to her. Her breath caught when he reached up to tug his tunic off.

"Garen," she whispered, reaching out to touch a spot below his shoulder. Across his back was a fox with three tails that shifted into the fire that circled around it. The fox was simultaneously fierce and wise. At various points the flames burst into swirls of lotus flowers like the ones in the willow pond in Rowan Reach.

A flower that grew from the mud.

Their failings are not your own.

Renna brushed her thumb along the fox's face, and Garen shivered in response. Underneath the ink, scars mapped his skin. *I knew where every mark and cut would be and why it was being done.*

Garen shifted to face forward, and she drank in the details of the tattoo across his chest, the crisscross of scars along his torso: more intricate swirls of flame and flowers, faint traces of runes beneath. Renna tilted her head, realizing something had been nagging at her. She'd seen his bare torso a few times now—only fleetingly, to be sure, but how was it that he walked around Loxley bearing a tattoo that could be considered heresy? "I couldn't ever make out the details before."

"Is there a question in there, lishka?"

Renna fixed him with a look. "Do you ever make anything easy?"

"Would you like me to?"

Heat swooped low in her belly at the underlying taunt, the air all around them warming a few degrees. Garen held her gaze, his eyes two pools of silver with flecks of blue, like storm-tossed waves. They'd gotten closer together, though she didn't remember moving. It was as if he was the moon and she was the tide, powerless to its pull. Their mouths hovered a breath away from each other.

"It's part of the enchantment," he whispered against her lips, answering the question that she no longer cared about.

The wave overtook them both, and their mouths met. Renna sighed into the kiss, melting into him. One hand palmed her hip, his fingers slowly spreading wide. Garen's other arm slipped around her waist, pulling her closer until she was sitting on his lap. They traded kisses like secrets. Their bodies pressed together, slipping into quicksand. Garen's kiss was devastating, his embrace worshipful. He trailed his knuckles down her back, sending a cascade of pleasure rippling along her spine. Then his hands began to rove over the planes of her body like he was memorizing every moan, every rock of her hips, each response he pulled from her.

His fists curled, bunching up the material of her dress until it pooled around her hips. He trailed lavish kisses down her neck, and she dropped her head back to give him better access. He brushed his hands against the sides of her breasts, trailing below them and then back up across her collarbones, not touching her where she desperately wanted him to. Teasing her. She pulled back to catch her breath, and he chased her mouth. Renna rolled her hips against his, capturing his bottom lip between her teeth. His breathy laugh of surprise made her toes curl with pleasure. He nipped back at her, one hand squeezing her ass while the other cupped the nape of her neck.

Tension coiled low in her core, her whole body vibrating with need and want—the crackling air just before a storm. Inescapable, like the moment before she'd dipped into the power of the Velmir. Even with only his trousers and her thin dress, there were too many clothes between them; she needed to feel his skin on hers. Renna pulled at the hem of the dress, and he helped lift it over her head, tossing it aside. Garen's jaw went slack as he drank in the sight of her. He brushed her hair over her shoulders, trailing his fingers down her back. He looked at her like she was the sun and he would die without her warmth.

Or perhaps the moon, because the darkness surrounding her did not scare him.

Garen held perfectly still beneath her. "Take what you need, lishka."

The same words as when they'd been in the meadow of her mind, now eliciting heat and fondness and something more. His meaning was clear. Renna was in control—he would give her whatever she wanted. It would be her choice. She wound her arms around his neck and kissed him deeply. The space between them evaporated. Garen kissed her like he needed her in order to breathe. His tongue delved inside her mouth, and she let him take and take and take, teasing pleasure out of her with every swipe, nip, and stroke. They moved together now, hips rocking. Garen's hand slipped between them, gliding up her stomach, the heat of him melting into her very bones and lighting her up from within. He palmed her breast, and she dropped her head back at the sensation, a breathy moan escaping her lips.

"Gods, Ren, do you have any idea how much I've dreamed of hearing that sound again?" Garen buried his face against her neck, and she arched her chest toward his mouth. He responded with devastatingly light kisses across the tops of her breasts, over her collarbone, tracing up and around her scars. "Of tasting this constellation of freckles right here."

She was dizzy with his touch, with his words, the reverence and yearning in his voice. He ran his tongue up the column of her throat before latching on to suck at her pulse point. He captured the taut peak of her nipple in his mouth, rolling the other between his thumb and forefinger. "Tell me what you want, lishka."

Her cunt clenched, aching for him. "You."

Garen flipped her onto her back, one hand cushioning the back of her head, his weight grounding her. His kiss turned languid. "You already have me."

Then he was moving down her body, dropping kisses along her neck, over her breasts, below her navel, on the curve of her hips. His voice rumbled low, his breath raising the hairs on her stomach as he dropped to his knees. "May I?"

"Yes."

Garen tugged her hips to the edge of the chaise, kneeling between her legs. He lowered his mouth to the soft inside of her thigh, fingers spread wide on her opposite leg, holding her open as he explored the sensitive skin. She could feel the cold press of his ring against her. His face was open and hungry, intent on her, as he dropped more open-mouthed kisses higher and higher. Garen brought his mouth closer to her core. "Okay?"

"Yes." Renna was practically panting, writhing beneath him.

"You are fucking radiant."

Renna's vision whited out as he pressed his tongue flat against her core, tasting her in one long stroke. All she knew was his mouth between her legs. His tongue was just as devastating at this as when he was kissing her. His eyes burned like molten silver as he slid a single finger inside her, watching her face. The tension in her core grew as he worked her with expert movements, as if he had studied her the way he'd trained and studied mettlemancy—as if his life depended on it. Her fingers tangled in his hair, gripping it hard at the roots as she cried out his name. Garen added a second finger, curling them as if he were drawing back the string of his bow. The pressure was exquisite. A string of pleas tumbled from her lips, and she was vaguely aware that she was calling out to the gods she'd never believed in.

He looked up, grinning wickedly at her. "That's blasphemous, love."

Renna pushed up onto her elbow, reaching for the laces on his trousers. She began to protest when he pushed her back into the cushions. "But you need—"

"Trust me, this is what I need." He punctuated his words with more delicious pressure, fingers crooked inside her as he gently sucked her clit, pulling an embarrassing whimper from her. Garen's eyes flared. His free hand squeezed her breast and plucked her nipple. A wave of pleasure was building inside her, washing away everything else. Renna's back bowed off the chaise as the wave swelled and crested. Her orgasm bloomed through her like a star exploding, scattering sparks across the universe, and forever altering the night sky.

When the world stopped spinning, Garen crawled back up her body, pulling her against him. Renna's muscles were soft and pliant, and she allowed herself to be tucked under his chin, her ear against his heart. Their legs intertwined as if they'd always fallen asleep like this, like their bodies knew no other way. Their hearts beat in sync as they lay in the magical afterglow. Renna's eyelids were heavy as he dropped a kiss on her temple. "You're safe, lishka. Sleep."

CHAPTER 36

Nastasia Bogdanik's white cloak glowed against the fading night as she led the small battalion of armed guards, Keepers, and Trissaia through the trees of Sherwood Forest.

She was sure she'd sensed Renna's presence back at the castle, but the red clerics had not found a trace of her before Nastasia had needed to leave. Hers had been the last group allowed to use the causeway out of Loxley before the tide swept in, a furious storm on its heels, and they'd moved as quickly as they could over the last few hours.

When the woods became too dense, they all dismounted, tying their horses to the wicked trees. A solid hour passed before the Keepers to her left began to huff under the strain of carrying the heavy palanquin. One of them cursed in a whisper.

Nastasia stopped, turning on her heel, one hand coming to rest on the whip coiled at her hip. "Is there a problem?"

"Are you sure…I mean, I thought the orders were for us to go west." The man who spoke had beady eyes and sweat pouring down his face. A bit of acne marred his left cheek. Nastasia eyed him coolly, waiting long enough that the man began to visibly regret his words, shifting his feet and dropping his gaze.

"I was not aware that you heard the voice of the Mother, Keeper."

"I apologize, Trissaia Bogdanik. My tongue got the best of me. T-truth is in the blood."

Nastasia quietly enjoyed the ability to make men tremble and cower. "Yes, well, perhaps your tongue would better serve the Mother if it were removed. The instructions we were given were meant as a cover for our true purpose." She paused, touching the aurem bracelet around her wrist. An old habit, as it was no longer an active conduit meant to ensure that everyone thought Renna could channel finnikfire. Nastasia felt an odd pang of loss for the power she'd always felt while wielding it. "Our aim is east, not only to find the outlaw witch but to strip the vedra of the last vestiges of the blasphemy they call magic. Today we will secure the Mother's victory in the impending fight against darkness."

Nastasia ran a finger along the palanquin, a thrill going down her spine at the raw energy emanating from inside. The golden aurem around her neck thrummed with power, its sinuous magic sinking into her veins, coating her throat like honey. She imagined the bloodstone pulsing as her voice took on a distorted quality and the eyes of those around her glazed over.

"Your orders are these: destroy the tree that the witches and druidhen hold dear. Fail, and your lives are forfeit."

CHAPTER 37

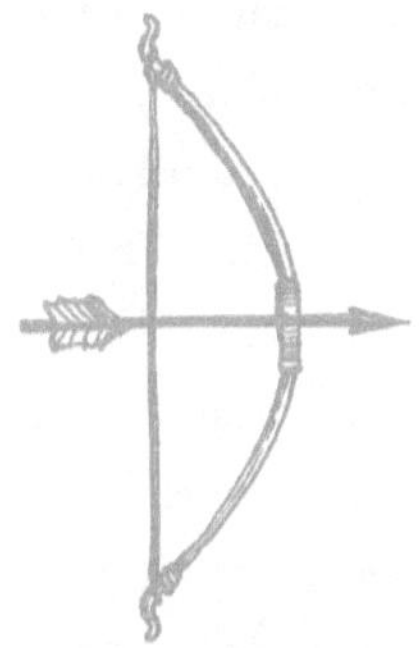

RENNA AWOKE WITH GAREN'S ARMS STILL CIRCLED AROUND HER, HEAVY AND STRONG AND WARM. THE WIND OUTSIDE HAD DROPPED TO A LOW HUM; THE STORM HAD SETTLED SOME TIME AGO.

His cloak was slung over their tangled bodies, and one hand was trailing up and down her back, idly tracing patterns across the tattoo and scars there. Such a simple touch, considering all that had happened before, but still it was one that Renna had never allowed herself. Her naked body, stripped of all barriers, was curled around him. He wore only his trousers. Garen's eyes were closed, but the moment she stirred, he was alert, eyes searching her face.

There was a delicious ache in her throat from when she'd cried out in pleasure, so Renna signed to ask if he'd slept at all—before realizing he couldn't understand her. "I'm going to have to lend you the learning cards Sif made me," she said, stretching her arms overhead.

Garen took advantage of her movement to kiss her shoulder and collarbone. His stubble tickled against her skin. "Sif is the non-hearing child, yes?"

Renna nodded, settling back into his arms, her cheek against his heart. She ran her fingers through Garen's blond chest hair. She furrowed her brow, the memory of Sif's horror at the blood gems still not sitting right with her. They'd been unable to destroy them, so they'd kept them locked in a chest where they kept the training weapons. "The palanquin we ambushed that was meant to be carrying the Blood Tithe…I can't help but think that it's somehow connected to whatever is happening beneath the Mother's Flame."

"How so?"

"When we first brought the blood gems back to Rowan Reach, Sif was horrified in a way that reminded me of being down there. Underneath the Flame…it was like no one could hear me. Except Yana."

Renna craned her neck to look at Garen. His brows were drawn together, considering her words. "It was the same for me," he said. "So the people kept down there are either Silenced or deaf. Why?"

All the books she'd been reading in Sherwood flooded her mind: tales of men being lured to their deaths by the rusalka's song, of wood wraiths speaking poison into people's minds. The witch slinging herbs in Wendsvik before the contest. That had been when she'd recognized the scent of moonshade, though at the time she'd not been able to place why it was familiar. What else had the woman said, though? There'd been a yellow flower that would protect one from the gaze of a basilisk, the massive serpent-like creature that could turn its victims to stone. It was like the way they'd used beeswax to resist the wood wraiths' whispers while seeking the Flowering Fern.

"What if…what if the blood gems upset Sif *because* she couldn't hear?"

Understanding of what they had to do next unfurled between them.

Garen slipped out for nearly an hour, heading to a safe house to collect dry clothes, midnight-colored cloaks, masks, and a few weapons. The streets in Nottingham were still covered in water up to Renna's calves and empty of people. If this was how bad the flooding was now, what would the devastation be like when the Endless Tide came?

He and Renna climbed to the rooftops. They would make their way back to the castle and access the cavern beneath the Mother's Flame through Keeper's Keep. It was slow going, and they had to incapacitate several guards once inside the Keep, but within a few hours they were at the entrance to the tunnel. They stopped their ears with beeswax, staying close together and using rudimentary hand gestures to communicate. Mettlemancy was too much of a risk down here; they needed their shields to be flawless.

They slipped into the quiet procession of people carrying buckets of blood. The workers paid them little to no mind as they crept along in the shadows. Renna took in details of the faces around her. The deaf workers must have been ripped from their homes, chosen because they could not hear. All this and more had been done under her watch, with her silent agreement; she had trusted that those in power before her had done what was right instead of taking a real look at the lives of those she was meant to protect and serve.

Renna was done with looking away, done with being silent. Magic shivered across her back, coating her throat and chest. *I will find a way to get you out of here.*

The pressure in the air built as they went deeper into the tunnel, reaching a painful level by the time they reached the massive cavern. Once more the smell of rotting meat filled her nose, and a wall of heat bore down from above. The charmed acorn in her pocket pulsed hot, almost frantic. *Ren, where are you?* The message felt a world away.

Because now she could clearly see the immense chrysalis growing in the center of the cavern. The swelling mass could have engulfed the entire grove where the Oakheart stood. Its carapace looked like a patchwork of dead skin: greenish greys, sallow yellows, ruddy browns. The mass pulsed as blood from above splattered over it. Some of the people were rewetting sections of the chrysalis that were dry and flaking, soaking it once more with buckets of blood. Large tentacle-like offshoots sprouted from the thing, climbing the walls of the cavern like vines, snaking their way up through the grates to the Mother's Flame.

Horror and revulsion choked Renna. Garen was rooted to the floor next to her, rage emanating from him. He gripped her hand, and she tore her gaze away from the ceiling to look where he pointed.

At the very base of the monstrosity knelt about two dozen acolytes, gathering thousands of blood gems that were spilling from the chrysalis. They were the same as the ones that the Keepers had brought into Sherwood. The acolytes appeared to be inspecting each gem with strange tools that they struck against the face of each rock, then held up to examine. One hunched woman, her white skin sallow, marked the section she'd pulled a gem from with some kind of chalk. When she moved to inspect a different pile, a man hurried over and began harvesting the rocks she'd just left, piling the hewn pieces onto a tray that other acolytes held.

Something was horribly wrong. The acorn in her pocket was burning against her skin, the tapping too fast for her to catch anything other than *attack*. Renna was trembling. Her tattoo was buzzing, her vision narrowing, and her knees buckled. Garen caught her as she slumped against him. The images before her were cutting in and out. She saw flashes of the forest one moment, and then she was back in the cavern. Garen's lips moved, but she couldn't hear him.

Alita.

Her mind was burning, and so was her back.

The cavern disappeared.

Alita whinnied, crying out.

Renna was in Sherwood, inside Alita's mind, seeing through the mare's eyes.

Heat and cold and wind and a loud rending noise swirled in a terrifying cacophony as the sky *split*, coloring like a bruise as the Throne Crown wards crashed down. Flaming arrows rained all around, the red fire setting the trees alight. Screams filled Rowan Reach, and Alita tossed her head, veering away from an arrow that landed a few feet in front of her. The finnikfire quickly ate through the grass, making a path toward the books in the library.

Soldiers broke through the trees, swords glinting as they charged. Nastasia, swathed in Trissaia white, had a glint in her eyes that Renna had never seen. Fire crackled in her palms, wreathing her arms. Alita charged a soldier, cracking his skull beneath her hooves. She barreled over three more, buying the outlaws some time.

Little Jon appeared first, a wild look on their face, quarterstaff whirling. Magic clung to the staff, leaving an imprint in the air briefly as the druid dealt swift blows to their enemies. An arrow nicked Alita's flank as it flew by, and Renna gasped at the pain. Alita ignored it.

Thrown daggers caught unsuspecting Keepers in the gut, or the arm, or in one case, the eye. Blood stained the fallen leaves as Scarlet pulled out her sword.

Alaini was wielding the musical longbow. She took out the nearest Keeper who was setting fire to the trees, her voice raised above the din of battle, plucking notes between shots. Vines erupted from the ground, snaking around ankles, dropping enemies.

Terror and disbelief churned through Alita and Renna, their minds melded into one. Smoke burned their lungs. Realization sliced through her gut. *No. Please, no*, Renna begged, struggling against the tether that tied her mind to Alita.

The location of Rowan Reach.

The way through the wards.

That was what Ulrik had found in Renna's mind at the ball.

Her wail was echoed by Alita's high-pitched scream, and then Much leapt onto Alita's back, armed with his bow, his quiver, and something else that he clutched tightly as he pressed his heels into her sides. "We have to protect the Oakheart."

Out of the corner of their vision, Renna saw Nastasia and several Keepers pursuing them.

There had been a persistent itch behind Alita's shoulders for weeks now, and it burned as she galloped through the trees and jumped over a fallen log. The lay of the land was a part of her soul. She skidded to a halt in the sacred grove.

The Oakheart was on fire. One section blazed, the flames eating away at the leaves, devouring the bark. Much swore, throwing himself from Alita's back and charging toward the tree. With a flicker, he disappeared, then reappeared, tossing a bucket of water on the flames. Steam hissed, but the fire raged on. His form flickered again. He meant to wind-walk water from the spring until he doused the fire, Renna realized with horror. Much would burn *himself* out long before making a dent in the flames. Alita shook her mane, her fear and frustration palpable.

The group Nastasia was leading was not far behind. Storm clouds gathered overhead, and Renna's heart twisted. *Please rain, please. We need rain.* Thunder rumbled in the distance, swelling as the minutes went by too quickly. Much continued to wind-walk at a pace he could not sustain, fetching bucket after bucket of water. He slowed the spread of the fire, stalling it, though not for long. He swayed, bracing his hands on his knees as he gasped for breath, but when he heard voices nearing the clearing, he straightened. Alita cantered over to him as Much pulled on his cowl and hood, and readied his bow. Alita bent her front legs, allowing him to climb on just as Nastasia stepped into the grove. A sword was strapped to her hip, along with a whip and quiver, her bow in her hands. She wore her golden collar with the thick bloodstone at the center.

Alita's hackles rose. Renna stared in horror, utterly powerless as her cousin strode into the clearing, trailed by four Keepers carrying a familiar metal box. Much did not hesitate, shooting off four arrows in quick succession, pinning the hands of the first two to their cargo. His exhaustion was taking a toll, though, and he missed the other two shots completely.

"Is that you, Princess?" Nastasia's words dripped with a condescension that gutted Renna. Much remained silent, letting Nastasia believe he was indeed Renna.

No, Much. Say something. Don't do this. She was the one Nastasia wanted.

"You never did have the stomach, let alone the marksmanship, for the kill. I thought I'd find you here, hiding away with your beast while your friends do all the work."

Nastasia's voice took on a distorted tone as she addressed the Keepers. "You know the king's orders. See that it's done."

The two injured Keepers ripped the arrows from their hands, biting down screams of agony. Then the four of them began walking toward the Oak's roots, haunted, empty looks on their faces. Much released another arrow that Nastasia dodged easily.

She clicked her tongue. "Do you expect me to just stand still like I used to and let you shoot at me? I think you'll find that I'm not so submissive an opponent anymore." She crouched, walking in a slow circle, uncurling the whip from her belt. "I think I'll enjoy this."

"On my mark, girl," Much whispered low enough that only Alita could hear, his hand stroking her neck. Then he spurred her into action at the exact moment he wind-walked into the tree. Alita charged the Keepers, spinning around at the last moment to kick with her hind legs. The metal chest went flying as the Keepers were thrown like sacks of grain. It cracked open, scattering the thick blood gems across the ground, just the same as the ones in the cavern where Renna's physical form was now immobile.

"I see you've learned some new tricks with that vedra blood," Nastasia called, trying to spot Much through the branches. He shot three more arrows from the opposite side of the grove, catching two Keepers in the shoulder and arm. "You cannot stop what is in motion, Ren. The Blood Moon rises. Why don't you stop hiding and come out and face me?"

Even though one of the Keepers was bleeding profusely from the head, they all stumbled to their feet with glazed eyes. Listlessly they gathered the gems, compelled by Nastasia, and began to claw at the dirt between the Oakheart's roots. A deep primal fear surged through Renna, and she screamed, praying Alita could hear and understand. *Do not let those gems near the tree!*

Another pair of Keepers burst into the clearing, bows drawn, trying to figure out where the attack was coming from as Much flitted around the perimeter of the tree, staying out of sight, raining down arrows. Nastasia's expression was turning feral, her patience quickly deteriorating. A streak of orange shot through Alita's legs as Kit entered the fray. The fox sank his teeth into the meat of Nastasia's leg. She kicked the animal aside, and Renna stopped breathing as Kit crumpled to the ground.

Enraged, Alita charged, but Nastasia's whip struck quick as lightning. Pain exploded across Alita's face, and Renna's every nerve burst into flame. Everything was colored scarlet as blood dripped down into Alita's eye. The new guards threw ropes and nets at Alita, holding her back. Kit limped toward Much as he corporealized at the base of the Oakheart, his arm soaked with blood. He fumbled, catching himself on one knee. *Shit, shit, shit, you've done too much. Where are the others? Go find the others, Much! This is when you quit.*

Rain finally began to fall, and Renna heard the shouts of her friends in the distance. But it was too late, wasn't it? Kit crouched next to Much, and his familiar's nearness seemed to bolster the archer. Renna knew the set of Much's jaw, the dangerous and determined glint in his eyes. It was the same look he'd had when he'd entered her camp unarmed, and again when he'd suggested he masquerade around as her.

Renna threw herself against the confines of Alita's mind in earnest, pleading, *Much, run, please. Do not let her think you're me. It's me she wants. Please don't do this, please!*

Nastasia swung her arm overhead and brought the whip down with a crack. Much wind-walked a second too late, and another slash of red bloomed on his chest when his form appeared twenty paces behind the Trissaia. It was sheer determination that kept his bow from wavering as he shot an arrow aimed directly between Nastasia's shoulder blades.

Renna knew exactly what was coming and could only watch with suffocating horror as the other woman spun on her heel and snatched the arrow from the air mid-flight. With the move they'd practiced hundreds if not thousands of times as little girls in Loxley, Nastasia nocked the arrow and returned fire.

Much's feet stuttered back at the impact, the arrow making a sickening *thunk* through muscle and sinew, and then all Renna could hear was her own screaming. Much blinked in confusion, looking down at the arrow sprouting from his chest. A second arrow struck him in the shoulder. His bow fell to the forest floor, and he staggered back, taking a third bolt to the stomach.

Renna's harrowing scream mingled with Alita's as Much tumbled to the ground. The mental connection severed, and Renna was thrust back into her body.

PART
FOUR

CHAPTER 38

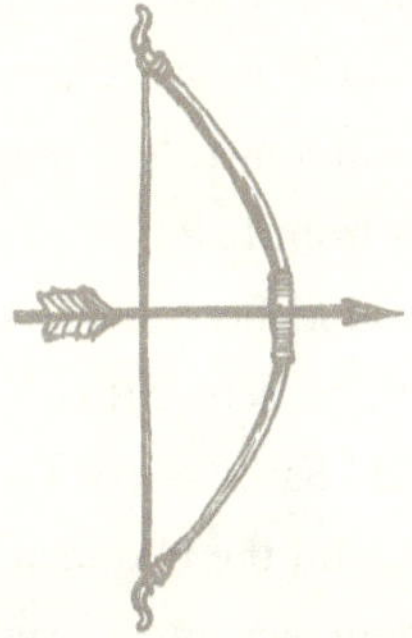

RENNA WAS BEING DRAGGED BACK THROUGH THE TUNNEL, AWAY FROM THE HORRID CHRYSALIS. GAREN'S HAND CLAMPED OVER HER MOUTH AS HER SCREAM SHREDDED HER VOCAL CORDS. ANGUISH CARVED HER BODY HOLLOW. Much…Much was…

Renna spoke into Garen's mind, shielding be damned. *They found Rowan Reach.* She twisted free, sprinting back toward the Keep, too full of panic to stop and explain, to ask questions. She had to get back. Renna clawed the beeswax from her ears.

Garen caught up with her easily as they breeched the tunnel. He snatched her wrist, and she wrenched it out of his grasp. "Will you stop for one second?" he hissed.

Renna whirled on him, teeth bared, shoving him in the chest ineffectively. "He was pretending to be *me.*"

"Who, Renna?" Garen's hands were heavy on her shoulders. "I cannot help you if you do not *let me in.*"

The truth was too raw; the words stuck in her throat like gravel. Despair cracked her anger. Her whole body trembled as Garen reached out with mettlemancy to see the image in her mind. The sorrow that flashed on his face caused her own to swell anew. Garen took a moment to compose himself. Renna could still taste the blood in Alita's mouth.

Now the acorn in her pocket was unnervingly cold.

Garen seemed to come to some conclusion. "Keep your shields up" was all he said.

The mountains around my mind protect the forest of my soul. Renna trembled violently as she followed Garen back through the Keep and out into the streets. Much was okay; he had to be. The others would find him. Little Jon could heal him. He had to be all right—

"Ren." Garen cut through her spiraling thoughts. They were in a deserted alleyway at the edge of the noble sector. The far end connected to a warren of small streets, where Kirin waited astride a massive Nozdravian. The mare was dark grey with spots ranging from black to white, a good two hands taller than Alita. Her hair was long around her hooves and waved in a peculiar pattern behind her shoulders, thicker and denser there.

"Are you sure about this?" Kirin asked in a low tone as they approached.

Garen gave him a look, and the two men shared a silent conversation that had nothing to do with mettlemancy and everything to do with being brothers in arms who'd fought their way through hell together. *I begged him to be the one to do it.*

Finally Kirin nodded. Garen grasped Renna's waist and boosted her up behind Kirin.

"The tide," Renna croaked, her vocal cords straining in protest. That was why she was here and not in Sherwood—she'd missed the window of low tide. Why she hadn't been there when…when…

Renna pushed her terror down into the invisible roots in her mind. Neither man answered. Kirin spurred the horse forward, and they hurtled down the cobblestone streets until they finally gave way to packed dirt. Salt gathered in the corners of Renna's eyes as the wind whipped her face. Kirin murmured something to the horse as they made their way into an abandoned stretch of field. Scorch marks pocked the ground, visible in the dawn light. Magic washed over Renna, a gust of wind that caused her to clutch Kirin tighter to remain seated, and her vision went grey.

Massive feathered wings unfurled on either side of the Nozdravian, jutting out from behind her shoulders. She flapped them in huge sweeps, gaining speed until she took flight.

Renna's stomach lurched as they flew up, up, up. Loxley was a speck below. There was no way anyone would be able to identify the shape moving high above, and even if they could, they wouldn't have believed what they saw. A winged horse…how long had…was Much…the Oakheart…and Kit…who else…he couldn't be…Renna could not form a coherent thought, everything slipping through her fingers. She focused on a spot on Kirin's back. Her teeth chattered against the cold, wisps of clouds parting and shifting around them until they changed to storm clouds. The horse dropped lower, the rain a persistent sheet, soaking them within minutes.

The horse banked right, heading toward Sherwood in the distance. Renna tried to relax her legs, to not grip the horse too tightly as she adjusted to the rhythm of flying instead of galloping. In nearly no time at all, they were speeding over the tops of trees toward the heart of the forest. A trail of dark smoke twisted up into the sky like a black river, marking their destination. The smell of burnt trees assaulted Renna's nostrils. Rowan Reach was visible through the shattered wards, and her heart lurched. *This is my fault.* The storm had doused the flames, but half of the Oakheart had been destroyed. Even from the air, she could see the crack that split the massive trunk, cleaving the sacred tree in two.

Shouts came from below, and the occupants of Rowan Reach pointed to the winged horse as they circled once, twice, and then landed in the desecrated grove. Bodies of fallen Keepers littered the ground, their purple robes hiding the blood that surely covered them; half of them had fallen on their own swords, it seemed. Some tar-like substance, black and crimson, oozed over the roots of the oak, seeping into the ground where unholy blood gems glittered like spiders' eyes. Someone was trying to treat a gash across Alita's face, speaking in soothing tones to the horse, who was desperately trying to get closer to the base of the tree.

Little Jon, Alaini, and Scarlet were clustered together, Much's broken and brutalized body in their arms. Renna threw herself from Kirin's horse, stumbling over roots and through puddles of blood. Grief sliced through her torso, flaying her open. The drop to her knees jarred her, and dirt lodged under her nails as she crawled toward them, her final, desperate denial of what she'd seen shattering. Renna's shuddering wail came from someplace deep and unending as the truth sank its teeth into her soul.

Chapter 39

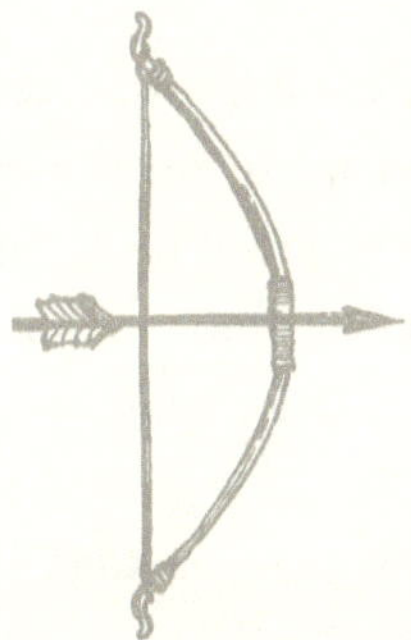

Funeral practice in Loxley involved laying out the dead on a pyre atop a bed of bloodsiphons. Perfunctory prayers to the Mother were recited. After the body was burned, the filled siphons were tossed into the Mother's Flame, the dead's final offering to the Mother.

He'd want to be by the willow and the lotus pond, Renna signed, and so they'd gathered under the weeping tree to honor Much and the four others who'd been slain in the raid. Renna had not known the others well, they'd only briefly been in the camp. But they had put themselves in harm's way to protect the children and youngsters. She committed their faces to memory. They would not die in vain. Alaini played Much's favorite ballad on her lute, tears streaking down her face the entire time, Kit pressed against her leg. Renna was hollow and cold. It felt like she was viewing all of it from far away—the song, the remembrances, the sprigs of flowers and sticks carved with runes that they placed on each fallen comrade's chest before they buried the dead.

The ritual was over too quickly and the crowd dispersed, but it was just as well. Even if they'd had endless time, none of them could've truly captured Much: the joy his company brought, the way he'd lit up dark corners of Renna's soul, the bravery he'd exuded until his last breath. To try felt like a mockery. Renna tucked each memory into the forest of her soul, deep in the earth, as if she could inter him properly in her mind, safe and protected and never to be hurt again.

Alaini had hardly said two words to her since she'd returned. Now she looked at Renna, her face twisted with grief and rage. "Where were you?"

The accusation gutted Renna, tearing her up from the inside out.

This is who you are, a voice hissed in her ear. *You destroy the things you love.* Blood welled in tiny crescents under her nails as she dug them into her palms. She was so selfish, so weak.

Her Thorns waited for her response. Despair and shame rooted her to the ground as she tried to answer the question. Renna wanted the forest to swallow her whole. She wanted to turn the tide back. Alaini's features were stripped of all warmth, teeth bared and eyes wide. "She was looking for *you*, Renna—"

"Alaini," Scarlet cut in, as if she could stop the words from spilling from the other woman.

"He was pretending to be *you*—you were supposed to be here."

Renna flinched like a kicked animal. "I lost track of time and missed the tide."

"What could you possibly have been doing that was more important than your friends?"

"I made a mistake. I thought…I thought Ulrik was controlling Nastasia, I thought she needed to be saved—"

"Much needed saving, not that pious bitch."

"Alaini." Scarlet snatched the other woman's arm, trying to rein her in.

Nastasia had done this. Nastasia had lied and betrayed Renna, plotted against her for who knew how long. Now she'd killed Much. He'd been the best of all of them, and Renna's cousin had slaughtered him.

Alaini was crying, thrashing to get closer to Renna, her words an onslaught. "The king knew the location of Rowan Reach because of you! Much is dead because of you!"

"Enough!" Little Jon roared.

"He got the location from Renna's mind, and now Much is dead!"

Renna had brought this pain and death to the only people who had ever really cared for her, accepted her for who she was. *You will destroy this kingdom and everyone you love.* The torment and rebuke on her friend's face was too much to bear. Her mind conjured the image of the broken aurem from her crucible. And like that day, Renna could do nothing but flee. She ran for the trees and blocked out the broken sobs that ripped from Alaini, the words Little Jon was calling after her, the shrill whine from Alita.

She would never outrun this, this curse and poison and destruction she spread wherever she went. Renna pulled her hair at the roots, feeling herself unraveling. She held on to a tree trunk to keep from falling, her chest heaving. Thorns bit into her palm, but she did not pull away. She deserved the pain, deserved the blood on her hands. Because even though she'd not dealt the killing blow, she had to own the part she'd played in Much's death. She'd deviated from the Thorns' plan for selfish reasons, refused to accept the truth of Nastasia's betrayal, and now she would never know if Much would've still been alive had she been there to fight with her friends.

She held tight to Alaini's blame and anger, pulling it into herself like a sword in the gut. The ring that connected her to Garen flared hot in persistent bursts. But voices roared in her mind, each damning thought chasing the next in a vicious whirlwind that left her gasping.

He was pretending to be you.

You are weak.

You will only bring destruction.

Do not let the darkness snuff out the light.

False Queen.

Unworthy.

You have no power here.

This is because of you.

Vedra.

Witch.

Renna sank to her knees. Ulrik had done everything he could to keep her small and powerless. He had feared the destruction she could bring. Garen's words echoed in her mind.

The way I see it, the only thing you might destroy is everything that is wrong with this kingdom. You get to choose what you believe.

The storm was coming from her, spinning out of her soul in a vortex that she could not stop. Her tattoo crackled with unsteady energy. Like a gathering storm.

"I am not powerless." She ground out the words. The storm surged inside her, and for once she did not shy away. Renna closed her eyes, imagining the river of power pulsing through the forest, threads of brilliant golden light coursing through the roots of the trees, washing all of Sherwood in its glow. She thought of the morglak's demand for blood. Renna grabbed a thorny bramble, pressing it between her palms, piercing her skin until her fingers were slick with blood. She sank her hands into the dirt like gnarled roots.

She gave no thought to a tether, to what would happen if she failed, to her fear of being consumed by the storm. Whether it was pleading, praying, or bargaining, she called on the magic of the woods.

Maybe truth was in the blood after all, because Renna belonged to the forest, and as her vedra blood seeped into the bracken and the roots, the forest answered her call.

CHAPTER 40

Tʜᴇ ꜱᴜɴ ʙʟᴀᴢᴇᴅ ʜᴏᴛ ɪɴ ᴛʜᴇ ꜱᴋʏ ᴀꜱ Gᴀʀᴇɴ ᴄʟɪᴍʙᴇᴅ ᴛᴏ ᴛʜᴇ ʜɪɢʜᴇꜱᴛ ᴛᴏᴡᴇʀ ɪɴ Kᴇᴇᴘᴇʀ'ꜱ Kᴇᴇᴘ. Tʜᴇ ᴏᴘᴇɴ ʙᴀʟᴄᴏɴʏ ᴏꜰꜰ ᴛʜᴇ ᴛᴜʀʀᴇᴛ ᴡᴀꜱ ᴡʜᴇʀᴇ ʜᴇ ᴡᴇɴᴛ ᴡʜᴇɴ ʜᴇ ɴᴇᴇᴅᴇᴅ ᴛᴏ ᴛʜɪɴᴋ, ɴᴇᴇᴅᴇᴅ ᴀ ᴍᴏᴍᴇɴᴛ ᴛᴏ ᴄᴀᴛᴄʜ ʜɪꜱ ʙʀᴇᴀᴛʜ.

The vantage point meant he could keep an eye on who approached the keep and the castle. There he could look out across the sea and imagine Wendsvik, and if he needed to, he could reach out to speak to Sindri. Only a few hours had passed since he'd sent Renna back to Sherwood with Kirin.

Nastasia had taken a contingent of Keepers and attacked Rowan Reach. How long had Ulrik been planning that? And why send a group of Keepers and Trissaia instead of soldiers? Garen scrubbed a hand over his face. He was missing something. And then there was the matter of what was growing under the Mother's Flame…

Garen pulled the chain with the fox eye stone out from under his tunic, centering himself. Connecting to his familiar was like wading into a river, and the moment he began, something loosened in his chest. Magic lapped around him like a gold-flecked current. Sindri appeared on the far side of the water, his brilliant fur a riot of white, orange, and red. The fox's three tails whipped fiercely before he came to meet Garen in the river.

Sindri did not waste time. *What's happened?*

Garen showed him what he'd seen under the Mother's Flame, the hidden monstrosity. Then Renna collapsing in the cave and the rush to get her to Kirin. Garen had suspected for some time that Alita and Ren might develop a familiar bond, given the way her tattoo had manifested and that her horse was a

Nozdravian like Kirin's mare, Aska. The attack Renna had seen through Alita's eyes had been devastating.

He'd wanted to go with her, but he could not risk blowing his cover. Even calling Kirin had been selfish and dangerous, but it was the only thing he could think to do in that moment. If she had made it off the island before the tide and the storm, Renna might have been killed as well when the Keepers had ambushed Rowan's Reach. Garen knew a wound like that could poison the soul.

Focus. Sindri's admonition cut through his spiraling thoughts.

Do you have any idea what that thing could be?

I will have to consult with some of the mages here, but it seems to be a beast that feeds on massive amounts of blood.

Revulsion shuddered through Garen. The river churned before settling again. A beast that required a steady supply of blood, an amount that could be fulfilled only by continuous bloodletting throughout the kingdom.

So what is Ulrik doing sending Keepers into the forest? Bleeding gods, he needed to find Nastasia and question her about what had happened.

You are not to do anything to jeopardize your cover, Sindri cautioned, sensing his rising anger. *Croyner has ordered you do nothing until we have more intel. The Endless Tide is coming, and we cannot afford to have the king hearing whispers of the Falsehoods' attack.*

I know what my orders are, Garen growled, mentally cursing Croyner, his commanding officer in the Falsehoods. He sensed Sindri's attention drift, as if he was listening to someone else Garen could not hear. Probably Croyner's familiar, a squat badger. His suspicion was confirmed a moment later when Sindri spoke.

I am to remind you of what is at stake. The Endless Tide is the best chance anyone will have for another century to successfully bring down Loxley.

The ever-changing tides that made Loxley land locked twice a day meant a successful seaborne attack was not possible, nor could an army march in and invade before the tide shifted. Next year, however, the Endless Tide would begin with a much longer low tide, and the Falsehood army—filled with water-adept vedra—would have a chance at a successful siege.

Garen was to do nothing until then. The beast that was growing in the depths of the castle, Much's death…these things changed nothing to the Falsehoods at this moment. The orders chafed like a leash, but one Garen would not cast off. Not while Sindri was bound to the Falsehoods.

Reaching out to touch Sindri through their mental connection was but a pale imitation of warmth and comfort. *Are you all right?* Garen asked.

The feeling of a flickering smile washed through Garen, though the fox merely gazed at him. *As long as you remain safe. I must go. Don't do anything reckless.*

The connection abruptly ended. The river vanished, tossing Garen out. He braced himself against the battlement with one hand, the other clutching the stone around his neck. *Pain is temporary. This pain will end. The mountain around my mind will stand.* He steeled himself, putting all the emotions, the fear, the unanswered questions into the valley in his mind, safe and guarded. His high sheriff mask was back in place when he opened his eyes.

Two streets below, Nastasia's contingent was returning. Her white cloak was stained with mud and blood, and only a few Keepers trailed behind her. People shied away from them immediately, giving the retinue a wide berth. Garen exited the keep's main doors just as they broached the small square surrounding the tower. Nastasia's lips twitched into a snarl, eyes narrowing at him. *The disgust I feel for you is equal, I assure you,* he wanted to say. Everything Renna had confided in him last night roared to life in his mind. Nastasia had bled Renna daily, letting her believe she could call finnikfire. What other betrayals had they not yet uncovered? There were always people so power-hungry that they would stab anyone in the back, but it still never failed to sicken him. Inside he was like a caged wolf, thrashing against his mental walls, wanting to rip out her throat.

The mountains in my mind will stand.

He maintained his unaffected expression as she approached. The Head Trissaia's mettlemantic connection lashed out at him like a whip, but she saw only what he wished for her to see: frustration at the Robbing Hoods' ability to slip through their fingers, the most recent man he'd interrogated, his desire for Loxley's glory above all else. Nastasia was not the type of person who considered it bad form to enter someone's mind without permission. After everything Renna had told him, it was clear that Nastasia felt that if she possessed the ability, it gave her the right. Meanwhile, Garen grappled constantly with the necessity of using his mettlemancy to maintain his cover and help save those he could.

It was worrisome that Ulrik had chosen only those with a strong allegiance to the church to enter the forest, not soldiers. He gestured to Nastasia's dirty clothes. "Was my invitation to all the fun misplaced?"

"This was a church matter."

"Apprehending that little witch who's caused so much trouble? Surely that is a matter for the high sheriff."

Nastasia managed to look down her nose at him despite his height advantage. "The king thought it wise to send me along with some devout Trissaia and Keepers."

"Are you suggesting that I am not devout?"

"I'm suggesting that if the king's choice is making you doubt your connection to the Mother, that's something you should ponder on your knees."

Garen kept his irritation tucked behind his teeth and inclined his head. "Truth is in the blood. May the Mother shine her Light on us all. Pray tell, where are the outlaws now?" When Nastasia said nothing, Garen tamped down the swell of hope in his chest. If Renna was dead, surely Nastasia would be gloating. "Ah. So perhaps you could have used my assistance after all."

Nastasia stepped closer, her eyes burning with a fervor that gave him pause. "Larger plans are being set in motion. She will meet her end soon enough."

Garen's heart iced over. Renna had risked her life several times over trying to save Nastasia, believing there was no way she was acting of her own volition. She did not deserve that kind of loyalty or compassion. He wondered what Nastasia knew about the thing growing under the Mother's Flame.

"Perhaps next time we might work together so as not to sacrifice one objective for another. That is the purpose of this union, is it not?" He gestured between them. A betrothal such as theirs was a deal brokered between men in power with little care for the interests of the parties involved.

"It would be good for you to learn sooner rather than later, Draic, that I am united first and foremost with the Mother."

And greed, he thought. He tipped his chin. "As you say, Head Trissaia."

"Now if you'll excuse me, the king has requested we prepare for a special hour of Silence to mark the Blood Moon tonight."

"Shall I escort you to the palace?"

She was already turning to leave. "That won't be necessary."

Kirin and Ilya were in the noble sector collecting tithes from the main houses when Garen found them. He needed answers, or he was going to do something foolish like ride to Sherwood himself, Falsehoods be damned. The fear in the eyes of each citizen as they opened their door to see the high sheriff and two guards hardly registered; joining the procession gave him an opportunity to speak to his friends with mettlemancy. No one they were visiting would be able to curb their anxiety enough to notice even if they spoke treason aloud.

Is she safe? was the first thing he asked Kirin.

Yes.

How many casualties?

Half a dozen injured and five dead. But there's something you must see.

Garen had endured endless days of torture, had been whipped and mentally ravaged by Ulrik, and had committed horrendous acts himself. But none of those had elicited the visceral fear he felt as he watched Kirin's memory of the blood gems fusing to the roots of the Oakheart, the exact same kind tended to by the acolytes. No good could come of those being introduced into Sherwood. Garen's mind conjured a chessboard, trying to figure out what type of treachery Ulrik was up to. But there were rules he didn't know, pieces he'd never seen, and more and more, it felt like perhaps the king was playing with a different board entirely.

They now knew that Ulrik had discovered the location of the outlaw camp months ago at the ball but had chosen to wait until last night to act on that knowledge. Why? Did he need the attack to be closer to the Blood Moon?

They found Rowan Reach. The terror and shame in Renna's voice when she'd said those words speared through Garen hours later as he lay in bed, on the edge of sleep. The realization jolted him fully awake. He had not been connected to her mind with mettlemancy in the cavern; it was too risky. Renna had used her own mettlemancy to speak into his mind.

CHAPTER 41

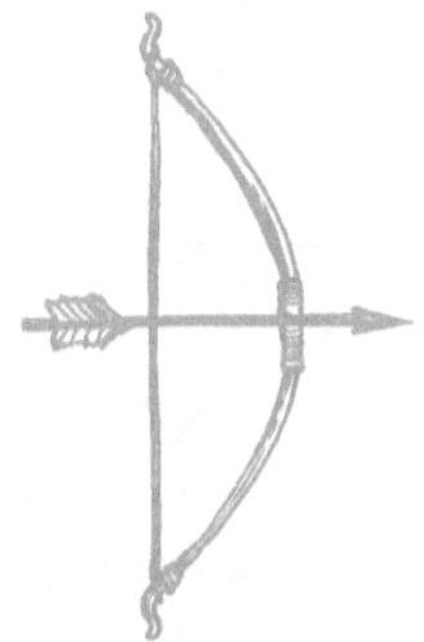

The moon was red as it rose in the sky after they buried Much.

All throughout Rowan Reach were pockets of charred and blackened trunks, foliage eaten away in an instant by the rancorous flames. The Oakheart had been desecrated. A thick, tar-like substance still wept from the trunk of the sacred tree, dripping in long ropes that seemed to be slowly strangling the massive oak. The stench of old blood hung in the air, the roots a disconcerting rust-red hue. The blood gems, identical to the ones under the Mother's Flame, had sunk into the roots like angry boils. Nothing they'd tried could keep them from feasting and growing on the majestic tree.

With the wards gone, a rotating watch had been organized. Bazyli and Asher were currently posted up just beyond where the wards used to start. Everyone not on duty had retreated to their beds. The silence and grief had its own gravity, leaving no one untouched.

Renna snuck around the camp like a wraith, readying herself. The power she'd drawn up from the Velmir pulsed through her body. Her ring had burned a few hours ago, Garen tapping a message to tell her there was to be an hour of Silence at midnight. Whatever Ulrik was planning, it would be tonight.

You cannot stop what is in motion, Ren. The Blood Moon rises.

Ulrik had sunk his claws so deep into her brain that she'd never questioned what went on around her, under her nose, or—worst of all—what was done because she'd ordered it.

Well, no longer. She was done being silent. She was not going to go quietly.

The baldric slung around her shoulder was getting heavier as she plucked vials and stoppered glass bottles from Little Jon's apothecary stash. A few fireworks leftover from the solstice had fallen behind some of the jars, hidden from sight. Renna hesitated, then stuffed them into her pack along with the scarlet robes she'd procured (and thoroughly cleaned) from one of their fallen attackers. Her quiver was full of arrows that had been crafted from oak wood and soaked in the fern flower elixir.

Next she turned to the delicately carved wands. Runes were etched onto them, and strands of leather lashed crystals to the ends or acorns to the handles. She ran her fingers along one made from a rowan tree, inspecting the runes: light, truth, clarity, strength. It was topped with a transparent crystal suffused with cloudlike tendrils of yellow gold—the stone Scarlet had picked up before the tournament in Wendsvik. The base of the wand had a large acorn nestled inside it. Tiny vines of ivy wrapped around the wand's length. Tucking it into a holster secured around her right biceps, Renna crept toward where Alita waited.

She could still taste the copper tang of blood in her mouth from being connected to Alita's mind during the ambush. Outwardly, nothing had changed between the two of them, but Renna could feel their souls interlacing. She tipped her forehead toward Alita's. The lash across the mare's face had very narrowly missed her eye. She brushed the space behind the mare's shoulders where the pattern of her hair swirled and waved, just like the coat of Kirin's winged mare. Renna moved to get a better look, fingers searching for…what, exactly? Wings?

One of Alita's ears twitched back, and she fixed one eye on Renna in a rebuke.

"I don't know how any of this is supposed to go," Renna huffed, feeling a little foolish. Kirin's horse had sprouted her wings seemingly from nothing. She should have pressed Garen for more information about the connection with a familiar, but they'd been tangled in one another's arms for that conversation. Getting answers had been the furthest thing from her mind. And then…

He was pretending to be you. Where were you?

Renna climbed onto Alita, armed with the forest and its magic running through her veins. She picked her way through the trees quietly, going the long way round so as not to pass Baz or Asher.

She'd not ridden far when three figures dropped from the trees above. Renna yanked on the reins, and Alita skidded to a stop as Alaini, Little Jon, and Scarlet drew themselves up. Each had a steely quality to their eyes in the red light of the moon.

"Going somewhere?" Little Jon asked, reaching up to pet Alita.

Renna worked her jaw. Her plan suddenly seemed childish and misguided. "I thought if I turned myself in, the rest of you would be safe."

"Only a fool would think that," Alaini snapped. Her voice was thick with emotion and had a gravelly quality.

"You're right to be angry with me. I couldn't…I can't let anyone else get hurt."

"Of course I'm bloody angry. Much—" Alaini bit down on her bottom lip. After regaining her composure, she said more softly, "His death is on my hands as much as yours. But being angry at you doesn't mean that I want you to go off and die too. Or that we're going to let you walk into a death trap."

"How did you know I was leaving?"

"You're about as subtle as Little Jon when they've had a few too many," Scarlet said. "We knew you'd try something ridiculously noble. We just had to follow and wait."

Renna had been so consumed by her grief that she'd reverted to her old patterns of thinking: that when it came to facing the dark parts of herself, she did not have anyone in her corner; that she had to hide her flaws and failings and bear them alone. Tears burned her eyes, blurring her vision.

Alaini's face was grim. "I think it's time the bastards in the castle feel what it's like when blood is demanded."

Every inch of Renna's body was pulsing with life and purpose and that river of gold from the woods. She and Alaini breached the upper level of the castle's tunnels. The bells chimed, signaling that an hour of Silence would begin soon. Unease spread through her. To call an official observation of Silence at midnight was unprecedented. Scarlet and Little Jon had exited the tunnels on the floor below and should be nearing the entrance to the temple soon, sweeping the halls for any guards or Keepers. They could not be sure how many bystanders would be inside the temple. Renna exchanged a look with Alaini. She pointed to the lute on her friend's hip then signed, *You sure about the spell?*

Sure or not, we're doing this, right?

Renna lit a match and held the flame to the spot that triggered the secret door to open. She and Alaini hoisted themselves into the private alcove at the front of the temple. Renna donned the red robes. Incense wafted into the small chamber as she hovered by the exit. She pulled a silver mirror from a pocket, angling it around the corner just so.

Thirteen Keepers, four priestesses, and two Trissaia, she signed to Alaini. All but the priestesses wore thick collars of aurem with bloodstones on their throats.

When a small cluster of Keepers passed near the alcove, Renna slipped into the group, just another pious follower of the Mother. Alaini stayed out of sight, waiting for the signal. Keeping her head down, Renna crossed to the front dais, kneeling as if sending a private prayer to the Mother. The short bow and quiver hidden inside the heavy folds of her cloak were cumbersome, but there was nothing for it. Moving carefully, she took out the first package she'd wrapped in dry paper and tucked it between the aurem plinth and the floor. Feigning interest in the handful of sculptures depicting the Mother, Renna moved through the temple surreptitiously to deposit the other items. When the bells struck again, she melted into the pillars and statues as the temple doors swung open.

Nastasia's Head Trissaia robes were pristine and pressed, free of Much's blood. A bruise was forming on her cheek, and her arm was freshly bandaged. Gisborne trailed behind her, looking like he'd swallowed something sour. A few guards followed next, none of whom Renna recognized. She couldn't determine whether the twinge she felt was relief or dread that neither Garen nor his companions were in attendance. She could not in good conscience ask for his aid and risk exposing his cover. But Renna wasn't loyal to the Falsehoods. She was loyal to her Thorns, to the people of Rowan Reach, and to the forest. There was a score she needed to settle with Nastasia and Ulrik.

The king, however, was nowhere to be seen as the doors were shut, and Renna's nerves prickled. The monarch always observed the Silent Hour within the hallowed temple. It wasn't strictly a rule, more of a tradition, but in the church that often counted for just as much.

At the front of the room, Nastasia invoked the Mother's name, and the crowd repeated the litany back in hushed tones. It seemed a lifetime ago that Renna had pardoned Yana's ward for breaking Silence. The way Nastasia had been so adamant that the girl should lose her tongue was no longer something Renna could justify as part of her cousin's devotion to the Mother and Her rules. All along, this had been her true nature: hateful, proud, and arrogant.

Much's lifeless form rose in her mind, and rage simmered through Renna, rumbling like distant thunder. She took an aurem lantern off its standing steel hook. When the bells rang once more, she used the noise to cover the sound as she stuck the rod of its base through the door handles.

The silence in the room was heavy, like it was meant to slowly suffocate every living thing.

Renna slipped her bow out of her cloak and touched the tip of an arrow to the aurem lantern. Then she took aim.

The dry paper around the fireworks would have caught easily from a single spark, let alone a flaming arrow. The explosion shook the temple, a plume of flame and smoke veiling the front of the room as the fireworks wailed and boomed, drowning out the screams. Rock and aurem shards went flying. Even though this was what she had intended, the result momentarily stunned her. Renna had braced for impact behind a pillar. Now the smoke cleared quickly to reveal a large hole in one exterior wall of the temple. Rain pelted in sideways, soaking the dais, making the floor and debris slick in a matter of seconds. A few Keepers had been thrown back by the blast, but no one was fatally harmed. Gisborne leaned heavily against the arch of an alcove, his eyes wide with horror. Over the chaos Renna could pick out the melancholy notes Alaini was playing, weaving her spell while she stayed out of sight. The Keepers nearest to her song slowly slumped into pews, exhaustion falling heavily over them.

Good, the spell was working for now. The fewer people interfering the better.

Renna lit another arrow and fired it at the next bundle. A second boom reverberated through the floor. The grinding sound of rock crunching and breaking was near deafening. The temperature dropped as the outside elements rushed in, wind and rain and noise greedily filling the space after being kept out for so long.

Renna stepped into the main aisle, bow drawn, and yelled over the din. "You want to fight me, Stasi? I'm right here. All you had to do was ask."

Guards drew their swords but Nastasia held up a hand. In a distorted voice, she said, "No one is to move. The pleasure of this fight is mine alone." The guards and Keepers stilled. Someone pounded on the other side of the door, attempting to break through, but everyone inside the temple remained frozen. Alaini's music had stopped abruptly, and cold dread slithered through Renna's veins. Her friend was hidden from sight but held by the invisible force of Nastasia's words. The space where Gisborne had stood was piled high with broken stone.

Nastasia took a measured step toward Renna, eyes narrowing like a cat's, a dangerous tilt to one side of her mouth. She plucked a ritual bloodsiphon dagger from her hip. A ball of finnikfire ignited in her other hand, burning bright.

Renna anticipated her cousin's mettlemantic attack, the pinch at the base of her skull barely registering. But she made sure to flinch how she always used to, watching herself through Nastasia's memory playing in her mind: her face tear-streaked and dull, her shoulders hunched. So terribly small. Someone to be pitied as she whispered her fears. *What if it's not enough, Stasi? What if I'm not enough?* Nastasia's reply smothered a deep resentment—*You will be, Ren.*

"I must say, I'm surprised you've lasted this long now that you're stripped of my power. Did you figure that out yet? It does feel so good to finally be able to speak the truth."

"Why did you do it?" Renna did not have to fake the anguish that cracked her voice.

"Did you really think the church would entrust the fate of the kingdom to someone with witch blood?" Nastasia laughed, and it was so different from the laugh Renna remembered, so much harsher and filled with vitriol, that it felt like a physical blow. Had any of the affection between them been real? She kept her arrow trained on the other woman.

"The king, in his wisdom as the High Trissaia, knew that the throne's position was fragile after your parents were murdered. He could not take the crown outright; there would have been riots. But you, pitiful and naïve thing that you were, willingly went under his wing, walked every step of the path he paved for you. If only you'd ever bothered to ask me what *my* Foretelling was instead of blathering about yours, expecting me to bend and scrape at your feet."

This was how her cousin had always viewed her, then. Never as Renna had, as equals. But there was a seed of truth to what Nastasia said. Renna had never inquired much about her cousin's life. She'd assumed that Nastasia craved the path of the church. Renna had been so wrapped up in her fears and worries that she hadn't been able to take on anyone else's. But that did not justify the harm she'd suffered at Nastasia's hands. Renna tried to hold the dissonant thoughts at the same time.

Two things could be true.

Nastasia took a step closer, forcing Renna back. "Still the same old Renna. Afraid to get close, lest someone see how woefully short you fall. Perhaps that's why I didn't notice that it wasn't you in Sherwood but your little friend. He fought like a coward too, staying back." Nastasia pushed forward the memory of the arrows striking Much.

"Fuck you, Stasi." Renna's hands trembled even as she pictured the words and the memory passing over her like water, like she was sitting in the freezing river with Little Jon. Behind the mountains in her mind, deep in the forest of her soul, she repeated Garen's lessons. *Control your emotions. Bait your enemy. Let them think they're in control.*

Nastasia's face shifted into something more sinister as she crouched a bit, holding her dagger out. Her voice distorted. "Let's see how you fare against me when I'm not holding back, shall we? Lose the bow."

Renna tossed aside the bow and took out her own dagger, letting Nastasia believe the warped words had compelled her. Nastasia immediately closed the space between them. She swung from above, and Renna took the slice on the outside of her forearm to protect her head. Her free hand shot out to grab Nastasia's weapon arm, bending the knife back toward her face. Finnikfire flared. Her dragonhide gloves protected her hands, but the flame resistant elixir she'd soaked her clothes in only held the fire at bay for a few precious seconds. Then the sleeve of her tunic was burning. he let go, frantically patted out the flame. Nastasia advanced, her pace brutal: cut, thrust, cut, thrust, parry.

The way you engage my blade tells me exactly what you're going to do.

Renna kept her focus on Nastasia, feeling for how their weapons met instead of watching the blade. She baited her cousin, taking another cut to her forearm, and then responded with a punch. Nastasia's head snapped back. Blood poured from her nose to join the red smears dragged across the stones from their boots. Renna lunged with an inside cut, slicing Nastasia's side while driving her other elbow up underneath Nastasia's jaw. There was a pained, angry cry and a fist gripped Renna's hair, trying to rip it out from the roots. Nastasia viciously twisted and Renna stumbled as an arm locked around her neck.

Panic washed through her. Renna hammered the hilt of her dagger backward into Nastasia's gut, striking anywhere she could connect. Hot breath was ragged on her face. The edges of her vision began to darken. Renna stabbed the dagger into the meaty flesh of Nastasia's forearm. The resulting scream nearly burst Renna's eardrum, but she broke free, making wild sweeps with her dagger as she spun to face off again.

Nastasia's arm cocked back in a blur and the dagger flew. Renna dove, bruising her body as she crashed to the floor. She scrambled behind a pillar as a ball of finnikfire whizzed toward her. There was a blast of heat on the left side of the pillar followed quickly by one on the right. Renna fought to catch her breath.

Nastasia spoke both aloud and in her mind. "You know, Princess, that this aurem around my wrist not only gave you finnikfire but allowed me to practice using compulsion on you."

The mountains in Renna's mind stretched higher. *Even though the storm rages, this tree remains safe.* Renna's weapons were discarded on the floor, out of reach. She could push off from the pillar and slide to the bow if she could distract Nastasia for long enough.

Nastasia stalked through her mindscape as she crooned, "You were so pathetic and desperate to be worthy. It was a little challenge for me, seeing what I could get you to do, how far I could get without the powers of the aurem. You remember your kitchen friend, Yana? That day out on the grounds, I forced her to take the fall for that witch storm. I only had to make her wave her hands around a little and she was marked."

Her mettle shields trembled. Renna did not shy away from the surge of anger and guilt, using it instead to fortify her shields. Her affection for Yana had put the woman in harm's way, had made her a target for Nastasia and Ulrik to exploit.

"I was ready to tip your hand if need be. But you ordered her tongue cut out all on your own, didn't you? You see, even though you were the one in line for the crown, I controlled you, Ren. The only power you ever possessed was what I *allowed* you to have."

"You have no control over me," Renna said through gritted teeth, her throat vibrating. Something was swelling. Building. The threads of golden magic responded to the words. The storm behind Renna's ribs expanded rapidly, calling forth the well of power from Sherwood. The wand strapped to her arm was growing warm.

Nastasia chuckled. "On the contrary. All those pretty little cuts on your back ensured your blood was bound so we could keep you under control." Nastasia pressed down on her mind: *Come at me, rush me, strike me.*

The command crushed against Renna's mind, grinding her bones, slowing her blood—an old visceral power meant to destroy her until there was nothing left but dust.

Behind the ivy-covered mountains, deep in the forest of her soul, a door opened, and a long-buried memory came flooding out.

Renna was twelve. She'd just received her Foretelling, and Ulrik had looked at her like she was something to be feared. He'd bound everyone present with an oath of secrecy punishable by death and whisked Renna from the room. She wanted to ask where they were going, but the wildness in Ulrik's eyes gave her pause.

Ulrik led her to the treasury, towing her through stacks of coins and gems. She struggled to match the pace of his long legs. They moved through the forge, and Renna stumbled, her head aching, woozy from the Foretelling. She'd never been down here, and there was too much to take in. She couldn't speak around the soft sobs choking her. Ulrik finally stopped before a pillar. It looked like all the others. But then he took her palm—the one still bloodied from her offering, the crescent-moon slashes weeping scarlet—and placed it on the stone. The world trembled, and a passageway revealed itself.

Ulrik pulled out a strip of cloth and tied it around her eyes. The press of the fabric against her face, the darkness that swallowed her vision, sent spikes of fear through her. This had to be a punishment for her Foretelling. Ulrik led her with his voice and hands down a steep stairwell. The wall she trailed her hand along was freezing. But when Ulrik steered her away from the steps, the air became sweltering. She could hear the shuffling of many feet, the subtle sound of brushing as if someone was painting. That didn't explain the smell of spoiled meat, though. Renna bit back a whimper.

Ulrik's grip on her shoulders bordered on painful, but Renna did not dare move as Ulrik finally spoke. "How is it possible that she carries witch blood and not Koravik fire?"

Renna flinched at the fresh words from her Foretelling. She'd failed. Then a primordial voice emanated from inside her head and all around her at the same time. The words grated on her ears, sending a quake through her body, the floor, the entire room.

"I warned you that it would not be so simple to eradicate the other magics. I can smell her blood. There is power there, but she has not yet called it. You must keep her from doing so."

Everything inside her screamed for her to run, but Renna's legs were locked, her eyes still blindfolded. It was so terrifyingly dark.

"Blood binding will hold for only as long as she believes in it. The Truth is what you say it is, sangeserre. Make her fear her power, and you have no need to fear her."

Ulrik's fingers closed around her wrist and he hauled her back up the steps. "Quickly, child," he hissed.

She tripped, banging her shin on a sharp edge. Once they were back in the forge, he tore the material from her eyes. Renna took a shuddering breath, ashamed of how the blindfold had sent her heart galloping. "Wh-what was—"

Ulrik cut off her question, crouching so they were eye to eye. The painful pinch of mettlemancy jolted her. He strode through her mind while his eyes bore into hers. *I am sorry, Rennavera. You won't remember this, but it is necessary.* The world grew fuzzy inside and out, her eyelids suddenly heavy. The terrifying conversation she'd just overheard deteriorated as it tore away from her mind in strips.

It was over in less than a heartbeat—the memory suddenly crystalizing like a fogged window wiped clear.

Renna was still huddled by the pillar, her bow, quiver, and dagger scattered. Everyone in the room was still held motionless by Nastasia's command. Outside the doors, metal on metal rang out. Little Jon and Scarlet would be close.

"Quit hiding, Rennavera."

The words passed over Renna, this time unaccompanied by the urge to obey. Even though Nastasia believed Renna was affected by the thrumming compulsion of the aurem and the blood binding, she was counting on Renna's need to prove her wrong. Renna realized that this was how things had always been between them: Nastasia using Renna's fears against her like a weapon. She'd let Renna inflict damage on herself then swoop in and stitch her back together.

Renna could finally see Nastasia clearly. Nastasia believed she knew Renna better than she knew herself. Her cousin did not understand how the forest had altered her, how her friends had slowly healed her wounds.

She reached her mind out. *Garen?*

Lishka. His relief was palpable even with the uncertainty in his voice. *I should have known you were the one blowing up the castle. We ran into two of your Robbing Hoods.* The connection wavered, as if his attention had moved to something else. Then he was back. *Are you all right?*

Does Nastasia know you removed the aurem?

What?

Does she suspect I am still under her control?

Most likely, but… Then, as if he sensed the mindscape she was casting, he said, *Wait, what are you doing?*

Playing chess.

Ren—

She dropped the mental connection to channel her focus. The smell of loam filled her, and she cast her mind deep into the earth, below the Velmir even, to that dark place she'd sunk all those nights ago in Sherwood without a tether, before Garen had pulled her out.

The real truths are sometimes the hardest to say.

Renna stepped out from behind the pillar.

The bow and arrows were off to the left. The dagger lay equidistant from her and Nastasia. Her cousin tracked her gaze.

"We both know you don't have the stomach to kill me." The bloodstone at Nastasia's throat pulsed as she palmed a tendril of finnikfire. Her voice distorted. "You will not touch that bow. Kneel."

Renna's knees buckled and she sank to the floor.

"How does it feel to be powerless?" Nastasia cocked her head, and Renna's mind was flooded with images of rushing to the dagger. Even through the mettlemancy, Nastasia's voice was distorted. *Come at me.*

Renna conjured a thought, letting it crystallize and take on life. She called up the Velmir, infusing the power into her mettlemancy, braiding it with who Nastasia believed her to be. Rennavera, who was tiring from the mental strain, collapsing under the compulsion, whose control was slipping with every hateful word thrown at her. Rennavera, who still doubted her own worth. Who was so completely enthralled that she would do as Nastasia said and lunge for the dagger between them.

Renna's muscles coiled to spring. Nastasia unleashed a blast of finnikfire, a red blaze that would have eviscerated Renna had she indeed lunged forward.

But Renna launched herself away from the dagger and toward the bow.

It was hardly a graceful move—more of an awkward roll and a scramble to rise to one knee—but her fingers were sure as she nocked an arrow and let it fly. It found its mark in Nastasia's dominant arm just above the elbow. A spray of blood spattered her face and torso as she screamed, her finnikfire doused from the sudden pain.

"You may have taken my power, but that doesn't mean I am powerless." As Renna said the words, a heavy chain unwound behind her ribs and pooled at her feet and she recognized it for what it was: a Truth. One that could not be given to her—it could only come from inside her. Magic churned through the winged stallion on Renna's back like it was summoning a storm—but she wasn't merely summoning it.

"I *am* the storm. And you cannot take my power."

The Velmir tore through her like a riptide. The golden river of power blurred where her body stopped and the world began. It swelled in her palms, and Renna threw her hands out as the magic erupted from her. Lightning, rain, and a volley of thunder drowned out all sound.

Time warped.

The world flickered.

Giant tentacles of decaying flesh filled the temple. They wrapped around every pillar, undulating and writhing. They snaked upward, weaving into the rafters above, bunching in corners and reaching over windowpanes. Corpses littered the ground where they'd not been a moment before. The air was putrid, the same reek that permeated the cavern below the Mother's Flame.

The nightmarish tableau guttered, the temple recognizable once more. Renna was seized with visceral horror as Nastasia screamed above the storm's roar, her face tilted to the heavens like a supplicant before a god.

Crimson geysers spouted from Nastasia's neck, chest, and stomach as she was flayed open. Her golden collar shattered, sending shards of aurem and bloodstone tumbling. Nastasia feebly tried to stanch the rivers of red spurting from the gashes, choking and drowning in her own blood as she crumpled to the floor.

CHAPTER 42

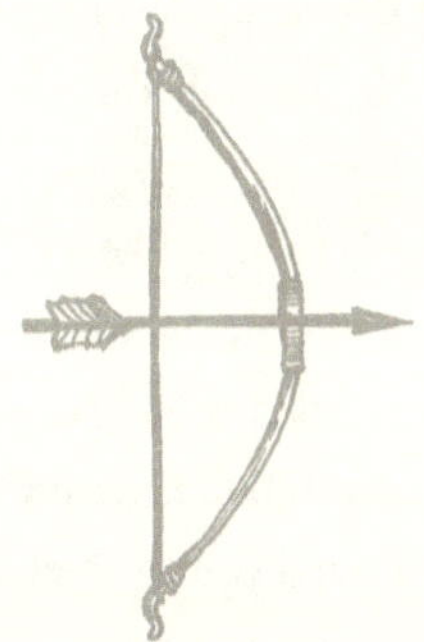

ENNA REMAINED FROZEN WITH HER PALMS OUTSTRETCHED. There had been that moment of internal detonation, the glorious relief as power had barreled through her, and then…and now…

Nastasia's body was sliced to ribbons, skin and muscle peeling back in a vicious, macabre bloom. The water around her swirled with bright reds and dark pinks as she bled out, spasming weakly.

A building pressure split Renna's skull, like a scalding dagger hacking at her brain. Her rib cage was vibrating, the back of her throat quivering. She collapsed on the ground, adrenaline and panic and whatever magic she'd just done draining her to the dregs.

Was she screaming, or was the raging noise coming from her mind? Renna's mettle shields shattered, and thousands of voices descended on her, tangling in a roar.

Renna.

Need to get this damn door open.

Bleeding Mother, there are witches in there.

I don't give two pricks about my cover, Sindri—

She killed her with without even touching her.

Please be okay, please be okay.

This is your chance to prove you ain't no tree-brained fool.

Garen, you do this and there's no turning back—

Look at me.

Surely they won't notice a few bloodstones missing.

Lishka.

"Lishka, look at me." Garen skidded to her side, masked as the Night Watchman.

Renna sucked in a ragged gasp as the chaos of her mind went silent. She was in the meadow with Garen. He was shielding her from whatever horror had just descended on her.

"Ren? I don't—your mind is acting like a lightning rod in a storm right now." His urgency cut through her panic. His hands were on her face, brushing away her hair, gripping the back of her neck, pressing over her heart to ground her. Renna sagged at his touch, struggling to rebuild her ivy-covered mountains.

"I've got you. I'm here. I need you to shield, Ren. *Now*."

The mountains of my mind surround the forest of my soul.

Combat surged around her. The temple doors were flung open. Garen nocked three arrows at once, angling his bow parallel to the floor, felling three guards at once. Little Jon and Scarlet, flanked by two others dressed like the Night Watchman, fought guards at the doors. Alaini had emerged from the rubble that had been the alcove, freed from Nastasia's words. With each arrow from her musical bow, the temple echoed with a battle song. Scarlet and one of the Night Watchmen moved like they could be twins, the former wielding her sword with the green gem and a dagger, the latter with a short sword and a hatchet with which he cleaved the sternum of an approaching guard.

Little Jon whirled their staff overhead, the carved wood and crystal pulsing with magic. Their fearsome visage, along with Scarlet advancing with a blade in each hand, sent the remaining members of the congregation scattering back, tripping over their robes to avoid the vedra, hands held up in surrender. Little Jon ducked under Renna's arm.

"Told you we'd make an outlaw of you," Little Jon whispered.

New friends? Renna signed, gesturing to the two other figures clad in Night Watchman garb.

Kirin and Ilya, Little Jon replied.

"We need to move," Garen said sharply, just as an alarm bell began to sound.

"The tunnels are blocked by the rock," Alaini said.

"Follow me. *Hurry*."

Renna couldn't tell if it was Kirin or Ilya who'd spoken, but they all obeyed. Strewn along the hallways lay unconscious guards, courtesy of her friends. Renna's plan would surely have ended with her death had her Thorns not insisted on coming with her.

It was all Renna could do to keep her feet under her and her shields in place. They made it to the throne room, the great oculus overhead, the red moon an angry eye in the sky. Armor struck stone as a swelling tide of soldiers rushed up the stairs. They'd breach the landing any moment. The future bloomed in Renna's mind. The sensation was akin to listening to the Oakheart, a deep intrinsic knowing: carnage would paint the walls and floor, flooding the castle with death. She and her friends would have to fight their way out amidst an agonizing spray of blood and viscera.

Bile rose in Renna's throat. Nastasia's butchered body. Much's lifeless face, his blood on her hands. The others they'd buried in Rowan Reach. What would happen to the people of Loxley as punishment for what she'd done here today? The cost was too much; they had to retreat, had to live to fight another day. Fight in a way that would liberate not only a few, but the many.

Sluggishly, she recalled the vials she'd brought and pressed one into Little Jon's hand. Renna thumbed open another and threw it toward the stairs. Smoke and vapor clogged the air, obscuring their view of the soldiers.

"Up," she croaked. "We have to go up."

"There is no up," Kirin argued.

But Renna pointed skyward to the great oculus, the huge bells, and the ropes stretched taut—to the metal rafters constructed for accessing the bells. She'd had the idea to use the ropes holding up the tapestries during the ball, but this was more reckless and dangerous by half. Her heart wrenched, knowing Much would approve.

They ran, pursued by the soldiers, until they reached the four thick ropes from which the bells hung. They paired off, two to a rope: Renna with Little Jon, Kirin with Scarlet, Alaini with Garen, and Ilya on his own. Alaini's face was ghostly pale, and Renna caught her eye.

Don't look down, Renna signed.

They hacked at the base of the ropes. Her stomach lurched as they were launched skyward, hurtling toward the oculus as the holy aurem bells plummeted to the Mother's Flame below. Renna's shoulders wrenched, tendons and ligaments straining to keep her arms in their sockets. The metal rafters grew rapidly before them. Renna tried and failed to banish thoughts of the awful tentacles snaking around the rafters in the temple.

Smacking into the small platform felt like being slammed down onto a boulder when grappling with Little Jon. The rope burned Renna's hands as it ripped out from her grasp, whipped through the pulley system, and disappeared below. Everyone scrambled to hold tight to the platform. Scarlet swung to hook her leg and pull herself up from where she dangled. Garen was hauling Ilya up. An immense clang shook the castle as the bells broke through each level, crashing and tumbling down. Too late, Renna realized their mistake. She cried out, praying that the bells had not smashed through the Flame to harm the people in the cavern below.

An arrow whizzed past her face. More followed, striking the ceiling, others flying out the wide opening. Below, guards gathered, pointing and aiming. Trissaia joined them, sending streaks of finnikfire at Renna and her friends. She scanned the rafters, grasping for a plan. The opening of the oculus was not close enough; anyone who tried to jump would surely end up landing next to the bells below. There was nowhere to go. Little Jon cradled one arm, which Renna, to her horror, realized was broken—they'd taken the brunt of the impact to shield her. Ilya was bleeding from a gash on his leg, and Alaini's lip was split. Garen's eyes flitted over Renna's face, checking for wounds. Kirin, neck craned, searched the night sky.

Movement caught her eye: soldiers were climbing the wall, using the ladder walk meant for servants to reach the metal rafters so they could clean the bells. One of Gisborne's annoyingly long-winded lectures surfaced in her mind.

"That climb takes ten minutes at a normal pace," Renna said, but judging by the speed of the guards, they would reach them in much less time.

"Quickly. Two can fit on Aska," Kirin said, and a horse whickered from above. Everyone's heads snapped up. The Nozdravian mare was there, her grey wings beating, sending gusts of fresh air against their faces. "Little Jon and Renna, you first."

"Why me?" sputtered Little Jon as Renna said, "I'm not running."

Kirin's tone was clipped. "Little Jon can't do any acrobatics with their arm broken like that. And you're the rightful heir to the throne."

Kirin had the same exasperated expression she was used to seeing on Garen's face, as she steeled her spine. "I came here as an outlaw, and I intend to leave as an outlaw. This was my idea, and I am not leaving first."

"Fine. Ilya, get ready," Kirin bit out. At Ilya's protests, Kirin gripped the back of the man's neck, hauling him closer, their faces mere inches apart. He spoke in a hushed, tender tone. Renna averted her eyes from the private moment, but she still heard Kirin's ragged whisper of, "Please, my heart."

Ilya conceded, and he and Little Jon readied themselves at the edge of the rafter. This would still leave five of them cornered, and the likelihood that the horse could return before the guards reached them was not good. Renna, Garen, and Alaini drew their bows and rained down arrows, providing cover for the Nozdravian as she swooped down to hover in place. Ilya and Little Jon climbed on. With a powerful beat of grey wings, Aska rose and disappeared.

Scarlet, Alaini, Garen, Kirin, and herself remained. Five minutes until the soldiers would reach them. Renna could make out their finnik leathers as they climbed. Alaini tried shooting an arrow with a grappling hook to the ledge of the oculus, but it kept sliding off the stone, never catching.

Garen stayed her hand as she reached for another. "Don't waste any more with that." Their quivers were alarmingly low.

"I've always fancied being forced to wait to die," Alaini joked weakly. "The anticipation really makes it special."

Garen continued to take out guards on the floor below, his lethal aim never wavering, but his arrows were dwindling. Kirin was back to watching the sky intently.

"*Fuck*," Scarlet screamed, jerking away from the edge. An arrow protruded from her left arm, just below the shoulder joint. Blood stained her tunic. Alaini cried out, holding Scarlet as she slumped. Much's body, riddled with arrows, flashed in her mind and Renna choked down the bile that rose. Garen moved quickly, speaking in calm tones for Scarlet to hold still as he snapped the extra length of the shaft. Scarlet whimpered, all the color draining from her face.

"Where is Aska?" Alaini yelled to Kirin, as more arrows struck the bottom of the rafters.

Kirin shook his head. "She's too far."

There would be no escape for them. Renna gripped Scarlet's sweaty hand in hers, squeezing.

"At least you made her pay," Scarlet said to Renna.

Renna blinked back tears. Much was still gone. She tried to picture the meadow in her mind to calm the panic lacing her veins. Grief and regret turned her limbs heavy. They should have fought their way out. It would be better to die fighting rather than sitting here, waiting for death.

Dying is dying, lishka. And you made sure some of your friends got out. Garen's voice was ragged.

Renna startled, checking her mettle shields. His presence wasn't in her mind, so how had he…

You're doing it, Ren, not me.

With a shaky breath, Renna realized he was right: she was in *his* mind, her thoughts all but shouted at him in the meadow. His meadow was similar to her own, but with subtle differences: the jagged mountains were an impenetrable onyx; the grasses waved higher; a small library spanned a mossy grove; the lake was nearly invisible, covered with lotus blossoms.

You first did it below the Mother's Flame, Garen said.

And she had. She'd not even realized in the moment, concerned only with conveying that Rowan Reach had been attacked. Reaching out her mind to his had been as unconscious as taking a breath. She'd lost the ability to speak into another's mind after her crucible. Or perhaps she'd never truly had it. Was that another power that had come only from Nastasia? The magic that had burst from her in the temple, though…that was something entirely new and entirely hers.

There was no more time to think on it. A ball of fire launched toward them. An oppressive wall of heat barreled over them, and everything went red as the finnikfire greedily lapped at the aurem lining the edges of the rafters. Everyone scrambled to the far end of the crowded platform, as far from the fire as they could get without falling to their death. Kirin's cloak caught the flames, and he tore it off, kicking it away. Garen hauled her behind him. Everyone's shouting blurred together.

Tears streamed down Renna's cheeks as she squinted against the finnikfire. Shadows darkened the oculus. Something soft and familiar brushed against her mind. Even though she'd never heard the voice, she knew it who it belonged to.

The druidhen are coming. Alita's words drowned out all the chaos.

A sob of relief ripped from Renna as Alita soared overhead. Fierce black wings jutted out from behind her shoulders, right where the swirls of hair had been. Where the persistent itch had been bothering the mare for weeks. Power and magic seemed to radiate from her, crackling like lightning.

Hello, Truth Sayer. Alita's voice was a balm that soothed Renna's battered mettle shields.

An owl flitted to the oculus's edge.

Briar Jain.

Then Myrryn Bjonir, the matriarch of the druidhen in her griffon form, landed beside the wyldling witch. The others cried out in awe as another creature appeared with the body of a stag, its head crowned in sharp antlers. It had massive wings and the face of an owl. A peryton—the creature whose antlers were used for the tattoo ritual. The creature last to arrive had the face and torso of a woman with the body of a bird. With vibrant feathers, she was stunningly beautiful, her features glowing and twisting Renna's heart.

One by one, the mystical creatures dropped through the oculus, each carefully gathering up her friends in their arms or claws. Garen helped Renna up onto Alita's back before climbing on after her.

Cries of outrage came as three guards breached the rafters and burst through the fire, their finnik leathers unsinged. Crossbows raised. Garen threw two daggers in quick succession, catching the first in the throat while the other sank straight into the second's skull. Scarlet's throwing star sliced the trachea of the final guard, spraying blood in an arc. The cost of the move with her injury was evident by the pain on her face.

Alita's wings carried them out of the castle, and Renna slumped against Garen's chest. His biceps flexed around her, his knuckles turning white on Alita's reins. The farther from Loxley they got, the more her grasp on the tumult inside her slipped away. Grief was a yawning hole beneath her, pulling her in as she took shuddering breath after shuddering breath. She couldn't bear to say the words aloud. Through the mental tether, all she could manage was, *Much is gone.*

I know. It's okay to break, Ren.

A sob cracked her open. The sky responded, raining down tears, thunder, and raging lightning as they flew toward Sherwood Forest. Even the tide below receded as if wary of the anguish pouring from the outlaw witch.

CHAPTER 43

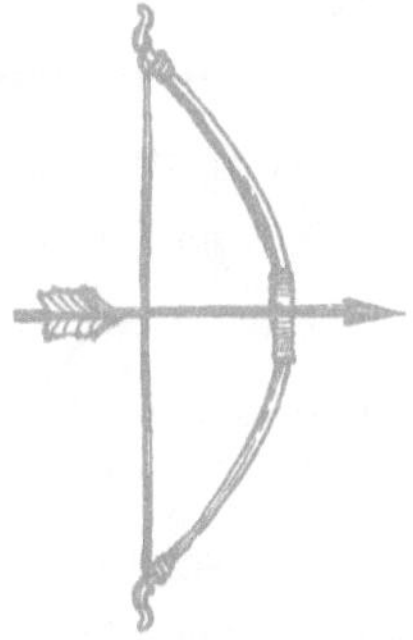

THEY LANDED BY THE OAKHEART, A STRANGE PROCESSION OF BEASTS AND HUMANS, BLOODIED AND BATTLE WORN. ALITA'S MASSIVE WINGS COLLAPSED, DRAGGING ON THE GROUND. Renna all but leapt off the horse, concern gripping her. *Alita?*

I am all right. Just tired, the Nozdravian replied through their bond. *Go. Check on the others.*

Renna was swaying with exhaustion, but she pushed everything that had happened in the castle deep into the forest in her mind, gave it to the roots of the trees. She could not hold it all. Not right now. Garen's hand rested on her low back, steadying her. Her chest hurt with a constant ache.

Ilya and Kirin were nearest, the latter sitting and inspecting his leg. Briar shifted from owl to woman in the blink of an eye, crossing to Little Jon, her entire focus on the injured druid. Alaini was doubled over with her arms on her knees, hair plastered to her face with sweat. Her whole body was ripped up from clawing out of the rubble in the temple. Scarlet's face was dusted with powder from the explosives and other people's blood. The snapped arrow still stuck out from her arm. Renna needed to be near them, to assure herself that the rest of her friends were safe.

Nastasia's butchered body flashed in her mind.

A harmonious voice pulled the entire grove to attention. "Children of Sherwood, I can sense the anguish in your hearts." The half-woman half-bird creature addressed the group. Her voice sounded like the melody of a harp and the resonance of a cascading waterfall. Her eyes were luminous and golden. She towered twice the height of Renna, and when her gaze landed on her, warmth washed over her like she was standing in bright sunlight. "Would you like me to take this pain from you?"

The offer was one that Renna had longed for so often in her youth—for someone to take the sting of the tithes, the loss of her parents, the pain of her looming failures. But even as the warmth bolstered her, she felt the memory of Much slipping from her, fading into the background. The grief at his death was love enduring on. Pain had forged her, made her, like the mud that nourished the lotus. No, Renna had not given away her choice or her power, and she would not give away her pain.

Her companions seemed to arrive at the same conclusion. It was Little Jon who answered. "You honor us with your offer, great corveth, and we thank you for your aid. For now, we will keep our pain."

The creature—the corveth—dipped her head, the motion simultaneously birdlike and human.

The griffon transformed into the druidhen matriarch once more. Myrryn turned to Little Jon. "Briar told me what was done to the Oakheart. Druidhen generally do not concern themselves with the acts of men. But when the forest is harmed..."

A chill settled over the grove as everyone looked at the desecrated tree: scorch marks on the ground, the splintered trunk, the sinister gems scattered among the roots. Much had taken his last breath right there. If the druidhen had only answered their call for aid earlier, perhaps…

Tension wrapped around Little Jon like a cloak, and Renna was viscerally aware of the pain her friend carried; each time their mother and their people had turned away or denied help had been a cut to the druid. Renna's back tingled. The pain of a thousand cuts could be crueler than one swift strike.

"We can see to the wards." Myrryn motioned to the corveth and the peryton. Renna half expected them to shift into druidhen as well, but they remained olden creatures.

"Will the others come?" Kirin asked.

A heavy pause. "Not all share the same mind about what is to be done."

"Are all druidhen in the habit of answering questions with non-answers?" Garen snapped, his patience clearly depleted. He pointed to the Oakheart. "This is just the beginning. More death and more destruction will befall Sherwood, Loxley, Wendsvik—*all* of Dravmir. No one will be safe."

The druid drew herself up, the air around her warping with power. "You speak as someone who knows. Perhaps your familiar has given you a taste but you do not truly understand what is coming. I admire your hunger, boy, but be careful how you speak to me. I will not ask my people to give more than they have already. Those who wish to fight will join us. More will come. But not because of your call."

Garen's familiar had given him a taste of what, exactly? There were so many things left unsaid in this exchange, and Renna's head was throbbing. Garen's jaw flexed, but he remained silent. The druid's gaze moved to Renna. Those leonine eyes seemed to see straight through her soul. The druid's mouth opened in a soft inhale. Renna tensed, ready for whatever the woman was about to say, hungry and wary at the same time. But the matriarch only said, "Rest, now. There is much to discuss later."

Renna was grateful that Garen followed her to the privacy of her tree house. Once there, she could only stand numbly, unmoving. He crossed to her, hands sliding along her jaw, tilting her face up to his. Tears slipped out of the corners of her eyes, and he brushed them away with his thumb. He helped her peel off her clothes, filthy from battle. He tugged the hem of her shirt out of her trousers, carefully pulling it over her head so as not to get any more blood on her face. Gooseflesh ran across her arms, prickling like tiny needles.

Garen gently worked her torn trousers down over her hips, kneeling before her to pull off one boot at a time. She trembled violently, like she would never be warm again. He left her side for a moment as she stared unblinking at her dirty clothes. Then Garen eased the large knitted sweater Edwine had made her for solstice over Renna's head. He pulled her hair free of the collar and guided her legs into a pair of loose trousers. Large hands squeezed one foot and then the other, strong thumbs pressing out the aches in her arches. Tears flowed steadily down her cheeks, wetting her neck, and soaking the collar of the sweater. Garen still knelt in front of her, settled between her legs as he peered up into her face. Renna slid off the edge of her bed and into his lap, arms wrapping around his shoulders as she buried her face in his neck and cried.

Renna was numb as she picked her way through the trees the next morning. Though she'd been wrapped in Garen's arms all night, sleep had eluded her.

So she'd slipped out at first light, careful to not wake Garen, intending to take Alita and go sit by the willow pond. The morning air was still, her eyes gritty and tender from crying. She was not the only one having trouble sleeping it seemed, for she ran into Kirin. He'd procured clean clothes, most likely from Asher, and was grooming Aska. Saddle bags were packed on the ground by his feet.

"Leaving?" Renna asked as she paused to pet Aska between the eyes.

"Just preparing. Garen will be too anxious to linger longer than necessary."

Renna nodded, her heart wrenching at the thought of him leaving so soon. Aska pushed her nose into Renna's palm. They had to return, of course. They had all been dressed like the Night Watchman, their identities still safe.

Kirin said, "Your friend, Scarlet. Is she—"

"Healing, thankfully."

Silence stretched again.

"Seems we have something in common, my lady. Nozdravians used to bond with vedra and druidhen frequently. It's much rarer now, especially outside of the druidhen."

Renna raised her eyebrows, and he rushed to clarify. "I am not a druid, no. But I spent a good deal of time around the horses growing up, which I believe helped to encourage a bond. It was not until I was in Wendsvik, though, that Aska became my familiar."

I begged Kirin to be the one to do it.

Kirin's eyes—one green, one blue—fixed on Renna. "It is no small feat to produce a bond like that. You should be proud."

Renna could not bring herself to do anything other than nod.

She fetched Alita, holding Kirin's words up to her memories with the horse as they went to the willow pond. Her strange dreams that had felt like Alita's memories; the way she'd always seemed to understand what Alita was trying to communicate to her; the magic of her tattoo manifesting as a winged Nozdravian. In hindsight, Renna could see the moments braiding themselves together. What had secured their bond, though? What had allowed her to see what Alita was seeing while she was underneath the Mother's Flame? Alita's wings had not come until after Renna had left to face Nastasia. Perhaps it was that moment of swirling intensity, the storm she'd unleashed from inside her.

When they reached the willow, Kit was already there, curled up by the patch of earth where Much was buried. Renna thought she'd cried all her tears the night before, but more came at the sight. They sat there—witch, horse, and fox—for a long time. Blossoms from a nearby cherry tree swirled and fluttered on the breeze, landing like pink snow over the freshly tilled ground.

"May I join you?"

Renna looked up into Myrryn's face. She was smiling sadly, and her likeness to Little Jon in that moment was striking. Renna gestured to the empty patch of grass beside her. The feathers in Myrryn's hair were those of an eagle.

"It has been a long time since I have seen a newly evoked Truth Sayer."

There was that term again.

Myrryn nodded to herself, looking out at the water. "You don't understand. How could you when the truth has been stripped from the world and so few are left to remember?"

Renna picked at blades of grass, holding them in her palm until the wind took them away. She'd spent so much of her life either not remembering things or trying desperately to forget them. Now there was this: the knowledge of what lurked in the castle, Nastasia's betrayal, the horrible conditions under which her people lived, Ulrik robbing her of her voice, her memories, and her magic.

"Will you tell me?" she asked Myrryn.

"Loxley has held its position of power for less than two centuries. The druidhen walked Dravmir long before it was even called such. We remember the way things were long before words were written down. Before kings and queens ruled. Even long before the Great Culling, when the fae and the mystical beasts lived among the vedra and the druidhen. But the greed of men is a deadly, pervasive thing that takes root and spreads, choking out anything unsuited to its desires."

Renna thought of the look on Nastasia's face when her cousin had commanded her to kneel, the strain around Ulrik's eyes as he'd stripped her memories of what lay beneath the Mother's Flame.

"At that time, your kind were known as Truth Sayers. Ah, yes, you are thinking I mean Trissaia. But Truth Sayers are as old as druidhen. It was only when the church came to power that they stole the moniker and perverted its meaning. You were taught that a Trissaia is the only one who can see the truth of another's soul, that only a worthy few can hold such power.

"They twisted what it is to be a Truth Sayer, claiming that to use a power source other than fire was blasphemous, wicked. They sought to cut witches off from the power that was rightfully theirs—the power of the trees, the oceans and rivers, the wind, and the sky. Not only fire, but every well of power."

The golden river below—the Velmir.

"Instead they shackled the Trissaia to one power source and began to feed the lie: that theirs was the only way to know your truth. But a Truth Sayer builds up a reserve of power from speaking Truths. The *hard* truths, the things that can topple empires and tear a person inside out, reforging into something purer."

In the castle, when Renna had claimed her power, it had been a moment of unleashing, unchaining herself. She'd known in her bones that certain Truths could come only from her.

The pieces had been coming together in a sluggish haze since the battle in the castle. She breathed in sharply as, all at once, words flooded her mind.

There is darkness inside you, Rennavera Koravik, that will destroy this kingdom and its people if you let it.

Garen's gentle voice: *The way I see it, the only thing you might destroy is everything that is wrong with this kingdom.*

Could it have been that simple and unsophisticated all along? Her Foretelling had never been about her worthiness or her ability to protect her people. It had always been about Ulrik controlling her, to keep her from exposing what he was up to. She recalled that horrible voice under the Mother's Flame: *The Truth is what you say it is, sangeserre. There is power there, but she has not called it yet.*

Renna wanted to lay down and weep. Because she understood now. The storm that Yana had been blamed for had been her doing. Renna, feeling so powerless and afraid that she would end up burning as well, had twisted the prayer. Not *Truth is in the blood*, but *Truth is in my blood*. In doing so she began to summon her powers.

Storms could destroy the kingdom Ulrik had built. He had used her Foretelling to speak *his* version of the truth. The "darkness" in her was merely her ability to call and wield storms. Underneath the Mother's Flame, they had only been able to see what was truly there when they'd had beeswax in their ears. The non-hearing were placed down there to work, to handle the strange gems that grew inside the chrysalis. Only when she'd called a thunderstorm and drowned out all the noise had she been able to see what was lurking in the temple.

A creature patched together from decaying, rotting flesh.

She recounted it all to the druidhen matriarch then, every detail, calling Garen and Alaini over to add what they had seen and heard in that secret cavern. Soon others joined them: Kirin, Ilya, Briar, Little Jon, and Scarlet. By the time they finished, the color had drained from Myrryn's face and the sun was setting. She thought of the morglak's bargain: safe passage in exchange for blood. Sangeserre weaving spells with blood.

"What manner of beast has Ulrik tied himself to?" Renna asked, feeling utterly spent.

Myrryn looked shaken. "The creature you speak of can be conjured from a lie and a blood sacrifice using malevolent magic. It is lethal and nearly impossible to kill. Like the corveth's cousin, the rusalka, its power is in its song. The beast sings a song that forces you to forget its very existence, hiding in plain sight. Such creatures are remnants of leviathan drakes and wyverns from the time of the fae. They're called silmorra."

A beast that could make you forget it existed.

The Blood Tithe. The hours of silence that everyone had to observe, the rush of ecstasy and belonging that followed. With enough blood and silence given, Ulrik could cast a spell on an entire kingdom so they would forget the monster in front of them.

You won't remember this, but it is necessary.

Myrryn's gaze unfocused, lost in concentration. Realization crashed over her features and she transformed into a griffon in the blink of an eye, shooting toward the Oakheart. They all followed, spilling into the ravaged grove. Myrryn had already shifted out of her griffon form by the time they arrived. In the growing darkness, a change had begun in the sickly gems. They were expanding, solidifying into one mass at the roots of the oak. Renna watched in horror as the roots of the tree began to shift, bark giving way to tissue and sinew. A thick black substance was seeping outward like a dark puddle of blood slowly spreading over the forest floor. Everything in its path seemed to choke.

Myrryn cried out, whirling her griffon-topped staff. Light exploded from its point, halting the progression of the poison, but the damage was done. She staggered, her voice reedy with exhaustion. "They used the Blood Moon to siphon the Oakheart's power for a second heart for the silmorra. Whatever power they had before is nothing compared to what they can wield now."

EPILOGUE

GISBORNE AWOKE TO PAIN LANCING THROUGH HIS ENTIRE BODY.
Rubble from the explosion had nearly walled him into the small alcove where he'd been thrown by the blast. The temple was deathly quiet. His hand was broken, crushed under a large chunk of the temple wall, and dried blood made the skin on his face tight. He coughed out the dust coating his lungs and fought to extract his bruised and broken limbs from the debris.

Everything came back in fuzzy patches. He'd been arguing with Nastasia as they made their way to the temple. She'd refused to tell him where she'd been or where Ulrik was, only that they were to hold an hour of Silence at midnight. Ulrik had not even come to bed the night before. The king had been so distracted and paranoid lately, only able to focus on the upcoming Blood Moon. Gisborne had felt him slowly pulling away, secrets building between them. The king hardly trusted anyone anymore, not even the high sheriff.

Nastasia was Ulrik's favored confidante now. "I only require council from the Mother and Her chosen," he'd snarled the last time Gisborne had pled with him to share whatever burden he was carrying. The king's face had been looking sallow, his eyes yellow, and a muscle twitched in his cheek frequently.

Gisborne had been distracted as he'd walked with Nastasia to the temple earlier that night while the Blood Moon rose; surely Ulrik had accomplished whatever he needed to do and would soon be back to his usual self. But Nastasia, like an insolent brat, had refused to say a word about the mission she had carried out.

And there was still no sign of Ulrik as they congregated.

They'd waltzed in like lambs to the slaughter. The fallen princess had worn red robes, barricaded the doors, and shown no mercy. Nastasia's use of the power of the aurem collar had both delighted and terrified Gisborne. His metallurgic process had been groundbreaking. Ulrik had been able to instill each collar with an essence of his power as a sangeserre.

It was treasonous, technically—Ulrik's unsanctioned magic. Yet how could they ignore the good it had done, or would do? Rules were meant to be used to their advantage. He understood the mechanics of a blood mage. The arcane knowledge went hand in hand with the aurem that built the city, and it had challenged his mind all these years.

"Think of all the glory we can bring to Loxley, the revolutionary advancements we can achieve if everyone bends to our will," Ulrik had whispered to him one night many years ago as they'd lain tangled in the sheets, when their love had been new and exciting. Ulrik's devotion to the church matched Gisborne's own for research.

But none of that had prepared him for the cold horror that had crashed through his body when Nastasia had used the power of the collar on him. He'd not been able to move a muscle, his mind and body warring against the compulsion to obey, to *not move.*

And then there had been the horrendous clash of thunder and lightning, and the monster he had known was there had been revealed.

From where he'd been frozen, he'd caught the monster's reflection in the water that was rapidly filling up the temple, seeping through the rubble to pool around his ankles. Unlike what he had imagined from Ulrik's descriptions, the beast had horrified him. Cold rotting flesh had covered the expanse of its long serpentine body. It had been adorned with a perversion of scales like its ancestors of wyverns or drakes, grey and putrid, leaving a trail of grime and blood and fluid in its wake. It seemed to cover the entire temple, winding itself around the pillars, through the rafters, strangling the sanctum. Gisborne had wanted to claw his eyes out, and even now, as he dragged himself up the small mountain of rocks between him and the rest of the temple, he felt the same intense desire.

This is so far from what we agreed on, my love, he thought bitterly, feeling his heartbeat in his crushed hand. The sense of betrayal grew in his gut.

There were footsteps. Gisborne pushed aside a slab of rock decorated with aurem shavings, creating a small hole through which he could see into the room beyond.

Bleeding Mother.

Nastasia's body was gruesome to behold, and he was turning away from the sight when Ulrik skidded into view, trailed by a few Keepers. His lover's name was poised on his tongue, but something gave him pause. Ulrik looked like he'd barely escaped death himself, his robes tattered and streaked with mud and blood. A harrowing cry tore from Ulrik's throat as he dropped to his knees, looking at Nastasia's flayed body.

"Don't just stand there! Go fetch a healer!" Ulrik snarled. The Keepers looked horrified, but neither risked the king's wrath by saying that the Head Trissaia was clearly beyond the scope of a healer. They ran, leaving Ulrik alone.

Again, Gisborne was about to call out, but Ulrik roared into the empty room, "You think you can leave me alone to deal with this?"

An awful, grating voice filled the temple. "I told you to get your house in order, Osric."

"That bitch has ruined everything," Ulrik was practically foaming at the mouth, spittle gathering at the corners of his lips.

Osric. The name of the first Trissaia rang in Gisborne's head as fear lashed through him. *What have you done, my love?* Gisborne could barely breathe around the tightness in his chest.

Something that had the cadence of a laugh but was not one echoed through the temple. "Surely you can find a way to use this to your advantage. Isn't one body the same as the next?"

Ulrik muttered fervently, his hands twitching in strange patterns.

And then the king reached up and gripped the hair at the nape of his neck. A horrid tearing, squelching noise rent the air. Gisborne swallowed down bile as Ulrik peeled his skin off, discarding it like an old cloak. The thing underneath was greyish and disfigured, its muscles twisted in ways that evoked thoughts of torture racks and malicious magic. Red eyes burned in the sockets of its skull, the skin of which looked like it had charred and melted several times over. Yellowing nails the length of Gisborne's forearm pierced through the stumps of the fingers that the creature now used to saw through the rest of the skin—the rest of Ulrik—with horrifying efficiency.

Ulrik's skin pooled on the floor like that of a dead snake.

The thing climbed onto Nastasia's broken chest, lowered its gaping maw, and began to drink the slain woman's blood. Gisborne was unable to release the scream building in his throat as he watched the thing that had been Ulrik peel open Nastasia's flesh and burrow inside.

With slow, deliberate movements, the thing that wore Nastasia's body climbed to its feet. The Head Trissaia pressed her hands to her bloodied chest, the wounds slowly closing themselves, the skin knitting back together.

Run, a primal instinct demanded. *Run away, far, far away from this evil.* Gisborne shoved his uninjured fist into his mouth to muffle a whimper. He could not let that thing find him here. His skin burned and crawled with shame and anguish, as if it was his own that had been peeled away. *What have I done?*

The logic and conviction that had fueled his choices, the schemes he and Ulrik had hatched, fractured inside him. He had reasoned away all manner of evil during his years in the palace. But nothing like this. Never this.

Gisborne jerked away, his soul—or whatever was left of it—shying away from the unholy, smiling abomination. An interior wall of the alcove had collapsed in from the outlaw's blast. Gisborne forced himself to move quietly, his body screaming in pain until he found a large fissure that opened directly into the tunnels that the fallen princess had been so fond of.

Behind him came voices and footsteps, no doubt the Keepers returning with the healer. They would see the thing that looked like Nastasia, whole. Someone gasped, and another began praying aloud.

"A miracle—"

"Long live the Mother's chosen!"

There were several heavy thuds—probably the onlookers dropping to their knees.

"Long live the Trissaian Queen—"

"The Bogdanik Queen!"

Gisborne ran through the tunnels. *The outlaws.* His soul was surely damned, but he would do penance however he could before he left this plane of existence. Yes, he would deliver himself to the outlaws in the woods, into the hands of the fallen princess herself.

But nothing dulled the awful chants of *long live the Bogdanik Queen* that echoed in Gisborne's mind as he fled to Sherwood Forest.

To be continued…

AUTHOR'S NOTE

Welcome to my Robin-Hood-lore-nerd-dump. There will be spoilers for book one in here, so if you've not yet finished, beware. (Also, why are you looking at the back of the book if you are not yet done?? Who hurt you?) When I was twelve, I visited the tidal island of Mont St-Michel in Normandy with my family. Mont St-Michel is 1300 years old, sitting on a natural outcropping of rock in the middle of a plain of mud and quicksand. The daily tides swell up to fifty feet. I vividly remember the mist that clung to the ground as we watched the tide slowly creep in to seal off the entire city. It is, to this day, one of the most magical places I have ever been.

Thus began my fascination with the Unconquered Fortress.

I knew I wanted Sherwood Forest itself to be a source of magic, as this is a high fantasy world. When I began brainstorming the world for The Outlaw Witch of Sherwood, that trip to Mount St Michel kept coming to mind. After hours of research (and one particular morning spent researching what would happen to an ecosystem after mass deforestation—spoiler, it's very depressing—I crafted the geography and history of what is now the world of Dravmir to give us our opening line: "There were no trees, of course."

Centuries before our story begins, most of Sherwood Forest was destroyed, and all the trees in Loxley scorched: burned by holy finnikfire at the behest of the Mother. This violent shift in the ecosystem made the outcropping of rocks on which Loxley is built to become a tidal island: inaccessible by foot during high tide, and surrounded by marsh and quicksand at low tide. Now I had a delicious setting for which to hang all the social, political, and religious trappings. I read many research articles on how trees communicate and talk with each other through their vast network of roots (dubbed the 'wood wide web ').

In my research of Robin Hood lore, I learned about Juraj Jánošík, who was a Slovak highwayman (1688–1713). He's a main character of many Slovak novels, films, and poems, and as he robbed from the rich to give to the poor, he is often referred to as the Slavic Robin Hood. This led to the Slavic influence and inspirations as I crafted the world of Dravmir. I wanted the world to feel adjacent to and inspired by both Slavic and Nordic mythology, while not explicitly lifting. It was a matter of a lot of research, blurring the edges, and using sensitivity readers.

I used the rusalka (water nymph that lured men to their death) instead of the more well-known siren in Greek mythology. For Alita (the name means winged one!), instead of a Pegasus, I went with a Nozdravian, a nod to the Calul Năzdrăvan. The Nazdravian is common in Romanian folkloric mythology, meaning 'flying horse' and 'advisor to the hero'. This type of mystical horse typically assisted the clueless and bumbling hero, performing most of the difficult and intellectual tasks. The horse will seem ordinary at first, only gaining powers of flight after a series of trials. Perun is the Slavic god of thunder, sky, storms, oak trees (among other things), so I used it for the name of the Sea. Devana is the goddess of hunting, forests, and the moon, worshipped by the Western Slavs.

I used the Elder Futhark runic alphabet, which is the oldest form of the Norse runic alphabet. In Celtic, Slavic, and Nordic mythology and folklore, Druids were said to have gathered under oak trees. The word Druid comes from the Celtic word for oak, 'Duir.' It is commonly translated to 'oak-seer' or 'knower of oaks.' This led to the moment when Little Jon tells Renna that originally Trissaia did not mean 'truth sayer' but 'tree sayer.' The Oakheart was heavily inspired by the sacred oak Yggdrasil from Norse mythology. As my nod to the foxes in Disney's Robin Hood, I use the term 'lishka' based on the Czech word 'liška,' which means fox. 'Nastasia' means 'resurrect' or 'will rise again' in Russian (insert evil laugh).

If you are a Robin Hood nerd like me (or my nephew, who is much too young to read this book), you would know that Maid Marian is the Nightwatchman. Did you guess that Garen (our Maid Marian counterpart) was also the mysterious vigilante? The early version of this story had Gisborne as the Sheriff, until I realized it would make the tension so much more exciting to have Garen hold the role, and to satisfy my own obsession with enemies-to-lovers and a sad-but-bad-boy who needs a redemption arc.

Speaking of Gisborne, if you've read my other novel, The Abandoned Realm, here is a fun tidbit: Guy of Gisborne is Guy in another world where his story is finished! Before you throw this book and scream, "Brittany, Guy would NEVER have done what Gisborne did," please trust me with his Inspector-Javert-identity-crisis (and see above: my love of redemption arcs).

If you've read all this way, I hope the next time you walk around your local indie bookstore with your favorite drink you find a pretty special edition on sale, and that your favorite artist drops new fanart today. Thanks for sticking around.

ACKNOWLEDGEMENTS

Oo-de-lolly, golly, what a day! There are so many people who are involved with making any book come to life, and I have some of the best people in my corner.

First: Brad. Love of my life. Thanks for always listening to my ideas, letting me read aloud to you, celebrating each milestone, and understanding that when I say, "just five more minutes," it means another hour of writing. You make it simple to write love stories. Thank you for grounding me when the storms rage.

To my family and friends, thank you for being in my corner and letting me wax poetic on Robin Hood lore. You know who you are, and I'm grateful for you. Scott and Nancy Hansen, for all the childcare and celebratory toasts along the way. Lexy and Nolan, you are also too young to read this, but I love you both so much.

Maggie Stiefvater. How do I put it into words? Thank you for your mentorship, coaching, brainstorming sessions, and sticky notes. Thank you for helping me hone my skills and reach for EXEMPLARY. Thank you for the Poverty Tour, House Night, and the transformative time in Hvammsvik. Everyone from the Hvammsvik 2024 Retreat, especially House Night—Abigail Cummins, Kelsey Carthac, Ariel Cash and (our honorary) Meg Shallman. Your feedback on this story is immeasurable. Thank you for loving these characters while drinking copious amounts of tea with me. I am incredibly lucky to have you in my corner. Thank you for the hours spent going over plot, all the serotonin faeries, and (of course) Dead Body Soup.

There is a veritable army of people who championed this book at every stage. My amazing early/beta readers: Sarah Martin, Jalene Ashland, Erin Himeno, Nicole Maddy, Jain Willis, Kannon Howerton, Jenna Ahlman, Mikelle Roach, Jenna Douglass, Kim Newman, Jillian Hicken, Sarah Hansen, , and Lexi Carr. To my proofreaders, thank you for being the final stand against my typos: Brooke Bishop, Jessie Peck, Brooke Lockie, Melissa Goodger, Brandy O'Bagy, Greg Bishop, Ghada Bishop, Justin Bishop, Rachael Stoll, Sharon Halpin, Jeff Bishop, Kristen Reuter, and Sam Coyle. Jamie Shawn Bassett thank you for all the support with writing non-hearing characters. Justin Peck, thanks for being my resident doctor for all things blood and wounds. thaNK You WeNdI maCKliN. Lacey

Peterson, I think you knew the heart of this story before I did. Thank you for helping me discover it.

My fellow writers who help me see the forest when I'm lost in the trees (and not in a fun Rowan Reach kind of way): Caitlin Jacobs, Megan Carver, Kaela Woodruff, Nico Vincenty (all the file conversions!), Bryce O'Connor, Dave Smurthwaite, Jess Coleman, Brooke Emery, Rachel Stoll, Meredith Coffman, Gillian West, Mackenzi Lee, Waverly Night, Ben Wagner, and Derek Williamson. Derek thanks for geeking out with me over worldbuilding when that call for a "quick question" turned into eight hours. MVP.

Sarah Batista-Pereira, your accountability group and level head when I'm spiraling was just what I needed. Jolene Perry—thank you for all the encouragement, developmental edits, and, of course, your horses. Alison Cherry thank you for working your magic on this manuscript. I am forever grateful for your assessing eyes and thorough edits. Megan Carver—I feel spoiled to have you not only as a resource for writing violence and intimacy, but as a friend. Thank you for nerding out with me, talking cool stunts, and the Marco madness. Michele Kirichanskaya—thank you for your discerning eye on the sensitivity read.

It's been an honor to collaborate with so many talented artists on this book: Andrés Aguirre Jurado (the map of my dreams), Annabelle (Avendell), Jane (Incendiosketches), Alice Powers, Marlie (Honeypears), Karina Giada Art, Jenna Ahlman (alemonleaf), and Kay Carthac.

Abril—this book would look way less cool without you. Thank you for your expertise, your support, the hours in the bookstores, holding my hand through marketing, and researching Robin Hood lore alongside me to make this a work of art. Tricia Day—it warms my heart that we get to continue working together on another project. Thank you for your voice and dedication. Rachel and Lexi over at The Nerd Fam, thank you for your enthusiasm and support with the launch of this book, and for indie authors everywhere.

And lastly you, the reader. If you read The Abandoned Realm and came back for another story, thank you. If this is the first of my work you've read, thank you for taking a chance on me. I am eternally grateful for every person who has expressed excitement for my books, made posts on social media, shared with their friends, and connected with my characters. It means the world to me. I hope you enjoyed this story even half as much as I enjoyed writing it.

You matter. Your story matters. Speak your truth.

—B

ABOUT THE AUTHOR

BRITTANY HANSEN grew up devouring books about magic, looking for doorways to fantasy worlds in tree trunks, and staying up late writing her own stories. She studied creative writing in college. Now she lives near the mountains in Utah with her husband, two kids, and two fur babies. When she's not writing (or spending time with the aforementioned fur babies, kiddos, and hubby) she can be found reading fanfiction, swooning over fictional characters, and nursing her coffee mug on the couch.

www.brittanyhansenauthor.com
Instagram @abritbookish
TikTok @brittanyhansenauthor

www.ingramcontent.com/pod-product-compliance
Lightning Source LLC
Chambersburg PA
CBHW020227010826

48973CB00006B/1408